ONE MAN'S TREASURE

Hell Yeah!
Equalizers – Jet's Story

By

Sable Hunter
and
Ryan O'Leary

This is a work of fiction. Names, characters, places and incidents are either the product of the author's imagination or used fictitiously, and any resemblance to actual persons, living or dead, business establishments, events or locales is entirely coincidental.

One Man's Treasure
All rights reserved.
Copyright 2015 © Sable Hunter and Ryan O'Leary

Ebook
ISBN-13: 978-1535005944
ISBN-10: 1535005947

Cover by JRA Stevens
© Markskalny | Dreamstime.com - Bow Of A Barkentine Sailing Ship Photo
© Byheaven87 | Dreamstime.com - Cruise At Sunset Photo

Jet is a hero—Special Forces, an Equalizer, a motorcycle riding MMA fighter who is part pirate and all man. No one messes with Jet.

He is formidable—the tall, dark, and deadly type.

In One Man's Treasure, he's on a quest for gold. Jet travels to Mexico to fight a challenger before he sails the Sirena to bring up a fortune from the sunken Spanish galleon, San Miguel. As usual, Jet is in control, master of his destiny. Until...

Jet meets Sami.

Sami waits tables at a club in Veracruz. Jet can't help but notice the slight, shy bartender. It angers him when customers give Sami a hard time.

Only problem—Jet assumes Sami is a boy.

Sami is actually Samantha. She's come to Mexico to find healing and the truth about what happened to her best friend. When she has to leave town fast, she stows away on Jet's boat.

Imagine his surprise when he finds Sami...and then discovers she's a woman!

Beneath a silvery moon, Jet watches a mermaid play in the sea and discovers that One Man's Treasure can be more than diamonds and gold.

One Man's Treasure is love.

CHAPTER ONE

"I want sex." Sami sighed heavily. "Amazing, hot, sweaty sex with multiple orgasms and lots of cuddling." She felt halfway decent today, a rare gift. Plopping back on her bed, she picked up one of the striped pillow shams and stared at her beautiful best friend. "Yes, I think that's the medicine I need."

"With me?" Marisol's expression was priceless. Eyes, wide and teasing, sparkled as bright as copper pennies.

Sami launched the pillow in her direction. "No. Not with you, silly, with a man."

"Have you had a lot of sex, Miss Sami?" Marisol teasingly asked as she saved a file on her computer.

"No, but I've hallucinated about it a lot." Sami didn't take offence. Instead, she giggled. Someone as desirable as Marisol probably couldn't fathom her level of inexperience.

Marisol frowned at her odd choice of words. "Don't you mean fantasized?"

Quickly, she agreed. "Yea, of course. Fantasized." Although she had experienced very vivid and realistic hallucinations before the last surgery, she wasn't going to burden her friend with that knowledge. Nothing like a brain tumor to make one's life exciting. "You know, I don't really dream about sex. I think more about dating, I guess. I've never been on a date. You know, getting picked up on a Friday night and taken to the movies, sharing a goodnight kiss on the porch." Sami lay on her back and studied her friend's face. "You look like a young Jennifer Lopez, did you know that?"

Marisol pulled her long dark hair up in a ponytail and fastened it with a leather cord. She'd come to study with Sami. They were about to take their final exam in a journalism class at the University of Houston. "Thanks, but I think my butt's bigger." She looked over her shoulder and down at her rear. "I understand about longing for a normal life, for dates and a boyfriend. My life hasn't been very stable either. I didn't really date until I came to the States."

Sami ran a finger down one of the seams of her burgundy bedspread. "We've both had a hard time." She knew Marisol's life had been a nightmare. Her brother had been killed by the Galvez drug cartel and now her brave friend had made it her mission in life to expose the identity of the drug lord known only as 'the Jaguar.'

Seeing that Sami looked depressed, Marisol took a notebook, opened it, and joined her on the bed. "Okay, we're masters at research. Tell me what type of guy you're interested in and I'll keep my eyes open. We'll find you a man."

Sami knew they were just pretending. She was too weak to wrestle a stuffed animal, much less make love—she was skinny and frail. That didn't stop her from thinking about it, though. "I love girl talk." Sami wiggled around, sitting up and leaning back against the headboard. "Now, let me think." She straightened the scarf on her head, then tapped her cheek as if deep in thought. "I want a big one."

"Ha!" Marisol wrote the one word down in large letters. BIG! "Mr. Big. Are we talking shoulders, arms, height, brains or cock size?"

Hugging herself, Sami imagined how nice it would feel to be held. "All of them. I want someone who can wrap his arms around me and keep the world at bay."

Marisol's smile died a bit, knowing what Sami needed saving from. "All right, duly noted. Any other requirements?"

"Adventuresome and brave." Wiggling down to lie flat on her stomach, Sami raised one leg in the air, balancing her pink flip-flop on the end of her toes.

"You want a hero." Marisol observed Sami with an indulgent expression, seeing a fragile, delicate, China-doll girl who'd seen more pain in her young life than anyone should have to endure.

"Yea, I want a warrior." Sami started to pick her laptop up from the floor. "Want to see?"

"Oh, you have one in mind?" Marisol leaned over to help her pull the computer over the side of the bed. Her friend was getting weaker by the day.

"He's my dream guy, man-candy sweet." Sami smiled as she accessed the bookmarked website. "Something sweet to look at and think about other than my unfortunate condition."

"Give me that." As soon as the image came up, Marisol grabbed the laptop to see what Sami was viewing. "I wouldn't call this guy sweet. He looks to be straight out of one of those barbarian movies. You really like these tattooed hero fighter types, don't you? My God, he is big."

"Jet Foster." She sighed. "Yea, he's perfect. Like you said, a hero, a decorated war hero to be exact. One of the Equalizers, not only is he handsome, he's a good guy. I think he even hunts treasure as a hobby, almost like a pirate."

"The Equalizers, what's that? It sounds familiar." Marisol scrolled through the website featuring Jet,

Sami looked up to see her face crumple. "What's wrong?"

Marisol began to sob. "I'll come today." She pulled a towel from the rack to wipe her tears. "I don't care. I have to come." In a few moments, Marisol closed the phone and looked at Sami. "They murdered my mother, gunned her down in front of the market. I have to go to Mexico."

Over the next few hours, Sami did everything she could to talk Marisol out of returning to Veracruz. She was so scared for her friend, but Sami knew how she would've felt if she hadn't been allowed to say goodbye to her parents. "I am so sorry for your loss."

"I know you understand, you just went through this yourself." Marisol looked sad, but resigned. "Since I'm going to Veracruz, at least I'll be getting my hands on more information, something really explosive, my cousin says. He wants to give it to me in person. Salazar has infiltrated the cartel. He says they make frequent visits to Texas to launder money. When I get back, maybe I can contact this new Governor and his task force with information to bring them down when they're here in the U.S."

"You're serious about this, aren't you, Lioness?"

Marisol looked her right in the eye. "I've never been more serious about anything in my life," she said through the pain.

Sami hugged her friend. "I know this is important to you, but you're important to me. Take care of yourself. Please."

Sami walked her to the door and stood at the front window of her mother's house, watching Marisol leave. Resting her forehead on the cool wood, her breathing was short and shallow. God, how she wished things were different. Life wasn't easy for either of them and getting shorter for her every day. While she stared into the street, a young family walked by. The mother pushed a stroller and her husband's arm was across her shoulders. Sami felt a pang of wistfulness slice through her. What she wouldn't give for a chance at happiness.

* * *

When she felt like it, Sami boxed up her mother's things to take to Goodwill. Violet had owned her share of designer clothes, but not as many as one might think. Her mother's life had been the hospital, head of the oncology unit at one of the largest cancer facilities in the nation. Since her passing, they'd named a new wing after her, but Sami hadn't felt like attending the ceremony.

Marisol called when she reached Veracruz and emailed her a few hours after that, promising to keep in touch. Sami felt so sorry for her. Her mother had been murdered in cold blood. Marisol said her father was taking it hard and he was begging Marisol to go away with him to relatives in Brazil. She'd refused. She said she was on the trail of Angel Andrade, one of the henchmen for the Galvez Cartel and the man believed to be her mother's killer. She was convinced Andrade had found out she was Leona, the blogger who threatened to expose them all. Her biggest revelation was that she now possessed evidence which could lead to the Jaguar's true identity.

But that had been three days ago. Something was wrong. All communications had stopped.

Sami paced back and forth in her bedroom, holding the phone to her ear. "Marisol, why aren't you answering?" She was terrified something had happened. "Hell." She threw the phone across the room.

Sami felt totally helpless. She was weak. There were times when her vision was blurry and the side of her head felt like it would blow off. At moments like this, Sami did the only thing she could do, the only thing that seemed to help. She stripped down to her underwear, laid her head on a heating pad, and watched online videos of Jet fight. In her mind, she let his opponent be her cancer—her enemy—and she let herself celebrate when he would defeat the challenger, make-believing he was her hero, that he was fighting the fight for her. "You're amazing." She passed a finger over his image, pretending she could touch him.

Last night she'd had a dream, the doctor might call it a hallucination, but Sami had been aware it wasn't real—it was too good to be real. She'd been lying on her bed, alone, her arm slung over her eyes, the ceiling fan cooling her fevered body when she'd heard him.

She knew his voice, she'd heard that sexy growl in videos. "Sami, what are you thinking about?"

She'd uncovered her face, surprised yet glad to see him. "You."

"Scoot over."

"Okay." Sami would gladly make room on the bed for his big body.

"Let me hold you."

With a sigh, she'd cuddled against him. Even in the haze of her pain, she hadn't presumed anything, content for him to cradle her body next to his.

Strange, she could still remember his heartbeat, the warmth of his chest under her fingers, the feather caress of his breath on her cheek.

Bang! Bang!

The sound of the door knocker followed by the peal of the doorbell echoed through the house. Sami jerked to full alertness, rose from the bed and padded barefoot from her room. As she made her way through her mother's house, Sami admitted she had never felt at home in the River Oaks mansion. She much preferred the country acreage where they'd lived with her father before she got sick, west of Houston near the Brazos River bottom. In those days, Sami had run free and wild, playing in the fields, swimming in the water. Until the day when a pain in her head had caused her to double over, hands over her face, confused and scared because she didn't understand what was happening.

The tap sounded again as she covered the distance from the stairs to the marble entryway. Opening the door, she saw it was the postman.

"Samantha Cabot?"

"That's me."

"If you'd sign here." The man handed her a pad, and she gave him her signature.

After she'd finished, he handed her an oversize envelope. "Thank you." She shut the door behind him and glanced at the return address. Mexico. "Marisol!" Ripping into it, she took out a sheet of paper with writing on it that looked to be hastily scrawled. Snail-mail? Sami wondered why not an email or a text?

Soon, she found out.

Sami,

I'm writing this quickly. They are onto me. My mother's murder was committed to bring me home. If I disappear, Angel Andrade has me. Here is a flash drive, it's not everything, I've left some items hidden at my father's. Don't let my notes go to waste. Please, don't put yourself in danger, but try and get them out to the world. Leona may cease to be, but if the truth lives on, it will be worth it. Take care of yourself, go to the clinic, get well and live a long and happy life.

I hope to see you again. Don't let me down.
Marisol

Sami pulled out a thumb drive and stared at it as if it were going to speak to her. "Mari, Mari, what have you done?"

She returned to her room and plugged the drive into the USB port. What she found shocked her. God, Marisol was in over her head. Without hesitation, she found Marisol's father's number and placed a call. There was no answer. Then, she tried an alternative number, a cell phone indicated in his daughter's records as an emergency number. It took a while to get through. She imagined he was sick with grief.

Sami prayed that Marisol's fear of being taken by Andrade was unfounded, that she'd find her safe and well. Like Marisol, she'd been through much in her life. Burying her folks had been horrific for Sami. She couldn't imagine her own death could be much worse. Her father had been near retirement age when she'd lost him, a laidback country boy from East Texas who'd made his fortune in the oil field. He'd pulled out in front of an eighteen wheeler and died instantly. Her mother on the other hand, was raised in River Oaks, educated at Rice and born with a silver scalpel in her hand. Her grandfather had performed one of the first heart transplants and her father had developed innovative surgical procedures named after him and performed all over the world.

And Sami? Sami had survived to the ripe old age of twenty-two. Survival was her claim to fame. Oh, she'd gone to the University of Houston and as of a few weeks ago, along with Marisol, had been awarded a Journalism degree. Instead of chasing jobs with newspapers, television stations or magazines, they'd chosen to take their enthusiasm and passion online and do investigative reporting on their own blogs where they were accountable to no one and under no one's thumb.

Marisol was committed to exposing the horrors of the drug cartels that held her homeland and her people hostage. Sami didn't know how often she had held her best friend while she cried, listening to her whisper how many journalists had been murdered by the cartels. Being a journalist shouldn't be the most dangerous job in the world, but that was exactly what it was shaping up to be.

Sami, relegated to doing most of her investigative blogging from the hospital or sick bed, had to choose topics or issues that she could research online or over the telephone. Short trips were possible on good days, so she'd decided to tackle a series of cold cases. Over the past forty years, thirty bodies had been found in a twenty-five acre patch of land off I-45 about thirty minutes southeast of her home. All women, all young. All had died long before their time. But their lives weren't taken by a disease such as the one that threatened Sami, they were snatched from this earth by a monster who prowled the interstate trolling for prey.

Since she'd begun the series of articles, a new interest had arisen about the cases. Relatives of the lost had come forward, memories were resurfacing, and Sami hoped someone with clues or testimony would come forward so the victims could at last find peace.

All of these things were running through Sami's head as she stared at the evidence Marisol had compiled.

"Hello?"

Sami jerked, the voice on the other end of the line startling her. "Señor Lopez?"

"Yes?"

"This is Samantha Cabot, Marisol's friend from school. I just got a letter from her. She thinks she's in trouble. Tell me she's okay. If she's there, I'd like to speak to her."

A broken sob was all she heard for a few seconds. "She isn't here. Her car was forced off the road and she is gone. The cartel has kidnapped my daughter, they have burned my home, and I have had to flee for my life."

"Kidnapped?" Sami was horrified, tears running down her cheeks. "Are you sure?"

"Yes, there was a note. They said she would be tried, judged, and punished for her crimes. It was signed by the Jaguar."

"I'm so sorry. I'm glad you're safe." They talked for a few more moments, but Sami didn't have sufficient words to comfort the grieving father. "Call me if you find out anything, please."

He promised he would, but the next few days brought no word. She spent the time reading through Marisol's notes, doing her own research and trying to decide what to do about her health situation. Without intervention, Sami knew she couldn't live very much longer. She had a reoccurring astrocytoma, a malignant brain tumor that had proved resistant to all of the treatments Western medicine could offer. The idea that Marisol had mentioned about alternative treatment at a Mexican clinic seemed like a pipedream. But what if she was right? What if there was a chance she could stall the growth of the tumor and buy herself enough time to help Marisol? Sami had no real belief there was a cure or that she could live a normal life, but maybe she could feel well enough to allow the Lioness to roar once more.

As she pulled up the website for the clinic Marisol had told her about, the phone rang. Jumping up, Sami held onto the dresser for support until her heart quit hammering. Once she was steady, she reached for the phone—hoping against hope. "Marisol?"

"Miss Cabot?"

Sami stiffened with disappointment. "Yes."

"This is Dr. Nicholas Rio with the Great Physician clinic. I'm calling to let you know we have an opening. If you can be here within the next two weeks, we can begin your treatment."

Sami almost fell to her knees. "How?" Even as she asked the question, she knew how. Marisol had done her best to take care of her. A rush of adrenaline fueled joy surged through her veins. Was it foolish to dream?

"A friend of yours came by and told us of your need. If you could send me your medical records, I'd be glad to look at them."

Sami only hesitated for a few seconds. Perhaps this would all be in vain, but she knew she had to try. She had to fight the fight. If she lost, at least she'd know she had tried.

* * *

The weather in Veracruz, Mexico, was warm and sunny compared to the stormy weather she'd left behind in Houston. Sami had taken a few weeks and liquidated her assets, sold the big house in River Oaks and her mother's car. When or if she returned, Sami would purchase things more in line with her own tastes. This journey was momentous, not only because she'd seldom felt like traveling but because she was also stepping out on faith.

She found the Great Physician clinic with no problem. The building wasn't as modern looking as Sami had hoped, but she wasn't ready to judge the book by its cover. Placing a hand over her heart, she tried to still her breathing. A fine sheen of sweat had broken out on her forehead. The jet ride had taken a lot out of her. She was as weak as dishwater, as her grandmother used to say. Taking a deep breath, she walked up the sidewalk and opened the door. As soon as she stepped inside, two smiling nurses came to greet her.

"Señorita Cabot?"

"Yes, I'm Sami." Her eyes darted around, taking in the mint green walls, faux leather furniture and the cheap prints of tropical flowers on the walls.

"Good, I am Rosa and this is Maria, we have been expecting you."

Hope is a funny thing. To Sami, it was almost tangible. She shook their hands and allowed them to lead her in, escort her to the back and introduce her to the doctor. Dr. Rio, a middle-aged man with a close-cropped beard stood to greet her, then sat her down to tell her what she could expect. His office was a tad better furnished, but it was obvious that money had not been wasted on décor.

"This will be a three-prong attack, Miss Cabot. First, I want to boost your immune system and work on breaking down the blood-brain-barrier so the drugs I introduce will have a better chance of reaching the cells we need to target. At the same time, we're going to change your diet and work on making you stronger, boost the fatty acids and focus on natural cancer fighting foods that will help us with our plan." He drew on a pad and explained how he would use a special virus to attack the cells, almost like a cancer for the cancer.

Sami tried to listen, but soon all of the words were flowing together. "I'm willing to try it all," she admitted. "I'm not expecting a cure. What I'm looking for is time to finish some things that need to be done."

Dr. Rio frowned. "This is not about buying time, Miss Cabot." He folded his hands. "I need your mental and spiritual commitment or we have no chance of making this work. We are going for a cure, not merely putting off the inevitable."

Sami struggled for words. "This is hard. My mother was an oncologist and I have endured much at the hands of medicine."

Dr. Rio seemed to soften. "I understand, but know this—I do not prescribe to the cut/poison and burn regime that you are used to. What I want to do is kill your *cancer*, not *you*."

Part of Sami rejoiced and part of her wanted to defend her mother's life work. Instead of discussing, she agreed. "Very well. We shall begin."

"I'm glad." His calm demeanor reassured her, so Sami turned herself over to Dr. Rio's care. "I want you to stay here at the clinic for at least two weeks. After that we'll see how you feel and you can find other accommodations."

For the first few days, Sami's body had protested the changes and she'd been too weak to do much more than endure and sleep. But after that, she began to feel better. According to the treatment plan, she would be under the Great Physician's care for at least three months. At the end of that time, a new round of testing would be done to see if the cancer was gone or if the tumor had shrunk. An evaluation would determine their next step.

Sami had no idea if the treatments would work or not. Refusing to let herself dwell on the possible outcomes, she endeavored to make the best of it. Rosa was very supportive and asked question after question about Sami's life in America. Maria was more standoffish, and Sami would catch her staring. Once she even picked up a photo on her desk and held it while she dissected Sami with her eyes. She'd tried to see what the picture was, but Maria had turned it over. Odd. On the whole, however, the experience wasn't as bad as she'd imagined.

As soon as she felt well enough to leave the sparse, clinical room at Great Physician's, Sami acquainted herself with beautiful Veracruz. In the cool of the evening she walked around the city, visited the Naval Museum and an old Spanish fortress that was once part of the town's defense. There was only one section of the original wall still standing, but Sami could get a glimpse of its history. Veracruz was a jewel of a city, there was still a colonial feel to it and a great sense of pride. The town square gave her a feeling of old Mexico where the locals stayed indoors until about dusk before they came out to party. She found that the locals celebrated music in every part of their life. There was even a couple practicing salsa music on the square. They had no music, it was all in their minds, but she couldn't tell by looking.

As soon as she could, Sami contacted Marisol's father and asked if she could come visit. He told her that he was staying in a neighboring village, hiding from the cartel. Loyola Lopez gave her his address and she prepared to go, walking some distance from the clinic before she attempted to hail a cab. Being from Texas, she spoke a fair amount of Spanish, but she still stuck out like a sore thumb. At least her hair was growing back. Sami ran her fingers through the inch long short curls that at least made her look halfway feminine. Once she was safely ensconced in a taxi, she held on for dear life as he raced through the narrow cobblestone streets.

The neighborhood where Señor Lopez was staying seemed crowded but nice. Once she'd paid the fare,

Sami walked a brick paved path to a modest stucco home bordered by cactus and fruit trees. With a delicate knock, she waited for someone to come to the door.

Once it opened, a middle-aged man with salt and pepper hair and a distinct paunch answered. "Sí?"

"Senor Lopez, I'm Sami Cabot, Marisol's friend from Texas."

"Sí! Yes, please, come in." He spoke in somewhat broken English. While his smile was welcoming, he had the look of a man who'd been through something horrible.

"I wanted to come see you. I don't know how much Mari told you, but I've been sick and she encouraged me to come here for help." The home was neat and decorated with dark mahogany furniture, while bright colors dispelled the gloom.

"Yes, she told me about your problem." He touched his head. "And the deaths of your parents." Tears began to form in his eyes. "I am glad you are here. They will help you." Loyola wiped his eyes. "There has been too much sadness, too much loss. My Sonia, Mari's mother, she was gunned down walking across the street in front of the market. Marisol was taken on the way to her aunt's house. And here I am, hiding out like a coward in the home of my distant cousin."

Sami rose and went to hug him. "I love Mari so much." She couldn't hold back her own tears. "She is my one true friend. Is there anything I can do?" He shrugged his shoulders. "Did she leave behind a computer or notes, files, discs or anything like that?"

Loyola frowned. "You do not need to get mixed up in this. We must let it die." When he said the last word, he broke down in earnest.

"Señor Lopez, Marisol wrote me a letter and asked me to continue her work until she returned." The words 'if she returns' remained unspoken between them.

He appeared to be struggling with the idea, rubbing his hands together and gazing at the floor. "I begged her to leave this alone. We live too close to the cartels. Our friend's children have gotten mixed up with them. It's hard to tell who to trust and who not to. Even at church, we sit in worship with them. The wheat and the chaff, the sheep and the goats—we do not know our left from our right."

"She told me of your trouble. The mass grave that was just found a few months ago, twenty-four innocent people killed, this must be stopped." Sami leaned forward and grasped his hand. "What are the authorities doing to find her?"

Loyola rose and walked to the door. "They say they are looking. But the policía, they are as hard to read as everyone else. Some of them are on cartel payroll." He let out a deep breath and faced Sami. "It is not like a father to give up hope, but Marisol is dead. We just have not been able to bury her yet."

Anger swept over Sami. She wanted to cry, but her sorrow would only fuel his. "I'm not ready to give up. Let me help. No one knows me. Give me whatever she had, tell me where to look for these people. If I were to be Mari's eyes and ears, where would I go?"

For a while, Sami thought Loyola wasn't going to answer her. She let her eyes rove around the room and saw items he'd saved from the fire, photos of Marisol's family on a table by the door. There was even one of her. Sami wrinkled her nose. She hated to see photographs of herself. Since being diagnosed with astrocytoma at sixteen, she'd been sickly, too thin and gaunt. Sami always thought she looked like a character from a Tim Burton movie.

Waiting on him to say something, she gazed down at the clothes she was wearing. Fashion wasn't her forte. Jeans and blouses had been her uniform for a long time. Sami had never developed a social life among the children of her parents' peers and once she'd gone to college, she'd spent more time taking classes online than on campus. Idly, she fingered the pearl buttons on the yellow cashmere sweater she wore.

Finally, he broke the silence. "Down by the waterfront. My nephew Salazar told Marisol that Andrade and his men hang out there frequently, especially at a bar named Espada Ancha, the Pirate's Lair. It's run by an American." Loyola let his eyes rake Sami from head to toe. "Very dangerous, much criminal activity. You have no business in such a place."

She wasn't promising anything. "My time is tied up with treatments at the moment. However, if you could see fit to give me any information Marisol might have left behind, I'll protect it and put it to good use."

Their eyes locked and Sami thought he might refuse her. But he didn't. He left the room and while he was gone, Sami wrote down the name of the bar so she wouldn't forget. When he came back, he handed her a large manila envelope. "Here. I can't emphasize enough for you to be cautious. These people are ruthless. They'll kill you without remorse if you get in their way. If they find out you are connected to Marisol, they will kill you. You have put yourself at risk just by coming here today. If they found out I have this, that I gave this to you, they'd hunt us both down like dogs."

She accepted the envelope and slipped it in her bag. "I understand. No one will know I have them. No one will know I am Leona."

"I'm only staying near to find out what happened to my Marisol. After I do, I'm leaving Veracruz forever. There is nothing left for me there but bad memories."

He remained standing, and Sami realized he was ready for her to go. Rising, she thanked him. "Again, I extend to you my hope that Marisol will walk back into your life, healthy and happy. Until then," she nodded down at her bag, "I will protect you and honor her." Señor Lopez watched sadly as Sami left.

Upon returning to the clinic, she was glad to find she hadn't missed her session. As soon as she opened the door, Rosa and Maria were ready to hook up the IV drip and give her the meds she needed. When she was all set, Sami used the time alone to review what Marisol's father had given her. To her shock, there was a photograph of a tall, bearded man whose face was in shadow. He was standing in profile, so his features weren't clear...but he did look familiar. Who was he? She turned the picture over and saw where Mari had scrawled 'The Jaguar.' It wasn't enough for her to identify him, but it was a start and gave her some leverage to play with. Using Marisol's login and password, Sami posted her first blog as the Lioness.

* * *

Back in Texas...

Jet Ivan Foster gunned the Harley Electra Glide down Interstate 45, heading to Galveston. He let the chilly sea breeze keep him awake. He'd just flown into Houston from San Augustine, Florida, and he was dog tired. Nemo had scared him to death. His father was a pain in the ass on a good day, on a day he had a heart attack he was intolerable. The man thought he was immortal.

They were scheduled to dive off the coast of Florida near Amelia Island in a little over a month to search for the long-lost Spanish galleon called the San Miguel. Together he and Nemo had brought up a jeweler's furnace in that same spot six months before and Nemo was convinced it was from the San Miguel which went down while trying to outrun a hurricane in 1715. Jet and his father had done their homework, pouring over all the research they could get their hands on about the ship's route, weight, and treasure. He smiled, recalling that the estimated value of the gold and silver bars, coins, jewels and other valuables on board to be upward of two billion dollars. Now that would be a haul by anyone's standards.

Nemo was a retired Navy helicopter pilot who'd found a second career in the treasure salvaging business. He and Jet had spent most of Jet's childhood on the open ocean, especially after Naomi Foster had left them both.

Neither had ever gotten over it.

This hunt meant the world to Nemo and the possibility he was going to miss it was unacceptable to either one of them. Jet cursed his timing, but there wasn't a damn thing he could do about it. He had put his money where his mouth was and agreed to fight Santoro. In a few days he and Micah were scheduled to sail from Galveston to Veracruz, Mexico, where he would face the mouthy Spaniard and prove once and for all which one of them was the best. There was no question in Jet's mind, now all he had to do was prove it to the rest of the world. After the fight, he was set to take his new lady on a honeymoon cruise—and he wasn't talking about a woman—oh, no. Jet's face broke into a big grin as he thought about his latest acquisition, a boat so fine he would marry her if he believed in the outdated institution.

Leaving Nemo wasn't ideal, but he'd left him in good hands. Tyson, his friend and another of the Equalizers, had flown over to stay with him and be there until Jet could join them. As soon as his father was up to traveling, Tyson would move the Seaduction to Nassau Sound near Amelia Island to await Jet and the salvage crew he was supposed to meet up with in Mexico. Nemo was beyond excited, he'd spent eighty-five thousand to have his seventy-one foot vessel overhauled. Outfitted expressly for treasure hunting, the Seaduction resembled a barge with large, adjustable pilings that raised and lowered the hull after the pilings were planted on the sea floor.

This time, same as last, the Equalizers were invested in the operation. Destry proved invaluable helping them meet government regulations. Obtaining the proper permits for treasure salvage operations could be complicated. They had to contend with environmental regulations, the Corp of Engineers and historical and archaeological requirements. All of those battles were won, but none of that would matter if the ocean didn't cooperate.

Driving between Pasadena and League City, Jet noticed an old red truck pulled off on the side of the road next to the Calder Oil Field. This stretch of road was pretty deserted, so he slowed down to see if someone could've had car trouble. As a guy who enjoyed custom work, he couldn't help but notice the 67 Chevy two-tone pick-up had been restored to perfection. Drawing nearer, he noticed an older guy walking out next to a cross standing in a field, the same type of cross prevalent along roadsides to commemorate the place someone had been killed. Easing to a stop, he called, "Hey, are you all right, mister? Need help?"

Waiting for an answer, his eyes roved over the truck and he noticed a Fish Toledo Bend bumper sticker on the back.

"No, thanks, I'm fine." The old man waved him on with his hat. Jet returned the wave and started up again. As he rode over the causeway from the mainland to the island, Jet admitted he was a man of passion. Joining forces with his friends to form the Equalizers made him feel useful. They were a force dedicated to helping those who couldn't help themselves. In the last year they'd located several missing children, rescued both men and women in hostage situations and provided security for others when they were being threatened in situations beyond their control. Diving for gold fed his sense of adventure, searching for the unknown and taking risks when the odds were against him was amazing, and the chance of reward was astronomical. Stepping into the ring to fight fed his need to compete…and sometimes he just needed to beat the shit out of something. These things served to give him purpose—to serve, to explore, and to conquer.

However, his last passion was the one he kept the tightest rein on. Women. He loved women. Plural. He loved how they smelled, the silky touch of their skin. Jet worshiped their bodies and delighted in giving them ecstasy. There was nothing better than knowing you gave a woman pleasure. But, Jet had rules. He never got involved. He didn't do commitment. One-night stands were his specialty. Women were beautiful, wonderful, delightful—but there was no room in his life for one on a permanent basis.

Regardless, he fed this passion with an all-consuming regularity. Sex was as necessary to him as breathing, but the word love wasn't in his vocabulary.

No, that was wrong.

As he pulled into the Galveston yacht basin, Jet admitted he was in love.

And her name was Sirena.

* * *

Meanwhile…in Veracruz…

Angel Andrade and the Galvez Cartel are strangling the life from Veracruz. They are poisoning our young, taking the lives of innocents and funneling money that should be stimulating our economy straight into their pockets.

I have an idea. Let's form a neighborhood watch. I am Leona, the Lioness. My email address is truthaboveall@yahoo.com. If you see a crime, witness a murder, know the name of someone who is working for or cooperating with the cartels—expose them. Inform me and I'll inform the world. I have a photograph of the Jaguar. I will discover his identity. Soon I will declaw and defang the beast.

Sami took a deep breath and pressed enter. Her third blog post was finished. The last two paragraphs she'd written would cast doubt on Marisol's guilt in their eyes. Her taunt about the Jaguar should bring him out of hiding. She hoped it would be enough to set Marisol free—if she was still alive.

As instructed by Señor Lopez, Sami ventured to the waterfront and found a small apartment. She no longer had to spend her nights at the clinic. Her strength was still low, but she hadn't experienced any nausea or headaches in over a week. Perhaps her optimism was premature, but Sami chose to start acting as if she might live. In the evenings, she'd taken to exploring the neighborhood, attempting to spot people who matched the photographs in Marisol's files. If she knew who she was up against, if she could recognize her enemy, Sami would feel somewhat in control.

Today the townspeople were celebrating a fiesta. She wasn't sure what saint or occasion they were commemorating but that didn't prevent her from joining in the fun. Dressed in a cotton sundress and sandals, Sami would have blended in if her hair and skin were a shade or two darker. The music was loud and mesmerizing. A parade that reminded her of Mardi Gras wound its way down the narrow streets. The only difference she could see was that the theme was darker, there were more skulls and frightening masks, and the participants seemed to be intent on pushing their way through the crowd even if they knocked over booths or people to do it. Sami didn't let that bother her. She paid a few pesos for a drink and a pastry, and continued to study every face she passed.

Most of the people she encountered were revelers, just out to enjoy the day. There were a few who appeared to be looking for someone. She guessed she fit into that category herself. Taking a sip of the tart beverage, Sami was about to swallow when she almost choked…ahead of her a man dressed as a court jester pulled a gun and shot another man point blank—just like in the movies. Another man swooped in and gathered the victim up in a blanket and placed him on a float and they just resumed the festivities. With the noise of the horns and guitars and drums, the commotion had been drowned out. But she had seen it with her own two eyes.

Sami swallowed a scream, because as she was observing the crime, someone was observing her.

A man held her in his gaze, memorizing her face. His expression hardened and he pointed and called out.

She didn't wait around. Sami realized she needed to run. She had witnessed something that no one was supposed to see.

Dashing through the crowd, weaving in and out, she fled, intent on escaping. Every few seconds, she looked back over her shoulder, fearing the harlequin would be upon her. With a hand on her chest, she pushed herself to run on until she neared her apartment. Cutting into a shop, she leaned against the wall and waited. Several minutes passed before she had the courage to glance through the window. When she saw no one who appeared to be looking for someone, she crept out the back and darted to the building where she'd rented a one-bedroom flat.

Her hand shook as she inserted the key. Once inside, she sank to the floor. Closing her eyes, she tried to remember what he'd looked like—the shooter. The makeup he'd worn obscured his features. Still, she had to try. Reaching for Marisol's computer, Sami logged on and brought up the file of the cartel's known members. With haste, she thumbed through, then went back through them again more slowly. Sure enough, there he was. The shape of his nose and the set of his eyes were unmistakable. Rey Olmos.

She'd been spotted. Just going outside would be dangerous now. What the heck was she going to do?

Fingering her short hair, she let herself fret—until the very strands in her hand made her smile. All she'd need was loose clothes, no makeup, tennis shoes and she'd have a disguise.

Sami was going to be a boy.

* * *

Espada Ancha, the Pirate's Lair, was filled to the brim with rowdy customers. Sami let her eyes roam the crowd. Hookers openly hawked their wares. Members of street gangs with various tattoos seemed to feel at home. Several well-dressed men smoked cigars and others huddled together talking and drinking, possibly selling drugs or information. Some of the people were probably legitimately there for a drink, but Sami felt they were a minority. A 'se busca ayudante' sign announced that help was needed. Remaining hunched over, going for a humble look, she approached the bartender. The clothes she'd bought for the occasion would have swallowed two people her size. They only touched her on the shoulders. Her breasts were flattened by a compression bra and the baseball cap she wore covered her short hair and left her face in shadow. Walking up to the man who appeared to be in charge, she spoke, "Excuse me, sir. I'm looking for a job."

The older gentleman eyed her like she was an unwelcome roach. He examined her scathingly and sneered. "Applying for the job of bouncer, big man?"

Sami didn't let his attitude dissuade her. "No, sir. I saw your sign. I'm applying for the bartender/waiter job, I can mix anything and I'll work for half of what you're offering until you're satisfied I can cut it." The job was worth more to her than money. And she wasn't lying either, she'd studied mixology as an elective in school. Mostly online, but her father had let her practice on him with his well-stocked bar. As she waited for his reply, her eyes took in the room. This was a man's domain with paintings of bare-breasted mermaids on every wall and three big flat screen TVs with different

33

sports playing on each one. A mahogany bar was polished so she could clearly see herself reflected there. She wondered if she was fooling anyone with her disguise.

"Let me see." Sami could tell by his tone that he thought he was calling her bluff. "Mix me an Ojo rojo."

"No problem." She took a cold glass, added beer, clamato juice, and tabasco. "There, drink up."

"Okay." He nodded his head begrudgingly. "Mexico Lindo."

Tequila, lemon, and Curacao. "Cheers." She handed the drink to him. Sami figured mixed drinks were a rare order in this place. This was a beer drinking crowd. Still, she was prepared. "Can I have the job? On a trial basis?"

"Do you speak enough Spanish, Little Gringo?" As he spoke, he wiped down the bar, handing beers to waiting customers who eyed Sami with veiled suspicion. One was a middle-aged woman who winked at him.

Sami answered in the affirmative and added a compliment about the lady to the left for good measure. She thought she might as well reinforce the fact that she was male.

The bartender laughed. "My name's Fred. The job's yours if you want it. You can start tomorrow, be here by six and expect to work eight long hours."

"Thanks, Fred, I appreciate it." She coughed, wishing her voice was deeper.

"And don't worry, we'll find you a woman." Raking a gaze over Sami, Fred smirked. "Even if you are a little light in the britches."

"Good to know." Well, great. So much for her manly attributes. Next time she'd put a rolled up sock in her panties.

CHAPTER TWO

Yacht Basin, Galveston Island...

"Oh my God," Hannah said with wonder as she gazed on in amazement. "It's so big."

A dry amused voice came from behind them on the dock. "Why, thank you, beautiful. But let's not say that kinda stuff in front of Kyle. Just to be safe. You know how sensitive he is."

Kyle Chancellor smiled. He didn't need to turn around to know exactly who had joined them. "So good of you to join us, Micah," Kyle offered as he kept his arm around his petite wife, letting his hand drift to the small of her back before giving a light pat to her firm behind.

"Hey!" Hannah jumped at the tease from her husband. "Down, boy."

Kyle winked at her. "It's never down with you around."

"For God's sake." Micah huffed. "Get a room, you two."

"Hey, Micah. How are you?" She hugged their friend warmly. "The room's a good idea, though. I've always wanted to do it on a boat." Hannah took Kyle's arm and tried to pull her oversize husband by the hand. "We've got time. Let's get on board and head down below. We can test the 'motion of the ocean'." The grin on her face was exuberant, but her man stood his ground.

"I do like the sound of that, believe me," Kyle growled, pulling her close for a kiss. "But I'm not sure the big old lug would appreciate us doing that on his boat."

"A case of loose hips, not loose lips sinking ships," Micah added under his breath.

Kyle cut a sharp glance at his old friend. Micah Wolfe had a bad habit of saying too much.

Hannah had no idea what they were talking about. "Why would Jet mind us making ourselves at home? He certainly has no qualms about crashing at our place." She turned to regard Micah.

Kyle jumped in before Micah could explain his comment. "Jet's kind of a crusty old sailor, Hannah." When he saw his generalization wasn't going to be enough of an explanation to appease his cute lady, he elaborated. "His father is old-school. He raised Jet to have the same sea-faring values."

"You know," Micah added with a wave of his hand. "Red sky at night, sailor's delight. Never answer a siren's call. Blah blah blah. All that weird mariner stuff."

"It's what he believes in, Micah," Kyle said in defense of their friend.

"And I'm fine with all of that," Micah returned. "But one thing I'm not fine with, is any rule that excludes women, for any purpose." He winked at Hannah. "I enjoy having the fairer sex close at hand."

As they stood in front of the sailing yacht, Hannah was getting antsy. Although she could have watched the exchange between the two men go on for hours, she loved the way they all got along—one minute at each other's throats, the next, watching each other's back—but she was getting more and more confused and wanted answers. "What are you two talking about? Excludes women?"

"Wanna tell her, or should I?" Micah asked with a raised eyebrow.

"I'll tell her." Kyle let out a long breath. "Thanks for this, by the way."

Micah offered a wry smile. "You brought it up, Dingus." His response drew a small chuckle from Hannah's lips.

Kyle frowned at his wife. "Please, don't encourage him. We have a hard enough time with Wolfe as it is." His look might have been stern but deep down inside, he loved how his wife got along so well with his friends, and hearing Micah make her laugh brought warmth to his heart.

Hannah looked her hunky husband up and down. "Spill it, the suspense is killing me!" She gave them both playful whacks on the arm.

"Okay. Jet doesn't usually allow women on his boat," Kyle told her while rubbing his arm.

"Really, that's strange, considering we're having a party here tonight where women will be present, including myself."

Micah jumped in to save his buddy from having to speak to his lovely wife about such delicate matters. "Well, Kyle said he *usually* doesn't allow women on board. This party's an exception." He hoped that Hannah would have gleamed what he meant with the raised eyebrows on his face, but she remained confused.

Kyle added to Micah's already vague explanation. "Normally, he only lets women on board for *certain reasons*."

They both watched for that moment of recognition to flash across Hannah's face, but when it didn't, Micah had had enough. "Oh, for God sake's." He put his arm around Kyle's wife and moved down to whisper in her ear, "Jet usually only lets women on his boat to have sex with him, Hannah darling."

Hannah thrust a hand up over her mouth. "Oh, my goodness." She gasped with a titter. "So why the ban on women? That's so unlike Jet," Hannah spoke with a bit of disbelief.

Micah sidled up to her, speaking in low tones as if sharing secret knowledge. "Jet allows women onboard when his boat is docked, never when he sets sail. He says a female is bad luck on a ship, she will anger the sea."

"And who wants to anger the sea?" A deep voice from above caused Hannah to jump. Jet leaned over the railing, shirtless, looking down at them with an amused expression. "You coming up or not, you limey landlubbers?"

Micah put a hand to his heart. "A joke? From Captain Blah himself? I never thought I'd see the day."

The brawny sailor flipped his friend off and waved them up.

"I'm not so sure I like the idea of you inviting my woman aboard your ship," Kyle said with a sly smile when they were on board.

"He's insulted you, Kyle," Micah drawled. "You're just going to have to fight him to get your honor back." Micah never gave up on a chance to try to get Kyle and Jet to come to blows, it'd been something he'd wanted to see since the day he'd met the hulking sailor who had saved his ass more than once in combat.

"You and I both know he wouldn't stand a chance." Jet pulled his hands up to cover his face in a classic boxing stance. His white linen pants hugged the thick muscles of his thighs, the drawstring loose around his waist.

Kyle brought his hands up to mirror Jet's. "Careful now, Jet. We wouldn't want to give Micah what he's been after for so long."

Micah stepped behind Jet. "That sounds like an insult to me, big guy. You'd better punch him."

"Nobody punches anybody. And of course, I'm welcome aboard. I'm family!" Hannah was in heaven. Although these three men weren't related, they were still brothers and it thrilled her to see them goofing off together so freely. Woe be to any man who attacked one of them, because there was a whole platoon of the Equalizers waiting to seek vengeance.

Jet winked at Kyle and Micah over Hannah's head. "That's right, you're family." He left it at that.

As they strode along the deck, she marveled at the beauty and majesty of the ship, Hannah ran her hand over the smooth railing. "I've never seen anything like this before. How long is it?"

Jet stopped to check on a winch. "One hundred eighteen feet. She's as sturdy as they come. I bet I could sail it around the globe twice and never feel a single wave in my sleep." The sails were down, bunched away in storage. They only came out in open waters, but the two tall masts near the center of the ship stood twenty-two feet tall and proud.

Kyle slipped his hand into his awestruck wife's delicate one. "What did you end up naming her, Jet?" They'd seen the large white sheet covering the name at the back of the boat when they arrived and even though Kyle knew Jet wouldn't tell them until the christening, he still gave it a shot.

Jet just snorted. "Nice try."

Micah stood looking down on a piece of decking that didn't match the rest of the broad expanse. "I see you've been busy."

"I had to go over that spot a few times to seal it. I'll have to go back and do a few more coats on the rest when I get a chance." The ship was two-toned with a dark teak stained deck and the bridge had a fresh coat of bright white on it. The hull was now a textured Aruba Blue that Jet had personally picked out. "A man's boat should blend in with the sea, that's what Nemo Foster always says." Jet could still hear him in his head. 'Those damn yuppies and their blasted cigar boats. Bright pink or yellow, it's just showing off, that's all it is.' But like with all things, Nemo Foster had been Jet's compass, his guide on the sea and the rest of the world. He carried most of his father's traditions and beliefs with him everywhere he went.

"I like it, you did a beautiful job." Hannah complimented her husband's friend.

"The Aruba Blue masked a god-awful Clove Patch green the boat's previous owner had neglected to touch up over the years. It took me three coats to fully cover the mess."

"I know you're proud, Jet." Kyle folded his arms and looked the boat from stem to stern. Micah had called Kyle on their way over with instructions. He'd told Kyle, 'Jet's been working really hard on his new boat. Try to act impressed.' But Micah as always, was just kidding. What Jet had accomplished was impressive. Kyle knew Micah had been with Jet each step of the way, even going along to the Galapagos Islands to look at the motor-sailor when he was trying to decide whether or not to purchase it.

"Yes, he did." Micah slapped Jet on the back. He would be accompanying his buddy on the maiden voyage and he'd wanted to be sure it was safe enough to be on for all those days on the open ocean.

'Would you stop your worrying.' Jet had huffed the first time they'd seen the boat and Micah had expressed his concerns about the watercraft's seaworthiness.

"I told you all she needed was a fresh coat of paint and some TLC." He stood back and admired his new love. "I fell for this lady from the first moment I saw her; flaking paint, rusted rudder and all. Don't get me wrong, I enjoyed the Viking Motor Yacht, but this vessel has something the other one sadly lacked. And that's character. It looks like it's seen some rough waters and if the anchor could talk, I bet it'd tell us some tales of depths yet charted and creatures never seen by the human eye. Yeah, this new boat is a salty old sailor just like my father and that's what I've always wanted."

"How is your father?" Hannah asked, holding Kyle's arm and watching Jet with pride.

"He's on the mend, Tyson is with him. I'm not worried."

"Good, I know you can't wait for him to see it." Micah folded his arms and looked around, imagining what it was going to be like riding the waves from Texas to Veracruz.

"He's going to love it, no doubt in my mind." He tossed a coiled rope to one side out of the way. With a half-smile, he admired the added footage of his new boat. Memories brought out a longing inside the stoic warrior. It reminded him of his formative years spent rushing up and down the deck of his father's boat, the Seaduction. Jet was fifteen before he even understood what the boat's name meant, but Nemo Foster had been seduced by the sea the very first time he laid eyes on it and his boat was aptly named. The Seaduction was where Jet had learned how to sail, where he'd learned how to swim, where he'd learned how to be a man and where his love of the ocean was born. Now that he had his own big ship, something within him wanted a little boy of his own to teach to love the ocean—how he was going to accomplish that within the realm of his 'rules' he didn't know just yet.

Jet took them around the deck. Never the type to brag, there was unmistakable pride in his voice as he showed off the handmade railings he'd crafted with his own hands, putting layer and layer of stain and varnish on to protect against the elements. He showed them the date, tomorrow's date, which had been stitched into the mainsail to commemorate the boat's maiden voyage. Right under the date his name was embroidered as well, with the word 'Captain' beside it, the C as bold and yet understated as the captain himself. "I had the winches made custom by a guy up in Maine." He ran a hand over the polished steel.

"What's with the two wheels?" Kyle observed, noting the big wooden ship's wheel at the helm and inside the wheelhouse, or cockpit, there was another more modern looking one.

"This one," he touched the wheel beside them, "this is for me. They both work, I guess you could say it's like having a choice between automatic and standard transmission." He smiled at his friends. "I tend to like old-fashioned things."

"Awww, Jet's a romantic." Hannah was touched.

Micah, seeing Jet was about to get embarrassed, noticed there were no other guests. "Hey, I'm always the one who likes to make an entrance. Where is everybody?"

Jet was showing Hannah how to tie an anchor hitch knot. "Nobody's here yet. You're early."

It was then out of the corner of his eye, that Kyle saw a figure making its way up the stairs from below deck. She stepped out of the galley door, all legs, dressed in a tight black cocktail dress that left no room for mistaking what she had in mind. She strode over to them with a smile, and even though there wasn't the slightest hint of a breeze, her hair was a mussed-up mess. "Hi, everyone." She stretched her hand out cheerily. "I'm Amber."

Hannah quickly accepted the gesture. She could tell Amber was nervous. "Hi, Amber. I'm Hannah. Pleasure to meet you." Hannah eyed Micah, raising one eyebrow. Micah had to cover his mouth with his fingers to hide his grin.

"Thanks, pleasure to meet you too." Relief washed over Amber's face like a tidal wave and the freckles dotting her cheeks became more visible when the blush dissipated.

Micah watched the look on Jet's face shift. He chuckled and shook his head.

Jet caught his knowing look and shrugged. Shit, he'd forgotten all about the girl he'd left in the cabin below. Poor Amber fidgeted as she stood there trying to make friends. Jet couldn't blame her, though, he'd really been giving it to her hard in his quarters only minutes ago. With Amber on all fours, he'd had his fingers dug into her hips, driving in and out of her with force, only stopping when he heard the familiar voices outside the porthole.

Amber moved toward Jet's side, eyeing Kyle a bit too long for Hannah's liking, so Hannah stepped to her husband. "Amber, this is Kyle. My husband."

Along with pride, there was a territorial tone in her voice that made Kyle's cock twitch in his pants at the notion of Hannah marking her territory. Even though he knew Amber would be gone and never seen again after tonight, Kyle still hoped there wouldn't be any trouble between the women.

Micah stepped toward the wide-eyed girl in the tight dress. "I'm Micah." He took her hand and kissed it. "So nice to meet you, Amber." He could see the impressions Jet's fingers had left on her left forearm, the big guy just didn't know his own strength.

Jet didn't react. These people were his family. Hannah was protective of Kyle and Micah was going to be Micah no matter what. He held court wherever he went and flirted openly with married women right in front of their husbands and got away with it. He was always pushing the limits, but love him or hate him, the Wolfe had a charm about him that let him do as he pleased.

Hannah almost gasped at Micah's forwardness. Sure, she'd seen him make such brazen moves similar to this in the past, but Jet was practically his brother and when the ink-covered warrior didn't even flinch, she needed to know why. Pulling Kyle to the starboard side of the ship, she demanded Kyle do something about Micah's actions. "You have got to say something to Micah. I know he can be a handful sometimes, but Amber is Jet's woman. He just can't hit on her like that, Kyle. It's not right. Jet is his friend."

Kyle pulled her close. "It's okay." There was still so much Kyle's new bride didn't understand about his friends. The other Equalizers were a little more forthright about themselves, but Jet was a tougher nut to crack. Jet was the quintessential tough guy. He didn't say much to anyone, only sharing himself with people he truly trusted and cared about. He'd told Kyle how embarrassed he was by the attention he received being a professional fighter and a champion at that. Kyle knew Jet often found himself in trouble with the fighting organization he represented. At times, he'd refused to do promotional tours or interviews. 'I'm a fighter, not an actor,' Jet would often repeat at mandatory press junkets before big fights. He hated the promotional side of the business. All he wanted to do was fight and Kyle knew the organization had been trying to force him out for a while now, they just hadn't found an opponent who could take his title from him. Jet had dispatched every contender they'd placed in front of him so far.

"It's not okay, it isn't right," she protested.

"It's kinda complicated, baby," Kyle told the sexy girl at his side. "Jet came up the old school way. His father is a real hard-ass. Nemo is as tough as a two dollar steak and as mistrustful of women as they come."

Hannah demanded to know more. "Why? What has that got to do with anything?"

Kyle took her hand in his and rubbed the pad of his thumb over her palm. "Baby. You know I love you and I trust you with my life. Jet's issues are his own, and if he wants to tell you about them, then he will. I can't betray my friend like that." His loyalty made her heart turn to liquid. "Some men just have a tougher time trusting a woman and letting them in. That's all I can say." He placed a finger under her chin and lifted it up to face him. "All right?"

Hannah felt a pang of guilt for trying to force him to tell her about Jet's issues, but the kiss Kyle laid on her made all of that guilt melt away.

"Now." Kyle stole her hand. "Let's go find that room Micah was talking about."

* * *

"And just where have you two been?" Micah wanted to know when Kyle and Hannah returned to a party that was in full swing.

"Ummmm," Hannah stammered. "We, uhhh..."

"Ummm, I understand." Micah smiled, the contented look on her face gave them away.

"I had a conference call," Kyle said rather unconvincingly.

Amber stepped toward Kyle. She'd clearly had a few drinks by now. "Oh, that's right. I remember now. You're our sexy new governor." She placed a hand on Kyle's forearm and smiled up at him with a laugh.

Hannah had felt sorry for Amber earlier. She was fairly certain from what Kyle and Micah had said, that Amber was only here for a one-night stand with Jet, but this was the second time she'd come on to her husband and this time, Hannah was over it. She laced her arm inside her husband's. "Excuse us, Amber. Where's Jet?"

Amber removed her hand and stepped back, pretending to survey the party.

"He's conferring with his fight team," Micah answered Hannah, then held out his arm to Amber. "May I get you a drink?" Amber gratefully accepted Micah's offer, and he eased her away from the first couple before Hannah's claws came out any farther. There were about thirty people there, all drinking and carousing on the main deck. The boat had been outlined with glowing blue LED lights, making it stand out in the harbor. Jet had scoffed at the idea when Micah had suggested it. 'The ship speaks for itself. It doesn't need lights.' But Micah had chosen to ignore his friend's words and everyone marveled at how good the lights looked when they arrived just as the sun was going to bed for the evening.

Below deck, in one of the six guest cabins, Jet sat listening to his boxing coach, Peter Donaldson.

"I just don't think it's the best idea right now," Peter said with a worried look on his face.

"Look, Pete," there was a finality in Jet's voice as he started to speak, "I know you don't want me to do this, but I don't have a choice. This jerk has been running his mouth forever. Telling people that I'm dodging him. Afraid to fight him."

"Everybody does that when you're the champ. Let him come fight his way up the ranks and face you in a sanctioned bout. He's just a punk."

"You know that will never happen, Pete. Santoro is a piece of garbage. He's been talking trash about me on the internet for years. He's a bully." He took a sip of his drink and fixed his coach with a stern look. "And I hate bullies."

Jet's manager, Rick Joseph, chimed in. "You won't get paid for this, Champ. Don't waste your time."

"Always about the money, huh, Rick?" Jet scoffed. "I don't care if I get paid."

"It's a street fight, Jet! It's not worth it."

"It's about respect, Rick."

Pete made one final attempt. "Come on, Jet."

"Save your breath, Pete. I've already plotted my course. We leave tomorrow."

"We?"

Micah stepped into the room. "That's right. *We*."

"You have got to be kidding me." Pete threw his hands up in the air. "This guy?" Jet shrugged his shoulders. "Why are you taking Wolfe? Are you going there to fight Santoro or seduce his wife?"

Jet turned his back, folding his arms across his barrel chest. "It's happening, Pete. Whether you like it or not. So I suggest you go enjoy the party or just go home, because you're not going to talk me out of this."

There was nothing else to say, the hulking sailor had said his piece. Jet could be single-minded in his approach to a problem and there was no use talking anymore about it. He'd made up his mind and that was that.

Micah deflected the angry glares Jet's team gave with a smile as they passed by. "Oh, yeah. It's my fault. Like I tell him what to do."

Jet paced the cramped cabin.

"You know," Micah thrust his hands into the pockets of his dress pants, "you told me this trip was about the San Miguel. It didn't seem like that's what your conversation was about."

"It is about the San Miguel." Jet sliced his hand through the air.

"And again. That conversation didn't sound like it was about sunken treasure."

Jet didn't want to hear this right now. Ultimately, the trip was about connecting with someone to help him bring up the treasure from the San Miguel. But there was another part to it, a part he hadn't told anyone else about, not even Micah. "Just wait until we get out to sea. Then I'll tell you everything."

"Wait till we've gone out past the point of no return?" Micah huffed with a laugh. "You know I don't know how to drive this damn boat and I don't want to have to swim a mile back to shore with sharks all around me."

The conversation with Pete and Rick and now Micah had gotten Jet's blood heated and he wondered where Amber was. "Just trust me on this one, Wolfe. I promise you it's nothing we can't handle. And by the time we get back, you'll be able to *pilot* the *ship*." He corrected Micah on his terminology.

"I'll trust you, big guy. Like I've trusted you so many times before. But I thought this was going to be a vacation of sorts, a trip to Mexico to consort with some sexy señoritas while you played Jacque Cousteau. I should be mad at you for not telling me the whole truth." He put his hand on Jet's broad shoulder and Jet turned to regard him. "But I'm not. I trust you. And if you say we can handle it, than we can handle it. And besides, I just bought a new pair of Top-Siders for the trip and I don't feel like returning them. So I guess you're stuck with me."

"It'll be fun, partner. I promise."

There was a sharp rap on the door. "You in there, baby?" It was Amber's sultry voice coming from the other side.

Micah grinned. "Speaking of fun. Enjoy yourself tonight, because it's going to be just you and me out there on the water for weeks and I don't want you to start looking at me funny. I know what those long trips with no women do to you sailor types. And, honey, I ain't got no plans of being your woman."

"You're too skinny for me." Jet snorted.

"Pig! I'm not even going to respond to that." Micah opened the door, and Amber was standing in the doorway, holding a champagne bottle up to her lips and practically licking it up and down.

Micah patted his friend on the shoulder and whispered in his ear, "That girl is in heat, good buddy. I'll hit the lights on the way out. See you tomorrow morning."

Jet eyed his bawdy female companion. She moved aside as Micah passed, paying him no attention as he went. It must have driven Micah mad, a woman not paying attention to him, but this little vixen only had eyes for Jet and she looked him up and down, rubbing the pad of her thumb over the tip of the champagne bottle and licking her lips.

Micah hopped up and clung to one of the huge masts in the middle of the ship. "You all know me," he shouted. "If there's one thing I love..."

"It's women!" three voices cried out from the crowd and a chorus of laughter ripped through the salty air.

Micah laughed it off with his cool grin. "Okay. If there's one thing I love *after* women, it's a good party. But this one unfortunately has come to a premature end. Something I know my good buddy, Governor Chancellor, is familiar with."

The crowd all turned toward the governor and even Kyle and Hannah had to join in the laughter. "One time!" Kyle responded. "One time!"

The crowd loved him because of moments like this, he was able to not take himself too seriously and again, Hannah reveled in the camaraderie of the two friends.

"But seriously, though, folks," Micah continued. "You ain't gotta go home. But you gotta get the hell outta here." He stepped down off the mast and started herding the crowd toward the exit. "Yeehaw!" He playfully slapped a woman in a red dress on the rump. "Move along now, ya hear."

"Sounds like the party's over," Amber said from her spot in the cramped cabin.

Jet stepped up, reached a hand over her shoulder and closed the door behind her. "Party's just getting started in here." He pulled her to him, and she crashed into the rock hard muscles of his chest.

Jet was big and overheating, the blood coursing through his veins after the discussion with his team had gone straight to his cock and it tested the fabric of his pants. He took the bottle from her hand and placed it on the porthole ledge. Already the lone porthole in the cabin was starting to fog over. Amber's eyes slammed shut and her lips were devoured by Jet's in an instant. The beast inside was pounding at the cage as he closed his hand tightly around her wrist.

"Ouch," she whimpered through gritted teeth as they kissed.

But Jet didn't loosen his grip, he tightened it and brought her hand in behind her back and then the other one to meet it. He encircled her slender wrists with one big paw, clamping down on it, controlling Amber's body while causing her to lose control of her breathing.

She jerked her hands out of instinct and Jet chuckled. "Going somewhere?"

Amber tried to pull free again but it was no use. He was too powerful. She was at his mercy and she knew it. If he hadn't been holding her up, she might have collapsed to the floor.

Jet pushed her head to the side with his, searing her neck with his warm breath. "Was I too rough with you earlier?" He ran his sandpaper tongue across her collarbone.

"I'm a little sore," Amber whispered between gasps. She moved back and forth on her feet, fidgeting with the attention he lavished on her neck.

"You know, if you spend the night, I won't be going any easier on you."

"I don't want you to."

"And what is it you want right now?"

"For you to let me go."

"Why would I do that?"

"Because I want that cock of yours."

"What are you going to do with it?"

Amber looked to the side and Jet's eyes followed their path. The champagne bottle sat on the ledge, gleaming, calling out to them like a siren. Amber smirked. "Oh, I've got an idea. Why don't you let me go?" She bucked her hips toward him and rubbed herself against the thick erection that stood proudly between them. "I'll be glad to show you."

Jet relaxed his grip but didn't let go entirely. He was riled-up and it would've felt good to release all that pent-up energy on Amber, tear her dress off, bend her over and fuck her into next month. But for the moment, he felt like letting her tend to him before he sent her on her way.

"Okay." He released her from his grip. "Do what you will."

Amber reached for the bottle, snatched it off the ledge and bounded up to whisper in his ear. "I will. And I'll enjoy it too."

Jet relaxed and let her do what she wanted to him. And what she wanted became apparent quickly. Amber's nimble fingers found their way to the drawstring of his pants. She looked up at him, biting her bottom lip as the drawstring came untied. Jet's throbbing cock forced its way out the top of his pants, the thick head already smeared with pre-cum.

Amber's aggressiveness spiked and she walked Jet the few short steps back to the bench in the cabin before dropping to her knees and pulling his pants down with her. "Sit," she ordered, licking her way up the length of his shaft.

He did as he was told, this was just what he needed right now. To be serviced.

Amber took him in her mouth, bobbing her head up and down. Jet often wondered what it'd be like to experience something like this while out at sea with the waves rocking them in an erotic rhythm. But rules were rules, no women were allowed on board the ship while sailing, so he'd always have to wonder.

He threw his head back. "God dammit, I needed this. Keep going."

Spurred on by his approval, Amber finally found the courage to do what she'd been planning.

"Don't stop," Jet moaned when she took her lips from around his pulsing cock.

With a sly smile, Amber tilted the champagne bottle and poured liquid all over his dick. The bubbles tickled Jet's cock as it washed down the shaft. His legs twitched, the sensation on the head was new and pleasurable.

"Want me to clean that up for you?"

Jet nodded his head in response, and Amber did as she said she would. With relish, she licked up and down the backside of his erection, dropping down to suck each one of his balls before licking and nibbling back up the side. She took him into her mouth and stroked while she sucked. The feeling was sheer bliss and before he knew it, Jet was on the verge of exploding. He laced the fingers of his right hand in Amber's silky hair and guided her up and down. "Don't stop. Don't stop!" His cries echoed in the small room, bouncing off the fog frosted window.

Pumping as she suckled, she drove him over the edge and Jet released his tension into her mouth. All the stress of the talk with his team melted away as he erupted.

Amber sighed, falling back into a sitting position against the wall, sipping champagne. She was still sore all over from their earlier session and now the alcohol was getting to her.

Needing some air, Jet stepped over her, doing his pants up as he walked out of the room. He strolled out to the bow of the boat and looked left, out over the darkness of the water. The moon hung low in the sky.

Tomorrow he and Micah would set sail, head south on a new adventure. Just like his life had always been, he was always looking to the horizon, uncertain of what the future would hold.

The same could be said of his life with women. Amber was down in the cabin, probably about to pass out, but sleepovers with a woman weren't a part of his life and as much as he would always blame it on maritime superstitions, Jet knew deep down, it was his father's lack of trust in women that had molded his own attitude toward them. The rocky relationship between Nemo and his mother had engrained a deep mistrust of the female of the species in Jet. A mistrust that had him marching back to the cabin on a mission. "Where are your keys?" Jet asked in a low tone as he helped Amber to her feet. "I'll drive you home."

CHAPTER THREE

Down in Veracruz, Mexico...

"Here you go, Mr. Andrade." Sami's hand shook as she pushed the shot of tequila at the man she blamed for Marisol's disappearance.

"Gracias." He didn't spare her a glance, for which she was grateful, just shook ash off his cigar and went to rejoin a lighter skinned man whom she now knew went by the name of Rey Olmos.

In the past two weeks, Sami had carved out her own little niche in the seedy neighborhood. Dressing as a boy gave her more freedom. Not that she'd been inundated with catcalls or come-ons as a girl, but she felt more free and safer in the disguise. Since eating the diet prescribed by Dr. Rio, Sami was gaining a little weight and some curves too. She still didn't linger in front of a mirror, but maybe she wasn't as gaunt and drawn looking as she'd been before. A little pink in her cheeks would be welcome. As her treatments progressed, Sami was required to spend less and less time at the clinic. Now, it was only four hours in the mornings so she was free to work in the afternoon and evenings.

In her spare time, she'd practically memorized Marisol's files and added some information of her own. Leona had published her sixth blog since Sami had picked up the mantle and from the buzz she could hear in the bar and around town, she was accomplishing her goal. Not only was the Lioness getting emails and comments, she'd heard several of the cartel issuing threats about what they would do to the 'bitch' if they ever found her. What she didn't hear was questions about why Leona had reemerged, which worried her. Sami had no clue what that meant.

"Hey, muchacho, give me a beer," an old man called out. 'Young man,' he called her. Good, at least her disguise was still working.

"Coming right up, señor." She fetched his beer and handed it to him. His younger companion held up a hand for a refill. While she was getting him another shot of Jack, they continued their conversation.

"Did you hear Jet Foster is coming to fight Santoro?"

"No me digas! To Veracruz? When?"

"Yes, to Veracruz. I don't know for sure. Soon."

Sami almost dropped the glass she was holding. She couldn't resist eavesdropping on the conversation if she'd tried. Sidling up to the two customers, she asked, "Foster and Santoro are fighting? Where can I get tickets?"

The first one laughed. "You like the fights, chico?" He did a few punches in the air toward Sami.

"Yes, I'd like to see Foster fight." Actually, the fighting was secondary, she really just wanted to see Jet—but they didn't need to know that. "Where will the match take place?"

"Who knows?" The second one gestured. "Word will get out, it will probably be in some abandoned warehouse or in one of the sugarcane fields on the outskirts of the jungle."

Sami's eyes widened. "If you hear, will you let me know?"

"Sí, sí," the older one agreed. "If I hear and see you, I will tell you."

A feeling of elation filled Sami. The thought that she might get to be in the crowd to see Jet Foster fight was an unexpected gift. In a happy daze, she made drinks, filled trays, and settled up tabs until a sultry voice to her left caused her to drop a glass on the tile floor, which shattered in a million pieces.

"Oh, are you hurt?" A chubby cheeked woman with a big smile and dark round eyes placed her hand over Sami's. "I've been watching you." She batted her eyelashes. "I can't keep my eyes off your cute little backside." Sami's eyes widened. She was tongue-tied but apparently the woman wasn't having the same problem. "I never liked to come here before. Having you here has made all the difference." She winked at Sami. "You're bringing sexy back."

Sami coughed, sweeping up the glass. "What can I get you, ma'am?"

"A margarita on the rocks and a kiss for starters." She leaned forward, her massive breasts lying on the bar.

All of a sudden, Sami was all thumbs. She'd never met one in person, but she presumed this was a cougar. "The drink is coming right up." Sami turned and busied herself pouring the tequila.

Fred, seeing everything, came over and elbowed Sami. "See, I told you we'd find you a woman. There's girls for men like you." Fred studied Sami. "You remind me of that Canadian singer, that kid. You know, the one they discovered on YouTube, he's got that high voice. What's his name?"

Sami bristled. Great. She looked like the Bieb. "I don't know." She finished preparing the drink and handed it to her admirer. "There you go, ma'am."

"I'm Carlotta." She patted the stool next to her. "Come sit by me, handsome. What's your name?"

"Go. I'll cover you for a while, you need a break." Sami didn't get a chance to refuse, Fred guided her around the bar. "This is Sam. He's from Texas."

Sami sat next to the woman, who outweighed her by a good thirty pounds. Her skin crawled a bit. She wasn't cut out to be a guy or a lesbian. "Hello," was all she could manage.

The woman was definitely in heat. Before Sami could move or protest, she had her hand on Sami's knee and started moving it fast up her leg. "I bet you're limber." She licked her lips about the time her hand closed over the extra-large tube sock Sami had folded artistically and put between her legs. "Oh, you like me already," Carlotta purred.

Sami's eyes widened. "Sorry, I have my eye on someone else." Pushing Carlotta's hand away, Sami darted back behind the bar.

Fred nodded his head. "I understand. You play for the other team." He slapped Sami on the back. "Don't worry, I know just the man for you."

"Just get me tickets to see Jet Foster fight. He's the only man I want to see."

Fred threw back his head and laughed. "I think you've set the bar a little high, Sami."

"I agree," Sami muttered under her breath. "But it doesn't hurt to look."

* * *

Back in Galveston...

Jet rolled over in bed, tossing the blankets off, his impressive morning wood greeting the world. A squeaky noise had aroused him from slumber. Raising a sleepy head, he regarded the lazy feline lying beside him in the bed. "Damn it, Polly. I told you not to sleep so close." He rubbed the drowsy black cat on the head. "I'm gonna roll over on top of you one of these nights and crush ya. Come here."

He patted his chest and the feline roused from the bed with a big stretch and a wide yawn, her pointy ears lying flat to her head. Polly made her way slowly up onto Jet's wide chest and lay there to start the day with some much needed ear rubbing.

The contrast was unique, a giant, tattooed sailor being so gentle with the big furball of a cat. The scene might have looked odd to anyone watching, but appearances could be deceiving. Jet might be a hard-ass tough guy, but he had a softer side. He was a pushover for children and animals. Jet fought for his country and he fought in the ring, not just for himself, but for all the little guys out there who couldn't fight for themselves.

Polly, a moniker bestowed on her by Tyson, was a big lumbering cat. Fourteen pounds, she was black as midnight and her belly hung low when she walked. She was surprisingly spry and agile for a feline of such heft. She spent the majority of her day asleep in the sun, or waddling around Jet's boat. If you weren't careful, you could easily mistake her for a rug and trip over her. She wasn't in the habit of moving around that often.

Four years prior, Nemo had found his ship cat nursing four kittens down in the engine room of the Seaduction just after he'd pulled into port from the Bahamas. One cat on board was good luck, they killed mice and kept the sailors company, but five cats were too much for Nemo to deal with. In a drunken stupor he'd told Jet over the phone that he intended to drown the four kittens rather than keep them and Jet had rushed over to the boat to save them before Nemo could do what he threatened. When Jet arrived, he found his father passed out on the deck and he silently slipped away with the four kittens, buying a tiny bottle and milk on the way home. He'd taken them back to his boat to bottle feed them, but unfortunately two didn't survive being away from their mother at such a young age. A couple of weeks later, when the other Equalizers had come for a visit, Micah had fallen in love with Polly's brother and taken the kitten home with him.

Polly had been on every one of Jet's voyages for the last few years. Micah's folks had been good enough to keep the cats while they were in service. But once he'd come back to Texas, they'd been inseparable. She'd lain on the deck with aloof disinterest when he'd raised treasure from the salvage of the S.S Panama and was always the first one there to greet him when he got home from a fight. The two would spend hours together when Jet was out at sea, Polly sitting on his lap with one of Jet's hands on the steering wheel of his ship, the other stroking the feline. A bag of cat treats, or 'crackers' as Jet referred to them, were never too far away.

The cat rolled over, exposing her belly to her master, confident he wouldn't hurt her. "Okay. Get off of me." Jet turned to the right, and Polly rolled down and off of him, crashing to the soft bed below with a thud and a snarl of protest. "Oh, knock it off." Polly lay there, looking at the big man standing at the bed beside her, blinking her eyes as if she hadn't decided whether to get up or not.

Jet pulled on a pair of dark jeans, but didn't do them up. His morning wood was still standing at attention as he went to the bathroom with Polly in tow. His furry little companion stood in the bathroom doorway and watched as Jet splashed water on his face. After Jet scrubbed his teeth clean, he spoke to the cat still watching him intently. "I'm not sure I should feed you this morning. You're lookin' kinda chubby." Polly just blinked and followed a strange sound with her ears. "Oh, who am I kidding? Of course I'm gonna feed you. Lord knows I'd never hear the end of it if I didn't."

Polly followed him up the stairs, her spryness on display, almost tripping him as she raced ahead. She ran to her bowl on the ship's kitchen floor and stood by it, arching her back and waving her tail wildly while meowing her disapproval at the empty bowl.

"Let me put a pot on first." Polly caterwauled her protest at the further delay. "You keep it up and I'll make you wear the little sailor's hat Destry bought for you. And we both know you hate wearing it." He topped off her bowl and gave her a little pat on the head. Jet knew she'd dive right in as soon as she could and be preoccupied with her food for the next few minutes. "Don't forget to chew," Jet reminded his buddy while he put on a pot of coffee and went about preparing a six egg western omelet. It took a lot of protein to maintain the amount of muscle he'd packed onto his body over the years. Eating many large meals a day was just a part of his life.

Polly joined him on the deck above, sitting at the edge of the boat looking out over the water as Jet stood at the railing eating his breakfast. "You almost ready to set sail?" Jet bent and stroked his first mate's head. Polly meowed her approval, her purring drowned out by the crash of the waves as they battered the boats docked at Galveston Bay.

"She's quite the beaut."

Jet and Polly turned around in unison and found Saxon standing behind them.

"Some watch cat you are." Jet huffed and went to greet his friend. "What are you doing here? I thought you were on the job?"

"I was. That's why I couldn't make it to your party last night. But I finished up early. You should have seen the protection these guys had. It was a joke. I could have hacked it in my sleep. I was going to spend the night in Tulsa, but I made the company fly me back on their jet." Saxon had a big brown paper bag tucked under his arm.

"I see you stopped for groceries along the way."

"Actually, I was planning on giving this to you when you got back, but Kyle came online last night and when I messaged him and asked why he was home so early, he told me Micah had shut down your little shindig last night at a reasonable hour and they never got a chance to christen the boat."

"Shit! I must be losing it." Jet looked genuinely disturbed.

"Don't worry. He said he and Hannah were coming back over. Apparently she was pretty upset she didn't get to do her thing last night. Kyle told me, and this is just paraphrasing of course, 'Hannah was plenty angry she didn't get to christen the boat, so she's making me take her back over there tomorrow morning to smash the damn bottle. And if Jet is already gone, she's gonna smash a bottle over his head when he gets back'."

Jet laughed. "I forgot all about the christening." The distraction of the sexual encounter with Amber and the uncomfortable trip they'd taken to drop her off at her place afterward had taken Jet's mind off the actual reason for the party. The captain forgetting to have his boat christened should've been a sign that this maiden voyage might be in trouble, but Jet convinced himself he was just so distracted with other matters that it was a forgivable oversight.

"Well, don't worry, they should be here in a little bit. I'd watch what you say to Hannah, she's awfully anxious to hit something with a champagne bottle."

"Noted. What's in the bag?"

Saxon took the parcel from under his arm, but didn't hand it over. "Now, this gift comes with a disclaimer."

"Okay." Jet loved gifts, he had to clench his fist to keep from reaching for it.

"I had it custom made right after I found out you got the boat. But you are really lousy at sharing information with people. I had to rely on Micah for information so this would be just right. He said every time he asked you for details, you dismissed him. I painted it a few days ago when he finally gave me the correct colors and literally finished putting it together on the jet back from Tulsa."

"What is it?" Jet took the bag with a curious smile.

"Careful!" Saxon barked when it looked like Jet was about to shake the package. "You big ox. Don't be manhandling it like it's one of your opponents."

"It's not a computer, is it?" A look of slight panic came into his eyes.

"*No*, it's not a computer. I know your aversion to anything modern that doesn't help you fight, sail or find treasure."

Jet had little use for any technology that didn't fit a direct need of his. He often scoffed and scolded the other Equalizers while they 'played on their phones,' as he put it.

"Can I open it?"

"I wish you would. Before you smash it."

Jet slipped a hand into the bag with great care and when it emerged, there was a box wrapped in this morning's Tulsa World.

"I like your choice of wrapping paper." He smiled, a twinkle in his eye like a kid on Christmas morning.

"It was all they had on the plane. Beggars can't be choosers."

"What is it?" Jet asked with a giddy smile on his face as he peeled back the taped edge of the wrapping.

"You'll find out in a second."

With great ease the muscle-bound mariner unwrapped his present. Saxon may have been justified in calling him a big ox, but this big ox could be graceful and tender when it was called for.

The box was heavy in his hand, it didn't seem like it could be as fragile as Saxon had insisted. "A new pair of shit-kickers!" Jet hollered when he had finally exposed the oversized brown Harley Davidson shoebox Saxon had wrapped with care. "How'd you know I needed these?" He turned the box around, checking the size on the side of the box. "Twelve holes. All right. And a size fourteen? You even got my size right."

"Try 'em on."

"I think I will." He tossed the lid off with a flip and let it fall to the deck beside his feet. "What the…" The box was full of tissue paper and Jet pulled it out in big clumps. Saxon had placed four cans of Red Bull in the box to give it weight. The real present was in the middle, encased safely in bubble wrap and more of the Tulsa World.

"Gimme one of those." Saxon dipped a hand into the box and took a can. "The Tulsa job was easy, but it was time consuming and I can't sleep for shit on planes." He popped the top and downed the energy concoction in one thirsty gulp.

Jet extracted the bubble wrapped gift and dropped the box on the ground to be with its lid again. In no time Polly would be surveying the intruder and more than likely taking up temporary residence in the box, wondering why the humans were looking at her funny.

The newspaper came off in a hurry and the bubble wrap followed. "Are you kidding me?" Jet was in awe. "You did this for me?"

In his hand, Jet held a ship in a bottle. His ship. Saxon had indeed had it custom made the moment he heard Jet had bought the motor-sailer. Micah had acted as recon on the mission and furnished him with the coloring details he'd needed to complete the project. Saxon had spent weeks putting together test ships so he'd be ready when the time came to put Jet's together. And it was a good thing too, because he'd only had a few days to build a tiny ship inside a small bottle with nothing but glue and tweezers.

"Don't go tearing up on me now, you big ox."

"It's perfect. I love it. Thanks, buddy." He pulled Saxon in for a big hug with his free hand, almost crushing his brainy buddy in the process. "This is going in the wheelhouse with me. Right on the wall above the wheel, so I can look at it when I'm up there."

"You're lucky he went with that gift." Neither Jet nor Saxon had to turn to see who the voice belonged to, they both knew it was Micah. He had a talent for just being places without people even knowing he was there. With Micah, you usually heard his voice before you saw him, a talent he'd used to his advantage as an intelligence officer. "I wanted to get you tighty-whiteys with little blue anchors on them." He bent to pat Polly on the head. "Thunderpunch says hello." Polly just lay there, raising her head only long enough to accept his greeting. "But after thinking about it for a while, I figured you probably already had lots of those."

"You're gonna be on here with me for a while. You might just find out first hand." Jet teased with a grin on his face.

"Now I won't be able to sleep at all tonight. Thank you." He took the bottle from the Captain's hand. "It turned out really good, Saxon."

"Careful!" Saxon warned. "The glue might not be totally set yet."

Jet took the bottle back and cradled it like a sleeping baby. "It's awesome, Saxon. Both of you. Thank you." He held it up to look at it one more time. "You even got the name of the ship right."

As they followed Jet up to the wheelhouse, Saxon spotted Kyle's big black SUV pulling up to the marina. Hannah stepped out with a bounce in her step and an oversize green champagne bottle in her hand. "All right. Where is this damn boat? I feel like doing some smashing." She swung the big heavy bottle around and almost lost her balance.

Kyle caught her with one arm and deflected the swinging bottle with the other. "Careful there, slugger. You almost took me out. That's a serious crime, assassinating a public official." He leaned in and kissed her on the cheek. "But I doubt any court would convict you."

"Why's that?" Hannah asked with stars in her eyes.

"Because you're just about the cutest assassin I've ever seen. You'd better hope you get an all-male jury."

Hannah reasserted her previous query. "Why?"

"'Cause no jury full of men would send you to prison. With me dead, they'd all want to go after your fine ass."

"There wouldn't even be a trial." Hannah looked a bit sad.

"No?"

"Nope. If I hit you with this bottle," she tried to extricate it from Kyle's hands, but her husband held it still with his powerful grip, "and you died. Why, I'd fling myself off the top of Jet's ship and into the ocean just to be with you."

"So what you're saying is, there's no escaping you? Not even in death?"

Hannah smiled and crinkled her nose. "Nope."

Kyle's smile disappeared. "Don't get mad. But I kinda thought this thing between me and you was a casual thing." He held back the urge to start laughing like a master politician.

"Casual thing?" Hannah pulled away from her husband and lifted the bottle up over her head. "Why I oughta..."

Kyle broke for the boat with his sexy little honey in pursuit. "I swear. She meant nothing to me, baby."

"Get back here, you bastard."

Micah, Jet, and Saxon watched the whole scene from the wheelhouse of the ship.

"You know," Saxon commented. "This could look really bad if the paparazzi get pictures of her chasing him with a champagne bottle. I can already see the headline. 'Governor caught with other woman. Wife tries to kill him with bubbles.' Those pics would be worth money to the tabloid rags."

Jet looked over the surrounding area. "I don't see anyone taking pictures."

Micah left the wheelhouse and went to the edge of the railing.

Saxon poked his head out of one of the windows. "What are you doing?"

"Making a couple extra bucks." Micah stood, taking pictures of the scene as Hannah chased Kyle down the dock, trying to control the giant bottle in her hands and giggling as she ran.

Saxon turned to Jet. "You know. I'm not totally sure he's joking."

Kyle skipped the stairs, instead jumping up the side of the boat and using the rail to pull himself up and over.

"Not fair," Hannah said from back down on the dock. "Why do you have to be so damn tall?" She huffed when she was finally on board with the rest of them. "Are we going to christen this boat or what?" She swung the bottle wildly again and all hands on deck scrambled for safety.

Micah's face was overtaken with a smirk. "I'm not sure you want to do that just yet."

"Why's that?" Jet wanted to know.

Micah pointed toward the road leading down to the dock and they all turned to look. "Because I think you're about to have company."

Jet watched as a little red convertible barreled down the road at a high speed. It wasn't the newest car anyone had ever seen, it was a little beat-up from a fender-bender or two and the driver's side mirror had a crack in it. Inside, the armrest had numerous coffee stains on it and beneath the driver's seat was a graveyard for empty diet Coke cans. But the only person on board the ship who knew this was Jet, and the only reason he knew it was because he'd been driving that same car only hours earlier, when he'd driven Amber home in it.

"Shiiiiiit," he croaked when the car pulled to a stop beside Kyle's and Amber bounded from it with a Dunkin Donuts bag in one hand and a tray of coffees balancing in the other.

Kyle pulled him aside. "I'd head over to her if I were you, before she gets on the boat. That girl has a thing for you and she might not react well when you do what you always do."

Jet just looked at him. He knew what Kyle meant. Last night had been a good time with Amber, but that'd been it, a good time. There was nothing more and even though he thought he'd explained that in the car on the way to her place last night, her presence now made it appear he had failed.

Racing down the steps and off the boat, Jet met her as fast as he could. "Morning."

Amber was all smiles and cleavage. "Morning, sailor. I brought coffee." She was nervous after their talk last night, but not the type of woman to take no for an answer. "Oh," she shook the bag in her hand, "and donuts. Hi, everyone." She waved up to the boat.

Hannah waved back to be polite but in her head she didn't want Amber to come aboard.

Jet had enjoyed the same short-term relationship with other girls that he'd had with Amber last night. As quiet and closed off of a person as he was, he couldn't seem to stay out of the limelight. Jet was an internationally famous treasure hunter and mixed martial arts champion, notoriety came with the territory and so did women like Amber. They came on strong and some didn't take no for an answer very easily. Destry referred to the women who flocked around Jet as 'flight attendants,' because they all wanted to ride the Jet, they wanted to be with him because of who he was or what he could give them. The coffee and donuts were just window-dressing. Amber was there to show off her legs and her tits. Being on the arm of Jet Foster was exhilarating, if only for a night, and Amber craved more of it and the perks that came with it.

"What are you doing here?" Jet was about as subtle as a sledgehammer and the smile dropped from Amber's face, but she regained it quickly. She wanted everything to be positive with her and Jet. "I just came to see you off."

"Thank you." Jet took the bag of donuts from her and extracted the apple fritter—one of his guilty pleasures.

She rubbed up against him. "What say we go to your cabin and I'll send you off in style?"

"I've kinda got company." She'd probably propositioned Micah already, and Jet knew she'd made a few passes at Kyle last night, so inviting her on board might make Hannah feel uncomfortable—and he didn't want to do that.

Amber didn't miss a beat, keeping up the sex kitten performance. "Okay. But don't forget about me." She cupped his package through his jeans. "I'd like to get my hands on this when you get back."

Jet peeled her hand off. "Will do."

He walked her back to her car in silence. A future meeting with Amber wasn't on the docket. She was a 'flight attendant,' another example of why neither he nor his father trusted women.

"You mind if I call her when we get back?" Micah asked when Jet rejoined them on the ship.

Jet licked the icing from his thick fingers. "She's not your type. There's no chase there. Seduction isn't necessary. You wouldn't have any fun."

"You know," Saxon started, "I'm still shocked you're going on this trip."

"What shocks you about it?" Micah wanted to know.

"It just doesn't seem like your kind of thing."

"Normally it wouldn't be, but it's new to me, so I want to try it. Besides, it'll give me time to work on my latest novel. I've been neglecting my writing duties lately and the fans are growing restless." Micah wrote erotic romance novels on the side under the name Don Juan. He didn't need the money but to Micah, it was another way to entice the female population, to seduce them by the droves. More than anything in life, he enjoyed the art of seduction and writing what he wrote gave him the ultimate ability to exercise that art.

"I don't want to tell the captain what to do." Kyle looked at his watch. "But I've got a pretty big meeting in half an hour and one hell of an antsy wife. Can we get this underway?"

"Sorry, Mister Mayor," Micah quipped.

"*Governor*," Kyle corrected.

"My bad. I think he's right." They all turned to look at Hannah. She was having an animated conversation with Jet, gesturing with the bottle in her hands. She was clearly excited. "Before she brains someone with that thing."

They made their way down onto the dock, the white sheet still shielded the boat's name from curious eyes. Jet stood in front of the small cluster of friends. "I'm not all fancy with my words like the good Governor here. But I have dreamed my entire life of owning a boat like this. My last boat was great and I loved it, but this right here," he ran his hand over the smooth finish of the hull, "this is my dream boat. She's salty and weathered. Just like my old man."

"You're not exactly polished yourself." Micah did his best Statler and Waldorf impression.

Jet held up his hand. "If the peanut gallery could hold it down for just a few more moments, please. As I was saying. This isn't just a ship to me, it's my hopes and dreams realized. This ship is everything I've ever wanted and I thank you all for being here with me to christen it."

"And all four of us are very happy to be here," Micah muttered.

"I was planning on giving that speech last night, Micah. But I guess you're right, it does kinda lose its effect with only four people present."

"I'd say so. And the crowd looks bored." Micah just kept on.

"Just grab the damn rope, wise-ass." Jet indicated the rope attached to the sheet and Micah took it in his hand and waited for his cue. "Without further ado. I give you." Jet dropped his hand, and Micah pulled the rope. "The Sirena."

The letters were as sharp as a knife with fat lines and swirling tips, it was everything the ship was, elegant but utilitarian all at once. Jet held a hand out and helped Hannah up onto the small platform Micah had insisted Jet build for the occasion. "Misses Chancellor. If you would please do the honors."

Hannah took the stage with his help. "Finally." She slung the big bottle back. "I christen thee, the Sirena." The body of the bottle collided with the ship's hull and broke into a dozen big pieces in her tiny hands. Bubbles splashed down onto the dock, tickling Hannah's bare feet and trickling over the edge and into the sea.

"Now let's get the hell out of here!" Jet cried out. "The San Miguel awaits."

Micah stopped at the top of the steps leading back onto the boat. "You sure you want to stick to your no women on board rule? 'Cause I know a redhead who loves the water. And she's got a cute friend."

Jet gave his friend a push up the rest of the steps. "Get up there or I'll make you scrub the poop deck."

"You think they'll find it?" Saxon questioned from the dock as the Sirena pulled out to sea with its captain behind the wheel.

"I don't know," Kyle responded. "But if anyone can, it's Jet."

* * *

Back with Sami...

Sitting in front of Dr. Rio, Sami folded her hands and listened.

"You've come a long way, Samantha. But we still have much work to do."

In the weeks gone by, trust had grown between them. From the moment she'd walked into the clinic, Sami had felt a sense of peace. Here was a place of healing, not only of the body but also of the mind and spirit as well. From the meals to the water, she'd been taught what would strengthen her and what foods were most beneficial. She found herself eating mostly a raw organic diet, starting out with lemon water laced with cayenne pepper. Fresh salads and fish comprised a large part of her regime and each night ended with fresh coconut water. Thursday was juice day. No solids that day.

"What's next?" She was ready for anything.

"We need to do a liver flush."

Sami grimaced. "That doesn't sound fun."

He patted her hand. "No, it's not that bad. Just drinking some stuff the girls will fix for you. How do you feel?"

"Pretty good." She pushed her hair behind her ear. It had grown, all of three inches now. Sami had decided she looked like Peter Pan.

"I want to give you a medicine that will relax the blood vessels in your brain. This will help the virus therapy to get to the spot where it's needed the most. We won't administer this unless you can be at the clinic for twenty-four hour blocks of time. "

"Okay," Sami agreed nervously. "I have a job, but I can make arrangements to get off."

"Good. Where do you work?"

Sami blushed. "I work at a saloon on the waterfront. I tend bar. The Pirate's Lair."

He looked surprised. "Very well." Checking the calendar, he chose a date. "See if you can arrange for time off and give me a call when you find out one way or the other."

"All right, I can do that. Are we through?" Sami felt like she needed some air.

"Do you have any family in town, anyone you can stay with or who could check on you when you leave the clinic?"

"No, not really. Loyola Lopez is the only one I know in the area," she mused. "But I wouldn't really feel comfortable asking him."

The doctor cleared his throat. "Very well. We'll just have to make the best of it. You'll need to give Maria your address so she can check on you at least once when the procedure is over."

Sami agreed to this and answered a few more questions. When Dr. Rio was through, she had to stop and let Rosa take some blood. Wanting to find out anything she could, she asked, "When will I learn if any of this has worked?"

"We'll be able to give you a preliminary answer to that question soon." She smiled big, making Sami feel somewhat relieved.

"Thanks for everything." She impulsively gave the nurse a hug.

Returning to her apartment, she buried herself in the next blog post for several hours. Since she'd begun working at the bar, Sami had picked up several bits of information. First and most horrific, she'd overheard a conversation that led her to believe the Galvez Cartel was responsible for the abduction and murder of several college students who had been demonstrating at a local community college. Second, she'd learned a local woman who confessed to crimes in police custody was tortured. Lastly, Rey Olmos had shown his ugly face and she'd learned the name of the man he'd gunned down and why—Jorge Morales had helped the cartel launder money across the border in Texas, until he'd made a deal with the authorities in exchange for names and details designed to bring down the cartel. He had paid the price for his audacious move. Now, Sami was systematically putting together information for the same purpose.

Sipping water as she typed, a bit of nausea rose in her throat. Sami tried to ignore it, but it was hard. As she gathered the evidence and prepared to reveal it, it hit her how Marisol had paid for the very same thing, perhaps with her life. What she was doing was dangerous. The only consolation was that she had no one who would notice her absence if something happened. Sami was an island.

* * *

Aboard the Sirena...

"Who were you talking to?" Micah asked when their friends were a distant memory back on shore. They'd been cruising south for about an hour. Watching the water was mesmerizing. Already a pod of dolphins was following along with them.

Jet had the satellite phone in his hand. He always had a radio onboard to keep in contact with the outside world, but the satellite phone was another way to communicate. He had no cell phone or computer that used internet, although his instruments were hooked in with the weather alert system and the AIS, a marine GPS guide for ship traffic. "I was talking to Peter."

"I suppose now would be a good time for you to let me in on what exactly we're doing on this voyage. I thought I was here to work on my tan, get some writing done and accompany you to meet your treasure hunting contact in Mexico."

Jet stood from his captain's chair in the wheelhouse. "You are."

"I don't know what exactly I walked in on last night, but you said you would let me in on the whole story and I think it's time you did. Why was Peter calling?" Micah moved over to check the radar. He intended to keep his eyes peeled for storms or icebergs. He chuckled at his own paranoia.

"They say they're going to drop me," Jet spoke blandly as if what he said was of no significance.

"Peter?"

"No, the company I fight for." He turned to face his friend. "Everything I told you about this trip is true, we are going to meet a contact of mine in Mexico. He runs a damn good salvage operation, he has state of the art equipment and I've worked with him before. I'm going to try and get him to join forces with me and Nemo. You'll get to work on your tan and do some writing. What I haven't told you is that there's another reason we're going to Veracruz."

"Santoro?"

"Yep."

"Finally had enough of him, huh?"

"Buddy, I had enough of him years ago. I'm gonna settle this once and for all." Jet poured a cup of coffee and held it up to Micah, who reached for it, then he poured another for himself.

"Just who is this punk?" Micah asked as he propped his feet up on the console.

Jet walked to the panoramic windows and looked out at the sun-dappled waters. "Well, Domingo Santoro is the self-professed 'King of the Veracruz streets.' He's a pit-fighter and even had a brief stint as a professional fighter in a few legitimate MMA organizations. Smaller promotions mostly. And you're right, Santoro is a punk, he never had what it takes to make it as a fighter. He lacks heart, he's a bully and a criminal, a street thug with a heavy punch that won him a few matches. He's been taunting me with online videos for the last few years, saying I'm scared to face him, calling me a coward and mocking me every chance he gets."

"What's his problem? Is this just a way to further his own interests or is this personal?"

"Both, Santoro has set up hate websites dedicated to me. He rails about the fact that I've fought for my country. He called me a terrorist and a mercenary for going to Afghanistan to defend my country and went so far as to question some of my salvage findings. Santoro is like an annoying gnat, he doesn't have a chance in hell against a real fighter. That's why I allowed him to get away with it for so long, but Santoro had gone too far this time, he's used his influence in Veracruz to get Nemo banned from the area. Nemo can't find a spot to dock his boat or a place to drink in Veracruz and that royally pisses me off. Veracruz has been one of the places he's always enjoyed, he has friends there. In the past he used it as the hub for his treasure hunting activity."

Micah held up his hands. "Look, I'm convinced. I just wanted to know what was going on behind those big old brown eyes of yours."

Jet returned to the Captain's chair and checked the readouts on the instruments. "I love cruise control."

Laughing, Micah drained his coffee cup. "I saw an old movie by that name, it was about a runaway ship."

Jet snorted. "I have it under control, Wolfe. Anyway, the trip is about the San Miguel, but dealing with Santoro is a bonus I can't pass up."

Micah dry scrubbed his face. "So I guess I'm cornering you for the fight."

"Not gonna need you to."

Polly came strolling into the cockpit, rubbed on her master's pants and promptly jumped up into Micah's lap. He absentmindedly began stroking her, studying Jet. "I know Santoro is a nobody, but I hope you're not taking him too lightly. Does he know you're coming?"

"Oh, yeah. He does. I had a guy I know down there set the fight up four months ago."

"So he'll be ready for you."

"He's been in the gym every day since, according to my guy down there."

"And you're just going to sit on your ass steering the ship until we get there?"

"No. You are." Jet smirked as Micah's face contorted with shock.

"I don't know how to drive a boat! I don't know how to plot a course, or where the fuck the North Star is, or any of that other sailor stuff. You know that."

Jet waved his hand over the varied and complicated looking controls. "You're gonna learn." He smirked. "Besides, you look the part." He pointed at the new yacht shoes and the navy and white hooded long sleeve shirt Micah was sporting.

Micah passed his palm down his shirt. "I like to look nice."

Jet shook his head but continued. "I have no plans of taking Santoro lightly. He's been running his mouth for years, trying to drag me down to his level and into a brawl, which makes him dangerous. Well, he's finally getting his wish, and I plan to be ready for him when the time comes."

Micah set Polly on the floor so he could pace across the cockpit. The sea was calm, still as glass just a few hundred yards off the portside. "How? There's nobody to train with. I mean sure, I'm not a slouch, but I'm also no Peter. I can't train you."

"You don't have to." Jet leaned forward and adjusted their speed. "I brought a punching bag on board. We'll drop anchor or put this baby on auto-pilot and the most you'll have to do is hold the mats for me or put on the mitts so I have a moving target. I plan on swimming beside the boat for a few miles every day to keep my cardio up. I doubt this fight will last long, but since it's not official and there's no time limit, Santoro might think dragging it out will help his chances, so I need to be ready to go for a while."

"I'm sure these waters are teeming with all sorts of sea creatures that would love a Jet sandwich for lunch. Any great whites in the area?"

"Actually, yes." Jet didn't react except to make some notes in his log. "Katharine and Betsy were sighted entering Texas waters a few months ago."

"Excuse me?" Micah stared at Jet like he'd lost his mind. "Who in the hell are Katharine and Betsy?"

"Tagged female great whites, both weighing over a ton. Stands to reason they aren't the only ones."

Micah shuddered. "The thought doesn't seem to bother you."

"Nope."

"All right. I'm sure you know what you're doing." Micah knew he didn't have to say it, Jet knew what could be below them right now. Just like going into combat, he knew and accepted the risks of what might happen. Even if Micah had wanted to put up a protest, he knew Jet would've shot him down right away, so he accepted that he'd be returning from this trip with a newfound knowledge of sailing a ship. "What are you going to do when you get back? I mean, about them dropping you."

Looking up, Jet met Micah's eyes. "Well, the first thing I'm going to do is fire Rick. Peter said he called the company and told them I was going to Veracruz to fight Santoro. Needless to say, they were not too happy about that."

"Only because they can't sell pay-per-view to a fight in a dirty warehouse."

"Exactly. But I'm not worried. They've threatened to cut me before. But they won't. They can't. I'm their poster boy. The soldier champion they can trot out anytime the country is feeling especially patriotic. In the first draft of my contract, they had it written in that I had to be available to fight at any event two weeks prior or following the fourth of July. They've even suggested that I wear stars and stripes shorts in the ring. These guys are ridiculous at times. So I'm not worried about them cutting me. I'd just go fight for their competitor and they'd lose millions of dollars. Unfortunately for them, I have the upper hand in this relationship and I don't plan to relinquish it any time soon."

Micah was impressed, which he didn't admit. "So. How do we proceed?"

Jet moved over to the wheel. "You see this gauge right here?"

"Yeah."

"Keep that little arrow pointed straight ahead unless something big gets in the way."

Micah's eyes widened. "Wait a minute. Where are you going?" He followed Jet out on the main deck.

"To work out." With that. Jet stripped off his jeans and dove over the side of the boat and into the water below.

CHAPTER FOUR

With Sami in Veracruz...

Fred threw a dishtowel at Sami, who caught it and began wiping down the tables. "Thanks, boss."

"How did your session go?"

"Good, no nausea today. I start the other treatment with the virus injection next week." She'd had to fess up to Fred about her cancer, although she hadn't revealed her gender. The fact that she'd been sick seemed to explain a lot to the bar owner. If he asked her how she felt one time a night, he asked a dozen. Who knew the gruff looking old curmudgeon had a soft heart?

A customer pointed at one of the TVs. "Hey, turn that up!" Sami moved to do as he asked. When she looked up to aim the remote, the soccer game was gone and a special news report had taken its place.

"The body of a young woman has been found..." Sami froze. She tried to listen, she really did, but the blood roaring in her ears drowned out the newsman's voice.

"Are you all right, Sami Jo?" Fred asked.

"No, no." She shook her head.

"Here, sit down, let me get you some water." He led her to a table, but all she could do was watch the pictures go by. They replayed the same video clip twice more. Sami felt tears slide down her cheeks. According to the report, the brutalized body of a young woman had been found in a shallow grave only five miles away. They hadn't identified the body yet, but DNA results were pending.

"What's wrong, boy? You look like you've seen a ghost."

The reporter went on to say no suspects had been detained, but it was believed the body was that of a missing journalist, Marisol Lopez. When she opened her mouth to answer, she saw every eye in the place was on her. God, she hated to lie, it seemed like a betrayal of Marisol. "Nothing, it's just so sad."

Fred patted Sami on the back. "Pull yourself together, kid."

Sami heard him and realized he was right, she was about to blow her cover. Straightening her face, she tried not to react to the words coming from the speakers. "In a state with a horrible record of violence against the press, and given the allegations of local political and law enforcement involvement, it's doubtful local authorities will seek justice in this murder."

"Hey, how about some service?" a man yelled from the bar, and Fred looked at her as he took care of other customers at the far end.

"Of course." She rose and went to take their order. As she did, she noticed two men walking in. Bile rose in her throat when she recognized Rey Olmos and Angel Andrade.

As if it were a soundtrack, the report on the murder continued. "Veracruz is one of the most dangerous states in Mexico for members of the press. If this is the woman suspected, it will be the fourth journalist to be killed in direct relation to their work here in the past year. Violence tied to drug trafficking has made Mexico one of the most dangerous countries in the world for the press. More than fifty journalists have been killed or have disappeared in the last five years."

Mechanically, she served drinks, sneaking glances at the duo who she knew were the muscle behind the Jaguar. Once she caught them looking at her, she turned swiftly, pulling the cap down farther over her eyes.

Could they suspect? Sorrow and fear waged war in her breast. Maybe Leona ought to lay low—just for a little while.

* * *

Sailing the Gulf of Mexico…

"You okay, buddy?" Jet had a smirk on his face as he poked his head into Micah's cabin, who was groaning from under the covers.

"When does this shit end?" He stuck his head out and spilled the little remains of his stomach into a plastic bucket Jet had left by his bedside.

Jet had already emptied the contents over the edge of the boat twice in the last six hours. "Don't worry, you'll get your sea legs soon enough. Just keep drinking the water I brought."

"What time is it?" Micah's voice was hoarse.

"It's seven, we anchored for a few hours and I resumed about four."

"God, I feel like I'm gonna die." Micah groaned when another wave of nausea hit him with the swell of the ocean.

"We're going to be at sea for some time, it's best you get this phase over with. Soon you'll feel like a babe in your mother's arms while the waves rock you to sleep."

"Can't happen soon enough," Micah muttered as Jet left him to rest. He dozed for a few minutes until the light coming through the porthole glared in his eyes. He could hear the pounding and crunching as Jet hit the heavy bag in the engine room below him. "Knock it off!" He pounded the floor but the noise continued.

Below, ignoring Micah's outburst, Jet continued to pound the leather, single-mindedly. Finding the San Miguel was his goal, but that goal could wait until he'd smashed Santoro's face in. He'd printed out a hundred pieces of paper with Santoro's image on them. Jet taped a picture to his punching bag and hit it until the page was nothing but pulp, then he replaced it with another. He had one hundred copies and he planned on destroying every single one of them.

A vicious left hook landed on the side of Santoro's visage, sending the eighty pound heavy bag reeling to the side and the paper flying off in pieces. Jet took a step back, catching his breath and retrieving another picture of his opponent from the pile. "Five down already." He taped another picture onto the bag.

The engine room was cramped and dank. A single bare bulb exposed to the elements and the rust of the pipes and engines offered the only light. Polly had come down there with him, but wandered off when the noise started to get too loud. Jet had attached the bag to a steel I-beam that ran the length of the room and the metal chain it hung from creaked and scratched against the worn steel every time he hit it. Four more worn-out, tattered and destroyed pictures of Santoro later and Jet was covered with a thick film of sweat. "I have got to put a fan down here." He leaned on the bag, swaying with it as it moved. "Where'd you go, Polly?"

A quick search of the engine room failed to produce his furry first mate. There were a million little nooks and crannies that Polly could have disappeared into. Jet only came down here every other day to work out, check on things or when there was a problem. If Polly wanted to make it her own, she was welcome to do it. "Oh well," he called out for the cat to hear. "I know you'll turn up when you get hungry."

The door to Micah's cabin opened with a flourish and Jet stumbled in. "Sorry about that, buddy. We musta caught a wave the wrong way." The boat had been drifting along while Jet was below working out.

Micah groaned his disapproval. "Take me back to land." He rolled over and clutched his stomach. "I can't puke anymore. There's nothing left in my stomach to evacuate."

"We don't make landfall for quite a while, land-lover, so I suggest you get over it quickly." He placed a new jug of water on the floor beside Micah's bed and a packet of motion sickness medicine on his nightstand. Micah scrambled for the pills as soon as he saw them.

Jet snatched them off the nightstand, hiding a smile. "Now, you can do that if you want. Pop the box and down a few pills, but it won't help you in the long run, partner. You've made it this far and if you take one of these," he waved the box at Micah, "all you'll do is reverse any progress you've made and have to go through this all over again later on." He dropped the box on the nightstand, knowing Micah wouldn't take them now. Honestly, he didn't know if what he was saying was true or not. "It's your call. I'll be up in the wheelhouse." Jet walked to the door. "I know it doesn't feel like it right now, but it's almost over. You just gotta tough it out for a bit longer and you'll be okay." A muttered curse made Jet laugh. "Recovery time is quick, so hang in there, Wolfe."

He left the cabin and went topside. The waters up ahead looked a bit rough, the whitecaps were starting to get bigger as they headed further south, and the clouds rolling in looked ominous. The Sirena was built for rough waters and all of Jet's satellite equipment indicated the storm would miss them to the east, but out of compassion for his friend, he gripped the wheel and moved it a touch. "Better safe than sorry." He'd snug up to the coastline a bit more to assure they'd miss the bad weather.

Micah was up and about a few hours later. Jet had suggested skipping a shower on the ship and instead taking the plunge into the ocean and washing up quickly. "You've been battling with her since we left, Wolfe. You might as well get in there and show her you're not scared of her."

Still feeling a bit queasy but finally starting to come around, Micah accepted the challenge, shucked his clothing and dove overboard.

"Don't get your dick bit off while you're in there," Jet called out, tossing him a bar of soap to freshen up with.

Micah scrubbed the bad feeling away and climbed back onto the ship.

"I hope you aren't going to make this a habit," Jet drawled, intentionally looking over Micah's left shoulder.

Micah stood proudly in the buff, dripping salt water on the deck, his cock swinging low between his legs with the swaying of the ship. "I have no idea what you're talking about." He placed his hands on his hips and struck a manly pose.

"Wipe yourself down already." Jet tossed a green towel at his friend. "I don't need to be seein' that."

"Don't be jealous, big guy." Micah wiped the briny water from his torso. "I didn't ask God to gift me so generously. He just did."

"You ain't the only one who got second helpings when they were doling out inches, buckaroo." A ringing up in the wheelhouse caught Jet's ear. "That's the satellite phone. I'd better go get it. Put some fucking shorts on, would ya?"

"Can't do that, good buddy. This is how the good Lord intended me and I think I shall embrace his intentions this trip. Which spot on the boat gets the most sun? I think I'll set up a towel and lay out for a bit. When you're done, bring me a mojito, cabana boy."

Jet didn't bother to respond. Micah thrived on the encouragement. Sometimes it was best to just ignore him. Only a small handful of people had the number to Jet's satellite phone, so any call was important. He finally reached it on the sixth ring. "Hello."

"We need to talk." It was Rick.

"Rick. So good of you to call."

"Jet, this is serious. The organization is threatening to strip you of your title. Somehow they found out about the fight with Santoro. They're livid. They want you to turn the boat around right now and fly out to Vegas to meet them. This is no joke, Champ. They're serious this time."

"How'd they find out about Santoro?" The next words out of Rick's mouth were crucial. Loyalty meant the world to a man like Jet Foster and his manager was already skating on thin ice, anything but the truth here would send Rick into the icy depths below his feet.

"You know what the fight world is like, Jet. It's small, people talk. Somehow word got back to them about Santoro."

"It was you, Rick. I already know you did it. Peter called and gave me the heads-up. You're fired." Jet hung up the phone and placed it on the charging dock beside him. Rick was a good manager, but his disloyalty this time had been too much.

The phone rang again. "We have nothing else to say to each other, Rick."

"Jet, be reasonable. I had to do it. For your own good."

"Listen. You and I have been together for a long time. You brought me into the fight game. You got me a shot at the title and when I lost, you got me another shot. I wouldn't be where I am today without you, but this is the last straw."

"What were the other straws?"

"I know about the Adidas sponsorship deal. I know how much I was supposed to get for it and I know that five grand went missing from that deal and I also know you took it." There was silence on the other end of the line. "I looked the other way because I know you've had some problems with gambling. But this, running and telling them that I'm going to Veracruz to fight Santoro, just to cover your own ass, that's too much. It was great working with you, but the time has come for us to part ways. I hope to retain you as a friend and I wish you the best of luck, but our business association is over. Goodbye, Rick." With that, Jet again hung up the phone. Rick had been there from the beginning, he'd been the only manager Jet had ever had and he wouldn't be the Champ today if it wasn't for him, but it was over.

The phone rang again. "Listen, Rick. I said we were done. Stop calling."

"It's not Rick." The voice on the other end was that of the governor of the great state of Texas.

"Miss me already, Governor?"

"Not hardly. How's the voyage so far?" Kyle asked.

"Decent." Jet stepped out onto the deck and watched the sun dancing on the waves. "Wolfe got sick."

Hello, Impostor. We have the real Lioness in a cage. We want five million US dollars and all of the evidence you and she claim to have. Only then will we release her. We will contact you with further terms. If you choose not to comply, we will kill her and you. How bad do you want to see your friend alive?

Was Marisol alive? Could she be ransomed? Sami rose and began to walk around the room, running her fingers through her short curls. Of course she had to follow their directions, she had no choice. Marisol was her family.

* * *

Corpus Christi, Texas...

Jet cranked the throttle on a pitch black Harley Davidson CVO Street Glide. The throaty rattle of the pipes roared to life, shaking the posters and calendars of scantily-clad women inside the body shop of Kenny J's Custom Hog Shop in Corpus Christi.

Jet beamed. "Purrs like a kitten, Kenny."

Kenny J was a local customizing legend. He'd trained in mixed-martial arts with Jet until a freak accident in the ring had blown out his ACL and ended Kenny's fighting career. He switched his focus to building custom motorcycles and had made a name for himself in the industry. Kenny took a long haul off his ever-present Marlboro and smiled at his friend. "It's yours for the day if you want it, Champ."

"This is all well and good." Micah stood there in nothing but a pair of light blue surf shorts and white sandals. He wasn't ready to fully get back to the world of the clothed. "But what the fuck am I gonna ride?"

Jet patted the bitch seat of the Harley. "Hop on, little lady."

"Fuck you."

Kenny and Jet chuckled in unison.

Kenny exhaled a puff of smoke. "There's a Hertz down the road where you can rent a nice shiny Corolla."

"I want that," Micah said with a point. Jet and Kenny followed his finger.

"The Suzuki?" Jet asked.

"Yeah, the white one with the stripes."

"The GSX-R1000?" Kenny smirked. "That's a fast ride, Chief."

"Do you even have a motorcycle license?" Jet wanted to know.

"I don't," Micah confessed. "But I've been riding dirt bikes since I was eight and horses since I was four. I know how to ride."

"That ain't some little 250 for bombing around the ranch, partner. That little crotch rocket can fly."

"Well, I'm not riding on the back of your bike like your old lady. And I'm not going to risk someone seeing me in a Corolla. Besides, the stripe matches my shorts. It's a sign."

Jet and Kenny exchanged a look. Kenny shrugged. "If he thinks he can handle it."

"You sure about this?" Jet asked Micah.

Micah walked over to the bike and ran a finger down the bright white paint on the gas tank. "Oh, yeah."

* * *

Back with Sami...

Sami threw up twice while she conversed with the Jaguar, if it really was him. She'd tried to be smart and left her apartment, seeking out what served as a coffee shop in the trendier part of Veracruz. Before she found one with free Wi-Fi, Sami had visited three and downed four cups of strong coffee. To say she was buzzing was fairly apt. The two times she'd upchucked, she'd had to grab her laptop and sprint to the facilities, causing a scene each time.

Now, she endeavored to word her response carefully.

I am willing to give you the money you seek in exchange for Marisol Lopez. There are some conditions on my part, however. I need to speak with her to ensure she is alive.

Waiting for an answer seemed to take forever. She figured they were trying to trace her IP address. The idea that these people weren't tech savvy was ludicrous. So, as soon as she hit enter, Sami moved again.

By the time she was set up again, she was weak. Just the act of hailing a cab and maneuvering down the streets and into the shop sapped her energy. When she was settled, she looked and sat there until the café closed. But there was no answer, that day or the next, and Sami was terrified to think what that might mean.

* * *

At the King Ranch...

"What took you so long?" Micah stood with his arms crossed over his chest. The white sport bike was propped up behind him at the massive front gate of the famous King Ranch.

Jet brought the Harley to a lumbering stop and gunned the engine once before turning it off. "I knew you'd drive like a maniac."

Micah had blown the first red light they'd come across, narrowly missing a collision with a brown sedan that was making a left on the amber. He'd swerved to miss the contact and not taken his hand off the throttle for the rest of the drive. Jet had just shaken his head when he'd seen the Wolfe blow the light. Jet had been in more than one motorcycle crash in his time and he didn't feel the need to get into another one today, so he'd cruised along, enjoying the sun on his face.

"Kyle called ahead for us." Jet propped the big Harley up on its kickstand and waited for Micah to phone the main ranch.

"They said come on up." Micah climbed onto his bike.

"Kenny was kind enough to lend us these bikes, so don't go bombing up the gravel road like a fool and fuck up the paint job."

Micah offered a salute. "Sir, yes, sir."

They eased up the long road at a crawl. The ground was gravel beneath them and a hazard to any vehicle on two wheels. Micah took it all in. As a Texan and someone who'd grown up on a good-sized spread, the King Ranch was infamous. Covering eight hundred twenty-five thousand acres, it was bigger than the state of Rhode Island. More than just employees, the men who worked the ranch were called los kineños or 'the king's men.' The ranch had developed their own breed of cattle, the Santa Gertrudis, bred a Kentucky Derby winner, made one of the biggest oilfield discoveries in history drilling thirty-seven hundred wells, branched out into the timber industry and wild game reserves, and owned and managed subsidiary ranches in seven foreign countries. This was no small operation. This was a kingdom.

on underneath the tattered jeans and torn red shirt he wore.

"I'm here with my associate. Mister Wolfe. He's gonna wait outside. Is it okay if I come in?"

Jet watched the old man squint to see him. There was a pair of glasses on the arm of the chair beside him, but Jet assumed the old fella was too proud to put them on and admit he had trouble seeing.

"You the fighter fella Mike has been going on about all morning?"

"I am, sir."

"Well, come on in then."

Jet pushed the doors apart and they squeaked on their rusty hinges.

"Any messages you want me to pass along in case you don't come back out?" Micah asked from his spot on the cooler.

"Yeah. My friend Micah is an asshole."

Micah mimed writing the message down. "'Horses are jealous of how Micah Wolfe is hung.' Kind of a weird last message, but I got it." He tucked the imaginary scrap of stationary into his pocket. "Have fun."

Randy was on his feet when Jet walked in. He didn't have a shotgun in his hand, but he did have a dog-eared old paperback. "I've read it about a thousand times," Randy said with a grin. Clearly he'd seen Jet give him the once-over when he walked in, maybe his eyesight wasn't as bad as previously assumed. "Have a seat."

The room was a bit messy. A fine sheen of dust covered the table, a side effect of the bat wing doors no doubt. Jet took a seat at the tiny kitchen table.

"Can I get you a drink?"

"Water would be great if you have it, sir."

"Got some in the fridge actually. Mike brought me some supplies this morning. That's when he told me you'd be dropping by. What can I do for you, son?"

Randy's voice had changed. The gruff unfriendly greeting he'd offered at first had disappeared. In its place was a pleasant register that was welcoming and kind.

"We're looking for information about a rodeo cowboy who passed through here years back. Fella by the name of Sebastian McCoy."

Randy placed a bottle of water down on the table in front of Jet and took the seat across from him. There was a slight sneer on his face at the mention of the name, a sneer that didn't go unnoticed by Jet and he thought this conversation was about to finish before it even started.

Micah sat out on the cooler, going over a scene from his new book in his head. His cock started to expand in his shorts at the thought of what he had his characters doing, but the sound of tires crunching on gravel pushed the erection away and a puff of dust announced the return of Mike.

"That was fast." Micah got up and adjusted the dwindling stiffness in his shorts.

"Dropped the hunters off and picked these two up. They cook up at the main house. Lola had something she wanted to give to Randy. He has a sweet tooth."

A woman in her early twenties bounded from the backseat of the truck. "I'll be right back. He loves my flan." She was tall and lean, of Mexican descent, and she looked Micah up and down lasciviously as she headed toward the cabin. "Hi," Lola offered a shy greeting to the handsome stranger without his shirt on and brushed her hair back behind her ear before finding the ground with her eyes.

Micah graced her with his usual grin. "How are you?" He couldn't help himself, shy women were one of his vices.

"Fine." She pushed past them sheepishly and tapped on the jamb next to the bat wing doors. "Randy!"

The woman who remained in the truck eyed Micah with suspicion. She had a paranoid look on her wrinkled face. Micah placed her age at around sixty. She got out of the truck and came toward them.

Inside the cabin, Jet sat patiently while the young girl and Randy visited.

"Mother is out in the car," the woman said after hugging Randy and being introduced to the stranger. "I brought you some dessert."

"Thank you, sweetheart." He pointed to the table where she sat down the sweet concoction. "I was just talking to this nice man about the years I've been here." Randy patted her on the cheek. "Why don't you go outside and have a seat? I'll be out in a minute."

The young woman grew shy. Micah had an effect on her and she didn't want to go back out there with him after her initial reaction to his shirtless body. "I'll just go wait on the recliner by the front door."

Randy turned back to Jet. "McCoy, yea, I know the fella you're talking about. He wasn't here that long. He was wild when he was here. Those rodeo fellas always are. Can't say I took a particular shine to him. Although I know he settled down and built a fine ranch. Tebow, isn't that the name?"

"Yea, that's it." Jet screwed the cap back onto his drink. "Do you remember if he had a woman with him? Maybe he went into town on the weekends? Had a girlfriend there perhaps?"

"I do seem to recall a woman with him. Blonde. Pretty type. The rich fellas always get the pretty ones, so that's no surprise really."

Back on the porch, the older woman in the truck had finally made her way over to Micah and Mike as they talked.

"Juanita," Mike started. "This here is Mister Micah Wolfe."

"Nice to meet you, Juanita." Micah extended his hand for a shake and the woman took it, but not without a hard look. She must have seen the response her daughter had to Micah and she didn't like it, she'd probably only gotten out of the truck to come over and check him out just in case.

"Juanita was born on King Ranch, she's been here her whole life. Maybe you should talk to her also."

"What is it you were talking about?" Juanita asked.

Micah put his hands in his pockets. "My partner and I are here to see about some information on a rodeo cowboy who passed through here years ago. Name was Sebastian McCoy. Name ring a bell?"

"No," Juanita answered hard and sharp. But there was something in her face that said she knew the name.

Jet came out a moment later with Randy behind him. "I'm sorry I couldn't have been more help. I remember the fella, just don't remember the woman all that well. If I think of her name, I'll give you a call."

Mike ducked his head into the cabin. "Time to go, Lola."

Lola came out a moment later. "But I wanted to visit with Randy more."

"We gotta go, sweetheart. Now into the truck you go."

"She got pregnant, some say McCoy was the father. After she had the baby, they left. Antonio was killed a few months later, foot hung in the stirrup, dragged behind a bronc."

Jet nodded, realizing Noah must have been the baby. "What happened to her after he died?"

Juanita looked around suspiciously and leaned forward in her seat. "Tampico," she whispered and leaned back.

"Shit." Jet nodded, knowing exactly what she meant. "Thank you for the information." He stalked back to the bikes. "Time for you to go home, little girl." He took Lola by the elbow and helped her off the white speedster. "Don't follow her," he said to Micah as Micah admired her walking away, a little extra sway in her hips as she went. "Cell phone."

Micah fished around in his pocket and handed it over. "Who are you calling?"

"Kyle." Jet hit the send button on the phone. "Things just got a whole lot more complicated."

CHAPTER FIVE

With Sami in Veracruz…

Sami barely slept. She kept waiting for the Jaguar to answer her email. The hesitation and delay unnerved her. What if the body reported on the news was Marisol's and the communication from Jaguar was just bait?

Finally, in the middle of the night, she heard the 'you've got mail' beep and she jumped up, her heart in her throat. Throwing on a robe, she went to the laptop and sat in front of it. She was almost afraid to look. Rubbing her eyes, she tried to focus on the bright screen in the dark room. Sure enough, there was an answer to her request. A video clip was attached to an email that just said PROOF.

Too nervous to be accurate, it took Sami two attempts before she got the arrow in the right spot to click the mouse. And when she did, Sami wanted to gag. Marisol sat on a chair in a dim room holding a newspaper with today's date. "Save me, Leona." The words coming from her mouth were hard to understand. Her face was swollen, bruised, and bleeding. Marisol had been severely beaten. Sami began to cry.

"You motherfuckin' assholes," she whispered.

Moving the cursor back up, she viewed the email.

Here's the proof you asked for. Meet us tomorrow night at midnight on the waterfront, down by the new dry dock. Bring your information and the money. Come alone.

Fury bombarded Sami. She could get the money, but she didn't trust them. They were after information they assumed she had, including the obscure photo and since she and Marisol had both seen it, she didn't trust them as far as she could throw them. Both she and Marisol would be killed, there wasn't any doubt in her mind.

So, Sami decided to gamble. She had an idea. Now to set it in motion.

Putting off the response for a few minutes, she went to get a drink of water. Since starting the treatments, Sami's mouth was dry all the time. Taking a bottle of water from the fridge, she went to stand by the window while she drank. Veracruz was a pretty city. If everything was normal with her, she would've loved to take an excursion out into the jungle and see some of the waterfalls. Holding the cool bottle to the side of her face, she considered what she was about to do. Perhaps she was being too romantic, or perhaps it was because Jet was an Equalizer, but she had this faith in the new Governor and his even newer Secretary of State. The inauguration and every tidbit of news made by him and his entourage had been all over the TV. Sami had consumed every bit she could, always hoping for a glimpse of Jet. She didn't know if her plan would work, but it was worth a try.

Going to the computer, she looked up a number to call the office of the Texas Governor. Getting to speak to him would be impossible, but maybe she could talk to a staff member and convince someone to listen.

* * *

Corpus with Jet and Micah…

"She's a whore," Jet said the words matter-of-factly.

Micah spit his beer out. "A whore?"

Jet hadn't filled him in on the details before leaving the King Ranch. He'd spoken with Kyle on the phone, told him what he knew and now they were sitting in Kenny J's shop sipping a cold one while they waited for Kyle to call back. The report that needed to be made to Aron was a sensitive one. Kyle would pass Jet and Micah's findings on to Saxon, who would then decide how to proceed.

"The older lady in the truck at the ranch told me she knew of the woman we were looking for. She said she didn't know where she was for sure, but she'd heard rumors about Tampico."

Kenny J nodded his head. "Awwww. Tampico. A place I know well."

"We both do," Jet commented with a swig of his water. He was in training for Santoro, alcohol wasn't part of his diet.

"Been there many times and all have been good." Kenny sighed.

"It's a red-light district, Wolfe," Jet piped up when he could see Micah had no idea what they were talking about.

This was the first time Micah had ever heard of the place. "And you're saying she might be there?"

"She might."

Kenny chuckled. "She shouldn't be hard to find if she is."

"Why's that?" Micah wanted to know.

"Well, an old white woman with blonde hair in a place filled with Mexican women, should probably stand out. And if that doesn't help, just look for the hooker *without* a dick."

"I'm not sure I want to know much more about this." Micah drained his beer, tossing the empty can into a trash barrel six feet away.

The phone rang in Kenny's office and he went to get it. "It's for you, Champ."

Jet had given Kyle Kenny's number. "Hey, boss. What's the word?"

"I passed the info along to Saxon after you gave it to me. He and I discussed it and we decided it would be best if we advised Aron not to say anything to Noah until we know more. It may be a lead that will help locate his birth mother, but the fact that the trail leads straight to a Mexican brothel isn't something we should just drop on him out of the blue—not till we know more."

"Good, so we're through now? We can head on to Veracruz?" Jet was anxious to resume his journey.

"Well, no. Aron is worried as hell about all of this and he's sending Isaac to meet you two in Tampico to see if you can find out anything more."

"Meet us in Tampico? We aren't going to Tampico."

"I need you to go and check this out."

Jet was frustrated. "Now hang the hell on. The deal was that I'd go to Corpus Christi and I did. You never said anything about a pit-stop in the land of possible cocks."

"I need you to do this for me, Jet. The McCoys are very influential in Texas and besides, they're our friends. For God's sake, Jet, the man just found out his whole life was a lie. What the fuck do you want me to do, tell him his real mother might be a prostitute and send him on his way? We decided to tell Isaac because it won't seem odd to the rest of them if he is gone for a few days. I need you to meet him down there and go with him. The guy is no shrinking violet, but Tampico is a dangerous place, you told me that yourself. I want you and Micah there to watch his back. Micah knows how to gather intel, if anyone can find her there, it's him."

Kyle had a point, Jet knew what it was like to not have a mother and he could empathize with how Noah must be feeling right now, like his mother didn't want him. "Fine, it's not that far from where I'm headed anyway. But one day is all I'm spending there and McCoy had better stay the fuck out of our way when we get there."

"I'll call him myself and pass along the message."

Jet slammed the phone down on the cradle and stormed out of the office. "Kenny. I thank you for the loan of the bikes and the hospitality, but we have to be on our way."

"What's the deal?" Micah asked when they were back at the Sirena.

Polly watched over the edge of the deck as they untied the ship from the dock. It was getting late in the day and the sun was starting to sink in the sky.

Jet moved up the steps to the boat with Micah behind him. He seemed eager to get going. Scooping Polly up, Jet grumbled, "Jesus. Did you gain weight while we were gone?"

The big docile cat just blinked her eyes and began to purr. He carried her up into the wheelhouse and placed her on the ledge to his left. Polly lay down immediately and watched as Jet maneuvered the boat away from the dock.

"You gonna tell me or not?" Micah stood in the doorway. "I'd Google it, but my damn phone is dead."

"Tampico has a tolerance zone, a red-light district like I said earlier. The Mexican government says they're in charge, they say it's regulated but everyone knows the cartels run it and anything goes. Kyle wants us to follow the lead."

"So, we're going there?"

"It won't cause much more of a deviation from our plan, it's on our way anyway. Veracruz is about seven hundred miles from there. I hadn't planned on sticking so close to the shore. I wanted to get my girl out into the open ocean and let her do her thing, but we can do that on the way to the San Miguel when we cross the Gulf." There was an unmistakable undertone of displeasure in Jet's timber. He'd already lost time and had to push his fight with Santoro back another day or two.

"How far is it from here?"

"Were you even listening when I went over the plan and maps weeks ago with you?"

"I was, but my mind tends to wander," Micah said matter-of-factly and without shame.

"Girls."

"Usually."

"We've got about eight hundred miles to go, so you'll have lots of time to write and we'll have lots of time to plan our strategy. Isaac McCoy is meeting us down there. We'll hold his hand, walk him through things, but he better not give me any trouble." Jet walked to the small refrigerator and took out two waters, throwing one at Micah.

Micah caught it, unscrewed the cap and took a big swig. "Isaac's a good man, he won't be a problem. What did Kenny mean back there when he said 'just look for the hooker *without* a dick'?"

Jet smiled wickedly. "What do you think he meant?"

"I was afraid you'd say that."

"They say don't drink the water in Mexico. In Tampico, they say, check under the hood before you buy a girl." Jet laughed out loud. "Do yourself a favor when we get there, Wolfe. Keep your eyes facing forward and don't be so sure you're going to know which ones are packin' and which ones aren't. A lot of them look like women, but they aren't. So don't be acting like *you* while we're there. We get in and get out. We ditch McCoy and get back on the sea. I've got to call my man in Veracruz and tell him I've got another delay, this time in Tampico Now go write something."

Micah responded dryly. "For some reason, I'm just not that inspired right now."

Jet laughed again and steered the ship out of the harbor. The ocean awaited and so did Santoro. It was time to make up some lost time.

* * *

Sami goes on the defensive…

Sami didn't waste time, she knew Marisol didn't have any to spare either. The thought that Andrade and the others were torturing her made Sami sicker than the chemotherapy. She sat near a window for maximum cell service and placed the call, keeping her fingers crossed.

"Governor's office, may I help you?"

"Yes, my name is Samantha Cabot. I'm a resident of Texas, living in Houston. At present, I'm in Veracruz, Mexico and I have a problem."

"Ma'am, excuse me." The telephone operator cut her off. "Perhaps you should visit the American consulate there in Veracruz—"

Sami didn't wait for her to finish. She could interrupt as well as anyone else. "No, just listen. What I

115

have to say is for the Equalizers' ears, as well as the Governor's. I have information that could possibly take down the Galvez drug cartel."

"Hold on one moment, please."

Now she had their attention.

In a few minutes, another voice came on the line.

"This is Kyle Chancellor, may I help you?"

Sami took a deep breath. "I hope so."

Kyle could hear the nerves and hesitation in her voice. "Miss Cabot, take your time. Explain to me what's wrong."

"Like I said, I'm from Houston. My best friend, Marisol Lopez, a fellow graduate of U of H is/was the Lioness, the blogger that was whistle blowing on the cartel through connections she had in Veracruz. She was doing this blogging from the relative safety of Houston until they became suspicious of her identity and lured her back to Mexico by murdering her mother."

"Shit..." Kyle muttered. "I'm so sorry."

"Well, yes, me too," Sami agreed. "When she returned to Veracruz, she was kidnapped."

"Poor woman." Kyle knew full well what the cartel did to journalists. "Okay, that's unfortunate. I understand your loss, but what has that got to do with you and bringing down the cartel?"

"That's where it gets complicated." Sami took a deep breath. "When Marisol discovered they were onto her, she mailed me a drive with all of the information she had and asked that I protect it and get more out if I could."

"Have you?"

"Yes, she was kidnapped not long after she sent me the letter. Recently the body of a woman has been discovered and many people thought it was her. But I've found out differently. I have been blogging in her place. I am the Lioness now."

"Don't you think that's a bit foolhardy, Miss Cabot?"

The censure in the Governor's voice didn't deter Sami. "I don't really have a lot to lose. I have cancer." When he started to say something, she pushed on. "The doctors couldn't do any more for me at MD, so I took Marisol up on her advice and came to Veracruz to seek alternative treatment at a clinic. When I began to feel better, I started doing some investigating on my own."

"My God." He let out a harsh sigh and a low expletive. "What happened?"

"I got a message from the cartel. I've spilled the beans for them on several issues. I have encouraged folks to send tips for me to post, exposing who they are." She paused to catch her breath. God, she'd forgotten to eat. Sami wiped her forehead where she was perspiring a bit. "One of the things Marisol was given before she was kidnapped was a fuzzy photograph of the Jaguar, the elusive head of the Galvez cartel. The authorities haven't been able to stop him because no one knew what he looks like—I sorta do."

"What did the message say?"

"I got a comment telling me that Marisol is alive and being held for ransom. They want to trade her life for five million dollars and all the info I have collected."

"Five million, hell, that's a lot of money."

"I have the five million, Governor. My father was Deke Cabot and my mother was Dr. Violet Cabot, head of oncology at the Cancer Institute."

"All right." Kyle knew of the Cabots, they ran in the same circles as the Chancellors. Now he had an image of Samantha, he'd seen her picture in some society article or another. "I understand. What do you need me to do?"

Good, he was willing to listen. "They want me to meet them tomorrow night at the waterfront here in Veracruz with the money."

"Well, that part of Mexico is a little bit out of my jurisdiction."

Sami snorted. "Yes, but not out of the Equalizers' jurisdiction, I'm sure." The knowledge slipped out. Jet would be in Veracruz, but she wasn't going to mention knowing that. Not waiting for him to respond, she continued, "I'm not asking for you to come to Mexico. I plan on telling the Jaguar that I'm sick, that I'm in Houston. If he wants his money and the evidence, he has to bring Marisol to Texas for the exchange. Can you help me? I can set it up. I can make sure you have the ransom money. Could you have someone there to make the trade and hopefully bring the asshole down?"

Kyle's mind was racing. "Let me talk to some folks. I'll go ahead and say yes. You throw out the proposal and let's see what happens. In the meantime, let me see what I can do on this end. Tell them to meet you in the parking lot of the Astrodome. That's wide open, but we can have help nearby."

"You'll have to get someone to play me."

"I can do that."

"Just make sure they're emaciated with no hair. Okay?"

Kyle laughed sadly. "Gotcha, I'll leave this line open and waiting for you. Call me the minute you hear from them again."

"Great, thank you." The relief was evident in Sami's voice. "I knew I could count on the Equalizers."

* * *

Meanwhile in Tampico, Mexico...

Isaac McCoy stood on the dock with a set of binoculars in his thick hands. He rolled the lens knob, bringing the tall ship off in the distance into focus. "Damn Tampico," he muttered under his breath. "Why did it have to be here of all places?"

He scanned the hull of the boat for a name. There it was, glaring out in the low setting sun like a lighthouse beacon on the sea. Sirena. The name buoyed up and down in the water, scrawled in small letters on the starboard side of the hull. Isaac could feel the natives' eyes on him as he watched the approaching ship.

This wasn't his first trip to Mexico and he'd heard of this place from friends back home, but being here was another experience altogether. He felt the thieves, pimps, and cutthroats' eyes searing a hole in his back. Who was this tall broad gringo in the black jeans and shit-kicking boots, they asked silently.

A small group of loud revelers approached from his right and Isaac's hackles came up. The binoculars came down and his chest puffed out. He had a knife strapped to his left boot, it was tucked up under the cuff of his jeans and he knew how to get it out in a hurry if needed. He only hoped the need never arose.

The noisy group quieted as they approached. They looked Isaac up and down, eyeing him to see if it was worth the trouble of mugging him. Isaacs's right hand balled into a fist at his side and a snarl creased his lips. The Sirena was still minutes away, if this group was looking for trouble, he was on his own.

The leader of the group caught his gaze. All around them business went on as usual. This was Tampico, a place for whores, thieves, and people looking to do wrong, nobody paid any attention to the situation and nobody would offer assistance to the American if things escalated.

Isaac considered striking first, there were only four of them and they seemed intoxicated, they must have started the party early and he figured taking the first one out would chase the rest away. He scanned the faces of the men standing before him. They were a rough looking cabal, all shorter than the McCoy. They had rough faces speckled with scars.

The leader still stared Isaac down. Mistrust was in his eyes and Isaac diverted his gaze to the man's tattered T-shirt and began to laugh out loud, bending over and placing his hands on his knees. He looked back at the group and realized that while they still looked like a tough bunch and a few were drunk, it hadn't been him that had drawn their initial attention.

"Waiting for the Champ?" Isaac asked and relaxed a couple of notches.

They looked at him and raised a hand each. "Jet! Jet! Jet!" They chanted in unison.

Isaac couldn't help but laugh out loud again. The leader who'd been giving him the stink eye had a Jet Foster T-shirt on. These men were clearly fans, perhaps fighters themselves. Somehow word must have gotten out that the Champ was on his way and they had turned out to greet him at the dock.

Isaac held the binoculars out to the leader. "Here. It's that one right there," he said with a point. "I just about messed myself. You know that."

The leader smiled and nodded his head as he looked out at the approaching boat as it cut its way through the gleaming waters.

* * *

Out on the Sirena…

Micah walked into the wheelhouse where Jet was piloting the boat. He'd been watching the shore with his own set of binoculars and had just spotted Isaac. "Looks like McCoy brought along the welcoming committee."

"As long as he and his buddies stay the fuck out of our way," Jet grumbled.

Micah left out the fact that he'd seen the Jet Foster T-shirt one of the men had been wearing. He thought it would be funnier if Jet discovered on his own that his foreign groupies were out in full force, following him around Mexico.

There had been tension between Isaac and Jet ever since they first met on that daring rescue mission to retrieve Aron McCoy from a Mexican ranch. Nobody from either camp knew the precise nature of the problem and the groups didn't find themselves coming into contact all that often, so nobody had made an issue of it, but the fact was known.

"There isn't going to be a problem with you two, is there?" Micah asked, ignorantly unaware that the tension had arisen from an offhand remark Micah himself had made to Jet during the planning phase of the Aron McCoy mission, something about which of the two giants was the biggest badass.

Jet waved his boat mate off with a dismissive hand. "Leave me alone. I need to guide us in. Get back out on the bow and spot for me."

Polly was already out at the front of the boat. Coming in to dock was her favorite part of every trip. Saxon offered a scientific explanation for it, saying that the approaching closeness of land drew her attention. Micah always said she was hunting a real sandbox.

121

But Jet had a simpler answer. "It's probably the little tub of lard's nose smelling the fresh fish stacked in every seaport we ever pull into." Who was right didn't matter. Micah wandered out to the bow of the ship and joined the portly feline as Jet masterfully nosed the ship to the pier.

Isaac and the Jet Foster fans watched as the Sirena sailed by them. Jet was looking for a longer stretch of pier to dock his boat at, but Isaac took it as an insult as the boat passed by sluggishly with the small cheering group racing off to meet it when it finally stopped.

Micah stood at the starboard railing in his Topsiders with pants rolled up at the cuff. Holding his arms widespread, he declared. "My people. You have come to adore me!" He tossed the ropes down onto the pier and Jet's fans scurried about, lashing the boat down so it didn't float away. "You love me." Micah blew kisses, holding Polly up over his head as if she were Simba. "You really love me!"

The boat pulling in and the enthusiasm of the men who'd turned out to see Jet had drawn the attention of the town and others began flocking to the ship to find out what all the fuss was about. Jet stepped out onto the deck and his fans roared, which caused the rest of the crowd to start applauding. "You did this, didn't you?"

Micah cradled Polly like a small child and continued blowing kisses to the crowd. "I didn't. But I did ask Kenny if he knew anyone down here he could put us in touch with. Apparently he had the number to your local fan club affiliate. I thought it might be a good idea to know someone here just in case. Never hurts to have backup. Now go sign some autographs and find out which one of the chicks in the crowd has his junk taped to his leg."

"Sorry, Sherlock." Jet waved to the crowd and started to make his way off the boat. "Figuring it out on your own is part of the fun."

"Typical," Isaac said to the woman beside him. The girl was clearly a prostitute, but Isaac hadn't looked at her long enough to have noticed.

"I think this one might have a dick." Micah materialized on his other side from behind. "McCoy." He offered his hand for a shake. "Good to see you. You going home with him?" Micah jerked a thumb to the girl beside Isaac.

It was then that Isaac turned to look at the person beside him. She was dressed anything but modestly, with an overblown and surgically enhanced chest covered with mere scraps of material. "Not tonight, hon," he said, pushing her away with a polite but firm hand. "Or…bro'. Or, whatever."

Micah had slipped off the back of the boat after returning Polly to her room below deck. "I think we should get this underway. We've got to get to Veracruz as soon as possible."

"What's the rush? I've been here for a day waiting for you. Did superstar there have to stop to sign autographs in every port along the way?" Isaac watched Jet shaking hands and posing for pictures. It wasn't jealousy that he felt toward the big warrior, but he felt Jet had an ego he kept hidden from the public.

Micah let it slide, he knew Isaac had been the worst possible McCoy to choose for this mission because of the tension between him and Jet, but he also knew Kyle was aware of that and only sent Isaac because there was no other option. So, Micah was fully aware he'd not only be working as an intel man on this mission, but also as a peacekeeper.

"Mister McCoy," Jet said with an extended hand after he'd finally escaped the throng ten minutes later. "Good to see you again."

Jet had a way of being overly polite and formal when he didn't particularly care for someone. Tyson had told him a long time ago that acting that way usually only made the person like you less, but Jet was who he was and he wasn't going to change.

They clasped hands, each tightening their grip the longer the shake went on. Micah stood at the ready to defuse any tension that might arise with a joke, but the handshake broke and Jet walked off in a hurry with his four bodyguards at his side, watching for trouble in the crowd.

"They're from a local gym," Jet told Micah, who strolled along between them. "You were right and Kenny agreed. They're here to watch our backs."

The snort that escaped Isaac's lips went unnoticed. Jet had people who phoned ahead to arrange bodyguards for him when he traveled? To him it was another example of his ego.

"It looks like they're here to drink more than watch our backs."

They stopped and watched as one of their bodyguards broke from his post and began chasing a prostitute down the street, nipping at her ass with wobbly hands and even wobblier legs.

"I guess three bodyguards is better than none," Micah commented dryly.

"Let's just get this over with," Jet grumbled and walked off, the crowds parting as the stoic warrior strode through on a mission.

Every street looked the same as they wandered the crowded walkways. In the late evening sun, the alleyways promised even more danger. The farther they ventured from the Sirena, the seedier the place became and the more unease crept in. Jet and Micah had been in plenty of hostile places in their lives, but unlike Afghanistan or the presence of a jealous rival, there was a lawlessness to this place. The words 'No Rules' almost seemed to echo through the dank and humid air, as if carried along by a vibrating cloud of terror.

More and more unfriendly eyes were beginning to focus on them and the need to get to where they were going grew more urgent. "How much farther?" Jet asked their guide in a calm but businesslike tone.

"Just up around the corner."

Jet placed a hand on his guide's shoulder. "Faster," he said, pushing him along.

Micah and Isaac might not have known it, but Jet knew this place was surrounded by lagoons and rivers and it would only take one false step, one wrong word, or one dirty look and they'd find themselves floating face down in one of the many bodies of water full of hungry crocodiles.

Vaquero Loco was a seedy spot off the beaten path. They'd left beautiful high rises and paved roads behind over ten minutes ago for narrow streets and rundown buildings. A crooked metal sign hanging above the paint-peeled door was all that let them know they had arrived.

The room they entered was alive with activity. At small round tables, dark skinned men sat with tawdry women on their laps. Every eye in the place turned to regard them when they walked in, but they were quickly ignored in favor of drinking and all-around cavorting. Vaquero's inteior walls were just as shoddy as those outside had been. The bar looked like it was falling apart and behind it a one-eyed man with an unfriendly scowl looked them up and down as he dried glasses with a dirty dishrag.

Micah surveyed the room. "Oh, she's got one for sure." He pointed at a tall, wiry, 'girl' who led a squat man in a grey suit off toward a curtain. "You owe me a hundred bucks, Champ."

"Good eyes, Wolfe. But that one was pretty obvious. And as much as I'd like to stand around here playing, 'spot the taped junk,' I think it's best we tend to our business and be on our way."

Isaac chimed in. "We'll take as long as we need to and find out as much as we can about Noah's birth mother." He already felt Jet wasn't taking this as seriously as he should and he didn't like the idea of them rushing off because Jet had a fight to get to. "I know you've got somewhere you'd rather be, but this is important to me and my family. So take it seriously."

Jet's back came up. The danger of the locals slipped from his mind. He and Isaac McCoy had clashed from the moment they'd met and even though he'd promised Kyle and Micah he'd behave when he was with Isaac, the way he'd just talked to him had Jet's blood boiling.

"What did you just say, McCoy?"

The temperature rose a few degrees and Micah acted quickly. "You two can stand here and measure your dicks if you want to, I'm going to the bar. I'd say it's hot enough in this damn place to risk contracting hepatitis."

Micah left the two mountainous men glaring at one another. Their entourage had already broken off, forgetting about the Champ once in the presence of eager to please ladies. Neither man spoke. Neither willing to blink or look away. It was entirely possible that neither could remember the origin of their dislike for the other and both would most likely agree that combined they'd be a force to be reckoned with, a duo of bad boy bikers blasting their way across the blazing hot hardtop of Texas, leaving rubber on the road and slack-jawed observers everywhere they went, but neither had that thought at the moment. This was about dominance and neither wanted to blink first.

Micah returned a moment later with three bottles of Tecate beer. "Is this really necessary?" He pressed a dripping wet bottle into each of their hands. "I really don't see how this is getting us any closer to finding Noah's mother. Or getting us to Veracruz. If you two don't like each other..." His voice began to rise. "Then why the *FUCK* are you wasting time and making it so you're around each other longer?" Both men looked away and at him at the same time. "Now. Bro hug this shit out. Or fist bump. Or do whatever the hell it is that you biker badass types do. But do it quickly, 'cause these lady-boys are starting to look better and better the longer I'm here."

"Listen, McCoy," Jet started. "We don't have to like each other. Hell, we don't even have to get along. But I'm here to do what I can to help you and your family find your brother's real mother. I take every job seriously and I assure you I'm giving this the same consideration. I'll be here as long as it takes, but I don't have to tell you, this is a dangerous place and the last thing I want is for something to happen to any of us."

The tension dropped.

Isaac took a draw off his beer. "I believe you, Jet. I didn't mean anything by it." He extended a hand for a shake, and Jet took it willingly. There was no stress in the embrace this time. No battle for superiority. Something had changed between the two men. Micah's words had somehow put it into perspective for both of them.

"I just have a tough time trusting a man who rides a soft tail in the heat of the Texas summer, Foster."

Jet laughed a hardy chuckle and clapped his leather wearing comrade on the back. "Come by my shop sometime, McCoy. I'll show you the wonders of customizing a bike. Teach you a thing or two."

Micah had come back to them. "You two figured it out yet? Or do I have to pay for a bunch of happy endings so you can bond over it?"

Isaac threw up his hands in defense. "No thanks, Wolfe. I already get the best happy endings there are at home. My little gal already does 'em like a pro." He frowned. "Which is kinda troubling now that I think about it."

Micah and Jet began to laugh and Isaac joined in. "How 'bout you, Champ?" Micah draped an arm over his broad shoulders and turned him to face the room. "See anything that catches your fancy?"

"I see a lot of things, but not a one that catches my fancy."

"Well, I don't think we're gonna find out anything from the bartender. I was over there with him and he doesn't seem like the chattiest fella. I guess we just grab a gal and head upstairs to the hotel and see what we can find out."

"I plan on touching as little in this place as I possibly can," Isaac quipped. "You two feel free to go upstairs. I'm gonna go see what the snarly dudes leaning on the wall with their arms folded have to say. I'm only a holler away if you need me."

Jet moved in to whisper in conspiratorial tones. "You strapped?" he asked Isaac.

"No gun, but I've got a knife under the cuff of my pants."

"I guess it's better than nothing. You watch your step when you're talking to those fellas, because you best believe they've got something more than a knife at their disposal."

"I'll be careful. What about you two?"

They both averted their eyes and watched as Micah headed off through a faded beige curtain with a prostitute leading the way. "Don't worry about us. I can handle myself and Micah can talk himself out of anything. I've seen that boy charm a jealous husband and a rattlesnake all in one afternoon."

The stairwell leading up to the second floor was small and cramped. The building was old and raggedy and apparently when the architects had designed it, they hadn't intended for a man of Jet's girth to be moving about in it. His wide shoulders rubbed the wall as he followed his escort up the steep steps. There was an extra wiggle in her step, something he might have found sensual had he not been aware of her profession and the possibility of her having extra parts.

A rusty bed with a light blue sheet on it awaited Jet on the other side of the door when his escort ushered him into the cramped space. Jet made his way over to the window and opened it. It looked to be about thirty feet to the ground below, but this might be his only way out of there if things went bad. Jet brushed away the prostitute's hand when she came close to him. "Sit on the bed. I'm not here for that. I just want to talk."

The girl got up in a snit. "Too bad, jerk. I'm not here to talk. So either pay me for my services or buzz off." She had dark hair and scars on her thighs, standing there with one hand on her prominent hip, the other on the doorknob.

Jet didn't know what the scars were from and he didn't care, he hadn't picked her because having sex with her interested him, she just happened to be the first girl he'd talked to who spoke English. "Calm down." He fished in his pocket and came out with a handful of American money. "This," he held up a twenty and placed it on the window ledge, "is for you. He fanned five more twenties out in his hand. "The rest can be yours too. But that depends on what you have to say."

She folded her arms across her chest. "What's to stop me from just calling the guards in here and telling them to shoot you? I could take all that money and anything in your pockets. This isn't Beverly Hills. You're a long way from home, white boy."

Jet folded his own hands across the expanse of his wide chest. "You could do that." He knew very well where he was and what the situation entailed. "But we both know the guards are just as likely to shoot you too so they don't have to split the money with you. So we can either do this the nice way, the way where you get all my money and nobody gets hurt. Or we can do this your way, the hard way, where you call your goons in and there's a fight. I already know I'm outnumbered, but who's to say I don't get the drop on your guys and kill them before they kill me. Do I look like a man who doesn't know how to defend himself? There's probably a few guys in a room down the hall." Micah and Jet had already discussed strategy before arriving and formulated a plan to get out if things went south. "I'd say three probably, maybe four. Chances are at least two of them are drunk or high. So now it's just me against two. I'm sure one of them is young, probably a new gang recruit. Probably never shot a gun in his life, he's just here because the gang offered him protection. So now it's just me versus one of your guys. Maybe he's a stone cold killer, but maybe I am too." He stepped away from the wall and walked over to the prostitute, who kept a calm demeanor. Clearly this wasn't the first dangerous situation she'd been in. "Listen. I don't want any trouble. All I'm looking for is some information. I'll ask you a few questions and you answer them. You look like you've been here a while."

Her face was still defiant, but the girl answered, "You could say that."

Jet placed a twenty in her hand. "See, that wasn't so hard. I'm looking for a woman who came through here years back. A white woman."

"We get a lot of those."

"She would have stood out. She was tall and blonde. Her name was Sofia, last name might have been Garza."

The girl shuffled a bit in place, a sign to Jet that she was about to lie. "Doesn't sound familiar. Sorry."

Jet took her by the elbow. "You're lying. Just tell me. I don't know your name. I'm not going to tell anyone it was you who told me."

She backed away, yanking her arm out of his grip but didn't make a move to leave or call the guards. "I know the woman you're referring to. I wasn't working here when she arrived, but I was born in this area, I know it well. We all saw her. She was beautiful. She stood out from the other girls and they all hated her for it. She must've made the bosses a lot of money, so I'm sure she was protected."

"What was her name?"

"I never met her or knew her real name. They called her Angel Rubio." Her voice dropped to a whisper and she looked around the room, as if searching to see if someone was secretly in the tiny room with them. "They say she helped many people."

"What does that mean?"

Discomfort crept across her body and the woman crossed her arms in front of her again, this time not in a defensive manner, but almost as if she were hugging herself. "I've already said too much."

"Where is she?"

"I don't know." She placed a hand on the knob and turned it, then told the truth. "I can't say."

Jet thrust a hand up and over her shoulder, slamming the door shut in front of her. "Take it." He offered the money he had enticed her with. "Get out of this place. I know you probably don't have many other options, but leave, leave tonight and don't ever come back. There's no future here for you. I'll gather my friends and we'll leave. Thank you for this."

She nodded and went to the windowsill to collect the lonely twenty that still sat there.

Jet watched her do this and his heart broke for her. She appeared younger to him now, less of a sexpot and more a lost little girl. If he could've taken her with him he would have, but he knew it was better if she left on her own. The gang wouldn't go after her if she left on her own, they'd simply replace her with another girl, but if he'd snuck her out and taken her on his boat, the gang would've pursued him with an army just to get her back and kill her for abandoning them.

It was easy to find Micah, all Jet had to do was follow the high pitched giggling coming from the floor above. When he opened the door, Jet saw Micah sitting on a rickety bed with three women in the room with him, they were all drinking and laughing as he regaled them with some sort of joke that Jet had come in too late to understand. "Time to go, Wolfe."

Micah got up from the bed, handed over a handful of crumpled money and followed Jet out as quickly as possible. He hadn't gotten any information from the women he'd been talking to and even though he'd appeared to be having a good time, he was getting more uneasy by the second.

Isaac McCoy was already outside. "Find out anything?"

Micah shook his head and Jet said nothing, he just put his head down and moved as swiftly away from the building as he could.

They jogged back to the Sirena, following Jet's pace. Cars going by honked, but Jet never broke his stride, he knew the girl he'd spoken to could've changed her mind and told the guards everything. As of now, Jet didn't know who Angel Rubio was but from the way the girl had acted, she was someone important and someone not to be spoken of. If the girl had changed her mind and told of their conversation, there could be a hit squad on their tails at the moment.

Jet worked furiously to untie the Sirena from the dock. "Get on!" He barked when the last knot had been untied.

Isaac protested. "My stuff is still back at my hotel."

Micah was already up on the boat and he pulled up the steps after Jet had ushered Isaac up onto the deck to join him. "We need to get out of here now."

"What's wrong?" Micah asked.

Jet headed to the wheelhouse and began to bring the Sirena out away from the dock. "Nothing for sure, but I don't want to stick around and wait for something to go wrong."

He gunned the engine the second they were out of the harbor and set a course for the open ocean. Whether or not Isaac McCoy liked it, he was along for the ride now. He was coming to Veracruz with them.

Once they were on their way, Isaac pinned Jet down. "So, what happened back there?"

Jet held on to a rope hanging from the rigging. "Frankly, I'm not sure what I found out. All I can be certain of is that Noah's mother, if that's who Angel Rubio is, had connections in Tampico. I can't say for sure if she's a madam or runs some kind of halfway house for whores."

"Damn, that sounds bad." Isaac leaned on the rail and looked at the receding shoreline. "I'll have to get someone down here who can nose around and find out without Noah being any the wiser."

"Don't you think he could handle it? Noah's a grown man."

"I'm sure he could, we just tend to be overprotective." Isaac motioned to Micah to look at Jet.

Micah followed his nod and saw that Jet was checking his pockets. "Lose something?"

"No, just making sure I still had my wallet. I gave the girl money, but you never know in a place like that."

Micah got a sly look on his face. "'Girl,' are you sure?"

"Yea!" Jet said as he checked the instruments. "I think so."

Isaac chuckled. "What else did you get for your money? A little something-something?"

Jet bristled. "Watch it, McCoy."

"Did he like you?" Micah sing-songed.

Jet shook his head and walked off, throwing his hand in the air. "If you two don't beat all. It was a girl and I felt sorry for her, I didn't touch her."

"Yea, but did he touch you?" Micah called out, and Jet slammed the door behind him.

CHAPTER SIX

Back to Sami in Veracruz…

"Next week we do a complete workup to see how you're doing. I want to schedule you for an MRI, a cat scan and a full round of testing on your blood." Dr. Rio smiled, a positive expression on his face.

"Good, I'm ready to know something." He had explained the last round of treatments, some electromagnetic therapy which scared the bejesus out of her, so it was probably best not to know the full story.

Rosa had greeted her with a smile, offering her a warm sopapilla filled with honey. She'd gratefully accepted it and ate it quickly. Maria had not been as friendly. Sami had no idea how she'd offended the girl, but she guessed it didn't matter. Her time at the clinic— for good or bad—was drawing to a close. Just a few more days and she could return to America.

If she wanted to.

Sami supposed it all depended on what went down with Marisol. Late last night, after talking to the Governor, she'd emailed the Jaguar with her counter demands. Halfway expecting him to send another video of a dead Marisol, Sami had held her breath. But as she'd figured, he wanted the info of himself bad enough to take a risk. He'd agreed, saying he would be in Houston in twenty-four hours at the designated place. After that, Sami had phoned Governor Chancellor and relayed the information. He'd had Destry Cartwright get back in touch with her and they'd ironed out the last details.

Destry had been helpful, easing the way for her to get the money for the exchange. "I don't intend for them to get away with your money, but it's best to have it in order to convince them we're legit." He'd told her they'd found a Houston cop who would act the part of Samantha Cabot. "Our goal is to get Marisol away from them. We've downloaded the information you gave us on a flash drive. I'm sure they'll want to see it, but it's got a virus built in and the info will disappear thirty minutes after they get it, no matter where it's saved."

"What about Marisol, can you keep her safe?" This was Sami's primary concern.

"Yes, and we'll want to talk to her once we get her all the medical help she needs."

"Good." Sami was anxious for this to be over.

"How about you? It makes me nervous that you're down there all by yourself. If they ever connect the dots and figure out who you are...or are you going to be someplace safe?"

Sami considered what she would say next. "I'm in disguise," she finally admitted.

"Really?" Destry laughed. "What's your disguise?"

"I dress as a boy unless I'm at the cancer clinic. They know the truth, they just don't know I'm Leona."

"I wish I could give you more help," Destry muttered. "One of our guys is going to be down there, Jet Foster, but he's got his hands full."

Ah, he mentioned Jet. Sami shivered with awareness. "I heard. I'm a fan. In fact, I hope to go see him fight. And no, I certainly wouldn't want you to bother him with my problems. What you're doing now is more than I could ask for."

Destry didn't say anything for a few moments. "You're very brave, Miss Cabot. I'll be in touch the moment things go down. In the meantime, take care of yourself. And know this, I'll be praying for your full recovery."

Sami had felt better after speaking to Kyle and Destry, she had done what she could. Until she knew the outcome of the exchange, Leona would not be posting any more blogs.

* * *

Sailing from Tampico to Veracruz…

Sirena with her sails unfurled was a magnificent sight. When they'd left Corpus and headed south, the green water near the shore had begun to change colors. Now the farther they went as they sailed south of Tampico, the bluer and clearer it became. It was easy to see down twenty feet. When night fell, Micah was amazed to see all of the oil platforms. They were everywhere. Most were lighted, but Jet still had to be vigilant on the radar in case one wasn't.

When morning came, Jet stood on the deck with his arms crossed and his face in the breeze. Isaac and Micah were fishing. He'd heard Micah curse once or twice and Isaac laughed, so he presumed one of them was having some luck.

So was he, but not with a rod and reel. Jet was learning more about his lady love. The mainsail was up and he was motorsailing into the breeze at an angle. He would probably have to throw in a few tacks along the way, but that was to be expected. Over the years, Jet had learned if he kept the main on the boat's centerline and flattened it as much as he could by tightening its halyard, outhaul and boom vang and easing off its topping lift, he could maintain a tight wing angle, usually less than twenty degrees while still keeping the sail filled. Because he was relying on the engine to create most of the drive, he could get away with a super-flat sail shape. The sail would stabilize the boat's motion and also add some extra speed. If he hadn't been in such a hurry, he would've put more shape in the sail, maybe even rolled out the jib. This would have given him more free speed, but not greater speed. Once he was through with Santoro and on the way to the San Miguel, he'd play more freely.

"Jet, look!" Isaac called out. He smiled, going to see what the big McCoy was hollering about. Since they'd left Tampico, things had calmed between them. Micah said the problem was that they were so much alike. Maybe so. Jet wasn't threatened by the badass, he had just felt that McCoy thought he was better than everyone else. Since spending some time with him, Jet's opinion had changed. Isaac was down-to-earth, he didn't mind getting dirty and he could laugh at himself with ease.

"What am I looking at?" He joined them and looked out in the water where they were pointing. "There she blows." He laughed with delight.

"What kind of whale is it?" Micah asked. They were all standing on the deck, mesmerized by the large body that surfaced every few seconds not fifty yards off starboard. At least Micah had on clothes, not many, but he had opted for another pair of shorts and sandals. They were all acquiring a tan as the sun beat down unmercifully on the ship.

"That's a Bryde's whale. Very rare. There are only about fifty of them in existence and they usually stay off the Florida panhandle. I've never seen one this far west," Jet answered as they watched the majestic creature jump, waving its big tail, sending playful spouts of water into the air before it dove, sounding into the depths.

"I'm enjoying this," Isaac admitted. "I didn't think I would, but I am. Usually I'm in so much of a hurry that I don't take time to just be."

"Your family has been through a lot in the last couple of years," Micah said. "Everything from kidnapping, murder trials, and accidents to weddings…lots of weddings." His voice had gone from sympathetic to teasing.

"Yea." Isaac laughed. "Weddings invariably followed by babies…lots of babies."

"When are you and Avery going to add to the growing McCoy clan?" Jet settled down on a deck chair to shoot the breeze with his friends.

"Soon, if I have my way. We're not really trying, but we're not doing anything to prevent it and I'm getting in as much practice as I can." He started to laugh and then jumped when his trolling rod bent and a fish started spooling his line.

"You got one!" Micah called. Isaac settled onto the stool and took hold of the rod. "What is it?"

Jet leaned forward and looked. "I think you've got a mahi-mahi. Reel him in and I'll fix some grilled fish and ceviche."

"Now I've got one!" Micah cried as he began fighting the big fish, pulling back on the rod. They had run into a school of mahi-mahi and soon they had one a piece, enough food for several meals.

Their time together passed swiftly. They talked about the fight, the San Miguel, and Isaac's new idea to sell Hardbodies and open a couple of clubs, one in

Austin and the other in Houston. "What kind of clubs?" Micah asked.

Isaac answered with a sly grin, "BDSM."

"Now you're talking." Micah raised a beer in salute.

"Are you a Dom or a sub?" Jet asked Micah dryly.

Micah huffed. "What do you think?"

"I think I know a Dominatrix I'd like for you to meet." Isaac leaned forward. He whispered as if there were people nearby who would hear. "She'd have you trussed up like a Christmas turkey in no time and you'd be begging for more."

"You know this firsthand?" Micah asked, his mind going to places he hadn't ventured before.

"No." Isaac shook his head. "I'm faithful to Avery and I don't have a submissive bone in my body…but…" His smile turned wicked. "I could see the appeal in letting a beautiful woman *think* she was topping me for a little while."

Jet slapped Micah on the shoulder. "I think you should get Isaac to set you up with this whip-happy honey. What's her name, Isaac?"

"Brynn."

Intrigued, Micah asked, "No Lady, Mistress, Madame?"

"No, just Brynn. I don't even know her last name."

"What's she look like?" Jet asked.

Micah cut his eyes at Jet, then back at Isaac. "Yea, what does she look like? Tall, dark hair? Black leather, six inch heels, fishnet hose?"

Isaac laughed. "No, she's petite, long blonde hair, dresses all in white." He lowered his voice. "But she's in charge and the men I've seen with her are happy to turn over the reins."

"You might have to hook us up for a night." Micah propped his feet up on the railing.

Jet lowered his head and covered his eyes. "Please, please do. I'll pay for it." He was chuckling. "I'd pay big money to see some woman plant her foot in his chest."

"Oh, like Isaac said, she'd just think she was in charge for as long as I wanted her to." Micah seemed certain.

"Brynn is the real thing, Wolfe."

Micah smiled a faraway smile as if he was seeing something the others could not see.

Later, when night fell, Jet was alone on the deck. He'd anchored for the night. Isaac and Micah were already in bed. They'd made good progress during the day due to a steady headwind and he was in the mood to take a moonlight swim. Shucking his shirt, he walked to the edge and dove overboard. Breaking the surface of the water, he let the cool sensation wash over him. Closing his eyes, he just went with it, slicing through the calm with a strong front crawl. Arm over arm, he swam away from the Sirena, immersing himself in the refreshing depths.

Suddenly, his leg brushed something and Jet tensed, thoughts of a shark hitting him like a bat. But when he opened his eyes, he saw it wasn't a shark. He was surrounded.

Surrounded by lights, beautiful greenish-blue glowing orbs. He treaded water, looking around at the fireflies of the sea, the much-ballyhooed so-called phosphorescence, the natural neon liquid laser lightshow that no fog could stop. They weren't an electric form of microscopic plankton as many seafaring folk believed, but a clear walnut size jellyfish called Leidy's comb jelly. When the water was agitated, these non-stinging little beauties appeared, pulsing in concert with one another and the rhythm of the sea. Jet lay on his back and moved slowly back toward the Sirena, surrounded by stars above and stars below.

"Jet!"

He jerked straight up and answered, "What?"

There was no reply. His heart was hammering.

The voice had been female.

He treaded water, waiting to see if he'd hear anything else. Nothing.

Jet reached the Sirena and pulled himself up. He'd heard the sirens call. For a few moments, he gazed out at the ocean, a fairyland of twinkling lights. It appeared mystical, magical. No wonder his imagination was working overtime.

* * *

Back with Sami…

"Jet!" Sami cried.

She sat up in the bed, panting. Shaking like a leaf, she realized it had been a nightmare. She'd dreamed men were chasing her down a dark street, shooting at her. Why she called out Jet's name, she didn't know. Maybe because she'd been thinking about him before she went to sleep. The men from the bar, the ones who'd told her they'd let her know when Jet and Santoro were to fight had come to tell her the date had been set—in two days, her champion would face off against the challenger and Sami wanted to be there more than anything.

Working the hours that she did, Sami slept when she got the chance. At times, she seemed to have her days and nights mixed up. Glancing at the clock, she saw it was nearing midnight. She'd lain down about the time darkness fell just to rest her eyes and sleep had overtaken her. Then, she'd had that god-awful bad dream. Sitting up, she ran her hand down the front of her sleep shirt. Her breasts had grown, filled out. They were fuller as well as rounder. Looking down at her body, she realized all of her was bigger. The change in diet and the treatments had made it possible for her to gain weight. Standing, she went to the mirror and stared at herself. She spent so much time in ill-fitting boy's clothes with her breasts flattened against her chest that she had very little sense of femininity left at all. Puberty had come and gone during the onslaught of cancer, so Sami had missed out on all the things that girls dream about and look forward to.

Now, did that mean she didn't have daydreams of her own? No, she did. But hers were unrealistic. She spent her time mooning over a man who didn't know she existed. Who would never know she existed.

But right now, she had something much more important to think about. In a few minutes, Destry and the faux Sami Cabot would meet a drug lord on the streets of Houston, and Marisol would have a chance at freedom. It had been a long time since she'd prayed, but Sami decided this was a good time to start. Going to her knees, she knelt by her bed and bowed her head, lifting Marisol's name up. "Please, protect Mari. Let her come home. Keep her safe. Keep everyone safe as they try to help her." When she finished her short plea, she didn't rise, she stayed on her knees counting the minutes. As the clock ticked and ticked, she rocked back and forth on the floor, so long that her legs began to cramp. Why didn't they call? What if it all blew up and Marisol was hurt or killed? What if they didn't show up at all and she was already dead?

What if?

What if?

Sami's legs had grown numb from kneeling for so long that when her cell phone rang she was barely able to scramble across the floor to grab it. "Hello?"

"Miss Cabot?"

She placed a hand at the base of her throat, feeling the pulse that was beating uncontrollably. "Yes. Mr. Cartwright?"

"Yes, this is Destry."

"Do you have Marisol? Is she all right?" She flung the words out and then it seemed like an eternity before she heard a reply.

"Your friend is alive, in our care and on her way to the hospital. But…"

But?

Sami didn't care about a 'but.' "She's alive?" Happiness bubbled out and she started to cry. "Thank God, thank God."

"It didn't go down as we planned. We made the exchange, your money and information for Miss Lopez, but that's when it got out of control. Like us, they had back-up and a firefight broke out."

"I don't know what you mean. Mari's all right? Was anyone hurt?" She was frantic that no one be hurt because of her scheme.

"Like I said, we have Miss Lopez. And we apprehended a low-level lackey, but we didn't get the Jaguar or Andrade and…they have your money." It was apparent by Destry's voice he was expecting Sami to be angry or disappointed.

All she was, was thankful. "I don't care about the money. Would you get me in touch with Marisol? Does she have a cell? Where is she? Could you get her to call me?" The questions just came pouring out.

Destry laughed. "I will personally make sure she calls you tomorrow. I can tell you this, your name was the first thing she said when we pulled her into the car."

Sami was weak with relief. "Thank you so much." She hung up and fell back on the bed, smiling big and feeling like she'd just won the lottery.

* * *

Jet arrives in Veracruz…

The Sirena had a rhythm, which was most noticeable at night. A surge into the wave then the plunge on the backside caused a white sound like the ebb and flow of surf. The calm of the darkness lured Jet out on the deck the second night. He listened for the odd call of his name again, but he didn't hear it.

Over the years, he'd found that every night watch had rewards such as meteors or satellites. Tonight he'd seen a star rise in the east just before twilight. At first he thought it was another boat's masthead light. Just before dawn, he could see the lights of Veracruz some forty-five nautical miles in the distance. The winds were practically non-existent and the swells from the Bay of Campeche were large, eight to ten feet but smooth and consistent. The boat was rocking so sweetly he knew Micah and Isaac were probably still sawing logs. Because he'd been here before, Jet expected a touchy approach to the port through the barrier reefs surrounding the city. There was a lighthouse on one of the nearby islands that he could use to make the approach. It had a set of lights below the main white light. From east to west they were red, white, green, white, and red. Each light gave the navigator a zone. Jet knew he could approach the inner harbor safely if he could see the white lights. If the red or green lights came into view, he was in danger of hitting a reef. The only problem was that before he could see the lights, he had to be within twelve nautical miles of the reefs. His charts indicated bearings and distances, but the light system did help.

By the time Micah and Isaac roused, Jet was ready to dock. "This is gonna be tricky," he told them. They proceeded to the Malecon to Med Moor. The Malecon is a concrete wall in the inner commercial harbor. "This place is pretty unfriendly to yachts." Jet directed them while they tied up stern to the dock. Micah dropped the anchor and payout chain while Jet motored like a bat out of hell toward the wall. At just the right time, Jet stopped the payout of the chain and worked to get the anchor set before the Sirena crashed into the wall. Isaac tossed the line to some young kids waiting to carry their luggage and they secured the boat. "Kamikaze docking." Jet laughed as he joined them on the deck.

There wasn't a welcoming committee this time. Jet had expressly forbidden his contact from announcing their arrival. He wanted some peace and quiet, a little time to get himself in the right frame of mind to face Santoro in a no-holds barred street fight.

"What's the plan?" Micah asked as they walked down the pier toward the quayside neighborhood. Warehouses provided a buffer between the berths where the boats were tied up and the hotels, bars, and shops that catered to the seafaring community.

"I think we'll do better to find a hotel room and a good restaurant. Later in the evening, we're supposed to meet Able, the guy who's arranging the fight here, at a bar called the Pirate's Lair. Shouldn't be far from here.

After the fight is over, we'll hook up with Victor Torres about the San Miguel."

Isaac clapped Jet on the back. "I'm afraid this is where we part ways, Champ. I used your phone this morning to arrange for a private flight. I need to get back to the ranch and see Avery and deal with this Angel Rubio information on Noah's mother. You sure you're going to be okay with just the two of you?"

Jet grinned. "We'll be okay. Chances are," he pointed a finger at Micah, "that land-lover won't be far behind you. I don't think he was meant to be on the water like me. I'd be surprised if he joins me on the voyage back."

Isaac looked Jet right in the eye. "My family will never be able to repay you and your friends for what you did for Aron and now helping to track down Noah's real mother. If you ever need anything, Jet, you just pick up the phone and a McCoy will be there to answer."

The men exchanged a hug. A friendship had developed between them in Mexico and neither could wait to get back together stateside and talk motorcycles.

Isaac hailed a cab, and Micah shook Isaac's hand. "Don't forget to get me Brynn's number. I might want to call her up one of these days."

"Will do, I'll even loan her the use of my dungeon." Isaac laughed as he crawled into the backseat.

They waved him off, then made their way toward the hotel and a big plate of enchiladas.

* * *

Same place...same time...

Sami was happy. She felt good, Marisol was alive, and all was right in her world. Humming as she worked, she couldn't think of a thing that could make the day any better…until *he* walked through the door.

Sami froze in her tracks, tingles of excitement dancing all over her skin.

He was here!

A smile as big as Texas came over her face. Jet Foster and another guy came sauntering into the bar. She supposed the other guy was good-looking, but Sami couldn't have told you what he looked like to save her life.

"There's the guy you've been wanting to see, boy. Get on over there and see what he wants to drink." Fred pushed her toward the table where Jet and his friend had sat down.

She walked over and stood there a second, just basking in his nearness. He smelled so good, fresh like the sea and he wore a tank top that fit his massive perfect body like a second skin.

Micah looked up to see the slight young guy standing next to them staring at Jet like he was a T-bone steak and he was in need of red meat. "Uh, Jet." He tapped his friend on the shoulder.

Sami cleared her throat. "What can I get you guys?"

When Jet cut his eyes at her, she smiled. He didn't smile back, his eyes slid off her and over to the bar. "Thanks, fella, I'll have a Pepsi, no ice."

Her smile faded.

Fella?

He thought she was a guy. Of course he thought she was a guy! Just her luck, meet the man of your dreams and he calls you 'Fella.' "Sure thing. What about you?" she asked the man with the nice smile.

"The Champ's in training, but I'm not. Give me whatever you've got on tap." Micah watched the young man give Jet one last look of longing, then walk away to get their drinks.

"I think you have an admirer," Micah whispered as he picked up a few peanuts from a bowl.

"What?" Jet asked, sounding bored. "Who?" He casually glanced around.

"The little bartender/waiter guy that just left."

"What can I say? He has good taste," Jet muttered dryly, watching the door for Able. When he was in training, he avoided sex like he avoided alcohol.

Micah snorted but didn't say anything, just shook his head.

Sami was almost hyperventilating as she poured Jet's soda and his friend's beer. She so wanted to say something to him, but she wouldn't. Mechanically she put the mugs on a tray, concentrating so hard she didn't see the burly offshoreman who was in need of a drink.

"Hey, what's a person have to do to get some service in this dump?"

Sami jumped. "I'll be right with you." She gave him a small smile and picked up the tray to take to Jet's table.

Walking from behind the bar, she skirted around to walk past the impatient customer.

"Hey! Don't you walk away from me, you little freak!" With a snarl, he reached out and grabbed Sami by the arm, sending the tray flying. The full mugs flew through the air, landing on the floor with a crash, splashing liquid over several bystanders.

Sami didn't have a chance to respond, the big smelly sailor slung her against the bar, her back slamming on the edge. The blow knocked the breath from her body and she didn't get a chance to get out of the way before he had her pinned down, a big hand clutching her around the throat.

"People like you think you can get away with anything. I won't be ignored by trash like you!" He squeezed her neck and pushed her backward until her head was touching the top of the bar. Sami couldn't breathe.

Sami clutched at his arm, trying to tear him off of her when suddenly he was gone, lifted off her and tossed to the side like so much flotsam.

"Leave the kid alone!" Jet stood over the downed sailor, whose nose was bleeding. "If you want to fight somebody, fight me."

"Hey, that's Jet Foster," someone yelled.

"He's here to fight Santoro!" another voice called out.

Micah pulled Jet from over the other man. "I think he's subdued. Come on, before we have a riot on our hands."

Sami pulled herself up and moved behind the bar, righting her clothing, stunned that Jet had come to her defense. The sight of him standing over her attacker, his muscles bulging, his face a mask of menace made her heart pound.

"Get Foster's order," Fred told her as he sent someone else to clean up the mess.

"Yea, sure." Sami pushed a lock of hair out of her eye. A small smile came over her face. The bruises she received were almost worth it. He would never know who she was, but she would never forget the moment. Once she had the drinks ready, she headed back over to their table. Jet and his friend were deep in conversation, so she tried to be as unobtrusive as possible. "Here, this and anything else you two want is on the house tonight." She had to remember to keep the register of her voice low and husky.

Jet looked up at the young guy as he set the drinks on the table. His hands were small and delicate and he had the biggest eyes and longest lashes Jet had ever seen on a male. His lips were soft...damn, Jet shook his head, dispelling the crazy thought. "Thanks, kid. That wasn't necessary."

Micah watched with interest. "My name's Micah Wolfe, what's yours?" He held out his hand.

Sami wiped her hand on her apron and took Micah's. "Sami Cabot."

Micah was amused. Her attention only stayed on him for a microsecond before she turned back to Jet. "Thanks for coming to my defense. He was already drunk when he got here."

Jet shrugged. "No problem."

Sami delayed another second, wishing she had something else to say, then it came to her. "I'm going to come watch you fight if I can."

Micah grinned, then decided to play devil's advocate. "I tell you what, Sami. I'll give your name to the guy at the gate and you can come in as our guest."

Jet narrowed his eyes at Micah, but he didn't add anything.

Sami blushed. "Oh, no. That's not necessary, but thanks." She backed away. "Just let me know when you're ready for more." She gestured toward their drinks and hurried away.

Micah bit the inside of his jaw to keep from laughing when he saw Jet follow Sami's progress back across the bar. "Something you want to tell me?"

"What?" Jet jerked his head back.

Micah guffawed. "Are you blushing?"

"No!" Jet hissed. "It's warm in here, jerk."

"First the tranny in Tampico and now this little fella, you're branching out, big guy."

"The girl in Tampico wasn't a tranny." Jet sat back and sipped his drink.

"Are you sure?"

Jet frowned. "I didn't feel between her legs if that's what you mean, I told you I only got information."

"Yes, but what did you have to do to get that information?" Micah pushed, enjoying himself.

"I gave her money." Jet explained patiently as if talking to a child.

"Which one did it for you best, the tranny or the waiter?"

Jet drained his glass, then slapped it on the table. "You know, I don't think I'll fight Santoro, I'll just beat the crap out of you instead."

Micah leaned back, just in case Jet reached for him. "Oh, look, that man has on one of your T-shirts, could that be Able?"

Jet growled. "Yea, lucky for you." He stood up to greet his contact. "Hey, long time no see."

"You ready?" Able waved for a beer, and Sami immediately brought it over and refills for Jet and Micah. Able tried to pay, and she waved it off.

He thanked her, and Sami retreated back behind the bar to watch Jet as much as she could without appearing too obvious. When she got the opportunity, she cleaned tables near him—not that she was eavesdropping, but she did hear that the fight was in twenty-four hours and just like the men had told her, it would be held at an abandoned airfield in the jungle just south of the city, about an hour's drive away. There was no way she could go alone, perhaps Fred was going. Oh well, it wouldn't hurt to ask.

A crowd came in and she got busy, not too busy to take over another two rounds to Jet and his friends, but she didn't get a chance to stare or hear anything else.

Rey Olmos came in and this caused her to stay behind the bar with her head down as much as possible. She wondered if he'd been with the group that had taken Marisol to Texas and if he was using her money to buy beer. She caught him looking at her once, but she stayed out of his way. The next time she looked up Jet was gone. A pang of loss went through her chest. Now she knew she had to go see him fight, she didn't want that to be the last and only glimpse she had of him.

When she got the chance, she edged up to the owner of Pirate's Lair. "Hey, boss, are you planning on seeing Jet Foster fight?"

Fred eyed Sami and smiled, a gold tooth flashing in his swarthy face. "You want to go, don't you?"

"Yea, I'd like to." She gave him a hopeful glance.

Smiling at her indulgently, he patted her on the shoulder. "Let me see what I can do."

"Thanks." She would have hugged him but that would have been a girly thing to do.

With a lilt in her step, she went about her work. Her eyes gravitated to the chair Jet had vacated. She was tempted to go sit there herself and just revel in being in the spot he had occupied a few minutes before. If she'd thought about it, she should've picked up the glass he used and never wash it, just sneak it in her coat and take it home to serve as a keepsake. But Fred had promised to take her and she'd hold on to that fact.

Sami's mind was full of happy thoughts until her eyes met Rey Olmos and the hatred she saw shining out of them made her blood run cold.

* * *

For the first time Sami was afraid as she walked from the Pirate's Lair to her small apartment two streets

153

over. She made certain no one saw her leave, then she stayed as close to the buildings as possible so she could walk in the light. Instead of taking the shortcut through the alleyway, she stayed out in the open and as near other people as possible.

By the time she locked her door and laid her head against the cool wood, she was panting—not from exhaustion but from nerves. When the phone rang out of the blue, she jumped. Moving to answer it, she flipped every light on in the place, getting to where she'd left it by her bed. The readout on the phone said *Anonymous*, which made her nervous, so she answered tentatively. "Hello?" A stream of Spanish and tears met her ears. "Mari? Is that you?"

"Yes, my dear sweet friend. You saved my life! How can I ever thank you?"

Sami sat down on the bed and hugged a pillow to her chest. "Just hearing your voice is payment enough. Did they hurt you?"

There was a pregnant pause. "Sí."

"Did they…?"

"No, no rape," Marisol answered quickly. "I am so grateful. You paid money for me."

Sami laughed. "You're worth so much more than money to me."

Marisol sniffed. "How are you feeling? They won't let me out of here for another few days. Do you feel like coming to see me?"

"I feel pretty good, but I'm still in Veracruz."

"Ah, Dios mío! You went!" Another stream of unintelligible Spanish, too fast for Sami to decipher. "Are you cured?"

Sami laughed. "I don't know yet. I've been going to the clinic and keeping an eye on the cartel. I posted the blogs to get a reaction from them and I did."

"You're in danger, Sami. Come home."

"I will, it won't be too much longer. I want to see the treatments through."

Marisol coughed, then came back on. "How are you keeping an eye on the cartel?" She sounded suspicious.

"I'm working at the Pirate's Lair, a bar close to the waterfront." She lowered her voice to a whisper. "I'm masquerading as a boy."

Marisol giggled. "I can't imagine that, you're a delicate flower."

"It's worked, though, for the most part. This one woman thinks I'm hot, but most just think I'm gay. I did see Jet Foster, though. He's fighting here within twenty-four hours, so that's one added bonus I wasn't expecting."

Marisol made a teasing noise. "Oooh, did you talk to him?"

Sami made a feminine sounding snort. "Let's see, I was tongue-tied and spilled his drink. How's that for an impression? Besides, he thinks I'm a guy." She sighed.

"Oh, I'm sorry, honey." They talked for a few more minutes until Marisol was tired.

"I'm so glad you're alive, Mari. Like you told me, this world is a better place with you in it and I had to do what I could to make sure you stayed."

* * *

Micah and Jet sat in a jeep Able had procured for them, parked in a field on the outskirts of Veracruz. A dirt road led deep off the beaten path where a makeshift airport had been set up by the government for high level use. Everyone knew that 'high level use' was just code for military operations and drug running. It was how things went in some parts of Mexico. The area surrounding this clandestine airfield was fraught with danger and the perfect setting for the showdown that was about to unfold with Santoro.

Jet stood on the side of the runway and watched a little Cessna charge toward the end of it. The landing strip was bumpy and treacherous, no more than two worn paths in a field, but the pilot managed to land with some room to spare. "Wonder who that it?"

"Some drug lord come to watch you fight, don't you imagine?"

"I'm not sure I want to know." Jet pointed a sturdy finger. "See that opening in the trees there?" Micah regarded the tiny throughway that looked no wider than a footpath. "Head for that and don't stop. The place is about a mile into the jungle. When we get there you say nothing. These guys might not appreciate your sense of humor. You just make sure you've got one in the chamber and the second this is over, we're vapors."

Micah put on his game face and dropped the jeep into first. He gunned the engine once, looking at the small opening that Jet had directed him toward. The urge to ask if Jet was sure this was the place to go was strong, but he beat it back, dropped the hammer to the floor and blasted off across uneven ground and a meeting with Santoro.

Their destination was deep in the tropical rainforest. Everything from raggedy dirt bikes and four-wheelers to limousines were parked haphazardly around a building that couldn't have been more than a couple thousand square feet in total space, but towered three stories into the air among the tall vegetation.

"Not a word." Jet reminded his corner-man before they exited the vehicle.

Micah left it in gear, slipped the keys into his front pocket, and patted the Glock in his backpack. There were matching revolvers and some concussion grenades in there as well to keep the guns company. Neither man wanted to have to use anything in the pack, but they also didn't want to get caught with their pants down either.

They walked past a cluster of men who stood near the front door smoking. Jet kept his eyes locked straight forward. His focus was total and complete. There wouldn't be time for a warm-up for this fight. There'd be no rounds, no referee, no rules, and no guarantee that they'd even be seen again. The only guarantee there was, was that Santoro would be inside waiting and he wouldn't fight clean.

The space they walked into could hardly be described as a room at all, it was a dirt floor surrounded by skids that had been turned on their sides and tied together to form an uneven circle. All eyes fell on Jet as he circled the pit. Santoro was already inside, his trademark scowl festooned across his scarred brow. He smirked at Jet once and then spit on the floor to his left.

It was the first time either man had seen the other in person and Micah was sure he saw a moment of fear skate across Santoro's face. Santoro was a big man, much larger than Jet or Micah had realized, but Jet was the Champ, he was an MMA legend and a man globally feared. If Santoro was having second thoughts about this whole thing, it was too late.

Jet stopped and a scruffy man who'd smoked his cigarette down to the filter moved one of the skids aside for him to get into the pit. Micah looked above him. The pit was surrounded on all sides by two tiers of balconies. Men crowded in around the rail to get a good view, spilling their beer and ashes down onto the dirt floor. God only knew what else these men had seen fight here, everything from men to cocks to dogs. The earth here must have seen countless battles and gallons of blood spilled on it. As he stared up into the crowd, his gaze got hung up on a small pale face and big eyes. Was that the young bartender from the Pirate's Lair? God, he hoped not. This was no place for someone like him. Who'd look after him? Hell. Jet shook his head, he couldn't worry about that now. He looked again and this time there was no sign of him. Good. Maybe it had been his imagination.

Jet stepped in and went to his corner. There was a portly old fella with a thick shock of black hair standing in the middle of the ring. He was as close as they would come to a referee, but the man's only job was to ensure the fight started fairly. Once the action got underway, he'd join the spectators on the outside.

Jet went to a spot across from his opponent and Micah pushed his way through the throngs to get to Jet's side. Jet turned his back on Santoro to speak to Micah. "One in the chamber. Keys at the ready. I'm gonna try to get this clown out of here as soon as possible."

Micah eyed Santoro over the Champ's shoulder, expecting him to come dashing across the ring at any moment. "Put him to bed and let's get out of here." He pulled Jet in for a hug.

Jet turned to regard Santoro. The big man pulled his shirt up over his head with one arm, flexing every muscle in his body as he did. Santoro was hairy, but it was clear he was in shape.

"Big fella's been in the gym," Micah said.

Jet scoffed. "Probably steroids." He pulled his own shirt up over his head and kicked his sandals off, standing there in nothing but a pair of black boxing shorts.

The 'referee' gave them one final look and a nod before exiting through the hole Jet had entered. The moment the skid was put back into place, the room erupted. The sound was deafening. Loud men with scraps of paper moved about the crowd, taking money and jotting down bet slips.

The combatants circled each other. Jet was in his traditional Muay Thai stance, coiled and ready to strike, but Santoro was cocky, hanging his hands at his side, smirking at Jet, playing to the crowd. He taunted Jet. "Come get me, phony champion." If he'd appeared rattled at the sight of the Champ, he was now projecting supreme confidence.

Jet ignored his taunts, sticking to his game plan.

"Wipe the smirk off his face," Micah called out through the noise.

They circled each other for a minute, the crowd growing more frenzied by the second.

Santoro threw a few pawing jabs, but Jet covered up with his arms and hands, deflecting the advances as if they were gnats. Santoro bull-rushed him twice, but each time Jet deftly sidestepped like a matador, frustrating his opponent and drawing a chorus of boos from the crowd. They were here for blood, not a technical fight, they wanted to see two men standing in the middle of the ring exchanging punches with no regard for their lives.

The crowd was now in full blood lust mode. Jet had mounted no offense in the first five minutes, instead conserving his energy and using little of it to deflect Santoro's clumsy punches and advances. Twice Santoro had reached for and gotten a hold of Jet, but both times the muscled sailor had shucked him off and pushed his would-be attacker into the skid wall.

Santoro was getting frustrated. "You coward."

These were his people he was amongst, people who had come there to watch their local fighter dismantle this phony, television created champion. The boos turned into insults quickly and Micah was forced to watch on and listen as Jet's integrity and even his home country were slandered. Oh, how Micah would've loved to punch out a few of the onlookers, but that wasn't an option, all it would do is get them both killed.

Jet lunged in when Santoro wasn't expecting it and landed a heavy jab to the left side of his face. The big Mexican stumbled back and immediately his eye began to swell closed. Panic overtook him and he momentarily looked for an escape before composing himself. But the moment hadn't gone unnoticed by his opponent. Jet had faced down tanks and angry guerilla fighters in some of the most hostile places on Earth and he knew what he'd just seen, Santoro's heart was gone, his courage chased from him with one well-placed jab. He lunged in to take Santoro down, and Santoro unexpectedly sidestepped him. When Jet turned around to face his opponent, Santoro sprang forward and wrapped his arms around the Champ, pulling him in for a bear-hug.

There was no denying Santoro's strength and he squeezed with all of his might, trying to suffocate Jet. Jet flexed every muscle in his body and broke the hold, but as he stepped back, Santoro's long reach came into play, he struck out a hand and poked Jet in the eye. Santoro had lived up to his dirty reputation. Jet's vision instantly went blurry and Santoro threw a head kick that Jet barely avoided. He retreated back from his attacker and covered up with his hands, needing a moment to recover.

Deep in the crowd, standing on a section of skid, Sami was tense, fists clenched, chewing on her lower lip. "Go Jet! Hit the son-of-a-bitch!" she yelled, knowing he couldn't hear her, but it made her feel a helluva lot better to say it.

Fred tugged on her shirt. "Easy, boy, don't fall off your box."

Sami smiled over at him, adjusting her cap. Her hair was so much longer now, she should get it cut. But she was so glad to have it back, she hesitated to do so. "I won't." Sometimes it seemed Fred treated her with such care, surely he must realize Sami was a girl. Maybe he was just a good man.

Back in the ring, Santoro rushed in, spurred on by the applause of the crowd. He delivered a left hook to the body that doubled Jet up. He leaned forward, every ounce of breath in his body evacuated all at once. Santoro threw a knee that Jet deflected and used the time to get back to his feet. It had become evident to Jet in that moment that Santoro was nothing more than a street brawler, a man who'd made his reputation fighting in bars and unsanctioned bouts like this one. Santoro had no formal training, no technique, and no chance against a fighting machine like Jet Foster, unless he fought dirty, which was what he seemed prepared to do.

Jet stepped back against the skid behind him, playing possum as Santoro unloaded with everything he had. His shots landed on Jet's arms and did little damage. Jet was content to use this time to recover and let Santoro punch himself out. Sure enough, Santoro's labored breathing became evident in no time. He'd expelled so much energy trying to finish Jet, that he was now zapped. If Santoro hadn't spent so much time running his mouth and insulting Jet, he might have felt sorry for him, but Santoro had done the crime, now he needed to be punished.

Jet's killer instinct took over, he moved with a bob to his left and came across the top with a heavy looping right hand that Santoro never saw coming. The blow jarred his entire brain and drew a collective 'owwwww' from the crowd. Santoro wobbled back on unsteady legs and put his hands up. Jet moved forward and feigned a jab to get Santoro leaning one way and when he did, the shin of Jet's left leg met the side of his face. Teeth flew from Santoro's face in a spray of blood. The fight was all but over, but Jet dragged it on for another seven minutes, punishing a wounded and bloody Santoro. He landed vicious leg kicks that had Santoro limping after three of them and delivered so many unblocked punches to Santoro's side that he was sure the man would piss blood for a week afterward.

The reaction in the crowd was mixed. Some were all but silent now, they'd come here to watch their hero vanquish the champion and when it quickly became apparent that wouldn't happen, they lost interest. But some were cheering him on. "Yes! Jet!" It seemed he could hear the siren's call. Jet shook his head, maybe he got hit harder than he realized.

"Finish him," Micah said under his breath.

Almost on cue, Jet stepped to his left, avoiding a lazy right cross thrown by Santoro. He planted his foot, leaned back and delivered a kick that caught Santoro square in the jaw, felling the giant once and for all. Santoro twisted, coming up off the ground and landed with a sickening thud as his face bounced off the dusty ground.

The mood in the room wasn't difficult to read. Micah slipped a hand into his bag and motioned for Jet. "Let's fucking go."

Jet stood over an unconscious Santoro with his hands on his hips, looking out at a crowd who for the most part wasn't happy. He turned to see Micah with his hand thrust into his backpack and knew right away it was time to get the hell out of Dodge. Taking three big strides, he hopped the skid wall and moved at a hurried pace toward the exit. Micah moved through the crowd, only stopping when he came across the path of two men who looked very familiar. He'd seen them in the bar the night before. One was short with curly hair and an ever-present cigar, the other a handsome light skinned fella. He almost looked American, and his face told a story of many battles fought. Micah looked them both in the eye. The men remained stoic.

Jet bellowed from the front door. "Let's go, Wolfe!" The situation had grown dire, they needed to make tracks post haste.

Micah broke the stare with the two men and moved quickly toward Jet, his gaze landing on another familiar face—Sami from the bar. He was all smiles. Micah raised his head in a nod—there was something so strange about that little dude. Continuing on, he darted in and out of the crowd goers, some noticing him, others too drunk to even know where they were. He knocked a few men over, but put his head down and kept moving.

Jet was in the jeep when he arrived. Tossing the backpack toward his partner, Micah slid behind the wheel, thrust the key into the ignition and left in a cloud of dust, not taking his foot of the gas until they were safely back at their hotel.

CHAPTER SEVEN

The next night, the Pirate's Lair was full. Sami was on pins and needles. Something was wrong. If she didn't have to see Dr. Rio to get her results, she would've already been gone. Her sixth sense was screaming. Olmos was a constant presence in the bar and every time she looked at him, he was looking at her. Could he know? She'd taken precautions, packing a bag and keeping it under the bar. The bag contained her computer, all the information Marisol had given her and little else. If she had to run, she would.

The only bright spot had been seeing Jet fight the night before. He'd been amazing. She finished filling a tray with beers and reached around behind her back to pull on the compression bra. Since she'd gained weight the binding was beginning to be unbearable. Sami would be glad when she could be a girl again.

A smattering of applause drew her attention and she almost bit her tongue when Jet walked through the door followed closely by his friend Micah. This time they joined two other men who held up their hands to catch the Champ's attention, men she'd never seen before. Picking up the tray, she delivered the drinks to a table filled with guys with hookers hanging all over them, then ventured on to Jet's table. As she walked up, she could hear them talking.

"You should see my boat, Victor. The Sirena's as fine as she comes. I've got her docked down at the Melacon, not far from here."

The man named Victor answered, "I look forward to seeing her." His companion, a bald man with a hook nose sneered at Sami, but he didn't interrupt Jet and Victor's conversation and neither did she.

"So, you'll help me raise the San Miguel? My father had a heart attack not long ago. We'll have his boat, the Seaduction, but this is a big job. I'll need more divers and equipment than what we've got."

"I've cleared my schedule. My boat is in Cuba, but we can meet up with you along the way and sail on to Florida." He pointed at the man with him. "This is my first mate, Rafael, he's as good as they come. Has a nose for treasure."

"Sounds good to me." Jet shook Rafael's hand and pulled out a map.

"Let me see that." Micah grabbed at the furled up piece of parchment. "You actually have a map, a treasure map? Does X mark the spot?"

"Don't touch it," Jet snarled, holding the paper close to his chest. The other two stared at the map as if it was a snake that had them charmed.

Seeing an opportunity, Sami took their orders. "What can I get for you?"

Before anyone could say anything, Jet spoke up, "Were you at the fight last night?"

"I was," Sami admitted. "You did a great job."

Micah kicked him under the table, and Jet gave him a sideways glance. "Get us all your best beers, I'm celebrating."

"Sure thing." She didn't linger, just went to fill their order.

"There's something strange about him," Micah mused. "He sure does like you, Jet, no hiding that fact."

Victor looked amused. "Takes all kinds." He tried to get a look at the map Jet spread out, but he kept it framed by his big arms.

"We'll sail up the coast of Florida and meet Tyson and Nemo at Nassau Sound." Jet explained.

"Do you mean you're sailing through the Bermuda Triangle?" Micah asked.

"Straight through, I've done it many times. That's just an old wife's tale for the most part."

"I'm not so sure," Victor mused, rubbing his stubbly chin. "I've seen things there I couldn't explain."

His partner fidgeted in his seat, looking over his shoulder. Micah followed his gaze and saw him make eye contact with two men who'd been at the fight the night before, one of which was waving a cigar in the air. He didn't say anything about it, but he took note. In reference to the Bermuda triangle remark, he chuckled. "That settles it. I'm flying out of here."

"You were flying out anyway," Jet drawled.

Sami walked back up with their drinks. "Here you go, enjoy." She turned to take another table's order.

"Bring us a magnum of your best wine. We're celebrating." A man sat with a group of businessman, smiles on their faces. Nodding, she went to get it and some glasses. Lingering near Jet and his group would have been preferable, but she had no good excuse.

When she got behind the bar and found the wine, she filled a tray, and started back…when a commotion of shouting and crashing chairs drew her attention.

"Cheating gringo!"

Sami was alarmed to see Santoro and an entourage of his friends waylaying Jet. They had pulled him from his chair and already flying punches had been exchanged. Micah and Victor were up and ready to fight, but she didn't see Victor's companion. In just moments, the Pirate's Lair was a mass of confusion. Some were trying to get out of the way—the businessmen, the hookers, a few tourists—but most were picking sides, throwing blows, picking up chairs and tables to use as weapons.

In horror, Sami watched Santoro go after Jet. He had compadres framing them, keeping back anyone who would help the American. Two big men grabbed Jet, one by each arm, and Santoro moved in. When she saw a knife in his hand, she knew she had to do something—anything. Picking up the big bottle of wine, she moved out to the crowd, dodging blows and narrowly escaping being pushed to the floor.

When she drew near, Sami could hear Santoro snarling, "You're in my country, you Yankee bastard. I will spill your blood, you will not live to fight another day." With that bitter vitriol, he lunged and she attacked, raising the bottle of wine over her head and bringing it down with all the force she could muster right onto the back of Santoro's head.

He dropped like a stone and for a moment her eyes met Jet's and she saw a look of gratitude before he tore from his captor's grasp and laid them out like cordwood. Having done what she could, Sami retreated. But just as she did, Angel Andrade grabbed her arm.

Taking advantage of the chaos, he leaned in to whisper, "I know who you are, Miss Cabot. The Jaguar wants you, dead or alive."

He yanked on her, and Sami screamed, not bothering to mask her feminine tone. Wrenching from his grasp, she ran, taking shelter in the thrusting bodies and mayhem. Making her way to the bar, she ducked down behind it and found her backpack. It was now or never, she had to find a place to hide. Neither the Pirate's Lair nor her apartment was a safe place.

Keeping low, she crept to the end of the bar and tried to see where Rey or Angel were located in the general bedlam. With terror building in her breast, she saw they were coming toward her. There was no time to hesitate, she had to get out of here and find some place to lay low or she wouldn't be alive to see the sunrise. Dashing for the back, she pushed her way out the rear door of the bar and out into the night.

Jet and Micah traded blows with anyone who wanted to fight. Victor hung in with them and by the time they were able to take a breath, the place was in shambles. "Shit, this place is a mess," Jet muttered.

Micah panted, wiping blood from underneath his nose. "Let's get out of here before the cops show up."

"I don't think cops come to places like this." Jet looked around for the small waiter, but he was nowhere in sight. "Did you see that little guy down Santoro?"

"Yea, I did." Micah helped Victor up off the floor.

"I think it's time for us to go," Jet admitted.

"Can you take me to the airport?" Micah asked Victor. "There's nothing on the boat I need."

"Sure." Victor nodded. "Rafael, I'll meet you tomorrow and we'll get lined up to fly to Cuba."

"Sounds good." Jet kept looking around, wishing he could see what happened to his little friend.

Micah knew exactly what he was doing. "I'm sure he's fine."

Jet spotted the owner. "Hold on, I gotta take care of something." With a few long strides, he caught up to the harried looking man. "Hey, I'm sorry about this."

Fred waved his hands. "Not your fault, Santoro is scum."

Jet reached into his pocket and pulled out his wallet. "Here, take this." He handed him a wad of hundred dollar bills. "Replace your chairs and glassware. Tell Sami I said goodbye and thanks for saving my ass out there."

Fred took the money and smiled. "I'll do it. Thanks." He waved the greenbacks in front of his face.

Micah called out. "Let's go, Jet!" Several of their opponents were gathering themselves off the floor and he didn't want round two to start before they could get out.

"All right." Jet took one final look around, then left the bar to begin the rest of his journey.

* * *

Sami sought the shadows, trying to disappear, blending in and keeping her head down. She didn't know which way to go. Her heart was pounding so loud, she couldn't think. Almost blindly, she darted down an alleyway and ran as fast as her legs could carry her. Thank God, she wasn't dizzy or nauseous. Tonight her adrenaline was rushing and she let the high energy carry her over the distance, up one street and down the other. The only times she stopped was when she could dart into a doorway, looking back to see if she was being followed.

So far, so good.

When she got her bearings, Sami could see she was at the waterfront. Dozens of boats were moored at the pier. Frantically, she looked around for an open door on a warehouse, an open shipping container—anything. And then she saw it…the Sirena.

Jet's boat!

Did she dare?

She could get on, hide somewhere and then leave as soon as dawn broke and the coast was clear.

Shouts in the distance spurred her on. "Please, let this be okay."

Throwing her backpack over the side, she took a running jump, propelling herself from the dock to the top of the railing, grabbing hold and vaulting over. As soon as her feet touched the deck, she exhaled. She was torn, needing safety but hating to trespass. Oh well, she wouldn't hurt anything, she'd just hunt a dark nook to hide in and no one would ever know the difference.

Easing along in the shadows, she found the steps to go below deck and held on to the rail, all the while knowing she was in Jet's domain and wishing it were under entirely different circumstances.

"Meow!"

Sami jumped, almost tumbling headfirst into the darkness below when a big fat cat wound its way round her legs.

She bent to stroke its soft fur. "Hey, pretty thing." Sami loved cats. A loud purring noise came from its chest and she could hear it making up dough on the carpet, the breaking of threads a sign the cat was glad for the attention. "Were you lonely?"

"Meow."

"Well, show me a place to curl up and I won't take up much room or bother anything that belongs to your owner. Promise." Sami couldn't help it, she smiled.

Jet had a cat!

Now, she knew she was in love.

When her eyes adjusted to the darkness, she saw she was in the part of the ship that had bedrooms and the kitchen and a big dining room. Not wanting to be found, she moved on down the hall to hunt a more inconspicuous spot. When she heard the chugging of a bilge pump, she headed down another flight of stairs and found herself in what must be the engine room. A punching bag hung from a chain and over in the far corner a few tarps lay folded. "That looks like a good spot." Now that she was safe, a lethargic feeling of weariness washed over her. All she wanted to do was curl up, shut her eyes and pray everything would be all right.

* * *

"I hate to see you go," Jet admitted to Micah. "But I understand. I have a long haul across the Gulf and around to Amelia Island, thirteen hundred nautical miles."

Micah stood in front of his friend. "I've enjoyed this, you'll never know how much." He shook Jet's hand. "I'll be waiting for you when you get back. Kyle called this morning, said he wants to meet with me as soon as I get back, so I'm sure we have a lot going on. If you get over there in Florida and need help counting all that gold you're going to find, let me know."

"You'll get your cut." Jet grinned at his friend. "Call me when you get to Houston."

"I'll holler at you." Micah turned to go.

Victor and Rafael stood outside the wheelhouse, examining the workmanship on the Sirena.

"You're going to enjoy taking this lady across the Gulf, I'm almost jealous," Victor murmured as he ran a hand down the handmade railing.

"We'll be getting to know one another, that's for sure." Jet put his hand where Victor's had been.

"Ready?" Victor asked Micah.

"I am."

"And I'll meet up with you near the 80th Meridian West." Victor slapped Jet on the back as he named a navigational landmark both were familiar with. "Here's to the gold of the San Miguel, all two billion of it." He raised a bottled water in salute.

"Hell yeah." Jet nodded in agreement. "The grandest lost treasure yet to be found, and I'm the man to do it."

He followed the others to the gangplank, seeing them off, feeling a bit sorrowful to see Micah go. "He's an entertaining nuisance," Jet mumbled to Polly, who was winding around his legs. "Where have you been? Having a catnap?" Jet weighed the anchor, untangling the lines and went to turn on the engine.

Soon they were clearing the jetties and he set a course due east. "That's one fight I'm glad to put behind me." Picking up his friend, Jet held her under his arm like a big furry football. "Ready for something to eat?" His only answer was a head bump and a tail lash.

"I call dibs on the steak, you can have some tuna."

Down below, Sami slept peacefully, unaware the Sirena had set sail and she was now a stowaway.

When she awoke, her stomach growling, she sat up and rubbed her eyes. How long had she slept? A movement on the rough tarp startled her until she saw it was the cat, a big black cat with soulful eyes and a pink tongue. "Oh, you're cute. What's your name?"

She'd no sooner bent to kiss the purring feline when an uneasy feeling came over her. A rolling surging flow.

The ship was moving!

"Oh, no. God, no. Please no." She jumped up, grabbed her bag and made for the stairs.

Trying to be quiet, she tiptoed until she reached the second floor where she heard someone in the kitchen. It was Jet! And he was whistling. Taking one step at a time, she made it up the next set of stairs until she found herself on the deck—with a huge wide blue ocean on every side and not a bit of land in sight in any direction.

"Well, damn."

What was she going to do now?

Embarrassed and ashamed, Sami walked in a circle. Should she go to him and confess?

Should she just hide and hope to stay hidden until they reached port?

And then what would she do?

She stared over the side, jumping overboard was tempting. When she heard Jet's heavy footsteps coming up on the deck, she ducked around the side of the wheelhouse and leaned against the wall, breathing heavily.

How in God's name had she gotten herself in such a mess?

Jet was in a good mood. He had a plate of fried eggs and bacon, a big glass of orange juice and a copy of the latest Playboy. Life was good.

"Polly? I have bacon!" he shouted in a voice he thought would be seductive to a hungry cat.

A few steps away, Sami's stomach growled. She wondered if she might sneak some food and him be none the wiser. Making her way to the kitchen, she surveyed what he'd left behind. No bacon, she sighed. There were four oranges, so she took one and there was a loaf of bread that she didn't feel too bad about sneaking a piece of. Finding a glass, she filled it from the tap, then held her breath wondering if he could hear the water going through the pipes.

Sami halfway expected to hear Jet shout and come bounding down the steps. For just a moment, she let herself enjoy the fact she was here with the man of her dreams—right here, occupying the same space! Almost immediately, a sinking sense of guilt stole the joy. She was trespassing and stealing. Sami glanced at the food in her arms. But what choice did she have? If he knew she was on board, it would only make him upset.

Hopefully, she could hitch a ride, jump off at his next port of call and phone Marisol to arrange a way home.

Looking around, Sami didn't know where to go. Should she disappear downstairs or stay close enough to Jet so she could keep tabs on him and stay out of his way? With a sigh, she opted for the latter, refusing to analyze the reasons very closely, afraid that she just wanted the chance to be near him and to catch a glimpse of him when she could. Creeping back topside, she moved near the wheelhouse until she was even with a window, yet near a pile of rope to hide behind. Careful not to bump anything, she eased down and made herself comfortable, munching on the bread.

Inside the wheelhouse, Jet sat with his feet propped up on the table, ankles crossed, his Playboy on his lap. Draining the last bit of the orange juice, he flipped pages and snickered at a cartoon showing a husband and wife trying to set up a new password for their computer. The husband put in the letters 'mypenis' and the wife laughed when there was an error message saying 'too short.'

"Not my problem." Jet chuckled as he turned the page and looked at the centerfold. "Mercy," he whispered, gazing at the well-endowed brunette, bending over to show her best side. He turned the photo first one way and then the next, his hand moving down to take his cock out of his pants. "Oh yea, that feels good," he moaned as he began to stroke his dick in his fist. He leaned his head back and let the feeling overtake him, the rocking of the boat, the sensation of his cock growing and filling, a hunger for more making his hand move faster and faster. For a moment he kept the image of the centerfold in his head, then it changed to a big pair of blue eyes in a gamine face and Jet sat straight up with shock and stared at the brunette again, chasing the other memory from his head. "What the hell?" he whispered. He hadn't even been at sea long enough to blame it on solitude. He brought the magazine back in front of his face and let the erotic vision do its job. "What I wouldn't do to that ass of yours," he growled at the photograph as he pumped his cock furiously.

On the other side of the wall, Sami finished chewing the last bit of orange. She tossed the rind overboard into the water and closed her eyes as the cool sweet juice ran down her throat. And then she heard it— grunting, moaning—Sami jumped to her feet and peeped into the window. "Heavens to Betsy," she whispered. One of her dearest fantasies had come to life and was displayed in living color before her eyes. Jet was leaning back, his magnificent manhood was unsheathed and proudly erect and he was pleasuring himself. "Oh, this isn't fair," she breathed. How she'd love to slip in there and go on her knees and take him in her mouth. "I'm right here." She had to hold on to the window ledge to keep upright. Her whole body flashed hot and her nipples rose to hard peaks. Since she was right behind him, Sami could see the photograph he was staring at, and what she saw made her sad. The raven haired beauty with the voluptuous body was the type of woman to turn him on. Not her—never her.

But she couldn't look away. Fascinated, she stared as his hips bucked, his neck bowed, and his eyes closed. His hand moved faster and faster, his cries grew louder until he shouted and plumes of white cum shot from his cock and drizzled down the shaft.

Sami licked her lips. If she was prettier, if she was sexier, if she was confident—she'd go to him and offer to set his world on fire. Sadly, she stared down at herself. Heck, she was still dressed as a boy. With disdain, she tore the baseball cap from her head and tossed it out to sea.

What she needed was a bath.

Jet stood, stretched, neglected to zip his pants and wandered downstairs to freshen up. He passed through the kitchen and stopped…something was amiss. He was a man of detail and on his ship, everything had a place and was in its place. After messy Micah had left, Jet set about to put everything where it belonged and he knew damn well he'd had four oranges. Four oranges, six plums and three papaya—no bananas, bananas were bad luck on a boat.

Where the hell was his other orange?

"Polly! Did you knock an orange off the counter and bat it under the cabinet?" He stooped down to look, and Polly didn't say anything in her defense one way or the other, she just licked her paws and watched her human with a modicum amount of interest.

"Hmmmm, weird." He looked around once more and shrugged it off. "Claude strikes again." Jet smiled thinking of all the weird things that happened on ships at sea. "Oh well, just don't eat my cheese, Claude, do you hear me? The cheese is off-limits!"

Sami heard, vowing she wouldn't eat any more than she had to. Running her tongue over the roof of her mouth, she relished the last little taste of orange—it had been good.

But who the heck was Claude?

For the rest of the day, she stayed out of Jet's sight. It was hard. The man was everywhere! Several times, she just slipped around a corner with a hair's breadth to spare to keep from being seen. The cat—Polly, she learned—thought it was all a game. She'd dart between them, sometimes Sami just knew the portly pussy was about to give her away. When Jet dove overboard to swim and bathe, she sank down and peeked out between the railings, loving the sight of his big broad body cutting through the waves. She imagined meeting him with a towel and drying him off, then laying him down and kissing him from head to toe. Twice already, she'd adjourned to one of the far cabins on the second deck and touched herself till she came, clutching at the bedspread and burying her head in the pillows to muffle her cries.

Another time, he'd gotten on the phone with his father and she'd enjoyed listening to him laugh. It was easy to tell Jet loved Nemo. Sami smiled at how fitting the name was. Jet, in her mind, was Poseidon, king of the sea—and she, she was a little mermaid that he'd never notice, too obscure and shy to attract his attention. While he talked, she flitted about, exploring her playground, eager to commit Jet's sanctuary to memory.

Funny, she knew even at that moment that the smell of diesel and wet varnish mixed with a briny scent would evoke pleasant memories and a sense of security. Because odd as it may sound, only now—out of all the times in her life since she was a small child—did she finally feel safe. Jet was here with her and even though he didn't know she was here, it made her seem protected. The varnish smell was strongest near the mahogany railings, she'd heard Jet tell his father he had applied coat after coat to make them gleam like gold in the sunlight. When he would go down into the hull to work on the engine, the smell of diesel would cling to his clothes. She knew this because she picked up one of his shirts to rinse out and wear when she got the opportunity to change clothes. The pungent smell of the water would fill her nose when she lay belly down on the coarsely painted, skid-proof deck, head hanging over the side to watch the iridescent little fish swimming just below the surface.

In the afternoon, she hung back and watched in awe as Jet hoisted himself to the top of the mast in the bosun's chair as he shaded his eyes to look off in the distance in the glare that reflected off the metal spars.

When he was busy at one end of the boat, she went down into the cabin, hoping to find a spot she could sleep in while she was his uninvited guest. Like Goldilocks, she tried each unoccupied cabin, wriggling up the side of each bunk, testing the mattresses for comfort, then pausing a moment to imagine how it would feel to be rocked to sleep by the Sirena while she was being tossed about at sea. One she fell in love with had a skylight, mast above, reaching into the blue sky, an incredible view. When Jet came down to cook in the kitchen and use the bathroom, she went topside and swung on the boon, the smell of warm canvas and paint, mingling with the aroma of pure sunshine. Cable in hand to steady herself, Sami carefully made her way to the bowsprit. She could see the hazy, blue water far below as she balanced along the metal spar like a tightrope walker to the end, placing one rubber soled tennis shoe in front of the other.

Although she could swim like a fish, Sami had never been on a boat before, other than the Galveston ferry. She was amazed at the dolphins and flying fish as they seemed to play in the water below, just for her. Until night fell, she dozed on one of the bunks, rocked to sleep by the lilting sway. Jet had moored the Sirena when the sun set and she wanted to take a swim as soon as she thought he might be asleep. For several long hours she entertained herself with treasures and photos she found in a cabinet in the room—fan coral, its skeletal structure a subdued lilac, and a conch shell as big as her head. There was also a photo album with pictures of Jet as a child, doing everything from climbing the rigging with a sword in his hand to swimming in the Sargasso Sea.

Polly came to be with her, scratching at the door until she got up. Together they eased down the hall, pausing at Jet's door to hear him gently snore. "Come on." She motioned to Polly and she crept into his bathroom and filched a towel and a small bar of soap he'd taken from the hotel. Up on the deck, she stripped off her clothing and with a small squeal, jumped overboard. "Stay there, Polly, I'll be back up in a bit."

The water felt like the most perfect warm silk. She jumped and dove, swam on her back and stared at the stars. With the soap in hand, she lathered her body and rinsed it off, knowing her hair would have to be washed in the shower. Could she get away with that? Right in front of her something broke the surface and she bounced back, thinking she was about to be devoured by a shark, but it was a dolphin and she laughed with delight when it nudged her. She tentatively reached out to touch its smooth, cool skin. When Sami placed her hand over the fin on its back, it took off and she hung on, thrilled at the free ride.

"Oh, I like you," she whispered, enjoying the moment more than she had anything in a long, long time.

Looking up, she realized she was a little ways from the Sirena, so she swam back, its lanterns shining to light the way. The haunting sound of the cable gently clanging against the mast would stay with her forever. From behind her came a whop-whop-whop sound and she sped up, but when she safely reached the ladder, she looked back to find it was a school of flying fish soaring up out of the water, then belly flopping onto the surface before diving below. Sami smiled, it was an amazing sight.

Feeling chilled, she climbed the ladder and boarded the Sirena, pausing to wipe off with a towel before she returned below deck. The shirt she'd borrowed from Jet served as a sleepshirt, it was big enough to swallow two of her, hanging past her knees. Sami hugged herself and padded to the cabin, Polly making every step she did. When she was between the sheets, she sighed, pulling the covers up to her chin. The cat jumped up on the bed and they both nestled into the mattress and went to sleep.

* * *

"You're acting crazy," Jet told his cat as she stood in the doorway and plaintively mewed. "What do you want? I've already fed you."

He'd risen early, pulled up anchor and hoisted the sails. According to the weather report, there was supposed to be a squall this afternoon but this morning was supposed to be clear and warm. The sun was rising on the horizon like a big jewel in the sky. The only thing marring his morning coffee was Polly's insistent caterwauling.

"What are you trying to tell me?" If he didn't know better, she was acting like she wanted him to follow her. She'd walk toward him a few paces, meow, then retreated. "All right, show me what's bothering you." Once he got up from his chair and came toward the cat, she took off, her tail high over her back like a flag. She went down the hall to the far end, then stood in front of a door. "What's in that cabin? Did you leave one of your toys in there?" Some people would probably think he was crazy to spend so much time talking to a feline, but she was the only woman he'd ever really had a meaningful conversation with—except Hannah. He liked Hannah.

When he put his hand on the door knob, he grinned down at the cat who was right beside him, her eyes following his every movement. Opening the door, he watched Polly run in, expectantly. He followed, ready to pick up her ball or maybe see a mouse she could smell that had found its way on board.

"Come back to bed."

Jet froze.

WTF?

"When did you leave me?" A crunching sound from Polly's throat was her answer.

Jet took a deep breath, he knew that voice. Rounding the end of the bunk, he stared at his intruder. "What the hell are you doing on my boat?" he yelled.

Sami sat up so fast, she bumped her head on the bunk above. "Jet! I can explain!"

Oh, shit. Oh, shit. She scrambled around and grabbed the shirt she'd pulled off the night before and tugged it over her T-shirt, in an attempt to cover her burgeoning breasts.

"Get down and get your ass in the galley." He stalked out.

"Can I use the bathroom first?"

"It's the head, dammit, and yes, use the head first." Jet fumed his way down the hall.

He had a damn stowaway!

Sami was almost in tears, but she fought them back. He had every right to be angry. Meekly, she crawled from the bunk, straightened the sheets and cover and padded to the bathroom to do her business.

Jet poured another cup of coffee and tried to calm down. The kid had saved his life, he couldn't exactly make him walk the plank.

"I'm sorry."

"You should be." Jet stared at Sami. "Thank you for saving me, by the way." That needed to be said, now he'd said it.

Sami blushed. "You're welcome."

"Now, what the hell are you doing on my boat?"

Sami hung her head. "I didn't intend to be here, I was just hiding from these men who were chasing me."

"What men?" Jet frowned.

"Angel Andrade and Rey Olmos."

The names meant nothing to Jet. "Did you get their drinks wrong?"

"No." Sami shook her head, it didn't matter. There was no use burdening Jet with her sad tale. "Look, I didn't know you were leaving so quickly. I hid, fell asleep and the next thing I knew we were out at sea."

"Well, I didn't want to refight the battle of the Alamo with Santoro and his gang, so I thought it was time for me to cast off." Jet stared at the kid. He couldn't weigh a hundred pounds soaking wet. Yet, there was something about him. Something that bothered Jet, made him feel uncomfortable. "You'll have to stay out of my way. And you're going ashore the first chance I get to put you off."

"Okay." She looked up at his dear face. "Where will that be?"

"Cuba," he spat out, not really meaning it.

"At least the embargo's been lifted," she mused. "Okay, that will be fine."

Jet grumbled under his breath. "You ate my orange, didn't you?" At least he wasn't going crazy.

"I'm sorry. I won't eat anymore, just some bread, maybe." She looked at him hopefully. "Or I could cook for you if you'd let me, I'm a decent cook."

"We'll see." Jet got down another cup. "Want coffee?"

"Please."

Seeing his hopeful glance, Jet sighed. "Sit down." He set about to feed his unexpected companion. "If you're going to work around here, you need to eat. Looks to me like you need to fill out and put on some muscle."

Sami's expression didn't change. "I've gained some weight recently."

Jet snorted. "Really? I think you need to gain a lot more. Before we reach landfall, I'll have you hoisting the rigs and swinging the jib."

"Will you teach me to tie knots?"

As he put bacon in a pan, he glanced over his shoulder at the small guy. "Sure. Where are you from?"

"Houston."

"What were you doing in Mexico?" Jet broke a couple of eggs and added them to the bacon.

Sami's stomach was growling. She didn't want to tell Jet the whole story, there was no use. "I came down to help a friend."

He seemed satisfied with her explanation. Seeing some dishtowels to fold, Sami made herself useful. "If you'll tell me some things to do to help, I'd be glad to do them. I don't want a free ride, I want to work."

Jet appreciated the boy's attitude. "Well, I'll see what I can come up with. How old are you?"

"I'll be twenty-three in October." Sami knew she hadn't done a lot of living in that time.

Jet turned to face his guest. "You look younger." His eyes roved Sami's narrow shoulders, small hands, big eyes and…graceful neck. If he didn't know better…

When Sami saw that Jet was looking at her really close, she almost confessed. What would it matter if he knew she wasn't a male?

"You'd just better be glad you're not a girl." Jet turned back around.

What? Sami was confused. "Why?"

"Because I'd have to throw you overboard. I don't allow women on my ship when I'm sailing. It's bad luck. Very bad luck."

Sami pressed her lips together. So much for honesty. He couldn't know she was a girl. "What kind of bad luck?"

"Storms. Pirates. Shipwreck. Scurvy."

"Scurvy?" He turned to grin at her, so Sami knew he was kidding. "I don't think a woman could cause scurvy."

"No, more like STDs. Actually, they're a distraction, unless she's naked and then she'll lull a storm like oil on water."

"So naked is good?"

Jet handed Sami a plate and sat down with his own. "Naked is always good. Have you known many beautiful women, Sami?"

Sami fidgeted in her chair. "Well, I had one come on to me in the bar the other night. She grabbed my crotch."

Jet roared with laughter. "Good for you."

Sami ate slowly. She felt extremely self-conscious. Not only because she was halfway in love with the guy, or the idea of the guy since she didn't really know him. But she was also afraid he'd see through her lame disguise at any moment. She didn't have her breasts flattened by the compression bra, so she sat hunched over, but there wasn't a dang thing she could do about her small hands or feet. And she didn't have the stupid cap to pull over her hair. Taking a sip of the coffee he'd poured for her, she looked up and met his eyes.

Jet was staring, he knew he was.

Dammit!

Why couldn't he stop?

Shit, he was thankful Micah wasn't here. The arrogant *sob* would have a field day with this. Micah had always been able to read Jet like a book. He'd know in a heartbeat that Jet felt some sort of odd drawing to Sami.

Was he gay?

Hell, no. Jet Foster loved women. He craved women. He wanted sex—with women! This was probably some sort of protective big brother thing he was experiencing.

"What's on the agenda today?" Sami asked. "How can I assist you?"

Jet narrowed his eyes. Sami's lips were way too full for a guy's. Then Jet realized he was talking. "What did you say?"

Sami cleared her throat. "Give me something to do!" She spoke a little too loudly and was immediately sorry she had. "Sorry."

Jet chuckled. "Don't be. What can you cook? You can be my cabin boy."

Cabin boy, great, Sami thought. "Sure. I can cook a lot of things. Why don't I look in your refrigerator and pantry and see what I can come up with."

"Sounds good…" Jet was about to give him a few directions when an alarm went off.

"What's that?"

"Weather alert. You do whatever you can and I'll go to the helm and see what's going on." He put his dishes in the sink and went topside.

As soon as he was gone, Sami laid her head on the table and groaned. Her nipples were tingling, she was damp between the legs and her mouth was dry—God, she was horny and nervous all at the same time. With a groan, she got up and went to the sink, drew some warm water, added dishwasher detergent, and cleaned up. Next, she explored the provisions and found some stew meat she could quickly thaw and fresh potatoes and carrots to cook. The potatoes were beginning to sprout, so she thought she'd do a beef stew. Checking the cabinet for spices, she noted how everything had a latch on the door, better to keep things in place during rough seas, she supposed.

And speaking of rough seas, Jet gazed at the radar and cursed. "Son of a bitch!" They were about to go through a helluva storm. "Where in the sam hill did you come from?"

Well, there was no use bitching. He had to get ready. If he wasn't mistaken, the Sirena was in for gale force winds and rough seas in just under an hour. Jet checked all of his equipment, then headed out of the wheelhouse to tell his stowaway to start battening down the hatches.

"Sami!"

Sami had just finished adding the carrots and onions to the beef stew. She was quite proud of her efforts. Jet didn't have many spices to work with, but she could make do. "Right here where you left me!" she answered.

"We're in for a blow!"

Sami understood more from his attitude than his words that they were headed into a storm. "There's no going around it or outrunning it?"

"No, she's too wide. This isn't a hurricane, it's too early, but it will be an intense tropical storm with at least fifteen foot waves. We need to get ready."

Sami understood. "Tell me what to do." He did and soon everything was secure below deck. She followed him up topside and was shocked to see how different everything looked. There was a fog rising from the sea, a thick haze seemed to engulf them from all sides. "Wow, I've never seen anything like this."

"Visibility is down to probably less than a mile." Jet went to the wheelhouse to check the instruments.

Sami stood on the deck and stared out to sea. In the distance, she could see something coming toward them. "Look, Jet! What's that?"

Jet came out to where she was. "What the hell?" He stared through the low hanging clouds. "There's nothing on the radar, that's for sure." Turning, he went back inside and got his binoculars.

While he did, Sami stood up on the first rail and squinted her eyes, trying to make out what she was seeing. "It's a ship, an old looking ship." She put a hand over her eyes, trying to peer through the glare.

Jet rejoined Sami, put the glasses to his eyes and stared—and stared. "It can't be what I think it is. I've always heard of her, but I always discounted the old tales. But, here, look for yourself."

Sami took the binoculars and focused so she could see more clearly. "It looks like a pirate ship, but it's…is it glowing?"

"That's not a pirate ship." Jet took the binoculars back. "Unless it's some prank, which it could be, I guess—that looks to be the Flying Dutchman."

Sami trembled a little bit, not really from fear—more from excitement. "What does that mean?" They kept their eyes on the ship with its tall sails and wooden hull.

"I'll tell you later, but nothing good, seeing the Dutchman is usually a portent of doom."

Doom! "Sounds like my kind of luck," she muttered. About that time, the most god-awful wailing came screaming from the galley. "What was that?"

"Polly!" Jet took off. "Something's wrong with Polly."

Sami was right behind him. He took the steps at a single bound, while she came down a bit more sedately, but still as fast as she could manage.

They raced into the galley and found Polly, back up, hissing, her tail caught in one of the cabin doors that had slammed shut just as she'd apparently been exiting. Jet rushed to open it and swooped her in his arms. "Did you break it, girl?" He ran his hand over the now somewhat bent tail. "I think you did." Jet looked at Sami accusingly. "I thought you closed all the doors."

"I'm sorry, I fastened the galley doors and storage bins, I didn't think about the cabin doors."

Jet tightened his lips together, but he said no more. "There's not anything I can do except offer you a treat." He cradled the cat, and Sami was more than jealous.

Fetching the cat a cracker, he toted her under his arm, giving Sami a wide berth. She felt like she'd contracted a case of the pox. "I'm sorry, Polly." Following Jet up to the deck, they found the winds and seas had picked up...and the Flying Dutchman was gone.

"Do you think it disappeared into the fog?" Sami asked, trying to make her eyes see through the thick haze.

"Maybe, if it was ever there at all," he spoke low, as if in thought. "We'd better heed her warning and get ready for a mother of a storm."

CHAPTER EIGHT

Sami did everything she was told, not wanting to make any more mistakes like the one that had injured poor Polly's tail. In the next half hour, Sami had a crash course in securing a boat for heavy seas.

"The wind is going to be running against the current, that's what will be dangerous, we could encounter very steep, breaking waves with a short wavelength. Jet showed her how to check the standing and running rigging. They taped all pins, rings, shackles, and turnbuckles. He put up the storm jib, storm trysail and drogue. "Here, put this on." Jet handed her an inflatable harness. "If it gets bad, I'll tie you to me or the mast."

Sami's eyes widened. "Is it going to get that bad?"

Jet shook his head. "I hope not, but we're going to be prepared. After all, we saw the Flying Dutchman." He showed her where the life raft was and how to inflate it. "Just in case," he added.

Sami stood by Jet and watched the storm come in. It was odd, like they were careening toward a mountain and couldn't stop. They were stationary, but the storm wasn't. To Sami, it looked hungry and what she'd always imagined her cancer to be like. Rising cloud banks, dark purple, black and cobalt blue met and married sheets of rain. Ahead of the storm, smoke rose from the sea. "What's that?" she asked, amazed.

"Wind on the water." He looked concerned. "Go into the wheelhouse," Jet instructed her when the big drops started to fall and the wind began to rise.

"Not till you do."

He grumbled under his breath, but gave her a couple more things to do to help. Once everything that could be picked up, blown around or blown off was tied down or put away, they headed into the wheelhouse together. And when they did, the bottom fell out.

Sami held on and tried not to panic as she gazed into the gaping maw of the ocean. She couldn't imagine anything that could make one feel more helpless than for the very surface beneath their feet to seem unstable. A strong headwind battered them, the waves rose and broke over their boat time after time. Water ran down into the cabin. She was so glad Polly was with them. "Is this the worst you've ever seen?" she called over the howling of the winds.

Jet didn't answer, just nodded his head and held on to the wheel. "Look." He pointed straight ahead, and she felt her mouth drop open as a waterspout danced right in front of the bow. Jet didn't spell it out, but she knew this was serious. Sami watched him record the data—gale force winds, forty to sixty-five knots, and thirty foot seas attacked them for six long hours.

Several times Sami felt the boat tilt at an awkward angle and she prayed—she prayed as hard as the night that Marisol was being rescued. If this storm was her fault, she begged for mercy—not only for her, but also for Jet and the Sirena.

But when it was over, it was over. The seas and the winds died down and there was an unearthly dead calm. Jet got busy, checking everything out, seeing what needed to be fixed. The anchor had come loose and battered the hull, but the engine hadn't sustained any damage.

"Is it bad?" she asked, hopeful.

"No," he told her, as he knelt and examined the electrical system. Sitting back on his haunches, he looked up at Sami. "You look like a drowned rat."

Sami immediately looked down, taking in her drenched clothing. At that moment, she was grateful for the harness or her femininity would have been undeniable. Laughing at her own predicament, she agreed. "Yea, I guess I do."

Jet was impressed at how the stowaway had come through the storm. "You helped. Thanks. I would've had a hard time without you."

"Good, I'm glad." What he said made her feel better.

Polly had found a tight dark hole in the wheelhouse to hide in and when all had quieted, she came out stretching. "I guess it's too late for that stew."

She'd had to turn it off and secure it in the refrigerator. "Probably, but I'll fix it tomorrow. How about some sandwiches?"

"Sounds good."

As she laid out food for their meal, he sat at the table, a little too quiet for Sami's peace of mind. "So, you're off to hunt treasure?" she asked, trying to fill the void.

Jet hesitated. "How did you know?"

He sounded suspicious. Sami shrugged. "I overheard you talking to those men in the bar."

"If you overheard that, you knew the Sirena was my boat, didn't you?"

His face wasn't showing any emotion, but she could hear the doubt, the unspoken qualm.

"Yes, I knew. I heard you say the name. But I didn't know where you were moored and I didn't run down there looking for it—not on purpose. When I was fleeing from those two men, I ended up at the waterfront and the name jumped out at me, it seemed like an answer, a safe harbor." As she handed him a sandwich overflowing with meat and cheese, she added, "I didn't intend to remain onboard. I didn't know you were leaving Veracruz right then."

Jet took a big bite. "So, you're not working for another treasure hunter? Trying to find information about the San Miguel?"

"No." Sami shook her head. "I'm not even sure what the San Miguel is."

"Okay, I believe you," Jet said as he picked up his glass to take a drink of water. She sat down with her own meal and for a few minutes they ate in silence. "Do you have any brothers or sisters?" he asked.

"No, I'm an only child." She took a sip of water. "My best friend, Marisol, is like my sister. She and I went to journalism school together at the University of Houston."

"She your girlfriend?"

Sami almost choked. "No."

If Jet hadn't been so busy trying to ignore his dining companion, he probably would've asked more questions. "Good sandwich." He started on the second one, but Sami asked a question of her own.

"What do you think we saw just before the storm, that ship?"

Jet continued chewing, swallowed and then took a drink. "The Flying Dutchman is a ghost ship, which supposedly went down in the late 1600s or early 1700s. Captain Van der Decken, or some name like that, put his ship and crew at risk during a storm rounding the Cape of Good Hope. His crew tried to mutiny, to turn the ship around, but the Captain killed the ringleader and threw him overboard and the ship went down in stormy seas. It's said that because of his sin, he and his ship are forced to sail the seas for eternity, never making port, never able to go home."

Sami looked steadily at Jet, eyes wide. "That's the saddest thing I've ever heard."

Jet laughed. "I don't know if we saw it, but tales have been going around for centuries, the Dutchman has been seen by ships, planes, and submarines—even by King George V. Encountering the ghost ship always foretells disaster."

"But we didn't sink." Sami almost sounded argumentative.

"True," Jet said, then smiled. "Maybe I had some kind of luck on board to counteract the Dutchman." He looked down. "Right, Polly? Cats, especially black ones are said to bring good fortune for sailors."

Sami leaned her chin on her hand and studied Jet. She still couldn't believe she was here with him, her hero. Oh, the circumstances were crazy, but they were sharing the same space, the same food…she wished they could share more. With a sigh, she asked, wanting to do anything to give them more reasons to be together, "Would you show me how to tie some knots?" During their battle with the storm, she'd seen him use several different ones.

Her question came out of nowhere. "Sure, I'll do that." Anything to keep his hands and eyes busy. "There's a couple of lengths of rope in the storage locker located in the stern."

"The stern is the backend, right?"

"Yes," Jet answered patiently, finishing his sandwich. "Go find them and I'll meet you up there in a few minutes."

Sami hurried off and Polly took that as a cue it was her turn. She jumped on the table and Jet picked her up. "You know you aren't supposed to be up there." He didn't fuss much, though, he was just thankful they were alive and still afloat. This journey wasn't smooth sailing like he'd anticipated. He didn't know which was worse for him—the storm or the stowaway.

After feeding Polly, Jet made his way topside to find Sam sitting on the deck with the rope in front of him. He was already winding it around his hands. When Jet walked up behind him, the kid glanced over his shoulder and saw Jet coming.

"Is this how you do a bowline?"

Whatever he was doing, and Jet wasn't sure, but it wasn't right. "No, let me show you." He sat down on the deck next to Sami. "Watch." He formed a loop near the end of the line and ran the end back through the loop. While he did, he talked. "The bowline is the king of sailing knots, it's been used by sailors for over five hundred years. You use this to turn the end of your line into a loop so you can tie it around a post or fasten the halyard to the sail."

She studied his big broad hands while he ran the line around the standing end and back through the small loop. "Or to tie two lines together," Sami added with a smile. "Or hanging a hammock!"

Jet cleared his throat. Damn, it was hot. "That's right. Under pressure the bowline tightens, so it won't give way. It's impossible to undo while bearing a load. See." He grasped the end and pulled the knot tight. "There's the big loop, ready for use. Now you try."

Sami grinned and went to work. After two tries, he had it and Jet felt a sense of pride. After that, he demonstrated the clove hitch and the cleat hitch. When he was done, he stood. "You practice all you want. I'm going to hit the sack." Rising, he stretched, looking out at the smooth calm sea that had been so rough and deadly only a few hours before.

"Goodnight, Jet, sleep well." When he started away, she asked, "Can I use the same cabin I was in last night?"

"Sure thing, kid, don't let the bed bugs bite."

Sami's eyes followed him until he left, wishing she was lucky enough to be sharing his bed. Wiping her brow in frustration, she decided when she mastered these knots, she would reward herself with a cooling moonlight swim. And she was keeping the rope. She could practice tying knots later. A mischievous thought crossed her mind, she'd love to tie Jet up and have him at her mercy if she ever got the chance.

* * *

Jet rolled over on his mattress. The air in his cabin was stifling. He'd left Sami above deck practicing his knots and made his way to his stateroom hours ago and had major trouble falling asleep.

Groaning, he opened his eyes. "Godammit!" He'd finally fell asleep and something had disturbed him. He felt the heat of Polly's fur plastered up against him. She'd stretched and dug those dastardly little toenails into his back. "It's too damn hot for you to be cuddling up against me." He gave the feline a half-hearted shove, knowing full well that Polly wasn't going anywhere. She'd settled in for the night and wouldn't be moving until the sun crested the horizon.

Jet dry scrubbed his face, the calluses on his hand rasping against a week's worth of growth. The swelling from the fight with Santoro had subsided, but the cuts on his chin had left small scars that hadn't fully healed over yet.

A groggy, naked Jet made his way to the washroom and drank from a water bottle that had tipped over and fallen into the sink.

He looked at himself in the mirror. "You look like shit, fella."

Life was good, he wasn't complaining, but his body still bore the aches that came with fighting and he didn't sleep well because of pain most nights. What he needed to do was crawl back into bed and count sheep while he was still drowsy, and hope the sandman took him away quickly.

Returning to his bed, Jet placed a gentle hand on his furry companion's back and pushed. "Shove over, you old rusty barnacle." Polly sat her ground, passive as always.

He'd cracked the port window in his cabin before going to bed and a splash drifted in through it, followed by what he could only describe as a giggle. A feminine giggle. Memory of the siren's call came to mind.

With one foot still on the floor, he stopped. "Couldn't be." His mind conjured up visions of mermaids frolicking just outside his window. "I have got to get more sleep. I'm losing it."

Another splash caught his ears and this time, another unmistakable giggle followed it. Jet rose from his bed with slow unease. The aches and pains had a strong hold on him tonight. He strode to the port window and looked out just as the moon disappeared behind a bank of clouds. The water rippled a few yards off to his right and a tiny splash jumped from the water. He stood there and watched through bleary eyes for the splash-maker to break the water again and just as the moon peaked out from the clouds, something broke the surface.

Jet rubbed his eyes. "What the hell was that?"

He'd never be able to testify in court as to exactly what he'd just witnessed, but it sure as hell wasn't any fish he'd ever seen before. It almost appeared to be the shapely rear end of a female and an unclothed one at that. The object surfaced briefly again in another location, this time accompanied by the giggle Jet was so sure he'd heard before.

"Holy shit!" Stepping back from the window, Jet thrust a hand over his mouth. Sami was sleeping close by and he didn't want to wake him up. "A mermaid?" He turned to Polly, who customarily ignored him. "I think I saw a fucking mermaid, Polly. My God, I must still be asleep. There's no way a naked woman is frolicking in the middle of the ocean all the way out here." The tales Nemo had told him as a child all came to mind. Mentally, he reviewed their location. According to the charts, they were nowhere near land and no other boats were anchored within sight.

Jet returned to gaze out of the window. The being surfaced again, but this time there was more of it visible. The moon continued to play its fiendish game of peek-a-boo and disappeared behind the clouds. Jet strained to see the figure floating on the surface. "Damn." Two rounded mounds protruded from the water just below an indistinguishable face. The choppy waters rolled over the tantalizing globes and it quickly became apparent to Jet that what he was seeing were breasts.

Two unbelievable breasts!

He ducked down from the window like a child who'd just been caught watching the adult party from the top of the stairs when he should've been in bed. "This can't be happening." His logical soldier brain warred with the mind of the man who'd sat at Nemo Foster's feet and listened to him recount the legends of the deep. Who knew what wonders existed in the depths of the sea? His heart pounded, his pulse raced. "Please, Lord." He looked skyward. "If I'm dreaming, please, please, please don't let me wake up."

The man who'd stared down the barrel of enemy weapons and faced trained fighting machines while locked in a cage, now eased slowly back up to the port window, doing his best to stay out of sight for fear of discovery. It was nearly pitch-black out now, but Jet could hear his lifelong fantasy diving and splashing in the salty ocean just beyond his reach. He closed his eyes and conjured up images of tepid water sliding over the big beautiful tits he'd seen bobbing on the surface. The little mariner's dream outside his boat was as curvy on the bottom as she was built on top. His mouth watered at the thought.

Jet's cock stirred. "Down, boy." He scolded the ache between his legs but after a moment, he couldn't resist and embraced it with a fever.

Oh hell, how many chances in his life would he ever get to see a mermaid? Even if this was a dream, he might as well enjoy it.

His thick erection bumped against the polished dark wood of the Sirena as he moved back into position in the middle of the window. Jet's big hand wandered down to rub the heft of his shaft, pressing the palm of his hand against it roughly and drawing it downward toward the tip. Moonlight broke through the clouds and the mermaid's floating body came back into view, her head laid back so every delectable inch of her was floating on the now still surface of the water. Jet drank her in with his eyes, memorizing every glistening inch of her magnificent body. His gaze was drawn to the most feminine part of her, two succulent breasts that cried out to be nuzzled, to be caressed, kissed, lavished with attention. When the water streamed off those glorious peaks, he saw a set of nipples that were hard as diamonds and begging to be sucked.

Working his cock faster, he groaned. "Oh my God, baby. You're perfect. The things I would do to you if given half a chance."

Jet wanted to blast through the door, bound up the stairs and dive into the ocean to claim her. The only thing stopping him was his own self-doubt, this had to be some kind of dream, some hallucination fueled by low barometric pressure or bad cheese. If it was a mermaid, she would be bad luck just like Nemo taught him. And if it wasn't, this erotic mirage could lure him to a watery grave and Jet had no desire to join Davy Jones anytime soon. So, he'd have to be content with the stroke he had going and God, did it feel good.

Jet rubbed faster, pumping his swollen dick with long rhythmic pulls. How he yearned to be out there in the water, his big cock buried deep in what he knew would be the tightest little pussy imaginable. It'd been so long since he'd been with a woman, and as wrong as it felt to be masturbating with Sami so close on board, Jet couldn't help himself. He was past the point of no return, he needed release or he might never sleep again.

Working his cock slowly, Jet rubbed the pearly drops of pre-cum that flowed from the head, massaging it in a circle with the pad of his thumb around and around the tip of his cock. He placed a hand on the wall to steady himself just as the mermaid dove under water.

"Hell, no! Don't go!" Jet needed to finish, he was painfully hard, but he wanted his eyes to be on the luscious little siren when he did.

Patiently, he waited for her to resurface, knowing the moment she did, he'd paint the wall in front of him with days of pent-up and even a bit confused, sexual desire.

The moon returned full-bore, illuminating everything in its path and when the water only a few yards off starboard erupted with a splash, his mermaid appeared in full view and Jet's cock surged. Shaking the water from her hair, his mermaid's face came into focus for the first time and he stopped mid-stroke… his jaw dropping …

WTF?

"Sami?"

Jet's hand fell from his now fading erection as he stared flabbergasted at the beautiful woman who he'd believed, up until a few moments ago, to be male.

Frozen, he continued to glare at the person who'd deceived him. "What the fuck just happened?"

Confusion clouded his mind. What the hell was going on? Anger flared in his gut. She'd lied to him. The sexiest woman he'd ever seen in his whole life was living with him on his boat. His boat! This was against all of his rules.

Then—another truth hit him like a tsunami. A flood of relief washed over his body as he sank to the mattress. He laughed out loud.

Sami was a woman!

No wonder he'd been drawn to the little waiter. She was all woman and he was all man.

"Oh, thank God, thank God." He released a long breath. "I'm not gay."

Even though he would've denied it to his dying breath, the teasing from Micah had gotten to him. Jet had been struggling with the sexually confusing feelings he'd developed toward Sami, but this explained it all.

"It must've been a pheromone thing, or something," Jet mused to himself. "My eyes were deceived, but my body knew the truth the entire time."

His body was still paying attention, because another splash and a giggle from outside drew a familiar twitch from his dick. Within seconds, it was standing all on its own again. Sami was still outside the window, the draw to go back to it and peer out was too strong to resist. Jet rose from the bed, grabbed two brown towels and wrapped one around himself, holding the side to keep it from falling down. His cock was totally and epically solid, leading the way up on the deck like a dousing rod.

Despite his aroused state, Jet walked stealthily so he wouldn't alert his stowaway that she was being observed. When he came to the railing next to the ladder, he stayed in the shadows watching Sami as she floated on the surface, her magnificent assets on full display for the stars above. His mermaid might not have a fish tail for legs, but her siren call was impossible to resist. While he gazed at her, he replayed their encounters in his head—her scent, the softness of her delicate hands, all of it made sense now. Still horny as hell, Jet rubbed himself through the towel, which was now pitched like a tent, the skin of his cock tightening to an almost painful degree. He couldn't recall being this hard in his entire life and it was all due to the sexpot playing in the water before him. Unable to hold it in, Jet groaned at the sight. Somehow, the low noise caught Sami's attention over the lapping of the waves and she turned…

Their eyes met.

A small gasp escaped Sami's lips and she dropped under the water like a rock, concealing her body from Jet's view. Dread hit her like a run-away train. Oh, no! She'd only wanted to cool off, but she'd gotten carried away and lost her head, making too much noise and now Jet had seen her.

Of course she had to come up for air, she didn't have anywhere else to go.

Dang it, dang it, dang it, she repeated in her head.

For a moment she just floundered in the waves, not knowing which way to turn.

"You might as well come on board, little mermaid. Unless you plan on swimming to Cuba." His voice was even, dry, and cold as steel.

Mortified, Sami reluctantly swam to the ladder and climbed up.

Forcing himself not to react to her nearness, Jet helped a stark naked Sami from the water. "Care to explain yourself?" he asked tersely.

Feeling entirely exposed, she stepped onto the deck of the Sirena, dripping wet, one hand covering her private parts, the other doing its best to conceal a chest far bigger than her hand could shield.

Sami kept her eyes on the deck. "I'm so sorry, Jet."

Bending, he picked up the extra towel he'd brought topside with a trembling hand and held it out to her. "Why the hell have you been lying to me all this time?"

Wrapping it around herself, the piece of cotton did little to make her feel less vulnerable. Never before had Jet seemed so big, so formidable. Her eyes slid up his gorgeous body, dreading to meet his eyes. Her attention was drawn like a magnet to the fact that he appeared to be aroused.

Was that for her?

"I think you need a bigger towel." Quickly, she pushed the thought from her mind. There was no way a man like Jet Foster could ever be attracted to a common girl like herself.

"So do you. Now, answer me!" His voice rose with frustration as Jet stood over her with chest heaving, heart pounding.

When Sami finally looked up into his face, she was surprised by what she saw. His words and tone were stern, if not threatening, but there was an intensity in his eyes. An intensity that almost seemed muddied by desire. She clamped her eyes shut, certain what she saw was wishful thinking.

Wordlessly, they stood, neither sure what the other would do.

While his exterior might seem calm, he wasn't. Inside, Jet was a raging torrent of lust. He didn't know if he wanted to throw her off the ship, pull anchor and sail off or take her in his arms and make love to her all night long. "What are you doing to me?" he finally asked when it became obvious she wasn't going to answer his previous question.

"I'm sorry," she repeated herself, at a loss for words.

"Sorry?" Jet clenched his fists, wanting to pull her into his arms so bad he could taste it. He needed some type of explanation. "You lied to me, Sami. You stow away on my boat and I think we're friends. All the time, you hide the fact that you're a woman from me." He raked his hand through his hair. "I've been struggling with this weird attraction to you," he spat out. "And all this time you're female! Were you teasing me? Were you laughing at me? How can you do that to a man? Can you imagine what it's like? To lie in bed and want someone you're not supposed to want so fuckin' much you ache?"

By this time, Sami was almost in tears. She knew exactly how he felt, because she ached for him. He was saying amazing things to her but in such a mean voice, she was hurt and totally confused. "Yes, I know how it feels, exactly. But I didn't want to lie to you. I told you

I was running away from someone when I slipped aboard ship."

"But why disguise yourself as a boy?" He gestured toward her body, his fingers itching to see if she was as soft to the touch as she looked.

"I'm a journalist. I write a blog and I've been wearing a disguise in order to blend in so I could gather information on the cartel." She hugged the towel closer around her. "Besides, if you'd known I was a girl, you wouldn't have wanted me anyway."

"Damn right." Jet exploded, not hearing half of what she said. He was still hung up on what he saw as her deceit. "I ought to throw you overboard." He put his hand on his hip, narrowing his eyes. "I don't allow women on board my boat! It's my damn rule! No wonder we ran into that storm. You're bad luck—a Jonah! An albatross!"

"Enough!" Sami held up her hand. Crying, big tears rolled down her face. "I said I was sorry. I never intended for this to happen. I was scared. I was running for my life and I just needed a safe place to rest. Look, I'll pay you passage."

"Fat lot of good that's going to do me now. I'm stuck with you!"

She stared up into the face of a man she'd hero worshiped from afar and felt her heart break. "You know what? I did lie! I'm not sorry." She dashed the tears from her cheeks. "I knew who you were, Jet. I've been following your career in MMA for a long time. I admired you. I used the idea of you to give me strength." She laughed harshly, hiccupping. "Hell, I fantasized about you. You were my hero. I used to dream that if there was a safe place in the world for me, it would be with you." She got up in his face. "And you know what? I'm glad I got the chance to meet you. Know why?"

Sami didn't give him a chance to answer. "Because now that I know you, I won't waste my time pining after you anymore. You're an ass. You're a mean jerk, and a bully. If I thought I could swim to shore from here and survive, I'd jump overboard now!"

Jet didn't know what he was feeling, now he was just reacting. "You won't have to jump, I have a plank for just that purpose."

If Sami hadn't been hurt and angry, she would have watched her tongue more, but she was too distraught to think straight. "Oh, which plank is that? This one?" She pointed at his obvious erection straining at the fabric of his towel.

Her acknowledgement of his desire fueled him to lash out. He reacted without thinking, thrusting a hand out to weave his fingers in her short damp curls. "Let's see if you can find something else to do with that little tongue besides being a smart ass." Pulling her to him, he gave one last long look at her face. How the hell he'd ever entertained the notion she was a boy was beyond him. Those eyes. Those lips. "Look at you, damn you. You're gorgeous." Without asking for permission, he lowered his head, crashed his lips to hers and took what he needed. Her lips were warm and lush and the contact sent an electrical jolt over his entire body. Every nerve ending was painfully aware of his need to taste, touch…take.

Stunned, Sami didn't know what to do with herself. At first she struggled, but it was like pushing against a wall. She wanted to run, to get away, to hide. But even more she wanted—him. Finally, she relaxed into his arms and gave herself over to the mindless pleasure. Every fantasy she'd dreamed paled to the reality of being close to him, cradled in his arms, his mouth devouring hers. Sami wanted to give him pleasure, bring him to his knees, but she didn't know how. So she gave him what she could—kissing him back, eating at his lips, her tongue tangling with his. Hungrily, her hands moved over his arms and shoulders while whimpers of unfettered delight rose in her throat.

Jet was in full heat. Sami moved her hand up his body, curling it around his neck, pulling him closer and he went gladly. What started out as part punishment, part preservation changed to acute and utter desperation. He drowned in her kiss, his tongue mapping the inside of her mouth. Every other kiss he'd ever experienced with any other woman was forgotten. Wrapping his arm around her, he held her so close he could feel the pounding of her heart in time with his. God, this was so good. He wanted…he wanted…

Whoa! With one blinding moment of revelation, a sense of rightness hit Jet as hard as a rogue wave and that unfamiliar overwhelming sensation scared the living crap out of him. With every bit of will and strength he possessed, Jet placed his hand on her arm and pushed, breaking the kiss, forcing his lips away from hers.

"No, we can't do this," he mumbled, pushing her, doing his best to ignore the dazed soft sexy look on her sweet face. "Go to your cabin." When she didn't immediately move, he raised his hand and pointed. "Now!"

Sami jerked away, moving out of his arms as if he'd burned her. And when she did, the towel slipped, falling to the ground and the sight of her running from him, gorgeous, completely bare, would be seared into his memory forever.

Crying, Sami couldn't run fast enough, taking the stairs almost in one leap. Polly tried to catch her leg as she passed, but Sami didn't stop, ignoring the tiny prickle of the cat's claws. Throwing herself in the cabin, she slammed the door and sank against it, gasping for breath. How wrong she'd been. Facing Angel Andrade was a piece of cake rather than baring her body and soul to Jet Foster. Rejection stung to the very heart of her. What had she been thinking?

Throwing herself on the bunk, she let his words play over in her mind. He'd called her a Jonah and an albatross. Sami wasn't dumb, she understood his references. A storm had overtaken a ship until the biblical character, Jonah, the real reason for nature's fury, had thrown himself overboard and was swallowed by a great fish. The albatross was considered to be curse, a burden someone had to bear. She knew Jet didn't actually blame her for the storm, he was lashing out. What he did blame her for was being there at all, uninvited, a burden and a distraction he had to deal with. Bottom line—she was a nuisance. One minute she was castigating herself for lying to him, the next she was imagining that he thought she'd thrown herself at him, parading around nude. What she told him about the cartel hadn't fazed Jet. So, what else did she have to say? What other defense did she have?

Humiliated, she lay on her stomach with her head cradled in her arms, remembering how he'd pushed her away, banishing her from his presence. She used to think Jet Foster hung the moon, she'd conjure him up in her mind or watch videos of him to give her courage or solace. Now she knew he had feet of clay, he was just a man—a man who didn't want her around.

* * *

In his own cabin, Jet was a mess. Pacing from one end to the other, he rubbed his chest and debated with himself. He was hard, horny and felt like a fool. He wasn't sure if he'd been had by that mere slip of a girl or if he was letting a miracle slip through his fingertips. He'd felt off-balance from the moment he'd seen Sami in the bar, been attracted to her, then realized she was off-limits.

Only she wasn't.

He remembered jumping to her defense, he remembered her coming to his rescue—all ninety pounds of her. The memory had him smiling.

As he lay down, trying to relax, every moment they'd spent together came back to haunt him. How she'd caught his eye serving him drinks, how she'd taken care of the rounds at their table and braved the dangerous crowd to come to his fight. How she'd put herself in danger taking on Santoro with a magnum of wine. Now, here—seeing her curled up in one of his bunks, making him a sandwich, tying knots with those graceful small hands, even battling the storm with him shoulder to shoulder—all of it came together in one arousing montage of confusion.

When he'd seen her playing in the waves, her beautiful body fulfilling every desire of his heart, he'd been so damn relieved she was female he didn't know what to do. And the kiss they'd shared had been amazing! Hot. Completely satisfying. Even when she'd been angry and was telling him off—what had she said? That she'd followed his career, fantasized about him, she even called him her hero. Sami had wanted him, desired him—there wasn't a doubt in Jet's mind.

And he'd pushed her away because he was afraid he was enjoying it too much? Yes, he had rules. But rules were meant to be broken. No one said this thing had to last forever. What was important was today. Now.

Jet smiled. Well, there was one thing about it. Nemo Foster hadn't raised a fool. Rising from his bunk, he grabbed a pair of shorts, pulled them on, then strode out of his cabin and down the hall to hers.

Sami way lying in her bed with the pillow over her head. The tap on the door made her jump. God, no. He'd come to fuss at her some more. Rolling over, she peeked out from under the pillow. He was so big, he filled the entire door. "Go away."

"I'm sorry, I can't do that."

With a groan, Sami sat up, holding the sheet over her breasts. She hadn't taken time to throw on a shirt, all she'd wanted to do was get under the covers and pray an iceberg hit the Sirena so she didn't have to face Jet again. But there weren't that many icebergs in tropical waters. "What do you want?"

"You."

"No, you don't." Sami pulled her knees up to her chest. "You hate me." She wound her fingers through her hair. "I was telling you the truth, men were chasing me. I was just trying to hide."

The details of what she was saying didn't register with Jet. Soon, he would have to make her explain herself—but right now, he had more important things on his mind. "No, sweets. I don't hate you. I'm obsessed with you."

Sami didn't believe him. "You yelled at me, you pushed me away."

Going to her, Jet knelt by the bed. "You've turned me inside out. I saw you through the porthole window and couldn't believe my eyes. I thought you were a dream—a mermaid—sent to torment me with your beauty. And then I find out you've been under my nose all this time, Sami. You made me feel things I didn't know how to handle." He tugged at the sheet, but she held on.

"You're confusing me," she whispered, wanting to believe what she saw in his eyes, yet afraid to let herself do it. "I don't know what to do."

"Give yourself to me," he whispered, moving closer. Again he tugged on the sheet, insistent.

Sami wanted him too much to resist. She closed her eyes, gathering strength. Then she just let go…

The sheet gave way, baring all that creamy smooth skin. "Mercy." Jet swallowed hard, his hand shook. "You are so fuckin' unbelievable." The tip of his index finger danced across her bare stomach. "God, you're spectacular. How in the world did you hide these?"

Sami drew in her breath, her whole body shuddering. "I wore a compression bra."

"Did it hurt?"

"Ummm, a little. What are you doing?"

"I don't know," Jet admitted. "But I can't stop myself." His fingertip slid from side to side on her soft skin, from one hip to the other and slowly up between her breasts. Jet leaned down to whisper in her ear, his massive frame blocking out the light from the moon filtering through the window. "You aren't going to resist me, are you?" He kissed her neck right below her ear.

Part of her thought it would be wise, they didn't really know one another. And nothing would come of this—it could only be temporary. Sami also knew anything they shared wouldn't mean the same thing to Jet as it did to her. Heck, she didn't even know what her future held. If the cartel didn't kill her, the cancer might, she hadn't even been able to return to the clinic to get the final results of her treatments.

But this was Jet, *her* Jet, the man she'd dreamed about for so long. To turn him down wasn't something she had sufficient strength to do. "No, I'm not going to resist you," she whispered.

"You want this as much as I do." His voice held that same cocksureness it always did. The man wore confidence like a second skin, it fit him like a glove.

There was no use lying about it. "I do." She'd always imagined saying those words to a man, even though this wasn't quite the scenario she'd envisioned.

Jet leaned across her and turned on the bedside light. "I've got to see you, I don't want to miss a thing." His eyes grazed her exquisite form. "And to think you covered up all this beauty with those loose, sloppy clothes." He glanced down to find Sami watching him. She stared into his eyes, almost seeming to absorb him.

Slowly, he lowered his head, but to his surprise, she didn't wait for him to come to her. Of her own volition, Sami lifted her head, sliding her palm up his arm to his shoulder, gently rubbing his neck. Her soft lips were scant inches from his, her warm breath feathered his lips. Tentatively, as though she expected to be pushed away, she sought his mouth, turning her head to seek his lips.

Fuck. She didn't play fair.

At the first touch of her kiss, Jet stiffened, knowing how the previous one had almost brought him to his knees. Every fiber of his body tensed as she gently caressed his mouth. Carefully at first, then when he didn't stop her, she let her tongue explore the seam of his mouth, tempting him to grant her entrance. Straining to maintain control, he gave her what she sought, opening his mouth and accepting the light, dancing forays of her velvety tongue.

She was driving him mad with desire. He'd never felt such need with another woman. Unfamiliar feelings were mounting, giving Jet an incredible appetite to shelter, control, mark, and revere—emotions he had no business feeling and no capability of honoring. He was a Foster, he just wasn't made that way.

Warning bells sounded in his mind through a fog of erotic ecstasy. She was blameless. Vulnerable. Unlike his normal conquests, Sami wasn't flight attendant material. "Wait." He cupped her cheek, turning his face so she was kissing his cheek. Taking what she so sweetly offered without coming clean wasn't fair. "I need to tell you something." His conscience was fighting against the current of his overwhelming need.

"What, Jet?" she asked breathlessly. "I'm sorta busy here." Her lips sought his again.

For the first time, Jet could fathom Kyle's obsession with Hannah. He'd always thought he was immune to the impulse to wrap his heart and life up in one woman. But this water sprite was giving him ideas he had to put a harpoon in—for both of their sakes. "You do understand what this is, Sami, don't you?"

She looked at him with those big blue eyes. "What is it, Jet?"

Even as he said the words, he was tracing her delicate cheekbones, rubbing his thumb over those plump pink lips. "This is sex, baby, just sex. Temporary. When we get to Cuba, I'll buy you a plane ticket home." Jet steeled himself for feminine tears of protest. So many times when he'd try to lay out the boundaries to women, they refused to see reason and gave him unwanted grief.

Imagine his surprise when she calmly nodded. "Of course, I know and I agree wholeheartedly. Our lives are completely separate. We're headed in different directions. I have things I need to take care of back in Veracruz, people to see and bullets to dodge." She grinned, rubbing her hands on his chest and down his six-pack. "I love this scorpion tattoo of yours, so sexy." She touched the ink on his stomach.

Her calm acceptance of their temporary relationship irritated him in some weird way. "Good," he grumbled. "I just don't want any misunderstandings later."

"There won't be any, I promise." Solemnly, Sami agreed. "This is just sex, just for—"

Jet kissed her quiet. She didn't have to be so damn agreeable.

Sami smiled beneath his kiss. Finally. A trembling started deep within, and she couldn't keep her hands off of him. Every inch of his hard muscles deserved attention. Pulling away to take a breath, she murmured, "You'll have to help me, Jet. I'm not a siren or a temptress." She didn't know how to seduce a man with her body or words. "I'm just me."

Jet wanted to laugh, but he felt this might not be the best moment to do so. "You have no idea of your own power, do you?" Joining her on the bed, he took her hand and brought it between his legs. "Feel and learn how much I want you."

His words stole her ability to breathe. She flushed with the newfound sense of her worth as a woman. Molding her palm over his long, thick manhood, a smile hovered around her lips. How many hours had she spent fantasizing about touching him this way?

Countless.

Jet was fascinated. Since he'd discovered her camouflage, she'd morphed before his eyes. Now, she was a goddess, every delicate feature exquisite. Her eyes glittered and she winked—winked—at him. "You're huge." Licking her lip, she tilted her head inquisitively. "For me?" The idea that she'd been responsible for arousing this alpha male to rock-solid made her quiver with desire.

"For you." Jet moved his face right in front of hers and planted the softest, most delicious kiss imaginable on her upper lip before consuming her mouth whole, parting her lips with his tongue and twisting them together. He was in trouble, big trouble.

She placed her other hand on his face, keeping her connection with the most male part of him. "I've dreamed about you." A mischievous light came into her eyes. "Fight the fight. I borrowed those words from you. They may have saved my life."

Again, he knew he should be more curious about her, but right now other parts of his body were more demanding than his brain. "What did you dream?"

Jet wasn't a pretty boy, he was handsome but hard. Massive. Confident—like he'd seen the worst life had to offer and came out of it stronger. That bad-boy edge made him so exciting to her. If she were to answer truthfully, she would say, 'You slew my dragons for me.' If she were reading Jet correctly, those words would send him off the side of the Sirena, swimming as far and fast from her as he could. So, she gave him a different, yet equal, truth. "I tasted every inch of you." She put a bit more pressure behind her touch, rubbing him up and down. Through the fabric of his underwear she could feel his cock respond to her as it strained and pulsed in her hand.

Jet's breath hissed from his mouth. "You're dangerous."

She wasn't, but Sami liked the idea. Oh, she meant what she said, but the bravado she was displaying now was for the specific intent of feasting her eyes and sating her hunger for Jet Foster—naked, aroused, and hers—for just a little while. "I'm not dangerous. I'm a safe bet, a sure thing. The only selfish motive I have is…pleasure."

Lies.

All lies.

Sami was shocked that she felt possessive. If her life was different, if she was different, she would move heaven and earth to fight for this man, lay claim, and place her mark to warn off any woman who would dare come close.

She curled her fingers to test her claws, and Jet groaned. "You just said the magic words, minx." Fitting his body to her silken curves, he ran his hands around her waist and down to cup the globes of her luscious ass.

Sami trembled with anticipation. "Get naked for me, Jet. I want to look at you."

Who knew she could be so bold?

So greedy?

A decade of just wishing and dreaming had culminated in this banquet for the senses and Sami intended to take full advantage. Her untried sensuality was demanding to be sated. Her body craved this man. Other more tender parts of her like her heart and soul were more involved than she would ever admit, but that was her secret.

Jet shucked his shorts in one fluid moment and she couldn't have kept her eyes or hands off of him if she'd been promised a lifetime free of pain—he was just worth it.

Focusing her whole being so she wouldn't miss a thing, Sami allowed herself to learn Jet's body. She sat up and applied gentle pressure, pushing him to his back. Holding her bottom lip in her teeth, she gave herself up to this most pleasurable task. With hands and lips, she caressed and kissed him from his lips, to his shoulders, down that magnificent chest, over rippled abs until she came to the mysterious part of him that assured her beyond any doubt that he wanted her as much as she wanted him.

From the first brush of her fingers, he didn't hold back. Jet allowed her to see how much her attention affected him. His jaw was set, his eyes hooded, head thrown back, hips raised—offering himself up to her touch.

And she didn't disappoint.

"You're beautiful," she whispered, and he was. Bigger by far than she could reach around, thick, long, and distended. She played with him, loving the way he felt in her hand and nearly intoxicated with the idea of inviting all of this male heat deep inside of her. "I crave you."

Jet had always been afraid of phrases women coined that began with the word *I* and ended with *you* but this wasn't one of them. Being the object of Sami's lust could be addictive. "You have my undivided attention and my full cooperation."

While his eyes followed her every move, she placed her hands on his chest, her lips on his and straddled him. Sitting up, Sami took both of his big hands and placed them on her breasts. They were heavy and aching for him. To her delight, he rewarded her by molding and kneading them, massaging them, pushing the globes together and rubbing the nipples. She closed her eyes and leaned back a little, moving her hips so that the hungriest part of her scrubbed against the hardest part of him.

"Jet," she moaned, her nipples swelling and puffing out, begging for his lips.

He sat up, leaned forward and bent his head to latch on to one stiff peak and when he did, she whimpered, cradling his head so she could keep him right where she needed him. For long luscious minutes, she luxuriated in the feel of his lips tugging on her nipples, his hands plumping and shaping them. The hungry male sounds coming from his mouth as he sucked at her tits made her wet.

"Like that?" he asked as he moved from one tender tip to the other.

"I love it," she said.

Another phrase he found he didn't mind at all.

"Show me, Jet." Sami ran her fingers through his hair. "Show me how to make you feel good. Show me how to please you."

In all of his time spent with the flight attendants, in all of the wild sexual escapades he'd shared with the myriad women he'd had sex with—none of them had ever asked what he wanted, what he needed. They'd taken and he'd gladly given. But Sami…Sami was the most generous, giving lover he could ever imagine. "You please me greatly. Just touching you, kissing you, looking at you gives me pleasure."

"Really?" Her heart leapt into her throat to know she brought him a measure of joy.

"Yes. Now, let me work here." He pulled her down on top of him, nuzzling her neck, licking her collarbone, then joined his mouth to hers and sucked tenderly until Sami thought she'd pass out from the sheer perfection of it all.

Rolling her over, he moved on top of her. "Is it going to happen now?" she asked, giving him what she hoped was a seductive sassy look. Hoping to entice him, she opened her legs to make room for him and stretched her arms up over her head, crossing her hands, sending him a message of total surrender. "Please, Jet? I'm impatient. I've waited for you so long."

Sweet Jean Lafitte! "You have got to be the sexiest woman in the world." Jet's gaze raked over her body like a flamethrower. As if he was hunting erotic treasure, Jet explored her—from her lips, back to those glorious breasts, down that sleek tummy to the haven between her legs—that place he most longed to be. Gently, he parted her folds and proceeded to drive her insane. With lips, teeth and tongue, he gave her rapture. And when he sucked her clit into his mouth, she tore at his hair, clawed the bed and called out to the deity at the top of her lungs.

Begging for more, for relief, she held on, his name on her lips. "Jet! God, Jet!" The tension, the need, the drive to ecstasy was so close. "I need you, Jet. I want you!"

He wanted too, more than he'd ever wanted before. "I can't last another minute without being inside you." Rising over her, Jet covered Sami, making a place for him between her legs, pushing her thighs apart to fit his cock to her opening, sliding the head through her sweet lips before pushing in slowly a mere inch.

"Jet, it feels so good." She moved her fingers up his arms, relishing the way his muscles moved and tensed. "You're so strong."

He was strong, yet he was weak. Weak with desire. Grasping her hips, he lifted and plunged deep inside of her. The rightness of the ecstasy swamped him. But...

Full. Stretched. Invaded. Sami's eyes widened. Jet was a part of her and the burn of his possession made her cry out.

Jet stilled, realizing what he'd done. "You've never..."

She kept stroking him, one hand at the back of his neck. "I'm okay. Just give me a second, I'm a quick study." Sami wrapped one leg around his, the action seeming to help make room for him. "You're just so damn big." It seemed as if she could feel him in her chest almost.

"Do you want me to pull out?" It might kill him, but he'd do it. "Am I hurting you?"

"Yea, it hurts, but don't you dare move." She tightened around him as if to hold him in. "I've finally got you where I want you and I'm not letting you go."

Jet buried his head in her neck and groaned. "Don't do that, not if you don't want me to move. It feels too good." Sami giggled, and Jet made a face at her. "Are you laughing at me?"

"Yea." She moved again. "Believe me, I've had pain and this is entirely manageable." Again, she squeezed him.

"You're killing me. Do you know how hard it is to hold back?" Pressing his forehead to hers, he looked into her eyes.

"Then, don't hold back. Move." She raised her other leg and wrapped it around his. The burn had changed from uncomfortable to very, very good. "I'm okay now." Tightening her arms around his neck, she lifted her body and moved her hips, rubbing on him like a cat. "Show me your fancy moves, Foster."

Jet threw his head back, a laugh mixing with a groan, nearly lost in the delight of the snugness he was encased within. "You're not playing fair," he growled as she began to kiss his shoulder, his collarbone, his throat, nibbling and sucking.

"I'm not playing," she confessed. "I'm serious about this sex stuff." Sami purred when she rubbed her cheek over the scruff on his jaw. "Move, Champ."

Jet didn't need any more coaching. Raising himself up on his arms, he pulled out slowly, making Sami moan. He didn't have to tell her to hold on, because she was clinging to him. He could feel her nipples poking him in the chest. Biting his lower lip, he slid back in, the pleasure so good, he had to shut his eyes to process it. "Better?"

"Perfect," she whispered.

With that word of approval, he sat up, adjusted her so he could control their movements and thrust so deeply she gasped. "You like that?"

With wide eyes she demanded, "Yea, I think you found the right spot. Do it again." Sami's heart jumped when he chuckled and his teeth flashed as a smile broke out on his face. "Did I say something wrong?"

He let his fingers play in her hair, caressing the short strands. "No, this is just new to me, that's all. I've never had such a good time during sex."

"Isn't that the idea?"

"Probably." Jet wanted to think about it, but he couldn't. Instead, he immersed himself in Sami, grunting as he slid in, moving his entire body up so their hips were lined up. He kissed her softly this time, plundering her with long, luxurious thrusts, his shaft dragging back and forth over Sami's pulsing clit with each plunge.

Her innocence was a barrier no longer, Jet excited her so much, she was overtaken by sensations she'd never felt before. "This feels so good," she keened, needing the relief only he could give her. A euphoric sense of expectation built in her sex. She closed her eyes as he thundered into her with such force she was sure they rocked the boat.

Jet felt her labored breathing and picked up his pace. Her greedy little channel rippled around him, giving him pleasure, sucking his cock deeper with every thrust. This wasn't something a woman could fake, he knew she was enjoying what he was doing, so he did more of it. "Cum for me, mermaid."

Sami pulled her mouth from his, dug her nails into his firm, sexy ass and gave herself over to the all-consuming climax—shaking, shivering, her world lit up by a fiery feeling so intense she almost blacked out. "Jet! My God!" The sudden release from the tightly wound tension was exhilarating—unlike anything she'd ever felt before. Cascades of blissful pulses electrified her pussy, her clit, her nipples. Every inch of her body radiated with delicious pleasure.

Just when she thought it was over, Jet picked up his pace. "Cum again for me," he demanded, looking down on her with a blaze of ferocity in his eyes.

"I don't know if I can," she protested.

"Yes, you can."

Their eyes locked together as he covered Sami, not an inch of her body was left vulnerable. Skin to skin, just as she'd dreamed, he was a barrier between her and anything that would threaten.

"You're going to make me explode," Jet said. "I can't take anymore. Cum with me. Now!"

His command thrilled Sami and her body instinctively obeyed. They erupted in unison, Jet emptying himself into her with force and a chorus of words that would make a sailor blush. He collapsed on top of her, both struggling to regain their breath.

Sami held on, his weight felt so good. She protested when he rolled off and gathered her near in the too small bed.

"Can I stay with you?" she asked, then wished she could recall the words. "Tonight, I mean?" Jet seemed to consider it a while before he answered.

Sleeping with a woman was entirely different from having sex, but this seemed a day for firsts. "Yes, but not here. Let's go to my quarters." He swept up the sexy sack of sugar in his arms and strode down the hall. "Come on, Polly. Bedtime."

Both knew there would be things to discuss when the sun rose. But for tonight, they'd sleep wrapped in one another, rocked in the gentle arms of the sea.

CHAPTER NINE

Sami lay very still, listening to the steady, even breathing near her ear, conscious of the warmth of the body next to hers. There was every possibility this was a dream. Or could this be one of those surreal hallucinations where actuality and imagination blended? She tested how substantial the cotton sheet was beneath the fingertips of her left hand—yea, it seemed real enough. Mentally, she reviewed her memories of the events of the night before, since they too were far from the realm of believability.

Did they actually happen?

Did she make love with Jet Foster?

Was she, even now, lying in his bed?

Very carefully, she turned her head, not wanting to jar the mattress if he was corporeal or burst the bubble of her mirage if he wasn't. Slowly, she opened her eyes, and the sight that met them made her breath hitch in her throat. Jet lay beside her, one big leg and arm out of the covers.

"My God, his muscles bulge even when they're relaxed," she whispered, easing up, propping her head on her palm.

Then, she took a moment to just stare.

As she had many times before, Sami studied Jet. His shoulders were more than a yard across, his chest expertly sculpted, the dips and valleys so perfect they could have been rendered by an artist intent on bringing Hercules to life. Yet he wasn't a statue. This wasn't a video or a still life.

224

Jet Foster was warm, he was real and he was magnificent.

And when he wasn't angry with her for masquerading as a boy or stowing away on his boat, he was a sweet guy who lived the most incredibly adventurous life imaginable.

In other words, he was her ideal man. Always had been. Always would be.

Her eyes followed the rise and fall of his chest, her fingers and lips were lobbying for exploration rights, but she held back, unsure of how her advances would be received.

A small smile played on her lips. He'd made her first time absolutely incredible. Jet Foster was all male, an amazing lover.

And he'd chosen her.

Just as soon as the thought formed in her cerebrum, she rejected it. Jet hadn't chosen her. She would have never been his choice under normal circumstances.

Sami was alone with Jet on a ship in the middle of the ocean. She was convenient—literally the only woman within five hundred nautical miles.

Sighing, Sami continued to stare...

Jet wasn't asleep. He was playing possum, like a stonefish pretending to be a rock so he could waylay some hapless shrimp. Parts of him were waking up faster than others. After all, his manhood was well aware that the current object of his desire was a mere six inches away. Desire was a weak description of what he felt for Sami Cabot, like he'd told her last night as he'd been trying to talk his way into her bed—he was obsessed with this enchantress.

Sami lifted her hand, the urge to touch Jet overwhelming. The sun shining through the porthole played along his skin, forming intricate patterns that she'd love to trace with her tongue. But she couldn't…she jerked it back and swiveled her body to get up from the bed, until she was halted mid-movement by an arm which hooked itself around her middle and tugged. With a breathy exclamation, she fell back against the same hard-body she'd been drooling over only moments before.

"Where do you think you're going, my naked little buccaneer?" She wriggled, still trying to get away, her lush little ass rooting around on his cock, causing him to groan.

"To cook breakfast?" She'd promised to help out in the galley and now seemed as good enough time as any, especially since she was feeling decidedly confused.

Jet had other ideas. "Hunger is definitely a problem, I can't argue with that logic." Gently, he moved her to rest on her back, his big body edging next to hers. Easing her head up, he ran one arm beneath it, leaving the other hand free to touch her anywhere he chose.

"What are you hungry for?" she asked, even as his fingers danced from her thigh to her waist, making her shiver.

"Seafood," he answered evenly, his big dark eyes flaring with an intense heat.

"Seafood, hmmm." Well heck, she was expecting him to say her or sex or something halfway romantic. "I guess you're in the right place," Sami quipped, trying to wiggle out of his hold.

"Nuh-uh." Jet stopped her, taking hold of both her soft cheeks in one big hand and tilting her lips to just the right angle. "You bet I'm in the right place. You look good enough to eat…" He pressed a kiss to her velvety soft mouth. "…lick, nibble, suck, munch on." *Fuck!* Her innocent sexiness just flattened him. "I see what I want and what I want is you."

226

Considering what she'd realized earlier—about her being the only available female—Sami really doubted what he said, but since he was the star of her personal fantasies, she couldn't manufacture much resistance. "Okay, you convinced me."

"You're so cute." Doe eyes framed by thick lashes. Turned up button nose. Full soft lips that would feel perfect wrapped around his aching cock. "We're three days out of Cuba and we can have a lot of fun in three days—that is if you want to?" Jet waited for her response.

"I want to." With a whimper, Sami threw her arms around his neck and planted that rosy little mouth right on his. Jet growled his approval, wrapping an arm around her waist and pulling her flush against him.

Nudging the seam of her lips, he swept his tongue inside, knowing exactly what to do to make her moan. Jet greedily swallowed the sound as he ravished her mouth, tasting and taking—luring her closer, then pulling back. Desperate, he kissed, nipping at her lips, only to pull back, meet her eyes, then lean in to devour her again as if he couldn't stand the thought of stopping.

A sweet pressure began to build between her legs. Sami hadn't known how wonderful feeling wanted and desired would be—even if it was for only three days. The next time he drew back to stare, she protested. "I don't think I can stand to stop kissing you."

She arched her back and pressed her plump tits into her chest, giving him ideas. "There's so much more to kiss." He began to work his way down her body. "You're a damn naked wonderland." Nuzzling her breast, he licked a circle around one puffy areola. "Look at those pretty nipples." He took one between his lips and scraped it with his teeth, causing her to arch her back, making the sexiest sounds, wordlessly cajoling him to continue. Jet sucked hard, flattening his tongue against her pretty nipple, teasing it till it was hard on his tongue.

When he dipped his hands between her legs, Sami almost passed out. It only took one—two—three swirls of his fingers and she flew apart, convulsing in his arms. "Jet, my God!" He started to rise over her, but she stopped him. "No, my turn. Please."

Jet relaxed back on the bed, smiling a sensual, knowing grin. "What do you have in mind, mermaid?" He took his cock in his hand and rubbed it up and down.

The sight made Sami's mouth water. "This." She shoved his hand away and took the hard, hot shaft in her own. Her fingers didn't even come close to meeting around his girth. Slowly, she moved her hand upward, rubbing the pad of her thumb over the purple head. Jet clenched his jaw and growled, so she did it again and got the same reaction. Like a puppet on a string, she could control his movements and responses just with the touch of her hand. A small smile of feminine power made her lips turn up at the corners. "I'm making you feel good."

If possible, he hardened even more in her hand and his hips lifted, a groan of absolute lust drifted from his lips. A tremor of excitement shook Sami from her head to her toes.

Touching was not going to be enough.

"I want my mouth on you," she admitted with a strained whisper.

Jet was hypnotized watching her hand move up and down on his aching cock. "Please, make yourself at home." Clasping her around the nape, he gently pushed her head in the right direction.

Sami licked her lips. "I'm a rookie at this." She smiled wryly. "Want to give me some pointers?"

"I'm not that picky." Jet crossed his arms behind his head, spread his legs and smiled indulgently. "As long as your lips are wrapped around me, I'll be happy."

"Okay." She let out a long breath.

To Jet, she was absolutely charming. He figured she'd have the same expression if she was about to sit for the SATs.

"You can't mess up, baby," he encouraged as she parted her plump soft lips and slid them over the aching head of his hungry cock—and that was the last coherent thought he had. "Fuck, yea," he exhaled, getting even harder when she fit her mouth over and down the engorged head.

Jet was no stranger to blowjobs, everywhere he went there were women willing to service him, have sex with him, give him what he needed.

This time was different, because Sami was different.

Gripping the sheet, he threw his head back and gave himself over to her. She took him deep, then slowly sucked her way back to the tip, tonguing him all the way. Expert she was not, but that didn't make a helluva bit of difference at the moment. He'd had girls go down on him who were more concerned about how they looked doing it or what he was going to buy for them when it was over, but Sami had no such expectations, he'd been open and upfront—she was doing this just because she wanted to—which was a damn sight, bigger turn-on than someone who had given so many they could do it with their eyes closed. Not that he'd turn her away…

Fuck!

What happened?

Looking down, he saw she had risen over him, giving herself a better angle. With renewed concentration, she seemed to find her rhythm, up-down, up-down—deeper, the upward motion accompanied by a tongue swirl around the head. And when she began to massage his nuts— "Shiver me timbers," he whispered. There was no way he'd last long with her doing this.

Taking her feathery-soft short strands in his hands, he gently urged her to raise her head. "You need to stop or I'm going to…" Jet didn't finish his sentence because she'd hollowed her cheeks and sucked hard. He felt his thighs tremble and his eyes rolled back in his head. Yesterday she'd said she was a quick study—she wasn't lying. "I think you've got the hang of it."

"I'm learning the ropes?" With a grin, she teased him, using a nautical term before licking the length of him—from stem to stern.

"God, yes," he hissed. "You're gonna be the death of me."

"Surely not, you're the Champ." She flashed him a seductive smile, before she enveloped him in the heat of her mouth, drawing on him, one hand pumping his cock in rhythm with her pulls, the other grasping his thigh. Sami reveled in the fact that she could make him shudder.

Jet couldn't take his eyes off of her. How beautiful she was, staring up at him through those long sexy lashes, bobbing her head as she worshiped his cock. He flexed his hips and watched her take him deeper. A dawning realization set him on fire—she was doing her best to give him what he needed. It wasn't an act, she was doing her best to please him. The idea made his head swim—because she pleased him greatly.

If she didn't stop...he needed her to stop or he was going to cum. "Sami." He tried to pull her up. She resisted, shaking her head and his hips agreed—rising, pumping, gliding into her hot sexy mouth over and over again. "God, this feels so good!" he groaned.

An answering whimper from her silken lips vibrated around his cock and he stiffened, pleasure boiling up from his balls. When his fingers tightened in her hair, she sucked him deeper, milking him, laving him with lips and tongue until he felt an amazing electric tingle surge through him.

Sami held on, holding him while he finished, loving the way his whole body clenched and quaked. Gladly, she accepted his release, swallowing, licking, petting, giving him everything she had. And all the while she burned, needing him so badly she ached. Surely…

A loud noise echoed through the cabin.

Sami jumped. What in the world? "What's that?"

"Satellite phone." Jet gave her a quick kiss on the forehead and crawled from the bed, his body protesting the activity. "Don't move."

She lay there a second or two, then decided she'd rather see what he was up to, something might be wrong. Not having anything else to put on, she grabbed her boy clothes and slipped them on. Polly seemed to be waiting for her, so Sami scooped her up and made her way topside. The sun was up and there was a breeze, she gazed out over the choppy waters. No land in sight. Jet came out of the wheelhouse. "I thought I told you to stay put."

"I was worried."

Jet's face softened. "No reason, it was Micah. Patience is not his virtue, he only lets it ring twice. Something must have distracted him, most likely a woman. I'll call him back in a while." Gazing at Sami, he loved the way she looked, the wind ruffling her hair, her eyes sparkling. Knowing how Micah had enjoyed tormenting him, Jet decided to have some fun. "Let me get my camera. I think we'll play a trick on ole' Micah."

He turned and bounded back down the stairs, Sami on his heels. "What do you mean?"

"Don't you have anything more girly to wear?" Jet called over his shoulder.

"Unfortunately, no. I didn't take time to pack while I was running for my life," she remarked dryly.

Jet snorted, assuming she was exaggerating. "Let me get you a T-shirt to protect you from the sun or otherwise you could just go naked." Grabbing his camera off a shelf, he kissed her quick on the way toward his cabin. "Wanna have a little fun?"

"Sure." Sami's life had been pretty devoid of good times, she wasn't about to turn any down. Hungrily she watched the play of muscles in his chest. "Wanna go back to bed? You owe me one." Her suggestion was met by laughter, not exactly the reaction she'd been hoping for.

"And I will enjoy paying my debt, just let me get the Sirena into the headwind and play a joke on my buddy."

Sami sighed. So much for being irresistible. "What joke?" She stood outside in the hall while he rummaged around in a closet.

Jet tossed her a shirt. "We're going to take a couple of photographs for Micah. Come on."

Sami tried to keep up, the man's stride was seriously long.

"What are we photographing?"

"You and me. Selfies!"

He seemed so happy, Sami hated to protest. "I'm not really dressed for a portrait."

"Exactly." Jet pulled her up the last few steps. "This is a prank. Micah picked up on my attraction to you and kidded me about it. I want to mess with him." Pulling Sami to his side, he turned on the video. "Hey, buddy. Look who's with me? I have a cabin boy." His voice dropped. "And…I just wanted to tell you that you were right, I couldn't resist." Running his big hand around her shoulders, Jet kissed her on the cheek. "I finally succumbed to temptation." Releasing the button, Jet doubled over in a hearty laugh. "That's gonna blow his fuckin' mind."

"You aren't sending that." She was a bit shocked.

"Watch me." He walked in the wheelhouse and took a USB cable out of a drawer. In a few seconds, he had the camera plugged into the satellite phone and the video was on its way.

"You're mean." She couldn't help but grin, he seemed to be having a good time.

"Now for the rest of the story." He tossed her the shirt. "Take off that shapeless garb and slip this on." Under his observant eye, Sami felt shy, but she did as he asked. When she unbuttoned the big shirt, it pleased her to see his eyes go dark with passion. "You have one fine rack."

"And you have such a way with words," she commented with a shake of her head. A buzz on the phone drew his attention and while he was looking away, she stripped off the rest of her clothes and had the T-shirt over her head when he turned back around. "Now what?"

"Let's get you wet." He went to a sink in the corner and pulled out a spray nozzle, pointed it at her, and before Sami could squeal, she was drenched.

With a squeal, she sputtered. "Jet Ivan Foster! Are you crazy?" While he was laughing, she grabbed the nozzle and turned it on him. And when Polly meowed from the side, she turned to spray the cat, but Jet caught her and jerked her against him, covered her mouth with his, his hands going between them to cup her now very obvious breasts.

"Crazy about these," he squeezed them, rubbing his thumbs over her nipples.

"Hmmm, why did you do that?" Her voice was weak because she was too busy feeling to process words.

"So we could do this." Holding her by the hand, he retrieved the camera and led her back on deck. Arranging her body against his, so Micah could see she was undoubtedly feminine but not any detail, Jet filmed again. "Pull yourself off the floor, Micah. My sexy little stowaway is a decidedly beautiful woman. Eat your heart out. Call me back when you can." With another chuckle, he went to transmit the second video.

"I'm going to cook breakfast," she called out.

"Thanks, I could eat. I'm going to check our course, adjust the sails and I'll be down."

His answer made Sami feel warm. So while she scrambled eggs, fried bacon and made toast, Sami let her imagination run wild. With a gentle pinch, she tested to make sure she was wide awake. "Ow." She giggled.

She was cooking breakfast for her and Jet!

Would wonders never cease?

Polly wouldn't be ignored, so Sami fed the fat feline before she dished up the food. Since Jet hadn't joined her, she found a tray and filled it with their plates and glasses. "Jet?"

In the wheelhouse, Jet moved to let Sami in seeing she had her hands full. He gestured that he was on the phone. "Hello? Micah?" He raised his eyebrows at Sami's semi-panicked expression, motioning her to sit down.

"I was relieved to see your paramour was a member of the fairer sex," Micah drawled. "I didn't know how we were going to spin your...newfound fascination."

Jet was amused. "I thought you'd enjoy my predicament."

"Speaking of," Micah continued, "how are you handling a female onboard? I'm surprised you haven't put her in the life raft and set her adrift."

"Well..." Jet hesitated. "I'm taking her to Cuba. You could help by asking Saxon to have a plane ticket waiting for her at a travel agent in Havana, a ticket to Houston."

"No," Sami spoke up. "I can get my own ticket. I'm returning to Veracruz."

Holding the phone, he questioned her. "Are you sure? I thought you were avoiding those two men? Don't you think you'd be better off in Houston?" He wasn't considering the less than fifty miles that would separate them. No, that made no difference at all.

"Make up your mind." Micah chided. "Her name's Sami Cabot, right?"

"Yes, Samantha Cabot. And I want her in Houston, get the ticket."

Sami rolled her eyes. "I can buy my own ticket to wherever I damn well please."

"Well, you heard that." Jet laughed. Sami's determination was endearing.

"That name...hold on." Micah moved away from the phone, but was back in an instant. "Ask her if she knows Destry."

"What?" Jet moved his gaze to Sami.

Micah repeated himself. "Ask Sami if she talked to Destry and Kyle, I think your little friend is knee deep in alligators and the Galvez drug cartel."

"What?" A chill ran through Jet. "I don't think so."

"Ask her. I don't know the details, but I think she's the same one who wrote the blog that called the Jaguar out of hiding. She and Destry arranged the rescue of another journalist, Marisol Lopez. I'd say that little girl has a price on her head as big as the national debt."

"I'll call you back," Jet growled and started to hang up the phone.

"Do that, but before you go, Isaac called again and they're taking steps to send someone down to find Angel Rubio. He said to tell you thanks."

"Good deal," Jet said. "Talk later."

Sami, unable to hear but one side of the conversation, was oblivious. "Here, come eat while it's still warm."

Jet joined her at the small table next to the porthole. He didn't know what he was going to do with her. Every time he thought he had this one figured out, she surprised him. Sami had more facets than a diamond. "Let's get to know one another a little better. I want to ask you a few questions."

"Okay, if you'll let me ask a few as well, I'm curious about you." She bit off a piece of crunchy bacon and wondered at Jet's reluctance to chow down since he was always the one who'd half cleaned his plate before she could even make a dent in hers.

"Sure, I'm an open book." He spread his hands. "Compared to you."

Sami's head jerked up. "What do you mean?" She didn't like his tone. He sounded suspicious again. "What's wrong?"

Jet took a slow sip of milk, leaving a thin white line across his upper lip that Sami wanted to kiss so bad she could taste it.

"I remember you telling me you came down to Veracruz to help a friend."

"That's right." Sami nodded, no secret there. "Her name is Marisol Lopez. She's my best friend in the whole world. We met our first semester in college, she's the one who inspired me to study journalism."

Jet felt a funny feeling in his gut. "So, you blog?"

"We both do." Sami considered telling Jet some of what happened. She needed to talk and he was here, they were both safe and he was heading away from Veracruz. Besides, he was an Equalizer, he'd find out sooner or later. As she contemplated what to say next, it hit her how odd it would be for him to see some report filed on her later, see her name in print and remember the time they'd spent together.

"What about?" Jet asked, bringing Sami from her daze.

"Well, I wasn't as successful as Mari. Of course, we were writing about completely different things." Lifting up, she brought one leg underneath her, settling in to be comfortable and share part of her life with the man she loved.

Wham!

Where had that come from?

Sami's feelings hit her full-force. Oh well, it was true. She'd had a humongous crush on Jet for years, but now that she actually knew him—had held him, kissed him—she was hopelessly devoted to him now.

"What did you write about?"

He seemed interested, so she opened up with a smile. "I've always watched true-crime shows on television and as a journalist, cold cases fascinate me." She took a bite of toast, then waved the rest of the piece at him. "You probably know this, but there's a place on I-45 between Houston and Galveston called the Texas killing fields."

Jet shook his head. "No, never heard of it. I was in Afghanistan and before then I spent a lot of time in Florida or with Nemo on his boat. I'm not originally from Texas."

"Good to know." She smiled at him, filing away that bit of information on him. "Between 1973 and the early 2000s, dozens of bodies were found dumped in that section of land. There was speculation that it was the work of one person, they called him the I-45 or Interstate Serial Killer. Let me show you. Hold on. Let me get my computer."

Sami got up and left him, sprinting off, and Jet took a deep breath. The very idea that Sami was involved in something so dangerous, and he wasn't talking about the serial killer mess, just made his blood run cold. When she came skipping back, he noticed how small she was, how defenseless, and he wanted to scoop her up into his arms and hide her from the world. "Whata you got?"

She opened it and pulled up the blog. "I know we don't have Wi-Fi, but here's my blog. There are even some comments I haven't taken the time to read yet."

She showed him the bookmarked blog, and Jet took the computer, quickly reading the article she'd written. "You're good," he offered, then it hit him. "I've seen this place. In fact, I stopped there on my way into Galveston right before we set sail for this trip."

Sami looked over his shoulder as he scanned down the page. "This is my third installment. I've been detailing and remembering the victims in hope someone somewhere would read it and remember something that would help uncover a clue so the cases could be reopened." Along with Jet, she read the comments. "Look, some of them are so sad."

My daughter was one of the victims, she was only fifteen years old. Her name was Sally.

Another read: *I remember this happening, I lived in Pasadena. We were afraid to leave the house.*

And another: *Who could have done such a thing? My dad always said it was a trucker, someone who came through, did the deed and moved on.*

And yet another jumped out at them: *Once when I was riding my bicycle by the field, I saw a red pickup, a Chevy, a man was pulling something from the back. I told the police, but no one ever questioned me about it. I've always wondered.*

Jet jerked his head around. "The reason I stopped was an old guy standing out in the field, looking at one of the crosses. He was driving a red 67 Chevy. Coincidence?"

Sami stared into his eyes, feeling a deep sense of camaraderie. "Maybe not. Can you tell me anything about him or the truck I could feed to the police?" She'd had some conversations with one of the detectives who kept the file on his desk in hopes something, somewhere would break.

Jet pressed his lips together. "I didn't really get a good look at him, although what little hair he had was white with traces of dirty blond in it, he held a baseball cap in his hands. He wore cowboy boots and..." His face brightened as he met Sami's eyes. "There was a bumper sticker on the back of his fender that said, Fish Toledo Bend. That's a lake in Deep East Texas next to the Louisiana border."

"Great!" Sami felt exhilarated. "Just as soon as I get on shore, I'll contact someone about the information." She reached over and kissed Jet on the cheek. "Thank you! Wouldn't it be amazing if you helped solve the case?"

He nodded. "Well, you're the one who laid it out, jarring people's memories, making them think of it again. Good job!" At that moment he was so proud of her, he felt like he was about to bust.

"That's why journalists write," she shared. "Mari always said that her job was to shine a light on things that had been shrouded in darkness." She smiled big. "I hope you can meet her one day, she's the bravest, best person I know."

If Micah had been right, it didn't seem to Jet that Marisol's friend was the only one who had been brave. "What's Mari's story?"

Sami brightened. "She's amazing, her family has been through so much. What she's told me..." She twisted in her chair, setting her fork on top of her knife, considering her words. "Her brother was killed by the cartel, a drive-by shooting, he wasn't even the target. Mari was only fifteen, but it changed her life. She started listening, making notes, learning who was who and what was what. By the time she graduated high school, Mari said she knew she wanted to help break the drug lord's hold on her country, on her city. So when she came to the States, she began to blog as Leona, the word in Spanish means 'the lioness.' As she was fed information, Mari gave it to the world and her power and influence grew. Her cousin and others fed her names and ties and dates, information that could lead to unmasking the Jaguar, one of the most powerful and elusive drug lord in the world."

The more Sami talked, the more nervous Jet became. If Micah was right, Sami was involved in this up to her gorgeous blue eyeballs and the thought horrified him. With smiles and gestures of her hands, Sami conveyed to Jet how important this topic was to her. Even though he was listening, it crossed his mind how much he'd underestimated this woman.

"I helped her when I could, as she helped me. We fact-checked every bit of the information she was given, staying in contact with informants by phone and email. Part of that time, I was sidelined with my personal situation at home and I took it upon myself to give her blog as much exposure as I could, to expand her readership, to get the blog quoted and cited in as many international magazines and news reports as possible. Soon, the lioness was well known, quoted and feared by the cartel." Sami took a deep breath, then smiled sadly. "It all seemed to be working until the cartel murdered her mother. They did it just to lure her back to Mexico in order to kidnap her."

Jet watched a myriad of emotions flit across her face.

"And it worked." Her voice shook a little. "The last time I heard from her before the kidnapping, she told me they were onto her and she mailed me all of her information."

Jet groaned. "What did you do?"

"I became the lioness."

Fuck. "What?"

"I came to Veracruz for…personal reasons… and to see if I could find anything out on Marisol. I met with her father and he led me to the Pirate's Lair. I worked there for the express purpose of trying to identify and keep an eye on the cartel members, especially henchman Rey Olmos and the Jaguar's second in command, Angel Andrade."

Jet's head was spinning. "How did you end up as a guy?"

Sami shrugged her shoulders. "I thought it would be some form of protection, but mainly because as Sami in a dress, I witnessed Rey Olmos commit a murder during a festival parade."

"Oh my God." Jet actually groaned. "So the night you hopped my boat?"

Sami nodded. "A few minutes after I'd cracked Santoro over the head, Olmos grabbed me and told me that the jig was up, he knew who I was. I had to run or I would've been dead."

"Wait, wait…what about Mari?" Jet was waiting, wanting Sami to tell him about Destry. He was pretty sure she knew he was an Equalizer.

Sami leaned forward and gave him a big, beautiful smile. "Mari's fine. I began to get comments on the lioness's blog, even some from the cartel. One day I got a note from the Jaguar indicating that Mari was alive and he would trade her for any information I had plus some money." Jet's eyes widened. "This came right on the heels of a news report about the recovery of a female's body that they assumed to be Marisol."

"So, what did you do?" Jet asked the words through clenched teeth, wanting to put her over his knee and spank her gorgeous ass until it was red.

"Well," she bit her lower lip and pointed at him, "I called the Equalizers. I knew our Governor and his Secretary of State were invested in the drug war and in trying to stem the flow of cartel money into the state, which is an ongoing issue."

All of a sudden Jet felt he was speaking to a learned correspondent. "You called Kyle." It wasn't a question.

"Yes, I did, and he and Destry set up an interception in Houston. That was the locale I had specified, I even gave them assurance I would be there. The governor made sure there was someone to stand in for me." She ran a delicate hand through her hair, forcing it up into sexy spikes. "The trade wasn't entirely successful," she sighed, "we didn't get the Jaguar." She smiled. "But we did get Mari back and that is the absolute most important thing to me. I've talked to her."

"What about the money?"

She dismissed the question with a wave of her hand. "Money is dyed paper, Mari is my friend."

Now, for the real question. "I'm an Equalizer, why didn't you tell me?"

Sami narrowed her eyes, a tiny line of concentration forming on her forehead. "Our association at the bar was very casual, you were there on business and it wouldn't have been proper."

"We've been on the Sirena for two days, why haven't you told me by now?" He did his best to keep any hint of anger from his tone.

She looked down. "I tried. I told you I was running from someone." When she saw that wasn't satisfying him, she huffed in frustration. "I didn't want to appear to be hunting an 'in' with you. The parameters of our relationship are clear."

"And what is that?"

Seeing she was getting nowhere fast, Sami changed her style. She batted her eyelashes at Jet, attempting to seduce him. "I'm your booty call, Captain."

Shaking a finger back and forth, Jet fussed, a smile coming to his lips that was part challenge and part invitation. "You're trying to distract me." Who was he kidding, her curves were wrecking his concentration. "Let me say this before I totally lose my mind and set out to do sexy things to you specifically designed to drive you crazy and make you scream."

"Say what?" She was ready for him to put her into an orgasm induced stupor.

Sampling her perfection was his ultimate goal, but he needed to make this point. "You will *not* be returning to Veracruz. It's too dangerous. You're too little. You will *not* put yourself into a situation where you might be killed. Again. *Ever*." He said the words slowly so she couldn't possibly misunderstand.

Sami couldn't stand it, she laughed. "Oh, I love when you're dominant." She rose and went to him, climbing into his lap, straddling his legs. "Not that I'm going to listen to a word you say, but I do like to hear you say it." She ground herself on him until his massive erection was notched into the tender vee between her legs.

"I'm gonna fuck you now, Sami, but if you think this is over, you're wrong." He framed her face with his hands and began kissing her hard, long and deep.

Sami was through arguing, she had other, more important things on her mind. Nudging her butt back and forth, she scrubbed her pussy against him, dragging her sweet spot over his hardness again and again—till she was panting, her fingers clutching his hair.

"Damn, you're hot, you're so hot," he whispered.

Hot?

She was a firecracker and about to go off. His cock was rubbing right against her core, her whole body was melting.

"I just want to eat you up," Jet's words whispered over her cheek. "You taste so damn good. So sweet."

"You're talking too much," Sami murmured as she let her hands move over his neck and shoulders, feeling his heat, storing up memories and sensations for when she was alone again.

Jet couldn't help himself, he laughed against her lips. "What would you rather I do?"

She felt his big hand move up her bare thigh to tease at the edge of her panties. Lifting her hips, she gave him room to work and soon he was rubbing the folds of her pussy. Reaching between them, she found his zipper and tugged. With his other hand, he helped, until she found exactly what she needed.

"Less talk, more action." She gasped as he guided himself into her.

"You want me." He said the words with wonder, as if this was a new thing.

Spreading her legs, she held onto his shoulders and worked her pussy down on his cock, impaling herself inch by inch. Pure raw pleasure flooded her body. "Of course I want you, I've always wanted you."

Jet growled, "Put your arms around my neck." When she did, he cupped her ass and stood up, carrying her to the counter by the controls, sweeping charts and papers out of the way. Gently, he laid her back. They were still joined. Clasping Sami behind the knees, he indicated for her to wrap her legs around his waist. When she did, he joined his hands with hers and began to move, flexing his hips, thrusting and pumping. "Is this enough action for you?"

"God, no." Never enough. "More." Jet was powerful, and she wanted to feel that power. Pushing her hips against him, she tried to get closer, urging him to take her harder. "I'm close," she confessed. Sami could feel the climax building, shimmering, a sweet heat radiating from deep within. She strained, locking her ankles behind his hips, watching his beloved face as he fucked her. "Harder, Jet. You're holding back."

How had she known?

He always held back. He didn't want them to see, didn't want them to know the real him. To let a person see the real you is to give them power over you, and he never wanted to relinquish power—until now. But he couldn't. He was big and she was so small. Maybe he could give her a taste, make her happy, make her think he was letting go.

"Hold on to me tight," he commanded as he began to take her, dragging his cock almost all the way out, then ramming it back in. God, he was in heaven. Jet felt her tighten around him, his dick getting squeezed from all sides. This woman was literally milking him dry.

Sami whimpered, she purred, she moaned for him—now she was the one who couldn't be quiet. "Good, Jet, it's so good." Closer and closer it came, until she sparked and the bliss swamped her, huge waves crashing over her again and again. "Jet!" she screamed, pulling him down on top of her, his weight crushing her deliciously.

Burying his face in her neck, Jet rubbed his body over her satin skin, his chest mating with the most perfect set of breasts he'd ever seen—not huge, just perfect. Sami quivered as she continued to pulse around him, and he held on, giving her every last bit of pleasure she could stand. And even then he didn't stop, keeping up the pace until he erupted inside of her, giving her everything he had, his body lighting up like a flare illuminating the blackness of night.

CHAPTER TEN

The next couple of days were all about lessons…

Never before had Jet laughed so hard or so often. "One of the most important things to remember when learning to sail, is to always know where the wind is coming from in relation to the boat," he explained as he brought the traveler up to catch the high winds. "Release the boom vang so it'll rise and loosen the leech." He pointed and held his breath while she followed his direction. "Now the top part of the sail will twist out."

"Yes!" Sami celebrated with a fist pump, then she ran behind him and jumped on his back. "I love sailing! How much does it cost a pirate to pierce his ears?"

"How much?" he asked indulgently, as he reached behind and cradled her butt in his hands.

"A buccaneer!" she shouted, and he pretended he was about to drop her.

"Funny." He chuckled.

She bent her head and nipped him on the ear. "What's a Southern sailboat called?"

"What?" he asked, ready for another joke.

"A yawl," she answered with a giggle.

"What am I going to do with you?" He pulled her around to the front and kissed her like he owned her.

After she'd let him have his fill, she came back with another. "News Flash!" She teased. "A ship carrying a cargo of red paint has collided with a ship carrying a cargo of purple paint. Last radio contact confirmed that both crews were…" She spread her hands…

"Marooned!" he yelled.

Sami pooched her lips out. "You've heard that one?"

He nipped her on the neck, making her laugh. "I've heard them all, you got them out of my sailing magazine."

"Yea," she admitted, then wrapped her arms around his neck, "just wait till I show you what I learned in your copy of Playboy."

"Deal."

Sami wasn't the only one who learned something. Jet learned he could have a woman on board—and the ship didn't sail over the edge of the world. To his surprise, he and his stowaway became friends. They talked and shared about everything imaginable—from politics to religion, from philosophy to history, from books to music. The only topics they seemed to avoid were certain personal ones, but since it was a mutual decision neither pretended to notice.

And they played.

Sami frolicked on board the ship and in the sea, and Jet was right there to chase her, catch her and kiss her at every opportunity.

In the dusk of the evening, Jet went on the deck looking for her and found Sami standing on the rail at the bow with her arms stretched wide. "What in the world are you doing, Sami Jo?"

"Don't kill my buzz, I'm having a Titanic moment." Since she was balancing precariously right on the edge of a fast-moving ship, in the front, where if she fell she could be run over right in front of him, he lost no time in pulling her back before she tumbled over the edge. "Hey!"

"I'm going to tie you to the mast," he warned her playfully. Tucking her under his arm, he carried her like a recalcitrant child.

"Bully," she protested weakly, mainly because she was upside down and feeling a bit queasy. She'd been feeling a bit off all day.

At first she'd thought it was seasickness, but it seemed a bit late in the game for that malady to strike. The sinking sensation in her gut scared her a bit, bringing back the reality of the cancer she'd been fighting for most of her life. Sami knew she needed to get back to Veracruz and go see Dr. Rio, find out if the treatments worked. During the time she'd been with Jet, her logic had been that she felt good. In fact, she'd felt strong and positive for the last few weeks. Sami knew she could've called Dr. Rio, but right now—she didn't want to know. She and Jet only had another day or so together and she'd rather keep the door closed on that boogeyman as long as possible. If the tumor hadn't shrunk, or if it had metastasized, she didn't want to know until Jet was out of the picture. There were a lot of things she dreamed of sharing with Jet, but pity about her condition was not one of them.

"Where are you hauling me?"

"To the galley, that soup you put in the slow cooker smells good enough to eat."

"Raise me up, please?" she asked sweetly, and he immediately complied.

When she laid her head on his shoulder, he cuddled her close. "Cold?"

"No, comfortable."

"Good, I want to talk to you."

He sounded serious and that made Sami nervous. "Why?" She leaned out to gaze at him. "Did Destry call, is something wrong with Mari?"

"No." Jet shook his head. "I want to talk about you." He eased her down in a chair, immediately going to the cabinet and fetching two bowls. Polly wound around his legs, and he stopped to make sure her bowl was full.

"That's going to be a fairly short subject," Sami mused. "I'm really boring."

"I doubt that. Don't confuse your lack of height with your appeal." Jet ladled soup into a bowl and set it in front of her. "Try me. Tell me something about you."

Sami dipped her spoon in the chunky vegetables and meat mix and blew on it. A standard delay tactic. "Well, I'm a spoiled only child of fairly well-off parents, my dad owned Cabot Drilling and my mom was a doctor."

"Was?" Jet joined her at the table, pulling out a chair and easing into it.

Sami nodded. "Yea, I've lost them both." When she saw the sorrowful look in his eyes, she covered Jet's hand with hers. "It's okay, I'm dealing with it. Before I left for Mexico, I sold the house and the cars. If I go home I'll start fresh." She smiled as if that was consolation.

If?

"So, you're alone?" Knowing what she was going to say, he beat her to it. "Except for Marisol?"

"Yea." She nodded, taking another sip of soup. "I've heard you talk about Nemo, he seems fascinating."

"Nemo is one of a kind, he had a heart attack a few weeks ago and is having to take it easy. I think the rest and recuperation is worse than the actual heart attack." Jet found it easy to talk to Sami, she really listened.

"But he's going to meet you at the wreck site?"

"We're planning on it, which reminds me, I need to call after we eat and check on him. My friend Tyson is with him. Tyson is a speculator, he plays the markets. I'm sure they've clashed on everything from the price of oil to the merits of hoarding gold."

"How about your mom? Is she still alive?" As soon as Sami breathed the words, she knew she'd made a mistake. His face closed, as effective as if a curtain had been pulled in front of it. "I'm sorry, I shouldn't have asked."

Jet waved a piece of bread in the air. "No, it's all right. I'm not ashamed. It wasn't my fault. I used to think it was, but it wasn't." At Sami's speculative looked, he explained. "She got tired of us. Left us before I even started school. No explanation, no birthday cards. I learned a few years ago that she remarried, had another family and lived within five miles of the house she walked away from. I have two half-brothers I've never met."

"Dang, that's rough." Sami felt so bad for him. "At least you have the Equalizers, you seem very close to them."

He was lucky, he realized that. "Yea, I do."

"Is how you feel about your mom the reason you're so against letting a woman get close to you...like on the boat?" she questioned with a slight smile.

"You're good." He laughed. "And the answer is probably. On the whole, women are selfish, they take what they can and leave when they've got what they wanted."

Sami was quiet for a moment, thinking, then she commented—just so he'd know. "I'm not asking for anything, you can trust me, I'll not be taking anything from you when I go."

This conversation was making Jet uneasy. When she left, she might be taking more with her than she knew. Determined to guard his heart, Jet dismissed what she said with a shake of his head. "Oh, I wasn't talking about you, you don't count."

Zing!

Straight to the heart. Story of her life. "Wow, good to know. I am a female in case you haven't noticed."

"No! Really?" He stared at her bug-eyed until she cracked up.

"You're so mean."

Wanting to push thoughts of his mother far from his mind, he leveled his gaze at Sami. "So, how did you end up a virgin at the ripe old age of twenty-three?"

"Ha!" Sami recognized a revenge subject change when she heard it. "Well." She sought for the right words. "I was waiting for you." At his stunned look, she giggled. "Gotcha!" What she said was partially true, but it wasn't the real reason. "My mother was very overprotective and I was sickly…up until recently." There, that seemed innocuous enough.

"Sickly?" Jet froze, his spoon halfway to his lips.

Oops. "How many women have you slept with?"

"What?" Jet had to stop and repeat the words in his mind. He laughed. "You have no filter, do you?"

"Not even a little one."

A further stall. "Good girls like you shouldn't ask questions like that."

Sami rolled her eyes. "If you think I'm good, I'm going to have to work harder in bed tonight."

"Oh, you're very good." He teased, his cock perking up, wanting in on the conversation.

"Yes, I am!" She stood and grabbed his hand. "Come swim with me. Who knows? You might get lucky."

He didn't have to be asked twice. As they ran, they stripped and when they dove over the side, Jet shouted. "Man overboard!"

Sami landed in the water with a splash. It was a windless day and the surface was as still as glass. "Look how clear it is." She dipped her face in and looked down. "How deep is it here? I can't see the bottom."

"Oh, about two miles."

Sami jumped in the water, still dog paddling. "What? Holy crap!" She gazed back down into the depths, sea monsters on her mind.

Jet looped an arm around her waist and pulled her to him. "Relax, I'm here. I won't let anything happen to you. Look down." She did as he asked. "See the big bands of sunlight streaking down into the deep?"

"Yes," she answered, not sure what was more thrilling—the view or being nestled close to Jet. Her heart was thumping wildly. "It looks like ghosts down there."

Jet slid a big hand up to cup her breast, tweaking the nipple lightly. "That's just a trick of the light reflecting off the plankton. It makes it look like figures swirling and hovering about."

"It's beautiful," she whispered as he kissed her neck, his whiskers sending rasps of delight through her body. "I used to be afraid of the water. Imagine that? I would cling to the shallows, stay on the steps. And here we are in the mother of all deep ends."

"I can't imagine that," Jet said. "You're fearless. When did you venture out, become brave?"

Sami held on with both hands to the strong forearm wrapped around her waist. "When I found out there were worse things in the world." Like cancer and death, she thought. "I love this, thank you." She impulsively held up her face to be kissed. "I used to dream of having an adventure and you're showing me how infinite the world is, how little I know of it."

"You're welcome, baby girl." He gave her the kiss she craved.

For a minute he let himself consider how lonely he would've been on this trip without her—and he wouldn't even have known what he was missing.

"In all my life, I've never seen this color of blue." She turned in his arms. "Dive down with me, just a few feet. Please?"

"Sure." He smiled.

They took a deep breath and dove as deep down as Sami could kick. When she opened her eyes, she was thrilled. Everything, everywhere was just the bluest blue, an unending, overwhelming, incredible blue. Sami twirled, dancing, her arms thrown out. The water was as clear as glass. She gazed at her own skin. Even it had a blueish hue. Here she could see the sunbeams up close, swim through them. They were like giant spotlights from above which disappeared into the limitless depths below. Swimming sideways, Sami looked down but there was no bottom, just an unending sea of blue.

Jet touched her arm and pointed upward, and Sami followed, gasping when she broke the surface. "That was amazing. I think I know what forever looks like now. Thank you."

Jet said nothing, he was at a loss for words. Heading back to the ship, he waited at the ladder for her to join him. Then he helped her up, his fingers grazing the velvety softness of her skin. Her body was a delight, from the tips of her breasts to the globes of her spankable ass. When he found his voice, there was only one thing to say. "I want to make love to you."

Sami waited until he stepped on the deck before she grabbed him. Plastering herself against his big body was one of her favorite things. "I love how you feel," she praised him, running her palms up his arms and over his shoulders.

Jet growled an unintelligible answer and moved her body with his as he turned. With hungry aggression, he ate at her mouth, sweeping his tongue inside and sliding it against hers, stealing her breath and ability to think. She stood on tiptoe, one hand gripping in his hair, the other reaching down between them to close around his cock, which was swollen and throbbing in her hand.

"Face the sea and stand on that ledge," he murmured, moving her so that she was cradled against him, her back to his front. An animalistic hunger raged within him. "You're so damn sexy, I can't get enough of you." He wound his hand in her short hair and turned her head so their mouths met.

The kiss was sizzling.

"Take me, Jet," she whispered against his mouth as he reached a hand around to cover her mound. Dipping his fingers between her legs, he massaged her slit up and down, spreading her cream up to her clit. "You only have to look at me and I'm wet for you."

Her breathy little confessions were ramping his need. "Hold on to the rail." Jet pushed two fingers deep inside of her, pulling them in and out, making her squirm. The other hand kneaded and plumped those incredible tits of hers, while he kept his lips busy nibbling on her neck. "God, you feel good." She was soft in all the right places and that tight, slick heat between her legs drove him fuckin' crazy.

"Fuck me, Jet. Please." Was all Sami managed to get out. She pushed her bottom back against him in invitation.

"Soon. Spread your legs."

She did, and he bent his knees a bit, pushing his cock between her pussy lips, not into her channel, but clasped inside her slick folds like a sausage in a bun, so he could slip and slide back and forth, nudging her clit with the tip.

"Faster," she begged with a whimper. Jet couldn't have turned her down even if he wanted to. She laid her head back against his chest and he pleasured her, rubbing her nipples between his fingers. "Jet!" Sami moaned loudly as she came unglued, her thighs pressing together, trying to trap his shaft in place.

"Bend over," he instructed, and she complied, resting her head on the cool wood. Pulling out, he took his cock in hand and spanked it against the cheek of her ass.

"Jet, swear to God, if you don't get inside me…"

Chuckling, he guided the tip into her juicy little pussy as he scattered openmouthed kisses across the silky expanse of her neck and shoulders. The sheer pleasure stole his breath.

Why did he ever do anything else?

"Deeper, you're teasing me. Slam hard, let me feel every inch." Sami ground her butt against him, tempting him to lose control.

"You're a demanding little mermaid." He pinched one nipple, making her squeal. "I'll give you what you need."

His body shook, he wanted her too damn much—which was an unusual feeling for Jet. He flexed his hips and bucked forward, impaling her in one powerful thrust.

Sami moaned, angling her head, seeking his lips, passion making her eyes even darker. "Sweet baby Jesus, give me more."

And so he did. He held her tight, hands roving over her front, from tit to clit, rubbing, massaging. He couldn't touch her enough. Jet fucked her wildly. No stopping. He nailed her over and over again, his teeth scraping the tender flesh of her neck as he bit down, sucking hard enough to leave a mark. She keened, her breath hitching with each pump of his cock in her pussy. Jet held her tits as he maintained the pounding pace. His efforts were rewarded when she climaxed, tightening around him, squeezing with quivering pulses.

"Damn, girl," he panted.

"Don't you dare stop," she pleaded, another orgasm hitting her so hard she reached back to grasp his thigh, needing to hold on lest she float away.

Jet couldn't last much longer, it was too good. Tightening his muscles, he closed his eyes, reveling in the bliss of being buried in her sweet heat. With a shout, he shot his cum inside of her in a series of jetting pulses that shorted out his thinking and made his whole body shake.

"Good, so good." He wrapped both arms around her and buried his face in her neck. "Are you okay?"

Sami went limp in his arms, letting him support her, fulfilling one of her dreams to just turn herself over to him. "Never better. You have to be the best lover in the world."

"Are you saying I fuck good?" he whispered in her ear.

She giggled. "Yea, you plundered me good, Captain." Sami picked up her well-worn garment and skimmed it over her head. "Next time I'm fleeing danger, I need to pack better. Hopefully I can find somewhere to buy a decent change of clothes before I catch that plane."

Jet frowned. What had seemed a good idea a few days ago now sounded totally unacceptable.

* * *

The wind had all but died down. Jet had been enjoying the nice, even sail they had going and he grumbled, realizing it was time to switch on a bit of power to keep them moving.

Sami just stood at the rail, sipping her drink. The sun was out in full force and they'd just gotten up from their beach towels. Jet's skin was an almost permanent olive color from all the sun he got, and she was finally seeing her skin start to turn a darker shade. The bright sun had not only been good for her skin, but it had lightened her hair a tinge and done wonders for her overall mood. The clock had been ticking since the first time they'd kissed and although Cuba was still too far away to actually see, Sami could feel it off in the horizon, a pulsing energy, drawing her nearer to the end of her voyage, nearer to the end of her time with Jet.

She watched Jet working the winches and booms and other shiny things she didn't totally understand yet. He commanded the big equipment with the same confidence as he did his own—be it a rope or his cock—he was the master. Sami felt a tingle between her thighs. Watching the muscles in his back constrict and expand was enough to make her dizzy and she gripped the railing with a strong hand for support, blaming the little twitch in her knees on a phantom wave even though the ocean was calm.

"Must have caught a swell," she offered despite Jet not asking.

He bundled the sails up and put them away. Sami continued to be amazed by how gentle such a big man could be. He handled the sails as if they were sacred, much the same as he had handled her in the bedroom, rough and forceful when needed, but never too out of control to know when to put on the kid gloves.

258

Sami's shoulders slumped at the thought. Although inexperienced with sex, she had always dreamed of what it would be like to feel Jet just let go, to totally and completely unleash on her. She longed to know what it felt like to be utterly dominated by the big man, to be taken, slammed up against the wall and used in whatever way would satisfy him completely. She needed to know what that felt like before she let him go forever.

Standing with his hand above his brow, blocking the glaring sun from his vision, he asked, "You okay?"

Sami felt her hand twitch. She wanted to reach out and follow a trail of sweat down between Jet's pecs with her finger. She wanted to undo his shorts with her teeth, drive him over the edge with desire and whip him into such a frenzy that he claimed her right there on the deck, took her with all the force in his mighty body. She wanted him to test her limits and if she had a safeword, make her use it.

Sami wiped a line of sweat from her forehead. "It's just hot out here." But it had been a different kind of heat that had encompassed her.

Jet scanned the sky, squinting into it. "Tell me about it. As much as I love lying out here on the deck with you in your underwear, I'd trade my left nut for a few clouds and some wind right now. I hate being listless like this and I don't want to use the motor, it's just too pretty." Jet began to whistle. He did it with such expertise that Sami just watched. "Do it with me."

Sami cupped her lips and nothing but air came out at first. "I'm out of practice." It was her desire for him that had made her mouth and lips go dry.

Jet began again. "You can do it." He whistled a high, consistent tone. Not a tune that Sami was familiar with, but one he clearly knew well. "That's it," he encouraged when she finally got the hang of it, matching him note for note.

"What are you doing?" Sami inquired when Jet had stopped and looked up into the sky, surveying it.

"Awww. Never mind. That's not gonna work."

"What's not going to work?"

"Whistling. The old-timers thought it helped the wind, but I can see it ain't working right now. Probably because I've got a woman on board with me." He offered a wink.

Sami chose to ignore the joking slight, the mention of Jet's nut hadn't been chased from her mind and it made her smile.

"What are you grinning about?"

Sami mustered up her courage and stepped closer to him and just as she was about to reach between his legs and hopefully deliver a line that unleashed the beast in Jet, a loud splashing noise caught both of their attention off the starboard side of the Sirena.

Frightened by the noise, Sami lost her balance and Jet had to catch her before she tumbled over the railing. "I'm so sorry." She gasped after she'd watched the glass that had been in her hand go tumbling over the side and sink right away. "I'll buy you a new one as soon as we make land."

"It's just a glass, girl. Let's go." He took her by the hand and headed toward the wheelhouse, pulling Sami along as he went.

Behind her the noise came again. "Where are we going?"

Jet didn't answer, he just scooped her up and slung her over his shoulder fireman style, placing her feet back down on the ground only after they were in the wheelhouse. "Hit that button," Jet said with a point, getting into position behind the wheel.

The boat lurched a moment after Sami had slapped the big red button with her palm. Up ahead of the boat, a blast of water came from the sea. "What was that?"

Jet pushed the throttle forward. "Let's go find out," he said with a grin.

The engines came to life and the Sirena started to move slowly, chasing another puff of water that was now further on up ahead.

Sami saw something black erupt from the ocean off the starboard side now.

Jet spanked her on her underwear clad rump. "Go on and get out there, girl. Spot for me, would you?"

This was exciting. Sami didn't know what she was going to look for, but she bounded out of the wheelhouse with Polly following. Polly gave Sami a wide berth as she skipped down the steps and across the deck. She came to the rail and saw what all the commotion had been about.

"How much room do I have?" Jet queried through an open window up in the wheelhouse.

"About ten feet," Sami called back with glee.

There was a cluster of dark objects in the water right beside the Sirena, following along, and Jet nosed the boat closer to it. They looked like stealth bombers and when one surfaced, Sami saw that they were actually stingrays, and big ones at that.

"Eeeeeeee!" Sami screeched with joy as the water rained down on her feet after a group of the big rays splashed up and out of the water.

She expected the feline at her feet to have fled the liquid assault, but Polly just stood there, water beading on her fur with the same aloof look she always seemed to have, watching over the edge of the ship with quiet awe as the dark objects in the water kept pace with the slow moving boat.

"Rays," Jet said from beside Sami as she wiped water from her eyes.

"They're huge. How many are there?"

Jet climbed up onto one of the main riggings in the middle of the ship. "I'd say about fifteen. Maybe twenty. Never can tell for sure unless you can get up high enough to look down and I don't really feel like climbing up into the crow's nest at the moment."

Sami was amazed at how at home Jet was on the boat, he knew everything there was to know. Oh, the places he must have been on his voyages, the things he must have seen.

Sami watched with a slack-jaw as three rays crested the surface. When the rays had gone back below it dawned on Sami—who was driving the boat?

Jet watched from his perch on the rigging, a look of amazement on his face. Sami imagined that no matter how many times a person had seen something like this, it never lost its wonder.

"Who's driving the boat?" she called up to her muscle-bound captain. "Are we on automatic pilot?"

"Nah, we're barely moving," Jet said in response. "Don't need a driver. I let Claude drive when we're going this slowly. He'll keep the course nice and steady."

There was that name again…the reference was lost on Sami. Surely there wasn't anyone else on board, or she would have known it by now. But she'd grown tired of feeling stupid when Jet talked about the sea and sailing, so she kept her mouth shut, she'd ask him to explain later if there was time.

They both watched a moment longer before Jet came down to stand by her. "No point in chasing them," he said as the rays switched course and started to move away from the Sirena. "Drink?"

"Please."

Sami followed him down into the galley. The boat was still moving, but Jet had been right, they were barely crawling. He took a key from his pocket and unlocked a cabinet adjacent to the table where they ate and started fishing books and notepads out. Plopping them on a table, he sat down and poured them both a drink.

Sami came and stood at his side, placing a greedy hand on his thick traps. "What's all this?"

Jet was working, spreading out papers and opening books on the table top. "Just some stuff I need to go over before meeting up with Victor."

It hit him like a ton of bricks, he'd be meeting up with Victor soon and they'd be off to find the San Miguel. The thought filled him with excitement, but it also meant he and Sami would be parting ways soon and that filled him with the exact opposite emotion.

Jet took a large piece of paper out of a cardboard tube and rolled it out over the table, anchoring it at the corners with books and a saltshaker. Sami saw it was a map of Florida and her eyes wandered up the Atlantic coast side, seeing markings all the way up from Key West, almost all of them scratched out as her eyes went further up the coast.

She suddenly felt uncomfortable. "I should go back up top."

"Why?"

"I don't think I should be seeing this. You might not want me to know what you know about the wreck."

Jet struck out a hand and took her by the elbow. "Nonsense." He pulled her down onto his lap. "You saved my life. I'd say if anyone can be trusted, it's you."

Sami settled in on his thigh. The thick, hard muscle gave her a nice place to sit and made her feel small, a feeling she enjoyed. "Where's the X?"

Jet tickled her. "We pirate types don't do the X thing anymore." Sami giggled and tried to fend off his invading fingers. "You pollywogs and landlubbers figured us out and started stealing our treasures."

When he let her go, Sami leaned forward in his lap and looked at the map. There were lines all over it that she didn't understand. This was like no map she'd ever seen before in her life. "Is that the Bermuda Triangle?"

Jet rose from the seat himself, pushing her away and coming around to the other side of the table. "It sure is." He placed his hands on the tabletop and leaned down right across from Sami. "See this?" He pointed to a spot where a flurry of scribbled lines was. "This is where I'm headed."

"So far up Florida?" Sami asked. "In my mind, I imagined the ship you were looking for was in some random spot miles and miles off the coast."

"A million miles down in some crevice deep in the Atlantic Ocean? Guarded by the Krakken."

Sami slapped him on the forearm. "Don't tease me, you big lug. I'm a land-lover after all."

"The word is landlubber, it means someone unfamiliar with the sea." Jet moved beside her and placed his hands on her tiny waist, positioning her right in front of him, leaning his big frame over and speaking in her ear. His breath and nearness made her loins stir. "This is Nassau Sound. This is where I'll go in."

"Where does it go?"

"Amelia Island. And hopefully right to the San Miguel. People always think these wrecks happen far out in the middle of the ocean, but most happen near the shore. It's a cruel twist actually. Proof that Mother

Nature has a sense of humor and can be unmerciful. Legend tells that it was a fleet of Spanish Galleons trying to outrun a hurricane sailing from Havana to Spain. Unfortunately they didn't make it and we think the San Miguel went down right here." He tapped the marked up spot on the map with a thick finger. "I'm confident this is where I'll find the San Miguel. I can only imagine the terror those sailors must have felt. Waves higher than their boat. Howling winds. They must have known they weren't far from shore. I bet some of them even had hope of surviving when they went into the water. Nassau Sound is teeming with sharks."

The weight of the moment fell heavy across both of them. The idea of those poor men thrashing about in the water, doing everything they could to keep afloat while their ship disappeared right in front of their eyes. There was no coast guard back then to come to their rescue. No signal flares to send up in hopes of being seen. No mayday sent out on the airwaves. No cruise ships in the area. It had just been those men, alone out there with nowhere to go.

Sami felt the drop in Jet's energy. "I'll make us something to eat." She slipped out from under his big body and missed it right away.

The feeling in the room had grown heavy and she busied herself with preparing some potato and asparagus soup to comfort them both while Jet looked over information.

They both worked in silence for the better part of an hour. Sami filled the time with dishes and cleaning up, all the while, watching Jet as he studied his maps and notebooks.

"They were carrying millions," Jet said out of nowhere.

Sami came to the table, drying her hands with a damp dishtowel. "The San Miguel?"

Jet pushed a tattered old book in front of her, and she picked it up. "Gold, silver, contraband. You name it, it was on that ship. They even had the Queen's Jewels aboard according to legend."

"What were those?"

"Magnificent jewels, Sami. Gorgeous. Timeless. King Filipe the fifth had them made for his bride. I can't tell you why they were on that ship, but word is that they were. What was worth millions back then, well, you can imagine what it's worth nowadays."

"How much?" Sami asked, unable to keep the excitement from her voice.

"A cool two billion," he whispered. That familiar look of excitement had returned to his scarred face. Sami knew those doomed sailors were still in the back of his mind, but Jet was exuberant about the ship when he spoke. "There's no telling what else is down there."

"Why are you so certain it's there?"

"Salvagers found coins there in the sixties. The easy stuff to find really. Stuff that probably washed in from the actual wreckage site. It's not uncommon. Some stray coins catch a current and float onto a beach. It happens all the time. A kid playing in the sand finds a plate from the sixteen hundreds. A guy out spearfishing sees a glimmer of light and discovers a ring or some piece of jewelry. Things from the San Miguel have been washing up on shore of the Amelia beaches for decades. We found the jeweler's furnace, I just know the actual San Miguel is there somewhere. I can't explain it, but I just know we're going to find it this time. I've had this feeling before."

Sami closed the book, placed it back down on the table and went to get him some soup. "And anyone can just go in and look for these wrecks?" She buttered a piece of bread and placed it beside the bowl on a plate.

"You have to apply for a permit, a lease, almost the same if you were going to mine for gold. There's a system, not that everyone abides by it. Pirates still exist." Jet moved a pile of books for her to place the food down and patted the seat beside him. "Enough cooking and cleaning for a while. Just sit with me. I want you close right now."

He wanted her close?

Sami didn't know what it meant, she wasn't sure if it was a sexual come-on or an intimate one. She took the seat beside him, unsure of how close she should sit. "You've done this lots of times before. I'm sure you're right this time."

Jet leaned back and rubbed his face. "It's a gamble for sure. Nemo has been after the San Miguel for years. For some reason he's always refused to take the artifacts that washed up on Amelia Island seriously. He can be a real fool at times. Lord knows he's dragged me along on plenty of his wild goose chases over the years. But he has to listen to me this time."

"It must be nice, having something you can share with your father."

Jet smiled. "My old man is a royal pain in the ass. Don't get me wrong, I love him to death, but he can be so stubborn. He can be a real pirate at times. Rough. Crude. Hostile. Which is the last thing you want to be when you're looking for treasure." He dipped the bread in his soup and brought it to his mouth.

"Careful." Sami leaned over and blew on it. "It's really hot."

The sight of her puckered lips drew a tightness in Jet's cock. "Keep doing that and you'll find yourself blowing on something else."

His words put an ache in Sami's clit and she wanted to reach under the table and free Jet from his underwear, but he dipped his bread again and she got distracted. "I'd think that being salty would be a good quality to have when you're at sea."

"Oh, it is. But you have to get out at sea first. Like I was telling you before, you wouldn't believe the hoops you have to jump through just to get the go-ahead to look. First, you need permission from the government where you're looking. For instance, I'll be looking in Florida, so I had to go ask the governor for permission to search his waters. Luckily the new governor there is more amiable to treasure hunting. And it helps to have a good buddy in government now.

"But it's not just my own government I have to ask permission from. Since the San Miguel is a Spanish ship, I also need their permission and I have to report anything I find to them right away. They want to know everything, so it's harder for me to steal something if I ever do find it. Then there's the antique dealers, rival salvagers and the crooked conmen who are out there forging antiques, selling false information and generally making it tougher to find this stuff. I hate politics, Destry usually handles that stuff for me, but even then, Nemo has come in and fucked me over. So yeah, being a salty bastard is great when you're out at sea, those guys are the ones who get things done, but rolling into a meeting with an ambassador and being drunk, well, that's not good for business."

"Can't change some people, I guess."

"No, you can't. Luckily, he didn't foul this one up. I'm actually really excited about this hunt. We have an ROV and Victor has this submersible that will make things a lot easier. I've never worked with one before, but it'll help big time with the heavy stuff."

"How heavy could a handful of gold coins be? Just put them in a bag and swim up."

Jet let out a hardy chuckle. "Oh, little girl, there's more than a handful of gold coins down there. The San Miguel weighed over a hundred and eighty tons. Hell, there were twenty-two cannons on it. Those cannons alone can weigh over a ton. It's not just the gold and silver we're after. The valuables are great, and there could be bars and bars of gold bullion on board, but it's not just the money we're after, it's the history. Those cannons alone are valuable, maybe not worth as much as the gold, but their historic value is immeasurable."

"So how do you get them up?"

Jet wrapped an arm around her waist and pulled her close to him on the bench seat. "I should consult you on that topic. From what I've seen the last few days, you're the master of getting things up." He offered her a sly smile, and Sami blushed. "There's lots of ways. Smaller stuff goes in a bag and we attach floaties to them. They float up on a guide wire and are collected at the ship. Big stuff, like the cannons for instance, well, those require a crane to get them out. The crane is attached to a salvage ship. Victor will have that. We hook straps around the cannons and lift them up. It's a pain at times because the straps can slip off and boy oh boy, you do not want to be under it when a two ton cannon comes falling down, even under water. Victor's sub and our ROV will make that stuff easier. He's got all these fancy riggings and pulleys on the sub, he's been showing me pictures and videos of how it works. I can't wait to see it in person."

Polly joined them and they sat and talked for hours. Jet told tales of his time behind enemy lines and about the people of Afghanistan. He talked about the Equalizers and how they worked together. When Jet told the story of his first fight in MMA and how he'd blacked out for a moment while being choked, but still managed to turn the tides and win the fight, he scared her to death. "Micah always says I was brain damaged that day. But I got the win, so that's all that matters."

Jet yawned at a lull in the conversation, and Sami's heart fell. Oh no, she was boring him.

"I think it's time to go to bed," he said with a stretch.

"I'm just going to clean up and then I'll go to my cabin."

Jet stood from the table and offered her a hand. "The dishes can wait." He pulled her close to him. "And like hell you're sleeping in your cabin. *Your* cabin, is *my* cabin. You're sleeping with me tonight. End of story."

The way he spoke shot a jolt of electricity down Sami's spine to zing right between her legs. "Okay." She looked up at him. Both of their eyes were sleepy.

Jet led her by the hand to his cabin, leaving Polly slumbering in the galley. They'd been on autopilot for hours while they talked, so Jet went to the wheelhouse to do a final check before going to bed.

Sami brushed her teeth and prepped herself for bed, slipping one of Jet's oversized shirts over her heated skin. Everything he owned had his unmistakable musk and Sami took a deep inhale from the shirt, her pussy creaming as he filled her senses.

Diving under the covers, Sami still couldn't believe she was here…with JET!

Although him showing her the maps and going over his plans made her departure real, she still hadn't let herself fully believe this was coming to an end.

"God, I'm tired," Jet grumbled when he came back in the room. "I had no idea it'd gotten so late."

Sami watched with rapt focus as he brushed his teeth in the tiny bathroom. The toothbrush looked like a tiny twig in his strong hands and his triceps flexed with one hand leaning on the edge of the sink. Sami's entire body kicked into overdrive, the dampness between her thighs had grown considerably.

Why the hell was he taking so long to get to her? It was torture. She wanted him near her right now.

Jet slid into bed a moment later. "Lie with me." He extended his arm above her head and Sami nuzzled into the crook.

"I'm sure you're going to find it, Jet."

Sleep was close to overtaking them both and Jet covered a big yawn with his fist. "I hope so. This will be the find of a lifetime."

Sami wished she was bolder, wished she had it in her to just reach under the covers and start stroking him until he was rock-solid, but even her better health had not filled her with complete confidence and when she heard Jet begin to lightly snore, she knew she'd be going to sleep unsatisfied.

"Damn it, Samantha," she scolded herself as she rolled off the big warrior.

Her time with Jet was coming to an end and as she drifted off to sleep all she could think about was the opportunity she'd just missed.

Sami dreamed of vast oceans spreading out before her. In her dream she was on Jet's boat, running up and down the deck with him in pursuit. When he finally caught her, he leaned her back over the railing and put a hand between her legs.

"Oh God, yes," Sami moaned in her sleep, rousing Jet from his sleep.

"What the...?" he asked through the haze of slumber.

Beside him Sami was on her back, her hips undulating beneath the covers softly. There was barely enough light in the cabin to see her, but what she was doing was unmistakable.

"Well, I'll be," Jet murmured to himself.

One thing a man of his considerable size had trouble doing, was being quiet when he moved, but he turned onto his side and watched the gyrating little honey for a few minutes.

"Naughty little girl," he said, lifting the covers up just enough to expose Sami's sweet little pussy to his eyes.

Her shirt had ridden up in the front and she moaned and whimpered softly while he fucked her in her dream. Her pussy gleamed in the moonlight through the porthole when Jet stealthy lifted the covers completely off of her. Her sex was swollen and ready for action.

"Fuck this," Jet mumbled to himself.

He sat up in the bed, careful not to disturb Sami from her fantasy. Slipping his swollen cock out the side of his shorts, he put a hand on either side of her and slid in between her parted thighs. The heat from Sami's pussy seared the tip of his throbbing erection as it hovered between them. He ran a finger through her velvety hot folds, coating it with her honey. The finger was gentle and he covered the top of his cock with her juices before inserting it fully in her.

Sami's mouth opened with a gasp. "Oh, God!"

In her dream Jet had been fingering her and the sudden introduction of his thick cock into her slippery channel was a delicious shock to her entire system. Her eyes snapped open and there he was, his gorgeous bearded face right in front of her. Sami did her best to focus on his face, but all the feeling in her body was located in her pussy and the glorious way Jet's shaft moved in and out of her.

Jet never said a word, he just stared into her eyes while he pumped in and out with slow deliberate strokes. The sensation of his invasion was sheer bliss and Sami could feel the crescendo building inside of her. She bit her lip and let the feeling take over, culminating in an ear-splitting orgasm that she released without apprehension.

Jet lifted up off of her and brought a hand up between them. Sami shimmied her hips and he maneuvered the hem of her shirt up over her gorgeous peaks.

Jet's tongue darted back and forth over her erect nipples. "God. I could suck on these for days." The stalk of his thick cock rubbed back and forth over her clit with each pump and Sami felt another orgasm coming on. "Don't hold back," Jet told her when he saw it on her face. "Cum for me, Sami."

His words set her off and Sami's insides erupted like a volcano. Jet plumped her tits together in one big hand and licked both nipples at once, picking up his pace as he lavished Sami's sensitive chest, devouring both nipples with greedy lips.

Sami's moans shook him to the core. She was amazing and Jet felt his balls begin to tighten. "I can't take anymore. Cum with me, Sami."

Sami tensed her insides, squeezing Jet's broad cock as she quivered, digging her nails into his wide back. She rode the wave of another orgasm with the sensation of Jet emptying himself inside of her.

"You okay?" Jet asked from beside her. "I didn't crush you, did I?" He wiped his face with the covers.

"Yes," Sami said in a breathy pant. "You…did…but I loved it." She rolled to him and gave him a kiss. It was salty and perfect.

"I'm all sweaty."

"So am I," Sami said, nuzzling back into the crook of his arm. "And I don't care a bit."

CHAPTER ELEVEN

The low rattle of the purr in Polly's throat woke Sami early. Jet was beside her and she stretched and greeted the day. "Hungry, girl?" Polly stretched her head to expose her neck for a quick rub. "Let's go get us all something to eat."

Sami rolled off the bed in silence. The covers were pulled back, revealing Jet from mid-thigh up. Even flaccid his cock was a sight to behold. Sami's palm itched to pet it, but a rumble in her stomach pushed her out the cabin door with nothing but Jet's shirt on.

After she'd fed Polly, Sami stood at the stove in front of a pan of crackling bacon. Tomorrow they'd arrive in Cuba and she'd be getting off the Sirena. She'd be going back to her life, a life that didn't include Jet Foster.

"Owwwww!" Sami hollered when a splash of hot grease splattered onto her hand. She dropped the spatula she'd been holding and went to the sink to run cold water over the burn. "Sami, you idiot." The spot on her hand stung, but not as bad as the pain in her chest.

The word 'CUBA' flashed in her mind in big, bright, red letters. She'd never been there before, but she hated that damn country for what it represented. The poor bacon sat bubbling hot in the pan when Sami returned to the stove. It was a charred and unrecognizable facsimile of its former self.

"Can't even cook right." A scream of frustration came out of her mouth.

The last thing Sami wanted to do was spend her last day with Jet an emotional wreck. Time was precious now and ruining it with dwelling on something that was out of her control seemed ridiculous, so she poured a cup of coffee and went up to the deck to gather herself.

It was later in the day than she'd realized. She hadn't checked a clock to know for sure, but Jet had taught her how to tell time by using the sun and to Sami, it appeared to be close to noon. It wasn't surprising it was so late, yesterday had been a long day, but Sami wouldn't have traded a moment of it for anything. Off in the distance there was a bank of clouds and the wind was considerably stronger than earlier. She scowled at the clouds, angry with the winds that would only speed up their arrival in Cuba. Sami wanted to scream at the impending clouds, rail against the wind, beat it down with her frustration, but she knew it wouldn't help. She'd been living a fantasy these past few days, but the clock was about to strike midnight.

"Stop feeling sorry for yourself. All you'll do is ruin the last bit of time you have with him." Sami steeled herself, determined to jam as much fun and memories into today as she could.

"Little crispier than I like it." Jet bit down on a hunk of black bacon. "But it is bacon after all, so it's still good."

Sami came right to him and wrapped her arms around his waist, placing her head on his strong chest. "I'm sorry." She was glad he couldn't see her face, because she felt like she was about to cry.

Although he may not have seen it on her face, Jet was intuitive and he could feel the emotions coursing through Sami's body as she held onto him. He stood in place, wrapping a big arm around her and just enjoyed the moment, the waves rocking the Sirena up and down.

He knew what he'd said, but with the reality of Cuba looming so largely, a war was waging inside of Jet.

"I should probably get the sails up," he offered with an awkward grin. "We should take advantage of this wind."

"Show me," Sami blurted out when their embrace had been broken.

"Show you?"

"Show me more. You've shown me how to tie off the boat, how to batten down the hatches, how to survive rough water, but I still don't know how to raise the sails or chart a course. Show me everything. I want to learn. I want all the experiences I can get before…"

The unspoken words hung in the air. Not even the ever increasing breeze could blow them off into the open ocean.

"Let me…uh." Jet stumbled for words. "I'll go get dressed and have something to eat. You might as well go get ready too. I'll show you in a bit."

There was a sudden tension between them. Two people who had grown incredibly close over the last few days, now felt awkward with each other.

"Hey," Sami greeted Jet after she'd cleaned herself up and joined him in the galley.

"I made you some toast. Jam's in the fridge. But you already know that, I guess." The big guy was flustered, almost as if he didn't know how to proceed with the day. "I'm gonna go up and check the weather. I'll meet you up on the deck in twenty."

The wheelhouse offered no respite for Jet from the awkwardness. He tried to lose himself in the readouts that came through. Cloud patterns, wind directions, they all seemed to make no sense at the moment. His head was somewhere else and he knew the reason was down below wearing one of his shirts and eating toast.

A little later, Sami stood at Jet's side. They were out front on the bow, looking back at the boat.

"First thing you need to know is that this boat is a motorsailer. There are different types of boats, but I'm not going to get into that because, well, because I know you're a smart girl, but sailing can be a confusing subject to even a seasoned vet like me who's been doing it all his life. All you need to know is that I choose this motorsailer because it's got shorter sails and is easier to manage. It can be run by a smaller crew and by smaller crew I mean me, Polly, and Claude."

Again, Jet mentioned Claude, but Sami was doing her best to focus, she wanted to impress him and learn to do what he loved so much. "I understand. I won't take it as an insult."

"Good girl." Jet gave her a pat on the rear and all at once, the awkwardness was broken, they were back to where they had been most of the trip. "Now. Sails are just big sheets that catch the wind. Anyone can look at them and figure that out. A sail works two ways. Either the wind comes from the side of the boat and goes around them and pulls the boat forward, or the wind comes from the back of the boat and pushes it forward. Easy peasy. You with me so far, rookie?"

Sami stood straight up and saluted. "My eye, captain."

"It's actually, *Aye aye,* captain, but I'll let it slide because you're such a cutie." He peppered her cheek with a kiss, and Sami giggled. She wanted him to explain, but already things were going fast and she wanted to be able to keep up. "We use multiple sails, unlike a yacht which would typically use a Bermuda sloop." Sami's lips moved while she tried to learn all the terms on the fly. "It just means one sail. Don't worry yourself with the details, pollywog." He moved around her like a drill sergeant. "None of this will be on the written exam."

Sami's shoulders slumped with relief. "Thank God. I've never been good at tests."

"Oh," Jet said from behind her in a whisper. "I plan on testing you later on, but it will have nothing to do with boats."

Sami's pussy clenched at the thought of the impending plundering from Jet.

"Turn around," Jet said a moment later.

Sami obliged like a good crew member. "What the heck is that?"

Jet held a harness in his hand. "Safety first." He ran a callused hand down her arm and up to cup her left breast. "I'm not gonna risk losing this overboard." He gave her tit a squeeze before dropping to a knee in front of her. "Leg up." He put a hand on her right calf and lifted her leg, placing it in the harness, then repeated the step on the other side before lifting the front of her shirt up and kissing the front of her underwear.

Sami came up on her tippy toes, steadying herself with a hand on his shoulder. "Good Lord. What was that about?"

Jet came up so he was face to face with her. "Just rewarding myself for being so safety conscious."

"I really wish I had brought another pair of pants with me, or shorts or something."

"I don't." He winked at her.

Jet definitely wasn't a robot or a boring guy, but he was usually Captain Serious and here he was cracking jokes, being playful, showing Sami another side that she'd yet to see. And she was loving it. If this was going to be their last day together, it couldn't have been going better than at the moment.

Jet handed her the end of a rope. "Tie it off." Sami took the rope and started to loop it together. "Nope. I want to see a poacher's knot. Let's see if you've been paying attention."

He left her to secure the other end of the line to the boat. There was no way Jet was going to let anything happen to her, but he felt better about her being secured to the boat just in case something happened.

Sami fussed with the rope, tying it off successfully once, but having to undo it when Jet told her the knot was wrong. "Close, but I said poacher's knot, not a Halyard hitch."

After a few minutes of trying, Sami finally achieved the knot she'd been ordered. Jet tugged on it. "It's probably not the best knot to use." But it had been one of the only ones he'd shown her, so it'd have to do. And besides, he couldn't have her untie it after she'd been so proud of tying it correctly in the first place.

Jet spun her around and kissed the base of her neck, sending a shock wave of shivers down Sami's spine. "You sure these little rewards are for you?"

Jet cupped her breasts from behind and took a long inhale of her essence. "Sure am. Time to unfold the sails."

It all happened so fast. Sami's head spun round and round. Jet showed her how to raise the sails, he showed her where to stand to avoid getting hit by the booms and he taught her new knots to use with the rigging. By the time it was over, she couldn't remember the difference between tacking or jibbing, or whether starboard was the right or left side of the boat, all she knew was that she'd been having the time of her life and she didn't want it to end.

"Now, I wanna learn how to fight," Sami said with a spring in her step after the sails had been raised and Jet had shown her how to chart a course.

Her words brought Jet down off the high he'd been riding with her today. She was alone. She had no family back in the States and with bad people after her, she was going to need to know a lot more than how to throw a punch. But he didn't put voice to his concerns, they were having a blast and her exuberance was infectious, so he took her down into the engine room and strapped her into a set of his boxing gloves.

Sami clapped her gloved hands in front of her face. "These are huge."

Jet stood beside her. "Sixteen ounces. Someone with small hands like you, all it takes is for a punch to land the wrong way and bam, you've got yourself a sprained wrist or worse. Now get your hands up like this." He stood beside her in a boxing stance and showed her how to protect her face. "It's not all about throwing punches, it's about avoiding them or deflecting them." He turned to face Sami and a deadly serious look overtook his face. "Put your hands down for a second." She did as instructed and watched him walk over to the bag. He tapped the underside of the bag. "You see this?" Sami nodded. "Kick it as hard as you can."

"Why?" Sami wanted to know.

"Just do it."

Sami stepped closer to the bag and raised her foot in a hard sweeping motion, catching the bottom with the top of her foot. "Ouch." She laughed. "Poor fella won't be the same after that."

"Do it again."

She did it and then he told her to do it again. "I already know how to kick a guy in the balls. I want to learn how to punch him in the face." She stepped back and threw out a few awkward punches, her hands colliding together as she did. "Stupid big gloves," she said with a giggle.

Jet came out from behind the bag. "Godammit, Sami. If you ever find yourself in a bad spot, you hoof that son of a bitch in the babymakers as hard as you can and get the hell out of there as fast as those little legs will carry you." The thought of someone assaulting her made him see red. "This isn't a game." He knew the danger she was in and when he turned around he unleashed all of his worries into one big left hook that took the eighty pound bag right up and off its chain, crashing to the floor in a puff of dust.

His intensity frightened Sami and she backed away a few steps.

Jet bent and retrieved the bag from the floor. "I'm sorry." He hooked it back onto the chain and patted the dust off.

"You don't have to worry about me, Jet. I might not have family, but I'm a survivor, I've been through a lot. I might be small, but I'm feisty." Sami popped the big warrior on the chin with her gloves and laughed.

Jet smiled. "That all you've got?" Sami brought her right hand up to hit him again and he dodged it with ease. "I thought you were gonna hit me."

"Maybe I should just kick you in the balls and run."

Jet sidestepped another punch and got in behind her. Wrapping one arm around her waist, he lifted her up and dropped her back down quickly. "The power comes from the legs."

"What?"

"Hands up," he spoke from behind her, his hands on both sides of her tiny waist. "The power in a punch. People think it comes from the arms. But it doesn't. It starts in the legs. That's where the power is generated.

You want to turn your whole body into the punch." He moved her hips until she was sideways. "Keep your shoulders over your hips and turn into the punch. Aim for the nose. Anyone at any time can knock someone else out if a punch lands in the right spot, but if you hit someone in the nose, you also take out their eyes because let me tell you from experience, it will make your eyes water like nobody's business. Then you kick him in the balls for good measure and run. Now roll those hips, soldier."

Sami put her hands up and threw a punch at the air, letting Jet's strong hands guide her lower body through the punch. She shadowboxed a few more punches before he moved her closer to the bag. "Take it easy for a few punches. Remember. Your entire body, top and bottom turns through the punch."

She did as she was told, receiving praise with each punch, praise in the form of Jet's hands creeping up her side. Sami fought back the urge to laugh as he tickled her with soft fingertips. "Is it wrong that you hitting a heavy bag is turning me on like crazy?" her trainer whispered in her ear.

Sami pushed her backside into him. "Nothing is wrong about you being turned on."

Jet pushed her forward with the weight of his body, reaching above her head to still the heavy bag. "Hug the bag."

"Yes, sir." Sami wrapped her arms around the bag, pressing her face into the rough, warm leather.

Jet held the bag with one hand and let his other snake down between her legs in the back. Sami came up on her toes and gripped the bag tightly, trying her best to maintain her balance. Jet's finger probed the surface of her underwear but didn't linger for long. He slipped a thick thumb in the side and teased her soft opening.

"Oh, God." Sami sighed in a low register into the hard leather in front of her.

Jet prodded her opening, sliding his finger up over her clit for a quick massage, while his thumb found her backdoor. He swirled his thumb around Sami's ass a few slow times, giving her a sensation she had never felt before.

Jet moved in close to her ear. "If I want it. I'll take it." He drew a long, slow circle around her backdoor and plunged a finger into her hungry pussy. Sami grimaced at the delight of the intrusion, and Jet moved his finger in and out of her hot aching hole while still stimulating her backdoor with pressure.

Sami held onto the bag for dear life. She wanted him to invade her with his big cock, but she was too lost in the feeling of the moment to dare ask him to stop.

He fingered her with long deep strokes. His finger could never match the girth of his thick member and Sami was aching for it. "God, Jet. Please fuck me," she panted.

"Little girl." He pushed his finger deeper inside her. "I plan on fucking your brains out soon enough. But right now you need to be good and cum for me." He twirled his finger inside of her. "Will you do that?"

Sami nodded her head. "Aye, aye, captain." Even if she'd tried to stop from exploding, she couldn't have, the pleasure was too extreme.

Jet rubbed her backdoor and pushed his finger in and out, and Sami blasted off. Her mouth opened and her teeth rubbed across the tough red leather of the punching bag. Her words echoed off the walls of the dank engine room as she bucked and ground her hips down on Jet's powerful hand. He held her in place until he thought she'd regained enough composure to stand on her own. Retracting his finger slowly, Sami gasped and lost her grip on the heavy bag. Jet caught her before she could fall to the floor.

"I want you to go freshen up and meet me in the galley. It's been a long afternoon and I don't know about you, but I'm hungry."

Sami was on Dream Street, eyes still not fully open. "I'll make us dinner once I'm done."

He untied her gloves and pulled them off for her. "I'll whip us up something, you just go get freshened up."

Sami went to the cabin in a haze, unsteady legs carrying her there.

"What kind of cheese do you want on your burger?" Jet asked when he came into the cabin twenty minutes later.

Sami had her duffle bag out on the bed and was going through it. Yet another reminder of their imminent split. "I have to go get my bank records when we land in Cuba tomorrow," she said with a book in her hand. She looked into the mostly empty bag. "And some clothing. I've been wearing your shirts for so long that I forgot I basically have nothing."

She tossed the book down in frustration. This had been such an emotional day for Sami. The ups and downs had been almost unbearable.

"Burgers are on the table. Help yourself."

"We aren't going to eat together?"

"I have to check…the rigging…and some other stuff. I'll join you in a bit." He placed a gentle kiss on her cheek. Jet felt like he was caught between the devil and the deep blue sea, he had to come to terms with himself before he'd know what to do next.

The rigging was fine. The Sirena had been cruising along for hours at a nice comfortable clip. He'd ease back the sheets and bring the boat to anchor for the night in a little bit, but there was no rigging to check, nothing needed to be checked, Jet just needed some time to himself to think.

He stood at the wheel, looking out into the dark night. Beside him on the ledge, Polly rolled over for a belly rub. "I just don't know what to do, girl." Polly reached for his hand when Jet pulled it away. "You are lousy at giving advice, you know."

Sami sat in the galley, eating her burger. Well, eating her burger wasn't really correct. She picked at it, tearing chunks of bread off and nibbling on it. She didn't have an appetite at the moment. It felt like Jet had simply disappeared, gone up top and slipped off the boat and was swimming for shore. Sami felt alone. She fought with herself whether or not to go look for him.

Would it be too forward?

Maybe he was avoiding her because he wanted her gone already?

A million different scenarios ran through her mind and none were positive. Perhaps the best thing to do would be to just go to the guest cabin and finish the trip as it had begun, with her sleeping alone.

Jet spotted her making her way up from the galley. She had a plate in her hand with two hamburgers and a large helping of pasta salad she'd made yesterday.

He took the plate and invited her in. "Thanks." They stood in silence for a moment, Sami looking out over the water, unsure what to say. "Storm's coming in." A bank of clouds off in the distance flashed high up over the water. "Saint Elmo himself if the weather updates are correct."

"I swear, I understand about twenty percent of the things you say."

"There's a super technical term that explains it. It involves the word plasma and fancy scientific stuff." Jet nodded toward the window. "Look."

Sami looked out the big bay window. "What am I looking at?"

Jet was in the doorway. "Come here." He tore a piece of beef off his burger and chewed it down. He didn't realize just how hungry he'd become. Sami joined him at the door. "Look up at the mast."

Sami's eyes followed the tall pole all the way up and what she saw amazed her. "It's glowing."

"Like I said. There's a big fancy scientific explanation for it, but basically it's just electricity in the air reacting with a tall structure. A lot of sailors think it's a bad omen."

"But not you?"

"I like to think it's a good omen, like there's some presence out there watching. Watching over to protect me. He is *Saint* Elmo, after all."

Sami looked on in awe as the top of the pole fluoresced bright blue. "The sea really is a magical place, isn't it?"

"I wish everyone could see the things I've seen."

"You'll never leave it, will you?"

"There'd have to be one hell of a good reason for me to. Any woman who wants to be with me has to accept that the sea is my mistress." He didn't stop to realize he'd never voiced the possibility of a special woman before.

Sami thought about it. She'd gladly accept Jet's love and passion for the ocean if it meant being with him.

"You had a pretty active day." Jet rubbed Sami's left shoulder. "Working on a boat is hard work, isn't it?"

Sami's head rolled forward. His strong but gentle hands on her neck felt good. She wasn't sore from the work, but she wasn't going to tell him that. "I probably need a nice long massage."

The moment seemed perfect. Rubbing Sami's shoulders did wonders to relieve Jet's own stress and when they finally found themselves below deck in his quarters, Sami was eager to return the favor.

"You must be sore from a long day running a ship," she said in a husky voice when he stretched out in the bed beside her.

Jet stretched his hand up over his head with a yawn. "It is hard work."

"Roll over," Sami ordered.

Not what the big guy had had in mind, visions of handjobs were dancing in his head. "Ummm. Okay."

Sami's fingers worked up and down his broad back, tracing the lines of his muscles. Jet twitched every time her light touch passed across his neck.

"Ticklish?"

"Nope. Just touches off every nerve in my body when you hit that spot." Sami carried on with the light touching, running her fingertip over his sensitive spot again and again, trying to draw out a reaction. "We gonna play this game all night, sugar plum?"

She sat up and climbed onto his back, straddling him with her already heated pussy. "Not sure what you mean, sailor."

Sami worked the thick cords of his neck and shoulders, kneading his smooth, firm body. She loved putting her hands on him. Jet sighed at the release of tension, and Sami creamed. She remembered similar noises in her ear when they had been joined together at the waist more than once in the past few days.

288

Unconsciously, she bucked her hips, riding his back without even knowing it.

Jet couldn't have possibly missed the movements she was making or the undeniable heat that sweet little pussy was giving off. "You best keep the movements to a minimum back there."

"Why?"

"Because you're making it tough for a fella to lie on his stomach, sweet thing."

Sami was feeling playful. "And if I don't?"

"Then I'll be rolling myself over and place you right smack-dab down on top of the distress I've got in my shorts right now."

The thought topped off Sami's desire. She placed her hands on his hips and started shimmying his underwear down. Jet took her cue and rolled over, Sami maneuvering herself so she was still on top the entire way.

Jet's cock was fully engorged and it stood at attention. "Lose the clothes," he ordered.

"Yes, sir." Sami pulled the solitary shirt up over her head and sat atop him naked.

"If you aren't just the sweetest, sexiest sight I have ever seen on a ship."

Sami sat and enjoyed the way he drank her in with his eyes. His cock flexed against her backside, smearing her bottom with a drop of pre-cum. The ache to get hold of him was too much to resist and she snaked a hand around her back and gripped it.

"Jesus H. Christ!" Jet groaned when he felt her touch. "Warn a man before you do something like that. If I die out here, you'd be stranded."

Sami rubbed the tip of his proud cock with the palm of her hand. "Oh, I doubt you'd die from it, big fella." And big he was. "God, you feel so good in my hand."

"Don't I know it. Enough with the teasing, baby. You need me to be inside you. Are you wet for me?"

Sami bit her lip and nodded her approval.

"Good." Jet placed his hands on her hips and lifted her easily. "Now put it where it needs to go so I can let you down." Sami positioned his big dick right below her tender opening and the tip of Jet's cock passed over her glistening lips.

"You are wet, aren't you?" Jet said with a smirk. "Rub it. Rub that tasty little clit with my cock."

He held her up, and Sami did as she was told, gripping the stalk of Jet's fat shaft and using the tip of it to massage her clit.

"God," Jet groaned as he watched her. "I can't take it anymore. I need to be inside you."

He lowered her down onto his aching member and Sami's channel quickly devoured him. She let out a low gasp and her entire body tensed as her pussy stretched to accommodate his size. The burn was exquisite as he opened her up, her starving femininity hungry for satisfaction. The invasion sent shock waves through Sami's entire body and Jet began to move her up and down on top of him. "Ride me, Sami. Make me feel good."

Sami's hands came to rest on his hard pecs. She worked herself back and forth, gyrating and pumping her hips as Jet's right hand came off of her hip and found her chest. He rolled her left nipple between his thumb and finger, pulling on it with the right amount of force to illicit pleasure.

"I'm going to cum," Sami confessed when the bliss became too much to ignore.

"Let go, baby. Cum all over my cock."

The sound of his voice lit the fuse inside her and Sami exploded, her gyrations ceasing for only a split second before Jet began moving her back and forth again. There was no time to recover, he kept moving her on top of his thick manhood. Inside Sami felt everything, his cock crashing into her walls as another orgasm washed over her while Jet drove up and into her with such force she thought she'd break into a million pieces.

When she opened her eyes she saw Jet watching her. His gaze blazed back at her with unabashed appreciation.

"Get down here."

He placed a hand around her throat and pulled her face down to his, kissing her with such fervor that Sami's jaw almost came unhinged. They were joined at the mouth and hips and Sami rode him harder, wanting everything he could make her feel. This would be one of their last times together and she wanted to ruin other women for him for the rest of his life. Their thighs rubbed together hard enough to cause a fire and Jet started to come unglued. Sami wanted their lips to part so she could hear him cum, but he held her firm, their lips locked in a dance of eroticism as Jet erupted inside her, the sensation pushing Sami on to another climax.

"I need a drink," Jet said as he gasped to regain his breath.

Sami sprang from the bed and ran naked to the washroom to get him one. "I'll get it." Any little thing she could do for him, she was more than willing to do.

Jet's larger than life frame lay sprawled out on the bed before her when she returned, his muscles still flexed from the exertion. What a sight he was. Sami paused for a moment before getting back in bed to get one last look at the pure definition of male in front of her. This image would have to get her through many lonely nights in the future.

He took a sip of the water offered. "You have worn me out, mermaid."

"I was trying to ruin sex for you," she admitted with a sigh.

Jet laughed and kissed her on the forehead. "I think you may well have succeeded. Now get some rest." He rolled her onto her side and wrapped a strong arm around her waist, engulfing her with his massive frame.

Sami stroked his forearm softly as Jet drifted off. If only she would be so lucky. The sandman wouldn't be visiting Sami tonight, she knew she'd be up all night, enjoying every second she had with Jet.

Because tomorrow, it all came to an end.

* * *

Rolling over, Jet reached for Sami. Patting the empty bed, he drowsily opened his eyes.

Where was she?

He was alone and hard as a rock. With a yawn, he sat up and stretched. Beside him, Polly stretched also, popping the mattress with her sharp claws as she kneaded the soft surface.

"Where's your mama?" Jet mumbled, then his eyes popped wide open when he realized what had come naturally to his lips. Furtively, he looked at the door to see if she'd heard him.

Where in the hell had that come from?

He rose from the bed, went to tend to his morning constitutional and patted his cock with a promise to see to its needs a little later. Once he was out of the shower, he toweled off, dressed, and headed to the wheelhouse to check the autopilot and the AIS system to make sure their course was still safe and clear.

When he was assured all was well, he came out and sniffed…and sniffed. "Pancakes," he smiled, "come on Polly, I think breakfast's ready."

When he made it to the galley, the sight that met his eyes made him smile. Sami was dancing. He'd given her a few T-shirts and she'd cropped a couple so she could tie them under her breasts. She wore this intriguing getup with a simple pair of panties. Jet had never seen a sexier ensemble. There was no music he could hear, but apparently wherever her head was, a band was rocking the house.

Sexy moves, seductive moves, swaying hips and snapping fingers. Even though Jet's stomach was swearing his throat was cut, he wouldn't have traded this moment for all the tea in China. He couldn't hear the beat, but he could feel it. Her lips were moving as she sang under her breath. And when she started playing air guitar, there wasn't a doubt in Jet's mind.

He was in love.

He'd fooled around and fell in love.

Not that he was going to do anything about it.

Yesterday he'd battled the reality of her being alone and defenseless in the world and that idea still bid thinking about, what he was feeling was fleeting like an ocean breeze, blowing one way one day and another way the next. He was sure of it. But as of this moment, he was totally entranced with the woman who had come onto his ship and into his life without permission. To his surprise she had made a place for herself, a place anyone else would have a hard time filling. But what was he going to do about it—hell if he knew.

Patience wasn't his strong suit, but today he had it in spades. He stood, enjoying her complete abandon till she swiveled in his direction and saw him. Her realization of his presence was as enjoyable as her rhythmic display. Her mouth formed a perfect O while her demeanor changed from total wantonness to shy innocence. She blushed a pretty pink and looked at him through those outrageously long lashes. "I didn't know you were up. Pancakes?"

"As many as you'll let me have." He gave her a big grin and sat down at a table already set with a steaming stack of pancakes in the middle flanked by butter and syrup. "I've never eaten this good on my ship before. There's pancakes in the freezer but they've never smelled like this."

"I hope you like them." She fed Polly before joining him. "They're Florence's recipe."

"Who's Florence?" he asked while she poured them both big glasses of milk, the last of it before he restocked fresh supplies in Cuba.

"Florence raised me. More than my parents, we can lay at her feet my personality disorders," Sami joked. "She believed in hard work, fresh air and taking responsibility for your actions."

"Sounds like a female Nemo," Jet said as he spread butter over the golden discs, then poured some of Vermont's best over them till it ran down the sides and puddled in a halo on his plate. Sami looked at the one lone pancake on her plate and the stack of four on his and wondered if she should get up and make some more. "Is that going to be enough to whet your appetite?"

Jet cut a big forkful and eyed it with relish, licking his lips. "I wanted sex, but these pancakes aren't a bad second."

A flash of fire warmed her blood and she felt desire pool between her thighs. "Oh." Sami cut a bite of pancake for herself and gave him a mischievous smile. "When you finish, I'll see what I can do."

After that, Jet enjoyed his breakfast, but he had more than pancakes on his mind. Yet, as much as he looked forward to loving on her, he was just as hungry to learn more about her. "What were you like as a little girl?"

Sami twirled the tines of her fork in the amber liquid, considering what to say. She never imagined she'd have the opportunity to bare her soul to the man whom she'd idolized, who had been the steadfast invisible 'felt presence' in her daily life. Sami had no problem rationalizing that she'd manufactured the ties, it was all in her hopes and dreams. But she'd clung to the idea of him, the power of him, tried to sync into the indomitable resolve by which he lived and draw strength into her own life. "I was a pesky little rascal," she admitted. "My parents worked long hours and we lived west of Houston in the Brazos River bottom. I basically ran wild, not that I was unruly, I was just...busy. Riding horses, swimming in the creek, hiking through the boggy trails and bringing home stray animals." She met his eyes, seeing his reaction. He looked...interested, so she continued. "At one time I think I had four dogs, six cats, a raccoon, a family of skunks, a white rat, and a turtle."

"Who's taking care of the menagerie while you're vacationing in Mexico?" Jet studied her face as he ate, wondering at the look of sadness on her face followed by a smile that he wouldn't describe as fake but more resigned. He knew she hadn't been on vacation in Mexico, he wasn't trying to pick a fight, he just wanted her to open up.

"I've never thought of it exactly like that, but I guess this is a vacation for me." Almost absentmindedly she rubbed the side of her head, the scars from her surgery were covered well, but they were a constant reminder of what she'd been through. "What I described was a long time ago. My dad moved us into the city when I was a teenager, mainly so they'd be nearer to their jobs…we left the animals for the next family except for one cat. I was able to bring Chancy with me, I carried her over my arm like a boneless cat. She went everywhere I did." In other words, the hospital, the outpatient children's center had allowed 'comfort' animals that boosted the patient's morale. "I love cats." Eager to move the subject away from dangerous ground, she asked a question of her own. "Why did you step away from your fighting career to go into the service?"

Jet scraped the last remnants of sticky crumbs off his plate and brought the fork to his mouth, licked it, then set it down. He met her gaze evenly. "I know you're expecting me to give you some cool story about how I was inspired to join up because I had a friend who died or I wanted to fight terrorism, but that would be a lie." Jet drained his milk and shrugged his shoulder. "It was simple, I loved my country and I wanted to follow in my father's footsteps. I decided there was more to fight for than a belt, I wanted to fight for freedom."

A thrill-chill shot through Sami. Jet was a hero, it was as simple as that. "I think that's the best reason of all." Calmly, she stood and cleared the table.

When he started to rise, she placed a hand on his shoulder. "No, stay. Just a little while longer." He wanted her near.

With a wink, she gave Jet a hard-on when she said, "I'll make it worth your while." He leaned back in his chair and watched as she spread a towel on the table, shimmied out of her clothes and draped herself in front of him like the greatest all-you-can-eat meal deal in the history of the world. "Have room for dessert?" she asked coyly as she poured a stream of honey over both breasts and then let it trail down to her smooth mound.

Jet licked his lips. "There's always room for Sami."

His response made her heart thump, wishing what he said was true. She pushed her breasts together, inviting him to take a taste. "What are you waiting for, Champ?"

"My heart to quit pounding." He stood up and placed a hand on either side of her shoulders, looking her up and down. "My God, woman, you have the hottest body I've ever seen in my life."

His approval made her nipples harder. Sami had expected him to go straight for her tits like a typical male. Instead, he began at her mouth, making her quiver with feelings she knew she needed to get a handle on before they consumed her. The kiss started off gentle but quickly got hot enough to melt concrete. So far, Jet wasn't touching her with anything but his lips and he poured more hunger into that kiss than she could have dreamed.

"Wow," she whispered when he finally lifted his head. "You have a very talented tongue."

"Think so?" Jet picked up her hand and placed a lingering kiss in the center of her palm, then brought her thumb to his mouth and nipped the soft pad. "Where would you like me to next demonstrate my prowess?"

"I'm hoping you have a craving for honey."

Sami arched her back, offering the drool-worthy tits, drizzled with honey. With a rumbling growl, Jet bent his head and licked the side of one generous mound, nipping and sucking the succulent flesh, circling the distended tip, avoiding the tempting morsel on purpose.

"You missed a spot, I think," she encouraged, even as he buried his face in her cleavage and began licking up the opposite slope.

"I have a plan," he mumbled against her bounteous flesh, nuzzling and kissing with abandon.

"To drive me crazy?" she panted. "It's working." So excited, she couldn't help it, Sami dipped her own fingers into her vagina and gave her clit a rub.

Her desperate self-pleasure didn't escape Jet's notice. He grabbed her hand and sucked on the tips of her fingers. "Sweeter than honey."

Sami trembled. "Sometimes I think the Jaguar's men caught me and this is heaven."

Jet smiled as he lowered his head to her breast. "I don't think I qualify as any kind of angel." Coming halfway up on the table with her, he muttered, "I need to get closer, I hope this thing is strong enough to hold us both up."

Sami laughed. "Me too, but the fall would be worth it." She was speaking from experience, since she'd fallen completely in love with him.

As he finally took her aching nipple between his lips to suckle, she grasped his head and held it to her, gripping his hair between her fingers. While he ate at her breast, his other hand was delving between her folds, rubbing the honey into her hungry flesh.

"So good," she keened, her body writhing in absolute bliss.

Once Jet was satisfied he'd attended to her breasts sufficiently, he moved lower. "I'm ready for the second course now. Spread your legs."

Sami gripped the sides of the table as he went to the end of it, placing his hands on her inner thighs to make room for his broad shoulders. "Mercy, you're pretty."

He held her open, his thumbs caressing the delicate cleft as he leaned in to stroke her clit with his tongue.

Sami almost came off the table. "Jet!" It felt too good to be still.

"Easy."

With long, slow licks, he stroked his tongue through her sex. The honey mingled with her own sweetness and his determination to go slow and savor went right out the porthole. Clasping her hips with both hands, he lifted her, pushing his stiff tongue up inside of her, spearing as deep as he could, licking the slick quivering walls of her pussy with a rhythmic motion that had her whimpering.

Sami's hand covered his as he endeavored to keep her still. "You are amazing, Jet Foster."

Her eyes rolled into the back of her head as he tongue-fucked her, in and out, then up to twirl around her clit before repeating the erotic process. She tossed her head from side to side, one hand coming up to pull at her own nipple.

Jet was driving her insane!

A fog of pleasure swamped her as that miracle tongue of his dove deep, withdrew, fluttered and licked until her thighs were trembling and she felt an incredible rise of anticipation wind itself up to an almost unendurable tension.

"Jet, please, please, I need you!"

He knew what she wanted, the same thing he had to have. Going to the end of the table, he clasped her behind the knees and pulled her to the edge. "Exactly the right height."

Spreading her legs even farther, Sami grabbed his cock and rubbed it up and down, loving how hard and smooth he was. But instead of guiding him inside of her, she lifted her hips and rubbed the head of his cock directly on her clitoris. "Look at me. I'm swollen, throbbing and all I want is you."

Damn. "You've got me." Coming over her, he picked up Sami's legs, draped them over his arms and drove into her hard, making the table squeak and groan in protest. They were both so aroused, it didn't take but a few hard strokes till he sent her over the edge, her whole world spinning out of control. She dug her fingers into his forearms, her pussy clenching down on his thrusting cock.

Jet groaned, throwing his head back. Sami didn't know which was better—the satisfaction he was making her feel or the gratification of watching him cum. The expression on his face was savage, yet she was unafraid. All of that power, all of that might was intent on giving her pleasure not pain. Afterward, he didn't pull out right away, Jet held her legs and moved in and out slowly, enjoying the last few pulses and aftershocks.

"Best breakfast ever," Sami said with a sigh, knowing that was the last time she'd be with him.

Best damn sailing trip ever, Jet thought—but he kept that revelation to himself.

CHAPTER TWELVE

"So, that's Cuba," Sami said, trying to hide the pain in her voice.

She'd cleaned up herself and the kitchen, then come up on the deck, only to see her first glimpse of land in days—a glimpse she could've gone a lifetime without seeing.

"Yea, it's not my first trip. I've been twice before, once to Guantanamo and once as a crew member on Victor's boat. We go back a long ways." He was taking care of a few housekeeping duties, oiling a winch and swabbing down the deck. "Things will be different this time, though. We can come and go as we please."

"I'm packed," she informed him, flatly. "I guess we're going to Havana? You can drop me off wherever. I'll slip back into my boy clothes when we reach port."

Jet cleared his throat, but didn't look at her. "I spoke to Victor a bit ago on the radio. He's going to be delayed a few hours waiting on a crew member. What do you think about bypassing Havana and dropping anchor off Playa de Jibacoa? The waters are beautiful there. I'll teach you how to snorkel."

A weight lifted from Sami's chest. The gift of a few more hours was welcome. "Sounds good to me. I would love to try."

"Great, I've got gear in storage. It'll be fun."

She helped him finish the deck, making him laugh when she and Polly made a game out of it, the cat scurrying out of the way when Sami would chase her with the mop. When they were near enough to the shore,

Jet dropped anchor and she studied the landscape, amazed that she was actually looking at Cuba.

"I never imagined I'd come here." Of course, she'd done a lot of things in the past few days she'd only dreamed about. Mainly Jet.

The beach was mostly deserted and the sands were white, a beautiful contrast to the blue-green waters and the backdrop of tangled vegetation and mountains in the distance.

"I asked Victor to bring some Cubans for the guys back home. They'll like that. Wait till you see the coral reef." He let down the ladder. "Have you ever snorkeled before?"

Sami shook her head no. Going with him to the storage bin, she took the mask, the snorkel and some fins. As he had been with all things, Jet was patient as he explained how to use it. There were so many things she wanted to ask him, and none of them had a thing to do with what they were about to do. But she smiled and followed his lead, wondering why they had sailed east of Havana, when she'd been expecting him to put her off so she could buy a plane ticket back to Mexico. She knew they would probably have another discussion about where she should or shouldn't be going, but he didn't know the whole story and she wasn't about to ruin their last few hours together by telling him. Sami had no desire for Jet to know about her illness, she didn't want his memory of their time to change or for him to look at her any differently as she told him goodbye.

"Stick close to me." He helped her adjust the mask before they dove over the side.

Once they broke the blue surface, an underwater wonderland awaited. A massive coral reef was laid out like ornamentation in a giant aquarium. At first Sami kept close to Jet, enjoying the fish he pointed out. She recognized some from her many hours of devouring the Discovery Channel—there were blue and yellow angel fish, black and white butterfly fish and a few orange damselfish. After she calmed a little, Sami ventured off, darting forward to check out first this fish and then that one, her excitement making the trips to the top for air something she put off until she was about to pop.

"I love it!" she announced with glee when they surfaced the second time.

"Ready to go in?" he asked, worrying if she was tired.

"Not on your life!"

The next thing he knew, her delectable bottom bobbed in front of him and he had to resist the urge to pinch it. With a smile, he followed her, loving the way she played, the happiness in her eyes. This was a good fish day, they managed to see an octopus, a Caribbean reef squid, a spotted scorpion fish, a porcupine fish, and an indigo hamlet. It was a good thing he stayed close, because a wavy movement in the coral alerted him and he saw a lion fish, a very poisonous specimen lurking in the coral. Grabbing her arm, Jet pulled her in the opposite direction. There was no danger from it unless she touched it—the very thought made him shake. Then when he saw a school of small fish behaving erratically, Jet expected more trouble and he took her by the hand, pulling her upward as a barracuda swam by. There was no use taking chances.

When they broke the surface, Sami gasped. "I'm not finished! Let's do it some more."

"We'll do 'it' some more, but it won't be snorkeling. Get your cute butt up that ladder." He patted her on the ass, loving the entrancing sound of her laughter.

"Thank you, thank you, thank you!" Sami threw her arms around his neck. "I enjoyed that so much!"

Wanting only to please her, Jet decided to move a little farther down the coast to get away from the danger. "Let's try a little deeper, we'll put on a light tank and I'll show you a shipwreck. Would you like that?"

She was ecstatic. "Yes!" Sharing things like this with Jet was amazing. She listened carefully while he taught her basic breathing instructions for the diving gear.

"What are we going to see?" Since she wouldn't be going with him to the San Miguel, this was the next best thing.

"In 1999, a team of divers investigated the waters around parts of Cuba and located over four hundred shipwrecks. This part of the world is a veritable treasure hunter's paradise. The last time I was down here with Victor, we checked some of them out. What I'm about to show you is one we spotted, but we didn't get a chance to look at closely. The likelihood of our finding anything is slim, but you'll enjoy seeing what's exposed above the sea floor."

They didn't move far, maybe a half mile before he dropped anchor and they were in the water once more. This time instead of a coral reef, there was more open water, seaweed and what looked to be timbers sticking up from the sand. Jet held out his hand, and she took it. He was watching her carefully and had leaned close to check the gauges on her breathing apparatus a couple of times. Swimming near, Sami's eyes bugged to realize she was staring at the skeleton of a ship, a ship that had sailed before the United States had become a country.

Jet checked everything out, making sure there were no sharks in the area before turning loose of her hand and letting her swim around. She was a brave little thing. He was surprised to find out how much he enjoyed doing this with her. Never a complaint, she didn't argue with him, followed directions and her enthusiasm was off the charts. Sami was a pure pleasure to be around—and he wasn't the least bit prejudice.

With a camera he had attached to his belt, Jet took a few photos for his files. Moving farther into the wreck site, he became absorbed with what he determined was part of the bow protruding from the sand. When something thumped him on the back, Jet jerked, whirling around, halfway expecting to face off a shark. Instead, he found Sami, gesturing wildly for him to follow her.

What had she found?

He swam alongside her, down the length of the wreck to a clump of rocks. When she moved to the bottom, tugging on something half buried, he came closer to investigate. Jet helped her brush aside some sand and what he saw amazed him—it was a Madonna, a statue of the Virgin Mary cast in what he assumed to be solid gold. Holy f—even thinking the word seemed sacrilegious at the moment. But Christ! He tugged at the piece. It had to be almost five foot tall and weigh over a hundred pounds. Giving her a nod, Jet gave a mighty tug and brought it out into view. Then, he pointed upward and followed Sami to the surface.

"We'll have to hook it to the winch, it's too heavy for me to bring to the surface."

"I'll help," Sami announced as she climbed the ladder. "Stay there, I'll hand you the rope."

As she ran to fetch the hook and line, Jet's heart was pounding so hard he thought it would burst from his chest. When she returned and jumped back in with him, she kissed him soundly. "Is this good? Will it help you?"

"Baby, you found a true treasure. We'll have to report it, of course, but this could make you a very rich woman." He dove back down and worked until he slipped a rope underneath the Madonna's outstretched arms and secured it with a knot. Swimming to the boat, he let Sami go up the ladder first, then together they turned the crank until the statue broke the waves. "Hold on, I'll pull it right up." Jet worked under Sami's smiling supervision and soon he had two ladies on board, Sami and the Madonna.

Kneeling next to him on the deck, Sami reverently touched the figure. "This is crazy."

"It'll be fun researching to see what we can find out about her."

"Yea, I can't wait." Sami looked up at him. "I don't want any money, I have everything I need. Whatever you get for it, you and Nemo keep it."

Jet didn't understand. "You found it."

Sami settled by him, her legs crossed beneath her. "You all but pointed me toward it, this is your site. I'm just glad you shared the experience with me."

Shaking his head, Jet was about to argue when he heard the radio. "Hold on, I'll be back." Grabbing a towel, he headed to the wheelhouse. "This is the Sirena," he answered the call.

"Amigo, this is Victor, where are you?"

Jet gave him the coordinates. "Rendezvous with me and we'll head into Havana and grab something to eat. I have a couple of errands to take care of."

"Will do. Be there shortly."

When he turned around, Sami was behind him.

Her eyes looked sad. "I think I'll go clean up, get ready to go."

Before he could answer, she was down the stairs, out of sight with tears streaming down her face. The time had come.

Sami didn't linger long in the shower. In less than ten minutes, she had on jeans and the original plain blue T-shirt she'd worn the night she'd run from Olmos. Wanting to look halfway decent, she put on the compression bra, mainly because it was the only one she had with her. Checking around, she made sure there was nothing of her left behind. Her computer was dead, due to the fact she didn't have a charger. But the drive with Marisol's information was safe in a corner zipped pocket. Other than that, she had no possessions to gather. Polly stood by, meowing plaintively, and Sami stooped to pick her up, kissing her dear black face and squeezing her so tightly she protested.

"I'll miss you so much." But she'd miss Polly's master much more.

Sami's heart was breaking, but she wouldn't let on. She had no intention of making Jet sorry she had spent this time with him.

Slowly, she moved back down the hall, stopping to gaze into Jet's quarters where she'd spent so much time in his arms. Next came the galley where they'd shared their meals and that last session of lovemaking. A swell of panic crashed over her.

How was she going to go on?

Running a hand over her scars, she wondered if she would live.

Did she even want to?

Shaking her head, she dispelled that thought. She was strong, she'd survive. But there was one thing for certain.

She'd never love anyone else but Jet Foster.

And she'd never, ever forget.

* * *

Jet stood on the deck of his Sirena and watched Victor's salvage boat, the Cazador, draw near. Painted dark blue and white, the forty-two foot custom hull with four diesel engines was equipped from stem to stern with everything a treasure hunter could conceive to need.

"Ahoy, mate!" Victor shouted over the waves.

He had a pair of binoculars and was looking right at Jet. Two crewmen were walking on deck behind him. One of them was Rafael, the first mate Jet had met at the Pirate's Lair. Jet raised a hand in greeting to his friend as Sami walked up beside him.

"I'm ready," she announced. "Before I leave, I want to tell you what these last few days have meant to me. You have been so kind and I won't ever forget—"

Jet held up his hand, halting her flow of words. Turning to her, he cleared his throat. "Sami…"

As he began, a shout was heard from the Cazador, drawing Jet's attention. To his disbelief, a shot rang out and Victor crumpled to the deck. Then another sounded out and wood splintered behind Jet. A bullet had torn through the wall behind them.

Instinctively, Jet grabbed Sami and he turned, shielding her with his body, pulling her toward a safe spot in the middle of the boat. "Get down." He pushed Sami to the deck as easily as he could. She tumbled with his shove, taking the impact with her palms mostly, but also bouncing her knees off the hard wood. Jet was crouched behind a piling near the galley. "I'm sorry, Sami." He reached a big hand out to her, but withdrew it when another crack in the air preceded more splintering of wood above his head. "Stay down." Jet looked up and over the piling and saw the Cazador barreling down on them, drawing closer and at a high rate of speed. "Fuck! Hang on!"

Sami gripped a coil of rope in front of her as hard as she could. The impact came a few seconds later. The Sirena lurched backward but stood her ground, taking the full force of the on charging Cazador. Jet lost his grip on the rigging he'd been clinging to and tumbled backward, rolling twice on the smooth deck before grabbing hold of a rail and pulling himself up. He popped up to take a look. Rafael was standing at the wheel of the Cazador. He gave Jet an evil smirk and waved a hand at him that now held a pistol.

"Son-of-a-bitch," Jet mumbled under his breath. He turned to Sami. "Get below."

"What's going on?" she cried. Another shot rang out. She didn't want to leave him.

"Mutiny!" He pushed her toward the stairs. "Go!" Sami ducked back into the cabin below. "There's a pistol under the bed. If anyone besides me comes through that door, you shoot first, ask questions later." He kissed her on the lips briskly and pulled the door shut. "Lock it and don't come out," he said through the door.

Jet wanted more than anything to go in and be with her, but he wanted her locked away and armed in case things went south.

Jet moved up and across the deck. He caught the sight of a pair of dark hands and a rope being tied to the starboard rail of the Sirena up near the bow. A gunshot rang out like a bell, punching a hole in the wood five feet in front of Jet.

When he turned, he saw Rafael standing on the roof of the Cazador's wheelhouse. In his hands was a rifle with a scope on it. "Permission to come aboard, Captain?" he asked with a laugh.

Jet scowled at the man. A traitor. He didn't need to see Victor to know he was most likely dead. Who Rafael was, Jet didn't know but the man had made it onto his shit list, and Jet intended to make him pay. Rafael's hubris was just the opening Jet needed to make his move to the wheelhouse. He flew up the steps and into the relative safety of the familiar spot. Under the steering wheel there was a loose panel. Jet gave it a quick yank and it came off with a pop. In a steel box he'd stored a nine millimeter and a hunting knife for emergencies. He strapped the knife to his calf and checked the chamber of the nine.

"No use sitting here waiting for them," he muttered to himself and crouched near the exit of the wheelhouse, peeking around the corner.

Two men had come aboard, both wearing red shirts with a black logo on the left breast. Jet didn't know what it said, or who they were. All he knew was that they were the enemy and if they were here to harm him, they would harm Sami too. He weighed his options quickly. Going back the way he came would get him back to Sami the fastest, but there were two unknown men on board with him now, it wouldn't be hard for them to cut him off before he got to her. Micah had joked about adding trapdoors to the Sirena while it was under construction, but Jet wished he would've taken him seriously right now. "You finally say something worth listening to, Wolfe," Jet mumbled to himself, "and I don't listen."

He popped out of his crouch and laid a row of fire on the two men in the red shirts. The first two bullets missed, but when the man on the left fell to the deck, Jet knew he'd made contact with the third and hopefully fourth shots. "One down, Rafael!" he shouted out the open door.

A rattle of fire volleyed in the air after his words and the bay window at the front of the wheelhouse smashed into a million pieces, raining down behind Jet. "I don't need help to take you, Foster!" Rafael called back. "I'll have you and your little cabin-boy lover. I know who she is. Olmos followed her and my sister identified her. Who knows? I might even make her put the boy clothes back on and enjoy her for a bit before I slit her throat."

He'd heard it all before, the taunts, the threats. Rafael was trying to draw Jet out by threatening Sami. But this wasn't Jet's first fight, he wasn't going to get drawn into doing something foolish and leaving both he and Sami exposed. "Why don't you put down the gun, Rafael? Tell your guys to back off. Be a man, face me one on one. Just think of the story you could tell when you got back. You killed the legendary Jet Foster with your bare hands. I'll even let you have the first shot."

Jet heard the squeak of a shoe on the deck below the steps. The other red shirt was close by.

Rafael got a hardy chuckle from Jet's words. "I like your offer, Foster. Almost as much as I like the fact that I know what you're after and where to go to find it. This is going to be a very profitable venture. Telling people I killed the great Jet Foster will just be an added bonus."

"I don't know you that well, Rafael, but any man who would turn on his captain and friend like you did, has got to be one hell of a lying, conniving dog. So I wouldn't put anything past you."

"Flattery will not save your life, Foster. Maybe I'll cut one of those pretty tattoos from your body and hang it on my wall. I'll tell everyone who comes to see it that I ripped it off you with my own fingers."

The red shirt below stepped on a piece of glass and Jet knew he was on the steps now, not far away at all.

"You know, Foster." Rafael's voice was closer. He must be up on the boat by now. "I think I'll use the money I get for selling your ship to buy my own. A luxury yacht. Maybe I'll take your tattoo off my wall and use it as my flag. My own kind of Jolly Roger."

Jet wanted to respond, but he'd moved to the back of the wheelhouse and slipped out a window. Not wanting to give away his position, he stayed silent.

Rafael stalked down the stairs. He had a pistol in his hand, but he tucked it at the small of his back behind his belt and took a filet knife out of a leather sheath before dropping it. The knife had rust on it near the handle, but was sharp enough to filet a tuna with no problem. He banged the handle against the door.

Inside, the noise frightened Sami. "Jet?" She gripped the pistol with both hands, ready to fire.

"Oh, yes. It's me, my love." Rafael mocked her from the other side of the door. "The bad man has gone away. Come out and give me a kiss."

Sami fired a round, but the gun moved in her hand and the bullet missed well wide of the door. With a squeal, she dropped it, covering her ears, the echo in the cabin deafening.

Rafael recoiled from the door. Now he knew she had a gun. Thrusting his body into the door once, it rattled on the hinges.

Sami's head was still ringing, a familiar sensation, but one she didn't welcome with nostalgic fervor. Rafael slammed into the wood again and the hinges buckled a bit. Three more slams and the door nearly popped off its hinges.

Slumping to the ground, her head pounding, she couldn't think straight. Sami knew the gun was there somewhere close by, but she couldn't focus enough to even think about looking for it. One last slam took the bottom hinge right off the frame and he pushed the door aside and stepped in. "Honey! I'm home."

His words sounded peculiar with his Spanish accent, but accompanied by his evil laugh, they were terrifying. "Come here, bitch." He snatched her from the floor by the arm and yanked her to her feet. "Look at me." He slapped her across the face when she looked at the floor and pulled her hair when she again refused to look up at him. "I just want you to know it was my sister who told us who you were. You thought you were so smart, disguising yourself as a boy. It didn't work! She came to me with her suspicions and we've been watching you ever since." He drew the tip of the knife up her arm, leaving an angry red trail in its path. "Before we're done, you will tell me everything. You'll tell me who your sources are. You'll tell me where the information is hidden. All of it. If you don't, I'll kill the big American and burn his ship to ashes."

Hurt Jet? "No!" she screamed. "Who is your sister? Someone at the bar?"

"That's none of your damn business!" Rafael slapped her again. "Don't speak unless I tell you to or I'll slit your throat where you stand!"

Sami pressed her lips together, but steeled her resolve. She wouldn't give this piece of garbage the satisfaction of seeing her fear. He pushed her out the door with the knife in her back. "Move, bitch."

Sami went willingly. Where was Jet?
Please God, let him be okay.

Rafael placed the knife to her throat from behind. "It was foolish to think you could escape the Jaguar." He stopped them only two steps out of the cabin. "I'll be taking your head back with me as proof to him."

Rafael's grip loosened suddenly and both arms dropped. A moment later he slumped to the ground behind Sami. The sound of his knife hitting the steps on its way down sounded odd compared to his body thudding on them as it slipped back in through the cabin door.

Sami spun around to see what had happened and saw Jet lying on the roof of the cabin. He was smeared with blood all down his left arm and the front of his face. "Not on my watch, asshole," he said with a snarl.

Rafael lay dead on the floor, a knife implanted in the top of his head to the hilt. Jet had gotten the drop on the other henchman, ambushing him as he crawled through the same window in the wheelhouse Jet had just slipped out from. He'd wrapped a length of cord around his hands and choked the man down in less than a minute. Unfortunately, he'd lost his nine millimeter overboard in the struggle. Rafael had either been foolish or sloppy enough to have just assumed his henchmen would do away with Jet and that was just what Jet was counting on when he eased around in silence and waited on the roof of the cabin for them to emerge.

It'd been heart-wrenching to listen to the way Rafael spoke to Sami, to hear the slap of his palm on her soft cheek and to listen while he threatened her. But he knew rushing in there would only put her in more danger, so he waited and when Rafael came within striking distance, he planted the tip of his blade as deep into Rafael's brain as he could. Death was instant and Sami was free.

"Jet!" Thank God! She rushed into his arms and hugged him tightly. "I'm so glad you're safe!"

He kissed her on the head, trying to step away an inch or two. "Careful. I'm covered in blood."

Sami didn't care. He'd saved her life and a bit of blood wasn't going to stop her from feeling the safety of being in his arms. She sobbed into his chest as Jet looked over the top of her head. Rafael's eyes were still open, he'd have to go in there and close them before Sami saw, but right now they needed to go check on Victor.

"I don't know what they did with Victor," Jet said. "I have to go check on him. I'd say stay here, but I doubt you'd do that. Would you?"

Sami pulled back and shook her head. "I'm coming with you."

Jet chuckled and led her to the bow of the boat where the Sirena and Cazador were tied together. They had to step over the first man Jet had shot. He stopped to quickly make sure the individual was dead and posed no threat to them. "Let me go first."

Sami balked, but she knew there was still uncertainty on the Cazador, it was best that Jet go check it out first.

Climbing down the line, Jet moved across the deck with caution. If there was anyone else on board, he needed to see them before they saw him. Sami followed him and clung to his side as he moved. He was so big he blocked her view as they proceeded. All she could do was stay tight against his back.

Jet went to secure the wheelhouse first, then circled the deck. There was nobody up top and they followed a trail of blood down the stairs of the Cazador and into the galley where they found Victor sprawled out on the floor, blood coming from a wound on his head.

Jet rushed to him. "Victor. Wake up."

The pool of blood beside his head didn't look good but when Jet rolled him over to check the wound, Victor groaned and they knew he was still alive.

His eyes opened a moment later. "Son-of-a-bitch shot me."

There was a graze on the right side of Victor's temple where Rafael had attempted to execute him, but the bullet must have ricocheted off his skull and bounced off without doing any real damage.

Sami rushed to the cupboards in the galley. "What are you doing?" Jet asked.

She rummaged through one cupboard, pulling boxes of cereal and bag of potato chips out in the process before finding what she was looking for. "First aid kit," she said triumphantly as she returned to Victor and started unwrapping the gauze she found in the white tin box.

Sami bandaged the wound on Victor's head and Jet lifted him to his feet. "We've got to get him into Havana to a hospital." The Cazador had rammed into the Sirena but unfortunately for her, the Cazador had taken more damage. Jet had been right, the Sirena was one hell of a sturdy vessel. "We have to get him on board the Sirena."

"What about his boat?" Sami asked as they helped Victor over to the rope that attached the two ships.

"We'll leave it here for now. I'll call the Cuban coast guard and let them know what's happened. They'll send someone out to get it. Victor's more important. It looks like he got lucky, but we have no idea if he has a concussion or not." As soon as Victor was comfortably situated in one of the cabins, Jet fired up the Sirena and headed for Havana full steam ahead. He didn't know the full extent of Victor's injuries or who else might be on their trail.

* * *

Havana turned out to be completely different than Sami expected. She'd seen pictures of the harbor before, but they hadn't done it justice. A narrow inlet leading into the bay opened up into a wider body of water where three natural ports dominated the landscape. The city clung to the shoreline, some of it more modern than others. Old Havana was one place she'd always longed to visit with its colonial architecture and rich history.

Getting Victor to a doctor had been priority, so they'd wasted no time entering the harbor and docking. Jet had called ahead to the port authority to report the incident and the deaths. An ambulance was waiting for them, which took Victor on to the emergency room, but Jet had been detained answering questions. Fortunately, Cuban officials were able to communicate with the Mexican consulate and verify Jet's story that Rafael and his friend had drug cartel ties. Victor would also have to make a statement, but his treatment came first.

The whole ordeal proved harrowing for Sami. When she'd been separated from Jet, she'd felt like her arm had been cut off, a feeling she was going to have to get over. They'd spent the night at the hospital, so there'd been no time for sight-seeing or anything else. Taking care of Jet's friend was priority. After that…it would be time for her to leave.

"Will he be okay?" Sami hovered behind Jet at the nurse's station.

The doctor had briefed Jet, but she hadn't been able to hear over the din of noise surrounding her. Apparently there had been a wreck involving a school bus and distraught parents were everywhere.

"Yea." Jet took her by the arm and led her outside. "The bullet just grazed his temple. Head wounds produce a lot of blood, but the damage was minimal. He's going to call in a different crew, two guys he can

I already have." Taking a deep breath, she announced, "I'll go to Houston."

Around them life was going on, traffic passed, people walked around them on the sidewalk. Horns blew. A slight wind off the harbor ruffled her hair.

Jet felt his control slipping through his fingers. "You're just telling me what I want to hear."

A tender warm feeling bubbled up in Sami's chest—he was worried and he was pouting. His lips were even pooched out a bit.

Impulsively, she got up on her tiptoes and kissed him. "No, I promise. I'll wait to go to Veracruz another time. There's a phone call I can make that will tell me what I need to know…at least for a while. I'll go to Mari and work things out from there. We'll decide what needs to be done as far as the cartel goes. I'm sure your friend Destry will have some recommendations." After the kiss, he hadn't moved a muscle or said a word. Sami took that as agreement. "See, I'll be safe and you can go on with your life, it will be like I never stowed away, like I was never there."

He huffed and grumbled, took her by the hand and continued on down the street. "No," Jet stated flatly—one word and that was that.

Sami was having a hard time keeping up, her legs were shorter than his and he was moving fast. "No?" What did that mean? "Where are we going?"

Jet lifted a hand, hailing a cab. "Like I said, we're going to hunt you some clothes and then we're going back to the Sirena and head for Florida."

"But…but…" Sami stuttered. Her bag fell off her shoulder and she almost lost it as Jet guided her to the curb to enter the small red taxi waiting for them. "Why?" she asked, the only word she managed to get out before he had her in the seat and was giving directions to the driver.

Once the taxi had pulled into traffic, he took her hand, folding it between his much larger ones. "Don't ask me a question I can't answer." He looked out the window away from her, as if he was afraid for her to see his face. "I have a bad feeling, like I can't let you go. It might be some damn omen or it could be indigestion, but I can't ignore it."

Sami felt his thumb move across the top of her hand, a petting motion. "Are you sure?" She hesitated to show him how she really felt, it would probably scare the bejesus out of him if she threw her arms around his neck and began peppering kisses profusely across his face. Instead, she sat very still beside him, almost afraid to move. "I mean, this time you'd be bringing a woman on board...willingly."

Jet chuckled. "Don't remind me." Then he picked up her hand and kissed it. "I'm not saying it makes sense, but I need you on this trip. You've turned out to be my lucky charm."

* * *

Once they were back on board, the first thing Sami did was clean the deck with bleach. Eradicating the evidence of blood where Rafael and the other man died was necessary before she could relax. She'd seen several people die at the cancer ward and the man Olmos shot right in front of her, but the violence of the attack and the viciousness of how they'd come at her and Jet made these deaths even more horrific.

"Here, let me do that." Jet came and took the mop from her.

Sami was very self-conscious. She didn't know if their relationship had changed or if they'd pick back up where they'd left off—sexually speaking. She smiled. Her own thought process amused her. Polly was glad to see her, and Sami was glad to see the cat, picking her up and toting her around like a fashion accessory.

Jet carried the assortment of clothes he'd bought for her to the cabin where he'd first found her. "Store these in that closet, you'll have more room." He hadn't given her a chance to go by the bank so she was further in debt to him.

"Thank you, this was all unnecessary. I'll pay you back."

He ignored her protest, copped a feel of her ass as he walked by, and instructed, "Put on that blue bikini and we'll call it even."

She couldn't help but giggle. Well, she guessed that answered one of her questions. "Okay, it will be nice to look like a girl again."

Jet had been about to go through the door. Instead, he turned, raking his eyes from her head to her toes. "You're completely feminine, one hundred percent woman, and I must've been out in the sun too long when I was stupid enough to think otherwise." Pulling her close, he kissed her tenderly. "I'm glad you're here." The embrace was brief, but it served to erase many of Sami's insecurities.

"I'll go put something on to cook."

"Good." He tweaked her on the nose. "I've got some phone calls to make. I need to tell Nemo we're on the way and check on him."

"Okay," she agreed, relieved they could step back into their routine so easily.

He smiled, moving away, still holding her hand, only letting it go when their reach wouldn't sustain the contact. When he'd disappeared around the door, Sami grasped her heart and spun around. She didn't really understand what was happening, but she'd be a fool not to enjoy it while she could.

After he'd patched the hull, a job that proved to be smaller than he'd feared, Jet checked out the engine and all of the controls, finally deeming them seaworthy. He navigated the harbor and was back out in the open sea, heading northeast. He took out the satellite phone to get in touch with everyone so they'd be aware of the Sirena's progress.

First call was to Tyson. He wanted to know the real scoop on his father. "Hey, buddy. How's it going?" he asked, a smile on his face.

"I want a raise, your father is a crazy man," Tyson answered flatly.

"Well, if I were paying you anything, I would. But double nothing is nothing." Jet knew Tyson was joshing.

"Truthfully, he's good. The doctor has cleared him to go on the salvage trip, but only if he stays on board, lifts nothing heavy, and sticks to the diet."

In the background, Jet could hear Nemo grumbling about 'fool doctors.' "Sounds good, let me talk to the old reprobate."

"Sure thing."

There were a few mumbles as the phone was passed from one hand to another.

"Hey, Son."

"Hey, Dad." Jet breathed easy, hearing his father's voice. "How do you feel?"

"Wonderful. Where are you?" Right to the point.

"Coming off the coast of Cuba. I'm heading straight for Key West to restock and then I'll head up the coast. I should meet up with you in three days max."

"Good, we have everything ready. That friend of yours is coming along. I'm teaching him the ropes. At first he was about as useful as tits on a boar hog, but he's learning."

Jet laughed. "Tyson's about three times as smart as I am, he's a genius, I'm sure he can handle anything you throw at him."

"Yea, as long as it isn't very heavy." Nemo continued to give Tyson a hard time, who was grumbling in the background.

"I'm glad you'll be joining me, I didn't want to do this alone." Jet turned serious.

Nemo laughed. "I doubt very seriously if you could do it without me. I'm the brains of the business."

Jet smiled. "Absolutely, Pop. We'll be all set when we see you. I have a really good feeling about this, I think the San Miguel is ours."

"What's this 'we' business, are you talking about that damn cat of yours or has Claude come out of hiding?"

Bowing his head, looking at the floor, Jet weighed his words. Might as well tell him now, he didn't want to give the old man another heart attack when he saw Sami on board. "Well, to put it bluntly. I have a woman on board. I picked up a stowaway in Veracruz."

"No, shit. And you're still afloat? Why didn't you get rid of the bitch in Cuba?"

Jet's hackles rose. "Don't call her that, Pop. Her name is Sami. You'll like her."

There was silence on the other end of the line. "So, it's like that, is it?"

Jet didn't know what 'that' was, but he wasn't going to debate semantics now. "Look, I need to call Micah. I'll see you in a few days' time. Take care."

Before his father could ask any more questions Jet couldn't answer, he rang off.

The next call didn't prove any easier.

"Micah, how are you?"

"Good. Where are you?"

"A few miles north of Havana, Florida bound."

"Where will you be docking?" Micah asked.

"Key West, Stock Island, I want to take Sami to see the cats at the Hemingway house, she'll like that."

"Whoa," Micah said. "Start over. Sami's still with you? I thought you were putting her off in Cuba. What happened?"

Jet pressed his lips together. "I changed my mind." He knew he didn't owe Micah an explanation and he wasn't certain the one he'd give him would make sense, but he'd try. "We were attacked. Victor's first mate shot him, rammed us and boarded the Sirena intent on killing Sami and stealing my map."

"Shit, are you all right? Is Victor dead?"

"Victor will be fine, he was lucky. Rafael and his friends are dead, and I decided to keep Sami with me until things settle down."

Micah didn't say anything for a long time.

"What is it?" Jet asked. He knew his friend well.

"The cartel doesn't settle down, Jet, you know that. What Sami and her friend are involved in is long-reaching. The Jaguar is not going to forget. There's not really going to be a safe place for those two."

"We'll have to protect them, see this shit through." Jet saw no other choice. "After all, we're the fuckin' Equalizers, it's what we do."

"Okay," Micah said.

Jet could hear the resignation in his voice.

"We'll do it your way, Champ." Then he blew out a long breath. "Ask Sami what she was doing in Veracruz."

"What do you mean?" Jet didn't understand. "She was in Veracruz for Marisol. I know why she was there."

"There's another reason," Micah declared. "Ask her."

"What do you know and how do you know it?"

"Look, I've got to go. Some of us will meet you in Key West sometime tomorrow. I'm not totally sure on the details yet. I'm about to call Kyle, we'll take his plane. Keep your eyes open. Your trouble isn't over by a long shot."

"I'll be okay," Jet said, his mind already mulling what Micah could have meant about Sami having another reason to be in Veracruz.

"Sounds like you need an army backing you. I might call Isaac and see if he or any of the McCoys want to join me."

"Whatever," Jet threw out, anxious to get off the phone. He hated when Micah was cryptic.

Why did everything have to be so goddamn complicated?

Jet made two more calls to equipment rental places and the guy where they bought fuel to fill up the tanks at their base marina just up from St. Augustine. All the time he was thinking, wondering what Micah knew that he didn't. When he heard Sami call his name, he was all set to get to the bottom of things. But when he entered the galley and saw her face, all thoughts of confrontation vanished.

She was crying.

"What's wrong?" She'd done as he asked, wearing the turquoise bikini with a filmy shirt thrown over it, the effect failing as a cover-up. To him, she looked like a confection, or a gift all wrapped up waiting for him tear off the pretty trappings.

Sami wiped her eyes. "Oh, I didn't think you'd come so quick."

Jet never hesitated. He sat down and pulled her into his lap. "Talk. Are you hurt?"

"No." She shook her head, but his kind eyes were her undoing. Throwing her arms around his neck, she buried her face against him. "I'm sorry."

Tightening his arms around her, he asked, "What in the hell are you sorry for?"

"All of this is my fault."

She started sobbing against him, and Jet didn't know what to do. "What's your fault, did you burn the bacon again?"

"No, we're having stew." She dragged the last word out as if in despair.

He patted her back. "Oh, that's horrible, just horrible." The mystery of a woman's mind would forever elude him.

"It's not the stew, it's everything else." She wiped her face with his shirt.

"Don't you get any Sami buggers on me," he cautioned, and she giggled.

"Snot what I'm doing."

Jet groaned. "Funny."

Sitting up, she sniffed. "If I hadn't stowed away with you, you wouldn't have been attacked and Victor wouldn't have been shot and you wouldn't be in danger." Sami touched his beloved face, running her fingers over the scruff of his beard. "I should have stayed in Havana."

"No," Jet disagreed a thousand percent. "You're right where you need to be. With me. I can damn well take care of myself and you."

"I know." She ran her thumb over his cheekbone as she caressed his face. "But you shouldn't have to. When we get to Key West, I'm going to Houston."

No way. Jet didn't feel like arguing. "Let's cross that bridge when we come to it." He looked at the stew pot. "Smells good." He thought about just skipping the meal and taking her to bed, but they were only a few hours out of Cuba and he wanted to keep an eye out in case Rafael had given information on their course to anyone else. "Let's dish up a bowl and go eat on the deck. You'll feel better after you've had a little sun."

"Okay." She stood and went to the cabinet, taking down three bowls, not forgetting to give Polly a small portion. Following Jet topside, they went to the wide expanse outside the wheelhouse on the starboard side. Sitting down together, they stared out at the blue ocean. "Can you believe people have tried to cover this distance on a life raft?"

Jet nodded. "There have even been a few who swam it, or died trying." He pointed overboard. "Look, what do you see?"

Sami went to her knees and gazed out at the water. At first she didn't see anything, then a fin broke the water—a huge, pale, grayish white fin. "A great white," she breathed in an amazed voice. "Isn't that a great white?" she asked to be sure.

"Yes, it is." Jet came closer to watch the majestic animal with her. "He's hoping we'll give him some scraps."

"Or fall overboard." Sami shivered. "I'll be showering in your bathroom tonight."

"I just hate it isn't big enough for two," Jet stated, for the first time wishing he had a house or an apartment to take her to. Living off on a boat had some drawbacks.

They watched the shark until it grew bored and swam away. "So, how close are we?"

Jet checked his watch. "Since we're using the motor as well as the sails, I'd say we're only a couple of hours out."

"Is that all?" She relaxed back on the deck. "I should have brought some sunscreen."

Jet gazed at her long legs, flat stomach, and the mounds of creamy flesh spilling from her bikini top. "You're turning a beautiful shade of gold. But it would be a damn shame if you burned." Rising, he went below, quickly returning with a good sized tube. "Lose the shirt."

Sami smiled. Soon, his hands would be on her and there was nothing better under the sun. "I get to do you next."

"I don't burn," Jet admitted, then he realized what he was saying. Was he a fool? "But it's best to be on the safe side."

They were sitting on a soft mat, so all Sami had to do was flip over and Jet licked his lips. "You have an epic ass, Sami Jo."

Sami smiled, folding her arms and laying her head down on them. "Sorta like your cock, huh?"

Since she'd never come out and said anything about his manhood, Jet decided to pursue the topic. "Do you like how I'm built? I think I've lost about five pounds on this trip."

Sami snorted. "I think it made its way to your cock. Of course, I remember the day that I showed your photo to Marisol, right before she came down for her mother's funeral. She said you ought to be in those barbarian movies." With a sigh, she finalized her critique. "You're perfect in every way." Then she chuckled. "Especially that cock of yours. You have no idea how perfect it feels sliding into me."

No, but Jet knew how it felt to go from flaccid to erect in no time flat. He eased down, the cotton drawstring pants a godsend. At least he wouldn't be strangled to death. Facing her, on his knees, he squeezed some lotion into his palm. "Maybe you'd better measure it to know for sure."

"You fill me up perfectly, that's all I need to know." She shivered in anticipation of what they were about to do.

"Tell me how it feels when I fuck you," he almost growled, rubbing his hands together to warm the lotion.

Sami could feel herself grow wet, her clit was beginning to ache. She fidgeted a little, her hips wiggling as she tried to squeeze her thighs together. "Uh, it feels so good. You stretch me perfectly. The burn is exquisite. Like the other night when you woke me up making love to me?"

"Yea?" Jet couldn't decide what to rub first, it all looked inviting. He was too busy listening to her voice. When she held up a foot and waved it around, he caught it. As good of a place to start as any. "I remember."

"Well, when we went to bed and you wanted to go right to sleep, I wanted you so much I couldn't stand it," she confessed softly. "I just shook with wanting you. I felt so empty and my breasts needed to be touched and sucked. My skin craved you and my pussy was so hungry, I'd like to have never gone to sleep. That's why I dreamed the way I did."

Jet threw the tube across the deck. With one hand he tore his cock from his pants and with the other he skimmed down her bottom. "On all fours. Now."

He took Sami by surprise, but she quickly caught up. "Now?"

"You think you can talk like that and there'll be no repercussions?"

Sami gasped as she felt his big warm body cover hers, his cock pushing into her from behind. "God, yes." She sighed, her arms shaking as she tried to hold up her weight midst the excitement. His invasion felt just as good as she'd described and with a few quick hard strokes, they both collapsed, satisfied.

Jet pulled her close. "Don't you ever lie in my bed and want me without telling me. No woman of mine will ever go to sleep unsatisfied. Do you hear me?"

"Yea." She heard. What she heard was 'woman of mine' and those were the sweetest words of all.

CHAPTER THIRTEEN

Before they knew it, the Sirena was pulling into Stock Island Marina. They had arrived in Key West—home of palm trees, Ernest Hemingway, and Tennessee Williams.

"This is gorgeous," Sami exclaimed, marveling at the sunny, tropical paradise.

To celebrate the occasion, she'd dressed up, her first feminine frilly garment to wear in front of Jet. A sundress made of gauzy yellow cotton, Jet thought she looked like a butterfly. "Let me get these things loaded onboard, and then I'm taking you somewhere. It's a secret."

"I love secrets," she admitted unabashedly.

Sami pitched in and together they filled the larder for the remainder of the trip. As Jet had ordered, the supplier had dropped crates of supplies off at the dock.

"You're good help," he praised her, winning a big smile as a prize.

"Thanks, now what's my surprise?"

With a chuckle, Jet took her hand. "Come on, have you ever ridden a motorcycle?"

"No!" she exclaimed. "Really?"

Jet handed her a helmet. "I had one dropped off for us. There's something I want to show you."

Climbing behind him on the big black hog, Sami wrapped her arms around his waist and felt a thrill glide up her spine. She didn't really care where they went, the getting there would be the best part. Sami pressed a solid kiss between his shoulder blades.

Jet smiled, he was liking the way her tits felt nestled up against his back. Why hadn't he ever ridden with a woman before? Hell, he couldn't remember. They left the marina, heading west. The island was only a mile wide and four miles long, so traversing it was a breeze. In no time flat, they were pulling into the driveway of 907 Whitehead Street in Old Town Key West. The Spanish Colonial structure built from native rock in 1851 with all of its history and significance was not the major attraction.

"This is the great novelist, Hemingway's house," Sami announced with amazement as she climbed off the motorcycle. "I recognize it from pictures." Her eyes were wide and when she looked at Jet, she grinned. "I want to see the cats!"

"I knew you would." Taking her by the hand, Jet led her into the gardens by the house. Tropical flowers grew in profusion everywhere—hibiscus, banana plants, birds of paradise, and ginger lilies. A pool shining like a jewel was set into the lush grounds.

But that wasn't what drew Sami's eye. There were cats everywhere! "How many are there?"

"Between forty and fifty," he answered indulgently. "All colors, all sizes, but all with extra toes. Polydactyl, it's called. All descended from Snowball, Ernest's own cat."

Nothing would do Sami but to learn some of their names and carry a few around, petting each one she came across. "Polly is going to be soooo jealous." She laughed.

Jet knew the feeling. He'd had to growl at several men he'd caught staring at Sami, especially her magnificent rack. Hell, when they went out, he might have to insist she wear that damn compression bra.

After she'd looked her fill, he took her in the bookstore and bought her some postcards to remember the day. Next time he'd learn to keep an eye on her, because when they arrived back at the boat, she presented him with a signed first edition of *The Old Man and the Sea*. She'd tucked it in her bag and he had been none the wiser.

Her gesture stunned Jet, he'd spent a few dollars on postcards and she'd plopped down nearly four thousand for a first edition—for him!

"I can't believe you did this." He touched the cover reverently.

"We're back in the States, I have access to my money again." And that was where she left it. "When will your friends be here?" she asked with a yawn.

"Tomorrow." Jet swept her up into his arms. He intended to take full advantage of this time before they faced the unknown with the San Miguel and the cartel. "But tonight is ours."

"I like the sound of that." She put her cheek next to his. "I didn't expect this extra time with you, it's a gift."

Jet cleared his throat, he wasn't choked up—hell no, he had a frog in his throat. "We shouldn't let it go to waste," he agreed. Hurrying, he bumped her head on the wall of the staircase, making her giggle—which made him smile. "Did that hurt?"

"No, I have a hard head."

"You won't get any argument from me on that fact."

She slapped him playfully.

Taking her to his bed, he laid her down gently, stripping off his clothes, then helped her with hers. "I'm not used to wearing so many layers," she confessed with a smile.

When he got down to a lacy bra and a pair of barely-there panties he'd picked out himself, Jet licked his lips. "You look like a Victoria's Secret model. I almost hate to take them off."

"How about this?" She pulled on the tops of the bra cups and tugged them down enough for her breasts to pop out the top, making Jet's eyes widen to the same degree.

Like a big cat, he crawled up the end of the bed, kissing her from the top of the tiny panties, up her stomach until he could tickle the end of her nipple with his tongue, making her wiggle. And when he started humming and singing the theme from Jaws, she got the giggles. "Remember that shark we saw today? I'm a bigger predator than he is. Dun-dun, dun-dun, dun-dun-dun-dun-dun-dun-dun, da-na-na!"

Sami was beyond laughter now, she had collapsed in a giggling fit. But when he grew serious and began worshiping her breasts in earnest, she melted. "God, I love your mouth on me."

"Me too." He chuckled and then covered one tip with his mouth and sucked hard.

A sigh of bliss escaped her, as she closed her eyes and reveled at the tug of his lips and tongue on her nipple.

Jet snuggled up to her, intent on giving her exactly what she needed. While sucking one breast, he caressed the other, then slid his hand up her neck to tangle in her hair.

And that was when he felt it.

A raised ridge of scar tissue. His fingers moved across it and Sami stiffened.

Turning loose of her nipple, he looked up into her face. "What's this?"

"Nothing." She shook her head.

"It doesn't feel like nothing." The look in her eyes told him more than her words or what he'd discovered beneath her silky hair. Micah's words came back to haunt him. 'Ask her, ask her point blank why she went to Mexico.'

"Why were you in Mexico, Sami? Besides helping Mari, why were you in Mexico?"

Sami sat up, pulled her bra cups back in place and picked the sheet up to cover herself. Staring at the bed, she tried to think of what to say. Here she was with Jet. He'd chosen for her to be with him, even if for a little while. Telling him would change everything.

Not telling him could be worse.

Glancing up into his eyes, she knew. Sami owed him the truth. "I went down to Veracruz to go to the Great Physician's clinic."

"What for?" Jet asked carefully. He wanted to grab her, hold her in his arms while they talked. But she'd edged away, keeping her distance.

"I have, or have had an astrocytoma."

Jet blinked, his heart hammering in his chest. He hated big words, they always cloaked the unthinkable within the unpronounceable. "What is that?"

Sami touched his arm. "A brain tumor."

Jet shut his eyes, pain cascading over him like acid rain. "What does that mean?"

Sami hated to say the word. It was a hated word, a word she took great pains not to say out loud. Just saying the syllables gave them power. "Cancer."

Jet swallowed. "What?" He stopped, unable to go on.

Sami tried to make it better. "I've had treatments, all kinds. Electrical, chemical, a new diet."

"Did it work?" Jet began to pray, an act he hadn't done enough to know the proper steps.

Shrugging, Sami brushed the tears from her eyes. "I don't know, the treatments were almost over when I...left on your boat. I didn't get the chance to go back and see."

"That's why you wanted to go to Veracruz," Jet stated in a low, even voice.

"Yes."

Dead silence.

Sami waited for him to say something...anything. All he did was stare out the porthole into the blackness.

When he didn't speak, she did. "I'm sorry, Jet."

Jet jerked from the bed, grabbed his pants and pulled them on, picking up his shirt on the way out the door.

"Jet?"

"I gotta go."

"Wait," she cried, grabbing for his arm.

He didn't stop. He couldn't. Jet went up on the deck and stepped off the ship, walking away into the night.

Down below, Sami curled up into a knot, arms wrapped around her knees. She should have kept her mouth shut. When something couldn't be changed, there was no use talking about it. She tried to imagine what he was feeling and she couldn't. Sami didn't have a clue.

And even if she could've guessed, she wouldn't have understood. Because Jet walked blindly, hands stuffed in his pockets. He couldn't breathe. The world didn't seem big enough to hold how he was feeling. Faster and faster he walked, until he was running. If he ran hard enough and fast enough, maybe he could outrun the pain, the reality, the possibility that that sweet gorgeous woman was sick. Jet couldn't process it. He didn't want to grasp it—all he wanted to do was get away.

For what seemed like hours, he walked, aimlessly, unseeingly, seeking only to escape. Until he came to a park where the shadows were deep enough he could sink to his knees and cry.

* * *

Back at the Sirena…

Sami stood on the deck, staring out into the darkness. She didn't know what to do.

Should she leave?

Should she call the police?

What if something had happened to him?

Feeling desperate, she picked up the cat and hugged her close. "What do I do, Polly?"

Sami stayed there until she was too tired to stand, then she sat down in the shadows to wait. Doubts and questions plagued her.

Had she disgusted him?

Did he not care?

She covered her mouth and bowed her head, wishing she could call back the words.

"Sami?"

Jet's voice sounded near her, he was back. She straightened up, realizing the lights from the boardwalk illuminated the deck well enough that she was visible. "You're back." The inane pronouncement stood between them like a barrier.

Jet took a deep breath, stooped down, gently picked her up, and started back down to his cabin. "Yea, I am. And we have a lot of talking to do."

"We do?" She held on to him, so glad he was back she didn't know what to do. "You scared me. I thought something might have happened to you."

Jet closed his eyes, trying to be strong. He sat down on the bed with her in his lap. "How do you feel? Really?" As he talked, he stroked her hair. "Do you hurt somewhere? Do you feel sick?"

Sami shook her head. "No, I've had a few nauseous moments onboard, but I think that could come from just being on the ocean."

Kissing her cheek and the dampness beneath her eyes, he gazed at her. "Tell me. Everything."

Sami didn't know where to start, so she just poured her heart out. "When I was in my early teens I started having double vision and headaches."

She probably didn't even know she was doing it, but Jet watched her rub her forehead as if she were remembering the pain. "Since your mom was a doctor, she probably recognized the symptoms, I'm guessing." He was inserting himself in her place, trying to imagine what she went through.

Sam grabbed his hand and held on. "My mother was an oncologist, a cancer doctor." She took a deep breath. "Which just made everything a thousand times worse. Because she understood, she knew—there was no sugar coating."

He could only imagine. "You've been fighting this a long time." Jet reached up and touched the spot on her head he'd found earlier.

"Yea, and my mother killed herself trying to find a cure for me."

"What do you mean?" His hands were never still, he felt like he had to keep touching her or she might disappear.

"She had a stroke after we learned the tumor had grown back this last time."

"If you were sitting there in Houston with M. D. Anderson at your doorstep, why come to Mexico?" He thought he knew the reason and he didn't know if he wanted to hear her say it.

He was right.

"The standard treatments weren't working. I didn't have much time left."

Jet shut his eyes, seeking strength. "What was the prognosis for the alternative treatments?" Sami frowned, and Jet wanted to soothe the line between her brows.

"Dr. Rio was very positive…and truthfully," she smiled at him, "I've felt good. Lots more energy and no nausea to speak of. When I get back to the clinic, they may have good news for me. You didn't know I was sick, did you?"

"No." God, no. Jet took her by the shoulders. "Okay, it's my turn to talk."

"All right," Sami said slowly.

"Everything's going to be okay." He said it with quiet, calm assurance and an unswerving determination.

"I know."

"We've got to find out what this doctor says, though. That has to be our first priority." He gently eased her off his lap and onto the bed. Standing, he paced across the room. "We'll call and talk to the doctor, explain what's going on and find out what he knows."

Sami started to protest. Jet just continued talking. "No, I have a better idea. As soon as Micah gets here, we'll take the Chancellor jet down to Veracruz. It's too dangerous for you to go alone."

"No," Sami said it loudly enough and forcefully enough to get Jet's attention. "No, please. I don't want this to stop. You've come this far and you've got to see this through. I refuse to be the reason you don't fulfill your dream of finding the San Miguel."

"Sami, the San Miguel isn't going anywhere." Jet tried to explain.

"You don't know that." She gestured, her hands waving in the air. "Bad people know about the treasure and Rafael knew what the plans were and where we were sailing. You've spent a lot of money to get ready, Victor is on the way and all the equipment has been rented. I can't let you walk away from all of that right now."

Jet was scared. He was confused. "Your health and life is important."

Sami started to cry. "I don't want this to stop. This journey with you is a dream come true for me." She rose and went to him, wrapping her arms around his waist. "Whatever my diagnosis is, going to Veracruz isn't going to change it. I've gone through the treatments, that's all I can do."

"You don't know that." Jet ran his hand through his hair. "There might be more. Another round. Something else."

Sami covered his mouth with hers, kissing him softly. "And I may be okay now," she said hopefully. "The point is...I don't want to know."

"What?" Jet asked, not understanding.

"If the news is bad, I don't want it to ruin what I have right now." Dare she be so bold? "What we have. I don't want the specter of cancer to overwhelm what we're sharing today."

"I don't know...it seems foolish." Jet was torn between wanting to make Sami happy and doing what he could to make sure she didn't die. "I'm used to going on the offensive, the attack, I don't like to wait and see about anything."

"I know…" she rubbed her hands up his arms, "fight the fight. You'll never know how many times I used your mantra as my own."

Jet swallowed hard, fighting more emotion than he'd even known existed.

"Please, Jet." If the treatments didn't work, she might not have much time left and she wanted to spend it with him if possible. "There's so much uncertainty in life. Cancer. The cartels. I've had more joy on this boat with you than I have in the rest of my life put together. You're the best thing that has ever happened to me—and I'm not ready for it to end. I want to complete this quest with you."

Fuck. He wasn't ready for any of it to end—especially her life. "You're killing me, Samantha Josephine Cabot." He bent to kiss her on the eyelids and then the lips. "Don't you know I'd do anything for you?" As Jet made his declaration, he realized it was true. "You have to live. You have to be okay." He tightened his arms around her. "I will accept nothing less."

Sami smiled. If her life ended tomorrow, this man had made living worthwhile.

She'd have no regrets.

"Thank you," she said, rubbing her face against his chest, taking comfort from his strength.

"Okay." Jet shut his eyes and sent a wish heavenward. "We'll go on as planned. But the second I see you starting to get weak or sick, I'm calling that doctor and we're on a plane to the clinic. Got it?"

"Got it," she agreed with a sigh.

"Let's get into bed." He pushed her in that direction.

"Will you finish what you started before?" she asked, a hint of seduction in her voice.

"With pleasure."

And he did, never turning loose of her till morning light broke the eastern sky.

* * *

"Permission to come aboard, Captain?"

Jet couldn't help but smile when he heard the familiar voice. "Identify yourself!"

He heard a few chuckles and some clanking.

What in the world?

"The Calvary's arrived!"

Making his way from the stern where he'd just finished refueling, Jet was glad to see Micah, Saxon, and Isaac. But what they were carrying surprised him. "Do you think you brought enough firepower?"

Isaac stepped forward to shake Jet's hand, patting him on the shoulder. "We've gone up against a drug cartel before. We came prepared." He waved his hand at the half dozen gun cases and ammo boxes spread on the deck.

Jet could see that. He greeted Micah and Saxon with a bro hug, noting that Saxon's hair was longer. He picked up a strand. "Are you going for a young Michael Bolton do?"

Saxon looked offended. "I had a girl say it made me look like Thor."

Micah punched him playfully. "If you're gonna be Thor, you need a bigger hammer." He winked. "Like mine."

"Hell, if we're gonna start measuring equipment, I've got you all beat." Isaac asserted.

Jet chuckled, watching Isaac take an AR-15 from its case. "I think that big gun you're carrying is your way of compensating."

Isaac grabbed his crotch. "Don't ever doubt the heat I'm packing, Foster."

Micah held another assault rifle over his head and sang. "This is my rifle." Then, he too grabbed his crotch. "This is my gun. This is for fighting, this is for fun."

Saxon groaned, and Jet laughed.

"Oh my God." A feminine voice sounded behind them. "A gun is not a penis extension."

Micah looked up and went slack-jawed. "Is this the cabin boy?"

Sami blushed. She'd wanted to look nice for Jet's friends, so she'd worn a lemon yellow sundress and strappy white sandals.

Jet didn't let on, but he was a bit taken aback. He'd seen her pick up a few items of makeup, but this was the first time he'd seen her wear any. She was more than gorgeous.

Holding his hand out, he brought her up close. "Guys, this is Samantha Cabot. Sami, you know Micah Wolfe, of course." Micah stepped forward and kissed her hand. "And this is Saxon White, another Equalizer, and our own private geek squad."

"I prefer computer genius." Saxon gave Sami a slight bow.

"Hello." Sami smiled demurely, her gaze moving to the other man, one who almost rivaled Jet in size. Clad in all black, he looked intimidating.

"This Johnny Cash look-alike is Isaac McCoy, aka the Badass of Kerr County."

She greeted him. "How do you do?"

"Honored." Isaac took her hand. "I didn't know Jet was capable of such good taste. I'm impressed."

Sami blushed anew. "He's being very kind to me. I've gotten myself into a bit of a scrape." She didn't know what else to say. Sami still didn't accept her role in Jet's life to be anything more than temporary and benevolent.

Frowning, Jet helped the guys with their stuff. "Head on down and pick a cabin, we need to set sail. Treasure's awaiting." To hear Sami dismiss their relationship as nothing more than a glorified security job for him hurt.

Sami watched the four good-looking men go below, still having trouble comprehending that she was here with Jet, an accepted part of this group—for now. All in all, Sami felt wonderful! It was as if a thousand pound weight had been lifted from her shoulders. She'd unburdened herself to Jet and he'd accepted the weight of her worries.

When Micah came back up on the deck, Sami approached him. "How is Marisol?" She'd wanted to talk to her, but she knew satellite calls were expensive out at sea and she'd still not replaced her cell phone charger.

"Mending well, she's returned to her apartment in Houston and Destry has arranged for protection until some plans are worked out." He didn't know how to tell Jet that Kyle was considering witness protection for both Marisol and Sami until the Jaguar could be dealt with.

"I'm glad, I can't wait to see her." Sami bit her lip, unsure of how to proceed. She had a favor to ask before they set sail.

About that time, Jet joined them, hooking his arm around Sami's waist. "Don't flirt with my girl, Wolfe."

Micah's eyes widened at his phrasing. "Wouldn't dream of it. We were just discussing her friend Marisol."

"I was wondering if I could use a phone before we leave shore. I'd like to talk to Mari and I'd also like to call someone," she looked at Jet, "about what you saw at the Killing Fields before you left Galveston."

"Sure." Jet motioned for Saxon to join them. "Go in the wheelhouse and make yourself at home. Use the phone, the computer, anything you need. Saxon can help you with any hookups or numbers."

Sami didn't argue, she thought she could've handled it alone, but she wouldn't turn away help. "Great, I'd like to get ahold of Detective Roundtree at the Houston PD, he's been my contact on the cold case."

Sami started to walk away with Saxon, but Jet pulled her back, whispering, "How do you feel?" His eyes looked deeply into hers.

She beamed at him. "Stop. I'm perfect."

"Better be." He held her gaze.

Isaac walked up to Jet and Micah as Saxon led Sami off to make her calls. "What's going on?"

"Come on, I want to go over some things with you." Jet led them down into the galley, pouring some coffee. "This may turn out to be more exciting than we first thought. It's gone from just a treasure hunting trip to possible war games with a bunch of ruthless pirates and a drug lord. If any of you want to back out, I wouldn't hold it against you."

"Are you kidding?" Isaac snorted. "That's why I came and reinforcements can be on the way with a simple phone message. It's your call."

Jet stared into his coffee cup. "I don't want to reassemble the group that went to Mexico after Aron, I don't think we'll be facing that much opposition—if any. I might be wrong. Rafael, Victor's former man, one of the guys I killed when they attacked us, worked for the cartel. He threatened Sami's life and spouted off some garbage about sending her head to the Jaguar on a gold plate taken from the San Miguel. Since he worked on the salvage ship, he had the coordinates and possibly passed them on to others."

Isaac lifted his lip in a snarl. "Let them bring it on, I could use some target practice."

Micah, not quite as warlike as Isaac, rubbed his chin. "We'll have to be prepared, those assholes fight dirty. I wouldn't be surprised if they didn't plant explosives on the ship."

Jet leaned forward. "That's my area of expertise, I'll deal with it."

Smirking, Micah pointed upward. "I'd say you have plenty to deal with. Sami seems to come with a little extra baggage."

"You let me worry about that." Jet frowned.

"What's she calling the police about?" Micah asked, watching his friend carefully. "Something to do with Marisol?"

"No," Jet explained patiently, going on to explain about the I-45 serial killer and the man he'd seen there. "Her series of articles has renewed interest in the killings and someone had recalled seeing a truck there years before like I saw."

"Hmm." Micah pursed his lips. "Interesting."

"I've heard about those killings, they're almost legendary in Texas." Isaac poured more coffee all around. "On the way here, Micah caught Saxon and me up on the dealings Sami and Marisol have had. Seems like your girl loves to live dangerously."

Jet smiled. "To be so little, she's fierce." He pointed at Micah. "Did he tell you about the time she cold-cocked Santoro in the bar when he was about to knife me?"

Isaac shook his head 'no.' "He did tell me that you fell for her when you still thought she was a dude."

Jet threw a lemon at Micah. "What can I say, I'm a pussy magnet."

Micah laughed. "For a while there, you were setting off my gaydar."

Isaac stood. "If you two comedians will excuse me, I think I'll go call Avery before we push off, if Saxon and Sami are through with the phone."

"Sure, mi barco, su barco." Jet raised his cup to Isaac as he passed.

When the big McCoy was gone, Micah bit the bullet and broached the subject he'd been dreading bringing up the Jet. "What's the deal with Sami?"

Jet didn't even pretend he didn't understand. He and Micah joked a lot, but now wasn't the time. He hung his head. "She's been fighting some damn type of malignant brain tumor for half her life." Clearing his throat, he said more, "I look at her and she's so full of life, like a firefly flitting around. I've never known anyone like her." Jet raised his head and stared at Micah. "She'd been getting treatments at some clinic in Veracruz, but we don't know if they worked, and she doesn't want to find out until we finish this 'quest' as she calls it."

"Are you setting yourself up for heartbreak?" There was a point where he'd assumed, as the rest of the Equalizers did, that Jet was immune to love. He wore Nemo's rules and his own stoic nature like a suit of armor.

Jet rose, putting his cup in the sink. "No, it's not like that."

"It's not?" Micah wondered how long it would take the big lug to realize he'd fallen hopelessly in love with the small woman who'd taken him by storm.

"Nope, I'm just helping her out. When this is over, I'll see that she gets to Veracruz and that she's safe and well." He turned around and faced Micah, one foot crossed over the other and arms folded. "After that, we'll both go on with our lives."

Micah felt the gate open for his revelation. "That's good because Kyle is thinking about putting Marisol and Sami into witness protection until this mess with the Jaguar can be sorted out."

Jet's stiffened. "Witness protection? You mean where they disappear and no one knows who they are and where they live?"

Micah nodded his head. "That's usually how it works."

Shaking his head, Jet responded, "I don't think so."

Micah enjoyed pushing the envelope. "Why?"

Jet was saved from having to respond when Sami came bounding into the room and straight into his arms. "I missed you."

The way Jet cradled her against him was more of an answer to Micah's questions than any verbal explanation could ever be.

"Did you make your calls?" Jet asked her.

"Yes, and the detective is going to have someone search the databases about the old red truck. He said there weren't too many of those on the road and it should be easy to find. He'll let me know if anything materializes out of our tip."

"And how's Marisol?" Micah asked.

"She's good. She left the hospital and went back home, but Destry thought it would be smart if she stayed somewhere else for a while. He sent her to stay in Tyson's RV."

"Does Tyson know this yet?" Micah enquired with a lifted eyebrow.

Jet snorted. "I guess he'll find out when he goes home."

Sami looked worried. "I'm sure Kyle or Destry told him, don't you think?"

"You don't know Kyle," Micah explained. "He takes being in charge to a whole new level." He sighed. "Texas will never be the same."

"Maybe that's a good thing," Sami said, nestled deep in Jet's embrace. "Sometimes change is for the best."

Micah met Jet's gaze over the top of her head and he got the Champ's message loud and clear. 'Shut your trap.'

Covering his trap with his hand, Micah followed orders and hid a smile at the same time.

* * *

In no time the men were settled and Jet had steered them away from Key West and they were journeying around the tip of Florida. There was excitement in the air. Sami felt exhilarated, helping Jet hoist the sails. She'd become a good sailor's apprentice—or at least that was her opinion.

Even with his friends around, Jet was quiet. He seemed happy, but every time she looked at him, he was studying her. A few times Sami wanted to ask him if her face was dirty or if her blouse was unbuttoned. She smiled—no, if her blouse was undone, he'd have her below and his hands would be on her tits quicker than a wink.

With three extra on board, she sometimes felt in the way, so for the last few hours Sami found a quiet place on the lee side of the bulkhead and sat down to write a new blog. This would be different than any she'd done before.

This one was on Jet.

Oh, she didn't plan to give away any of his secrets or expose anything he hadn't already made public. She just wanted to give her impressions of meeting a man touted as a hero and finding out he lived up to the name.

As far as Sami was concerned, the time was idyllic. She was happier than she'd ever been. Setting her computer down, she rose on her knees to look out to sea. There were times when Jet steered them out into the depths, the water was so clear that she could see an abundance of sea life—everything from rays to dolphins to turtles. The different shades of blue were awe inspiring. At other times, he brought them closer to shore. Turquoise colored water, mangrove islands, and sea grass meadows combined in a swirling display of color.

As Jet and his friends shot the breeze, Sami fixed food for them, a huge pan of lasagna. She wanted to carry her weight and cooking was one way she could do that. After they'd eaten, the men sat under the stars and smoked the Cuban cigars Jet had purchased.

"So, do you really expect to pull up two billion worth of treasure? Two billion?" Isaac repeated as if the number was bigger than he could comprehend.

"Sure do," Jet confirmed as he lay on a chaise with Sami between his legs. "Of course, we'll have to split it with the governments concerned, but we'll get to keep a good chunk."

"I'm a proud investor," Saxon chimed in, blowing a smoke ring into the air.

"What are you going to buy this time?" Micah asked. "You got that red convertible before."

Saxon took a long draw on his cigar, coughed, laughed, and answered, "I'm considering a small island in the Bahamas, actually."

"And a few dancing girls to go with it, I bet." Isaac sat up. "Isn't that close by to where we are?" Isaac sat up. "Let's sail by and look at it."

Jet laughed, shaking his head. "We're on a schedule. I'm already a couple of days behind as it is."

Sami stiffened in his arms, and he kissed the back of her head, whispering in her ear, "Not your fault, love."

Isaac understood. "Yes, Foster. And that's why I'm here. McCoys pay their debts." He raised a beer to Jet. "And we stand by our friends."

They were sailing along on a set course, guided by the auto-pilot and the built-in radar, enjoying the night air and one another's company when an alarm went off in the wheelhouse. "What's that?" Sami asked as Jet moved swiftly off the chaise.

"We're on a collision course with something," he said as he ran to the controls.

The others stood up to see what they could see. "It's black out there, nothing," Micah said as he looked ahead of them, out to sea.

"That's odd," Saxon noted. "The stars are gone, there seems to be a fog coming in."

They could feel Jet slowing the Sirena down, gradually bringing her to a full stop. Then, he came on board and went to the very front of the ship. The others followed. "What is it?" Micah asked.

Jet stared into the darkness. "Hell if I know. But the radar says there's a solid wall in front of us."

"What?" Saxon asked in amazement. "Is that even possible?"

Sami trembled and went up to Jet, slipping her hand into his. "I don't understand."

"I don't either, pumpkin." He rubbed the top of her hand with his thumb.

"Let's go closer," Isaac suggested. "It might be a malfunction in the equipment."

"Yea, I thought about that." Jet started off, pulling Sami with him. "You guys keep watch, I'm going to creep up there and see what this is, if anything."

Bottom line, Sami trusted Jet. Still, she was nervous. "Be careful."

"Always," Jet muttered as he turned the engine on and started moving forward at a crawl. He kept his eyes on the controls and marveled at what they showed. If they were correct, someone had built a damn wall from Florida halfway into the Sargasso Sea. How far it extended, he didn't know, it went out past where his radar could see. "This has to be a mistake."

"I see it!" Micah yelled. "Stop this damn boat!"

Jet eased up and cut the engine and grabbed a spotlight. "Come on."

"Back up or drop the anchor," Saxon said. "We don't want to ram that…thing, it might be charged or be a door into another…" His voice fell off.

Jet and Sami came to the bow and what Jet saw—he knew he wouldn't forget in a million years. Shining the light in front of them, they saw a wall. It looked to be a stone wall and as Jet shone the light to the left, to the right, and straight up—there was no beginning and no end. "My God," he breathed. "This is impossible."

"This is the Bermuda Triangle," Micah whispered.

"I'm backing off," Jet said, emphatically.

He returned to the wheelhouse and changed course, moving as quickly as he could from the anomaly. As he traveled, a thick fog seemed to inundate everything.

Sami was scared. "Are we going to be okay?"

"We will if I can help it, baby." He tried to assure Sami.

When he had put a mile or more between them and the wall, he stopped and once more went out on the deck. "How's it looking?"

"Like pea soup," Micah drawled. "This is spooky."

Jet went back down to the controls and what he found frustrated the hell out of him. "Hey, Wolfe! Come here."

"What?" Micah asked as he joined his friend. "Shit."

Even Sami could see something was wrong. She stood behind them and watched the instruments go nuts, gauges were whirling and digital read-outs were blinking from 0 to all 9's. "In the name of all that's holy, what is going on?"

Jet walked away from the spinning gauges and stalked back out into the open air. "Instruments have gone haywire," he announced to Isaac and Saxon.

"You know I've heard about this, but I didn't believe it," Saxon muttered. "Theories abound, everything from black holes to time warps to aliens."

"Electromagnetic storms," Isaac added. When Saxon gave him the eye, he added, "Hey, I watch the Sci-fi channel."

"Well, this isn't sci-fi, this is a fuckin' reality show. I just don't know what kind of reality it is."

For long minutes, they stared into the milky clouds, the thick shadows that cloaked them on all sides. "I swear to God, this is like an episode of The Twilight Zone."

Micah, who had stayed in the wheelhouse, yelled, "Get in here, Foster!"

Sami didn't know whether to scream or cry, but she did neither. She just had faith in the man she loved. Standing back, so she wouldn't be in the way, Sami waited.

When Jet stepped back in front of his dashboard, he was amazed yet again. Now the instruments and gauges were behaving normally and the radar was clear.

The wall had disappeared.

"It's gone," Jet breathed. "Gone."

"Maybe it's just hiding," Micah said. "Like it's cloaked."

Jet laughed. "Well, we're not going to take any chances. It's too deep to drop anchor, but I'm drifting till morning. But we're going to take turns keeping watch."

Micah looked over his shoulder and saw Sami standing there, pale as a ghost. "Let's divide the night. Why don't you take your girl to bed? She looks like she needs you."

Jet turned to look at her, worry clouding his face. "Do you feel sick?"

"No." Sami shook her head. "I'm fine, just unnerved."

"We all are, Sami," Micah stated flatly. "You two go rest, I've got this handled."

Jet clapped him on the back. "Thanks, man. Holler if you need anything or if a pyramid rises out of the depths or something."

With a shiver, Micah laughed. "Don't say that, I can face a battalion of armed men, take on a drug cartel single handedly, but I'm not fond of things that go bump in the night, especially ships bumping up against things that shouldn't be in the fuckin' ocean…"

Jet and Sami were halfway down the stairs while Micah was still fussing. "Are we going to be okay?" Sami asked as Jet picked up Polly and they went to his stateroom.

He pulled her close. "Nothing is gonna bother my girls while I'm around," Jet said as he held her tight,

Polly purring between them. Setting the cat down gently, he pointed to a pile of pillows in the corner. "Go to your bed, Polls, I need working room."

Sami hugged herself. "What was that out there, Jet?"

"I don't know, maybe some hallucination brought on by fumes of some kind." Even as he said it, he knew it sounded weak. "I guess we'll ever know."

Sami laughed weakly. "Well, hallucinations I understand. I've had a few of those myself." She blushed prettily. "Once, when I was really low, I thought you had come to me and was giving me a pep talk. You crawled in the bed with me and kept me warm."

Jet closed his eyes as if in pain. "How do you feel now?"

Sami rolled her eyes. "This is the third time you've asked me that." She spread her hands wide as she explained. "I told you, I'm fine."

"Good." Reaching behind him, Jet locked the door. He jerked his tank top over his head and tugged the drawstring that help up his pants. Giving her a sexy smile, he started sauntering toward her, giving her what she hoped was an 'I'm gonna nail you to the wall' stare. Licking his lips, he stepped out of his pants and underwear, tossing them over his shoulder.

Sami's heart skipped a few beats as Jet invaded her space. Expecting to be pushed back against the door and devoured, she was surprised when he gently framed her face and began rubbing his thumb across her lips—back and forth until she caught it between her teeth. She could tell he was holding back. "I'm not gonna break, Jet. This is exactly why I didn't want to tell you."

"I'm taking my time," he chided her playfully. "I'm not holding back."

"Better not." She teased, using his own words against him. "'Cause I need you to kiss me." She let her lips slide over his. "Touch me." She let her hands glide up his abs. "Take me." She nipped him on the chin.

Still staring, holding her gaze, he growled. "Who's in charge here? I thought I was the captain?"

"You are and I'm your first mate." She let her hand move down until she cupped him, stroking his erection. "*Mate* being the operative word."

Cupping the back of her head, Jet tangled his fingers in her hair and pulled her head back, exposing the gentle slope of her neck. Then he bent down and kissed her, leaving a hot trail of kisses along her throat till he came to her mouth.

Sami whimpered—this was different from any kiss Jet had given her before. Her mouth was being ravished. Thoroughly, completely, with immense attention to detail. With lips and tongue, he claimed her, branded her. Desperate need and a rising lust sizzled through her body. Jet pushed his leg between hers and pulled her tighter so she was riding the hard muscle of his thigh.

She was wet and the more he kissed her, the wetter she became. Jet chuckled between kisses. "If I'd known you were flouncing around out there without any panties on, I would've been all over you." With his words teasing her ear, he took hold of the bottom of her dress and pulled it up and when the waistband hung up on her bountiful breasts, causing them to pop out and jiggle, he groaned. "Damn, I love the way you're made."

Pushing her backward against the dresser, he began kissing and sucking at the tender flesh of her neck by her collarbone. Quivers of delight shimmered from every place he touched her and he swept the surface clean and lifted her up, going to his knees.

"Jet…" Sami gasped as he put her knees over his shoulders and tugged her hips so his mouth was even with her pussy. She had to grasp his shoulders to balance herself because the tips of her toes wouldn't even touch the floor. "Jet!" When his mouth touched her aching center, she threw her head back, clutched his hair and held on. "You are so good at this, if there was a belt to be won, you'd be the champ."

His only answer was a wicked wink before she felt him blowing his hot breath over the tender flesh, then ramming his tongue deep into the creamy folds in and out, faster, going as deep as he could go.

"Oh, my stars and garters," she breathed, closing her eyes tightly as he ate her out with complete and utter devotion to the task at hand—lapping, laving, using his teeth and tongue with more skill than any one man should possess. Sami surrendered, even if she would've wanted to, there was no escaping the orgasm he was intent on giving her. Her hips began to buck in a hungry rhythm as he sucked her pulsing clit. "Fuck…" she hissed as the bliss became so intense tears were running down her cheeks.

Jet glanced up to make sure she was okay, but when he saw the ecstasy on her face, he held her still and set out to drive her insane. It was a battle of the sexes—her demanding and him giving when and how he saw fit.

Before he was through, Sami was convinced that Jet knew best. The orgasm he gave her was cataclysmic—when it started, he didn't let up, he didn't relent, he didn't stop when she begged him to. He gave Sami exactly what she needed, pushing her from one climax straight into the next. She arched, she writhed, her fingers grasping the edge of the dresser so hard that Sami was sure she'd leave imprints.

And when he was through, he didn't just get up—he kissed her gently, taming her throbbing clit with soft butterfly touches. Nipping the inside of her thigh, then soothing the mark with his tongue.

"Jet, I need to hold you," was her plea and only that request brought him to his feet and he captured her mouth, slaking her thirst, letting her taste the sweetness he'd enjoyed.

"I got you." He assured as he went into her arms.

Loving the way he took care of her, she sought to return the favor, encircling his cock with her fingers, moving her palm up and down his shaft. "I love it when you make me cum, but this is what I need." Rubbing her face against his chest, she teased the flat brown disc of his nipple with her tongue. "I ache for you, Jet."

Panting, his body quaking with desperation, he picked her up and sat her down on his cock. Sami keened, her eyes widening at the invasion, her fingers digging into his hard biceps.

"You're mine," he declared. His power and size were never more evident as he began to move her up and down on his pole.

She wrapped her arms around his neck. "This feels so good," she whispered as she dug her heels in and held on.

Sami moaned, her pussy tightening and clenching, striving to milk him as he thrust in and out of her with every flex of his hips.

Jet buried his head in her neck, biting the soft spot next to the pulse point in her neck, the sensation of being buried in her snug creamy pussy almost too perfect to endure.

Sami could tell he needed to cum, she could feel how excited and near he was, huge and leaking.

Knowing he wanted her with him, she leaned forward and whispered, "Give me what I need."

"What's that?" Jet asked.

"You. Hard," she purred against his neck, giving him a taste of her teeth.

"Done." He walked her back to the dresser, anchored her ass and began fucking her with fast hard jabs.

When he came, he bellowed and when Sami felt his hot release jet inside of her she flew apart, clinging to him as he kept pumping inside of her, undulating his hips to hit just the right spot.

"You have made my life, Jet Foster," Sami whispered as she lay against him, her chest heaving.

He rubbed her back, keeping his lips pressed together lest he voice things he didn't fully understand.

CHAPTER FOURTEEN

The next morning when Sami awoke, she was alone, the ship's engine churning beneath her. They were underway. She rubbed her eyes and sat up, noticing that even Polly had abandoned her. Quickly, she rose and showered, dressing in a pair of baby pink shorts and a halter top. Jet had picked out all of her clothes and his taste definitely didn't require a lot of raw materials.

When she passed through the galley, it was obvious someone had fried ham and eggs. A plate covered with a napkin awaited her, but she left it, so uneasy that the sight of the food turned her stomach. A shaft of panic knifed through her. Automatically her hand wandered up to worry the ridge of scar tissue. Before Veracruz, Sami had been resigned to dying and now she wanted to live. She wasn't assuming Jet wanted more from her than right now, but he'd shown her how wonderful life could be and she didn't want to miss a minute.

Going to the coffee pot, she poured a cup and added sugar and cream. The motion of the boat seemed to be bothering her more today than before, so she wet a napkin and held it to her forehead. Once the wave of nausea passed, she made her way up on deck to find all of the men pouring over a map. "Hey, guys." Even though they'd made love and Jet had held her all night long, she hung back, feeling a bit unsure this morning.

But Jet had none of that. He held out his hand, and she took it. "We just heard from Victor, he's doing well and steaming this way."

"That's good news," she agreed.

Isaac, Saxon, and Micah were still studying the large document, but they each greeted her with a smile.

"Feeling okay today, Sami?" Micah asked.

At that moment, Sami realized he knew about the cancer and she felt heat creep up her cheeks. "Wonderful," she lied. "Never better." Placing a hand over her stomach, she vowed not to act like anything was wrong.

"Good." Micah smiled. "We're looking at a new map Saxon brought."

Saxon ran his hand over it, pride obvious in his voice. "Yea, this is the most detailed layout ever produced, using satellite imagery to show ridges and trenches of the underwater surface right off of Amelia Island. No ship has ever been able to do a survey like this. Data on slight variations of the pull of gravity over this part of the ocean are recorded with satellite altimetry and then they're combined to actually map the seafloor."

"Careful, Saxon, your geek is showing." Isaac patted him on the shoulder.

Saxon frowned, but he proudly stepped aside so Sami could see. "So, this is where we're headed?"

"Yea, and we'll be there in a few hours." Micah observed, checking the horizon.

"No more wall?" Sami asked, following his gaze.

Jet rubbed her shoulders. "We passed up that spot just after the crack of dawn. I got up early and ran tests on all of our equipment. We're okay."

"That's a relief," Sami said with a sigh. "I had bad dreams last night."

"I know." Jet kissed her neck. "You tossed and turned like a fish out of water."

"What's next after you find the San Miguel, Foster?" Isaac asked as he took a seat near the side and propped his booted feet up on the rail.

Jet pulled Sami with him and claimed another chair by Isaac. "I don't know, there's always more worlds to conquer. I'm sure I'll have another match or two lined up and I'd like to head back down to Cuba, there's a lot of unexplored wrecks there."

"What about you, Sami?" Micah asked. "What's next for you?"

Jet almost bristled, he knew exactly what Micah was doing. He wanted to ask him what his problem was, but he didn't want to embarrass Sami. So he settled on giving him a hard look which didn't faze Micah a bit.

Sami measured her words. "I have big plans. First I have to go tie up some loose ends in Veracruz, then I'll return to Houston." The rest depended on what Dr. Rio told her. "My mom had passed away shortly before I left and I sold our big house, so I'll be apartment hunting if all goes…well." She let her voice trail off and felt Jet's hands tighten around her waist.

As he heard her speak about the future, Jet knew he was in deep trouble. He either had to fish or cut bait. His rule of only one night stands was shot to hell. Usually it was the woman who feared getting hurt. For the first time Jet realized his own emotional wellbeing was at risk. He couldn't stand the thought of something happening to her. A world without Samantha wasn't a world he cared to live in.

"Houston's not far from Galveston," Micah interjected out of the blue and they all stared at him, wondering why he was stating the obvious.

"Nope, hasn't moved last time I checked," Saxon sniped, totally oblivious to the underlying currents.

All of a sudden Sami caught on. Ever so subtly, Micah was taunting Jet—over her. Jumping up, she excused herself. "I think I'll go make lunch." And she would have made it, if her head hadn't swum.

When she reached out to grab the rail, Jet saw her and made a grab for her before she tripped. "You're not going anywhere, nobody's hungry." His announcement was met by a few startled stares but no one argued.

"I'm fine," Sami whispered. "I need to go see to the food."

"No." Jet insisted. "You don't. Rest."

To her chagrin, Sami found herself confined to quarters, except it wasn't her cabin she was restricted to—it was anywhere Jet happened to be. Which wouldn't have been bad, if she'd felt he really wanted her there instead of being convinced she was about to expire or keel over. When she finally resigned herself to her fate, Sami kicked back and sipped a cold drink, basking in the sun.

As the men milled around, adjusting the sails and planning the salvage dive, Sami dozed. When a sudden noise jerked her awake, she sat up and realized they were nearing their destination. Jet was in the wheelhouse and he was blowing the Sirena's horn.

Standing up, she stretched, feeling better. A ray of hope brightened her outlook. Maybe all she was feeling was stress. After all, her life had been threatened several times in the last few days, she'd lost her virginity, and sailed across the Gulf of Mexico. A lot for anyone to deal with, much less someone who'd been through intensive treatments for brain cancer.

"Sami, come in here!" Jet called, and she smiled, heading in to see what he wanted. Micah was there and her countenance fell a little. For some reason, she didn't think he liked her. What had she done? "What's up?" she asked Jet, avoiding Micah's eyes.

"We'll be meeting up with the Seaduction within the hour and I wanted to show you something before we do." Sami came closer, curious to why they were both smiling.

Jet had an old book open on the counter. "We found some information on the Madonna. Listen." He began to read. "Although veiled in myth, tales abound of a life-size statue of the Madonna forged from Incan gold by Peru's Spanish overlords more than four hundred years ago. King Philip IV ordered a Peruvian goldsmith to cast the statue to be shipped home on a treasure armada. His last written words were a curse on the Incas who mined the gold beneath a Spanish whip. 'Let the imbeciles be destroyed forever'."

"Seems like his curse backfired." Micah observed dryly.

Jet continued reading. "In 1656, a treasure fleet of eight galleons sailed from South America for Spain. Aboard were wealthy colonists, five million pesos of gold and gems, plus the hidden Golden Madonna. At midnight one cold, cloudy day after Christmas, the ship hit a sand bar off the cost of Cuba, an accompanying ship rammed the first one, slashing into its hull. All crew were lost either by drowning or being eaten by sharks. Several times the Madonna was sought by the Spanish but storms befell them, every single one."

Micah chose that moment to make a creepy noise. "Wa-ooo-ooo," causing Sami to jump and Jet to laugh.

"So, this is your Madonna?" Sami asked Jet.

"Your Madonna," he corrected, "worth millions of dollars."

"I told you, I don't want the money. This was your find, I just happened to be along."

Micah leveled a look at Sami. "This is a lot of money, Sami. Don't tell me you aren't tempted. What Jet is offering you is a fortune."

Sami turned on Micah. What was his problem? His veiled insinuations forced her to reveal something she wouldn't have said otherwise. "I'm Cabot oil, I don't need anyone else's money."

Jet snorted, and Micah looked vaguely guilty. "I see," he drawled the words.

Sami just ignored him and hugged Jet. "Congratulations, your name is going to look amazing in the record books." Then, she turned and walked out of the wheelhouse, leaving the men alone.

Jet laughed. "I guess she told you."

"I just don't want you to get hurt," Micah mumbled.

"The only way I can get hurt is if something happens to her," Jet said. "There, I said it."

"I know." Micah clapped him on his shoulder. "I know."

"But she is going to be fine." Jet took a deep breath, holding his friend's gaze. "I have to believe that."

Out on deck, Sami stood with Saxon and Isaac. "I think we're getting close to Nassau Sound." Isaac pointed.

Sami looked toward the coast. "How far are we from the shore?"

"Looks to be less than two miles," Saxon surmised. "This is about as close as we can get. The entrance is obstructed by shifting shoals forming a shallow bar and there are occasional floating logs and stumps, both are a menace to navigation."

Isaac winked at Sami, then pinched Saxon on the arm.

"Hey!" Saxon yowled. "What'd you do that for?"

"Just wanted to be sure you weren't some damn cyborg or something."

Drawing closer, they saw another boat. "Is that the Seaduction?" Sami asked when they saw a vessel almost as big as the Sirena anchored ahead of them.

Steps coming from behind them caused Sami to look around. It was Jet. "Yep, that's my father. Nemo Foster. Brace yourself." He laughed. "My old man's a character."

* * *

Sami learned quickly that Jet didn't exaggerate. Describing Nemo as a character was putting it mildly. He was big, gruff and had no filter at all, speaking exactly what was on his mind. And the first words out of his mouth when he saw her were, "Good God, son, you not only listened to the siren's call, you brought one on the damn boat." Glancing at Jet, he scathingly barked. "It's a wonder you can even walk, boy."

Her cheeks went scarlet with embarrassment. Sami ducked her head, and Jet held up his hand, wordlessly telling Nemo that was enough. To his surprise, his old man listened. "Fine, whatever makes you happy. We have treasure to hunt."

Sami started to turn away, but Jet caught her hand. "Wait."

She tried to pass it off. "I'm okay."

"Look, what he said was nothing. Hell, that was Nemo being mild, he might as well be giving us his blessing."

"Blessing?" She wanted to know about this blessing.

"He's not going to give you a hard time." Jet tried to explain. "And Micah, don't pay any attention to Micah. He likes you."

Sami laughed. "Really? I think you're mistaken." She rubbed her hand down her arm. "It's okay, I get the feeling he's trying to protect your virtue. You'll have to explain to him our situation so he won't worry."

"Our situation?" How could he explain something he didn't understand himself?

A shout from Nemo drew their attention. "You have treasure to hunt, let me know if there's anything I can do to help. Otherwise, I'll stay out of the way."

Weaving his fingers through hers, he said, "We'll discuss this 'situation' later. For now, you don't want to miss this."

He was right. Sami was amazed at the activity. The two boats were cabled together and it wasn't long before Victor and his crew joined them. She found a comfortable spot to watch and just took it all in.

Nemo took the lead. "Our first step is to get beneath the waves and scout out the area. We'll send down Victor's submersible and two dive teams. We found the furnace in this area, but you all know as well as I do how things can shift and get moved around with tide and storms."

Jet put on his diving gear, and Sami couldn't help but admire him as he did so. Would she ever tire of looking at him? Not in a million years. Nemo's crew, two seasoned divers named Alan Parsons and Sid Franks, hit the water with an enthusiastic shout. Saxon was suited up, but Micah and Isaac appeared to be ready to work the winches. Victor was going down in the submersible, and Jet motioned Sami over. "Would you like to hitch a ride?"

She was shocked. "I'd love to." The opportunity to view the search up close and personal was a wonderful surprise.

"So, you feel okay?" Again, Jet asked and again Sami assured him she did.

"Please stop worrying. I'm good." She wasn't about to tell him of the earlier nausea. "I'll talk to Dr. Rio soon enough."

Jet grumbled something under his breath, and Sami laughed. "I would've never taken you for a worrier."

"So, Señorita Cabot is riding shotgun with me?" Victor came forward. Sami wasn't blind, he was one good-looking man with his olive skin and longish hair, a raffish face and big smile.

"Yes!" she answered excitedly.

While Victor was readying the small submarine, Sami's eyes were drawn to Nemo watching a screen. Putting on her brave face, she squared her shoulders and walked up to him. "What are you doing?"

Honestly, she expected him to tell her to beat it. To her surprise, he grinned. "I'm lowering a remote control vehicle, an ROV, equipped with metal detectors and a magnetometer. We're checking for metal just under the sand, be it a cannon, metal hinges on a chest or weapons." He stepped back so she could see. "You must be one special lady."

Jerking her eyes from the image before her, she asked, "What do you mean?"

"I've never seen my boy look at anyone the way he looks at you."

Sami didn't know what to say and he didn't press, he turned back and pointed. "With Victor's submersible, this baby and the dive teams, we'll be able to cover more territory in a shorter amount of time. This in essence is an archaeological excavation, so we have to be careful."

He went on to explain different techniques and what they hoped to find. "This is a once in a lifetime opportunity. What we might find here could rewrite the history books." He winked at her. "There's supposed to be a secret on board."

Sami's eyes widened. She'd known this would be an adventure, but she hadn't expected to feel so electrified. If someone had told her a year ago, when she'd been lying in a hospital bed taking chemotherapy that one day she'd be standing on board a ship with the ocean breeze on her face searching for sunken treasure, she would've thought they were crazy.

"Sami!" Jet called, motioning her to come.

"Thanks for being nice to me." She threw her arms around Nemo's neck and hugged him. "I can see where Jet gets his sweet personality."

Nemo coughed. "I wasn't aware he had one."

Giving him a warm smile, she ran to Jet. Goose bumps of anticipation danced over her skin. The sun was glinting off the water like diamonds and the salt spray in the air made her want to throw her arms up and sing. "Your dad's nice."

Jet looked as skeptical as Nemo had. "Victor's ready for you." He helped her step over onto Victor's ship and then down into the hatch of the ten foot submersible that was attached by a winch. "Hold on and you two don't elope or anything."

"We won't." She assured him as Victor took her hand to guide her the last couple of steps. Once she was settled in the seat, she was amazed at the thick glass on the window and the complicated looking controls and instruments.

"You'll have the same view a fish has, we'll be able to see it all."

Thrilled, Sami held on as the vehicle was lowered into the water. In a few minutes she felt as if she was on the most amazing amusement park ride in the world. They could watch the divers and she could pick Jet out—it wasn't hard, he was the biggest. As they moved around, she kept her eye on the ocean floor, anxious to help if she could. There weren't a lot of fish to speak of, most were scared away by all the activity. Still, the colors were enthralling and being a part of something so momentous was heady.

All of a sudden Jet's voice came over the radio and Sami jerked. "Victor, over here." She hadn't realized they were able to communicate.

"Be right there." He began turning the vehicle. "Maybe he's spotted something." They came nearer and saw Jet pointing at what looked to be a cluster of iron or steel on the sand. "I see it. Let's go up and get the excavator in place."

For the next hour or two, Sami just watched in awe. This wasn't some random half-hearted effort, these men knew what they were doing. They were experts. What appeared to be an underwater track-hoe was lowered into place and it began to move sediment, creating a hole about twenty-five feet wide and ten feet deep.

By now, she was watching the activity with Nemo, both of them sipping iced tea she'd made for everyone. He'd found her a hat to wear and she felt like a part of the crew. "Our method is different than traditional salvagers who use propeller blasts to blow the sand, we won't create a big cloud, we'll just move the dirt."

She watched in fascination as the divers entered the hole to see what they could find. "How did you know where to look?" she asked.

Nemo pushed his hat back. "At my son's urging, I've been studying this area for years. Coins have washed up on shore, we found that furnace a while back and we've read every bit of historical information we could on the San Miguel. About three months ago, I was walking the beach and found some ballast stones scattered along the shoreline and some encrusted copper nails and spikes that had been concretized together. Jet and I have been drawn back here again and again and when the permit finally came through, I knew we had to go for it." He rubbed his chest.

Sami remembered his heart condition. "Do you feel okay?"

Nemo huffed. "Now, don't you start. I'm tired of having a damn babysitter."

Sami sighed. "I hear you. Jet watches me like a hawk."

"Why?" Nemo asked, and Sami realized he didn't know. She kept silent for a while and he said, "Spill it, little one."

"I hate to talk about it, I always have." At his pointed stare, she relented. "I've been fighting a brain tumor for most of my life. After years of treatment and several surgeries, I'd given up. A friend talked me into going to Mexico for one last shot with alternative medicine." She brightened. "It's possible it worked."

Nemo looked stricken. "Cancer?"

"Yea." She shrugged. "That's how I met Jet, I was waiting tables at a bar he visited. I got crossways with some bad guys over a blog I wrote and hid on his ship." She smiled in apology. "He didn't know I was on board. I know you think I'm a jinx."

Nemo swallowed and cleared his throat. "Well, let's withhold judgment. When will you know?"

"I'm going back in a few days. Jet wanted me here…" She stopped and giggled. "I don't have any idea why he wanted me here to tell you the truth."

Nemo took her hand. "I think I do."

A shout caused them to whirl around. It was Jet. "Hey, Pop. I think we found something."

The divers had been using an underwater vacuum to aid in the search.

"What?" Nemo jumped up and went to the side of the boat where Jet was ascending the ladder.

"Hold out your hand." Nemo did as his son asked and Sami, who'd followed, gasped when Jet placed a gold bar into his father's outstretched palm.

"Well, I'll be damned," Nemo shouted and everyone came running. Divers began popping up on the surface.

"We're rich!" Saxon cheered.

Jet waved his hand. "Calm down, White. We've got a lot of work to do, this is just the beginning."

And what a beginning it was. Jet conducted a high-resolution video of the wreck site. Sami had no idea about the technical equipment at their disposal and the way her man stepped up and handled everything like a pro. They began bringing up treasure, some by winch, some in bags connected to a guideline. When it began to pile up on the deck, Sami sat cross-legged and watched, her eyes as big as saucers. What lay before her was amazing, a trove of forty-five gold bars, thousands of gold and silver coins, bracelets, buckles and broaches, glass stemware—even a perfume bottle.

"And this is just the beginning." The elation in Jet's face made Sami shiver with happiness.

"You did it."

"We did it." He grabbed her up, swung her around and kissed her in front of Nemo, God, and everybody.

* * *

After the initial excitement over the first load of treasure they brought to the surface, they settled down to a routine. It was slow work, excavating, locating and transporting. Everyone was involved. Sami even put on her diving gear and went down with Jet, staying close so he could monitor her. Tyson had joined them, this was his first time to witness something like this and he was over the moon.

Saxon was manning the vacuum equipment on board Victor's boat. He'd noticed the approach of two other boats, but he hadn't thought a lot about it. This was a fairly busy area, lots of fisherman and sight-seeing cruises. They were big boats, one looked like a luxury yacht, the other a commercial fishing boat maybe. It looked old and raggedy from where he was sitting. While the two strange vessels were out of the search grid and not bothering the excavation, he still kept an eye on them. He figured they'd come closer when they heard the hooting and hollering earlier, probably were a little curious. So far, they'd been polite and stayed away.

Saxon was adjusting the suction power when the sound of an engine roar caused him to look up. Out of nowhere a bright yellow cigar boat came tearing across the water not far from the Cazador. The wake it left in its path was ungodly and Saxon worried it might disturb the excavation below.

Far beneath the waves, Micah noticed the disturbance first, looking up at the surface after the boat had rocketed by. "What the fuck was that?" he asked from his spot on the sea floor.

All of the divers were wearing full-face masks equipped with radio communication. They could hear one another as well as Nemo and Saxon.

Saxon ran out to the bow and watched the intruder make a wide turn. "Some fucking asshole in a cigar boat," he spoke into the headset. "It looks like he's coming back around. Brace yourselves down there."

Jet came swimming over with Sami and Tyson behind him. "Everybody okay?"

Micah and Isaac were working together, loading their find into the bags for transport to the surface. The ripple above had made its way down to them and they were bobbing back and forth, trying to gain their footing.

"Like riding a bull," Isaac quipped. "Here he comes again." He pointed to the surface and they all watched as the hull of the speedster cut a sharp path through the water.

Saxon's voice came over the earphones in all of their helmets. "Hey, you fucking dick! I've got people in the water!" he yelled as the boat rocketed past. "What is this idiot's problem?"

Down below, something smelled fishy to Jet. People knew they there hunting the San Miguel—including the Galvez cartel. A niggle of unease tingled up his spine.

"He's coming over to the boat," Saxon informed them. "Hang tight a second. I'll see what this clown is up to."

Rival salvagers were known to pull crap like this at times. But a cigar boat? Those were damn expensive watercrafts. Jet knew that only two type of people normally owned cigar boats—people who raced them and people who used them to run drugs.

Jet grabbed for Sami's hand. In his earphone he could hear Saxon conversing with someone. "Get away from the rail, Saxon!" Jet yelled to his friend.

Saxon held a hand up to his headset. "Wait…what?"

Jet began to swim away from the treasure they'd been loading. "Run, Saxon! Nemo get your ass down wherever you are. Everyone scatter!"

The warning came too late, one of the passengers on the cigar boat had an uzi in his hand and he began emptying the clip toward the Cazador. The first bullet tore through Saxon's left forearm, bounced off the bone and exited at a ninety degree angle. By the time he was able to get fully out of the way, three more bullets had made contact with his body, two grazing his left hip and the last burying itself deep into his left thigh. Grimacing in pain, he stayed as low as he could to the deck, moving toward the center. "Back!" he screamed when Nemo and two of Victor's men jumped from one vessel to the other, running to see what had happened.

Nemo hit the deck but the two crew men were cut down by a hail of bullets where they stood. Saxon almost blacked-out from the pain, but he crawled over toward Nemo, who reached out to pull him to safety. "My God, boy, you're hit." Settling him into the wheelhouse, Nemo handed him a towel to hold over the wounds until they could do more for him. "Who are those fuckers?"

"I don't know," Saxon panted, sweat running down his face. "Get your gun, there may be more."

Meanwhile in the water, Isaac and Micah headed in an opposite direction from Jet, Sami and Tyson. They were shutting down the equipment just in case someone was trying to sabotage the operation. Each man was armed with a speargun and a knife but that would be no protection against automatic weapons up top.

Dragging himself to his feet, Saxon peered out the window. He noticed the yacht coming toward them from one side and the fishing boat from the other. At first it appeared help was on the way, but when bullets began to slice into the Cazador from both sides, he quickly realized they were surrounded. The other two vessels were with the cigar boat.

"Jet, don't come up," Saxon said into his headset. "Stay down. They aren't alone. I repeat, they aren't alone. We're under attack. Three boats from different angles. Stay under the water, get to safety if you can."

"Stay down, Saxon, I'm tired of this shit. My boy's down there, not to mention a king's ransom in gold." Nemo ran out onto the deck like a madman and began firing at the cigar boat with a shotgun.

His men tried to cover him, but one of them was hit. Nemo managed to hit the driver while the man with the uzi slid into the driver's seat and drove off as fast as he could, zigging and zagging from side to side as Nemo kept firing on him.

Under the blue, Sami's heart pounded in her ears. Fear wasn't an emotion one feels deeply when they've lived as long as she had with the specter of death always following, but being underwater and out of her element while all of this was going on was terrifying.

Jet could feel her anxiety. "Look at me, Sami." He swam close so she could see his face. "We're gonna be okay."

"What if they come down here?" She wanted to know. "We're sitting ducks."

Jet didn't want her to freak out, so he channeled his inner Micah. "I would've said, *it'd be like shooting fish in a barrel*." He gave her a smile. "Seems more appropriate considering our surroundings."

The joke went right over Sami's head, her mind was on escape and all of their safety. Jet remained calm as he watched over Sami's shoulder. Divers had entered the water and he watched as Micah and Isaac engaged in a battle right under the Sirena. They were outnumbered and their attackers had weapons, but Jet managed to beat back the urge to swim to them as fast as he could.

He remembered a cropping of coral he'd seen while scouting the location with Victor. "Stay right beside me. Tyson!" He motioned to his friend, took Sami's hand and they swam together, side by side for about a hundred yards until the coral came into view. "Stay here," he instructed Sami.

Sami latched onto his wrist. "Jet, no. Don't go."

Jet looked her in the eyes. His calm demeanor did wonders for Sami's nerves. "Tyson and I are going to swim back and check on things. You saw how easily I handled Rafael, and we have help today. Don't worry, I'll be back before you know it. Just stay here and don't move until I come back for you. Okay?"

He wasn't scared and his confidence made her feel better. "All right, but hurry."

Jet and Tyson swam off with a flourish, leaving Sami by herself out of necessity only. They needed numbers to fend off the attack. If Jet had stayed with Sami and did nothing, the bad guys would eventually come looking for them anyway. Safety was in numbers and right now he needed to fight with his friends.

Sami bobbed on the bottom of the ocean. Brightly colored fish swam all around her, ducking in and out of crevices in the reef, curious about her presence but smart enough to keep their distance. It reminded her of her scuba diving adventure with Jet, but fear hadn't played such a major role in that excursion, not like it was doing with this one. She tried to distract herself counting the fish, but her mind, heart, and prayers were with Jet.

When Jet and Tyson came close enough to see the melee near the Sirena, they could tell things had gone from bad to worse. Jet pointed out the man in full scuba gear who lay floating on the bottom of the ocean, blood tinting the water around him.

"This will bring more trouble," Tyson said.

Jet nodded. The blood would bring predators and this area was notorious for great whites. "Sharks."

Ahead of them, Jet could see four men locked in combat. When he swam closer, he could tell two of them were Micah and Isaac. Jet let out a long breath. The dead man was an enemy, not one of his friends. He swam up and slipped his right arm around the neck of the man who was trying to stab Micah. He squeezed until the man stopped kicking and then let him go. When the diver engaged with Isaac saw Tyson coming, closely followed by Micah and Jet, he dropped his knife and swam off.

Isaac went after him, but Micah grabbed his arm. "Leave him. We need to get up top to check on the others." Turning to Jet, he asked, "Where's Sami?"

"I left her by the coral, she's safe there." He was careful what he said, knowing she could hear every word they were saying. "Let's go." He pointed a finger at Tyson and Isaac. "You two hit that fancy yacht. Micah and I will head up and rendezvous with Saxon and my pop. These guys clearly mean business, so don't mess around."

The men broke and headed for the surface. On the way up, Jet caught the outline of a familiar predator in the water. It moved with quiet grace, but its menace was unmistakable. Jaws had arrived.

A crush of worry almost debilitated Jet. He felt torn. "Hug the rocks, Sami. I'll be there in a bit." Keeping her safe was his main concern, but the sharks on the surface were more dangerous than the ones below as far as he was concerned.

On the Cazador, Saxon had had enough shit. He was pinned down behind a pile of ropes, a towel bound around his bleeding thigh, an AR15 in his hand. When he saw someone emerge from the water off the starboard side of the yacht that was firing on him, he held his breath. Who was it? Micah's face appeared a moment later, his hand moving up to push off the diving mask. Despite the gunfire going on around him, Saxon was relieved to see the usual smirk on his friend's face.

"The Wolfe has arrived," he whispered. Springing up from behind the ropes, Saxon began lacing the yacht with gunfire, lying down cover for Micah, who took the opportunity to start climbing up the ladder on the side of the boat with a knife in one hand.

Up near the wheelhouse, Nemo and Victor were firing on the fishing boat. Nemo was fearless, or crazy, nobody could ever tell for sure as he stood with the shotgun in his hand. "Son of a bitch!" he shouted when a bullet grazed his right thigh, but didn't stop firing.

"You okay, Pop?" Jet asked from behind over the clatter of gun fire. He'd climbed onto the Cazador and was loading a shotgun.

Nemo kept squeezing the trigger. "Fine. Where's that gal of yours?"

Not taking time to answer, Jet yelled, "Watch it, more bastards are coming aboard!"

Down below, Sami clung to the coral. She'd seen the first great white that had wandered into the area and she was frozen with terror. "Jet?" she called into her headset. "Where are you?"

But up top, Jet had taken off his headset to fight and Sami was left alone. The great white swam above her slowly. It never looked down at her, but Sami knew it was aware of her presence. The blood in the water drew more sharks and before she knew it, she was surrounded. "Jet, where are you?"

Saxon could see the battle being waged inside the yacht, but they were all helpless to watch as the fishing boat was being filled with loot from the Seaduction. They were just too outnumbered to do anything about it. The bad guys were going to get away with some, if not all of the loot they'd excavated. This had turned into a survival mission now.

Nemo spotted the first load being moved from his ship and he nearly lost it. "You bastards!" When he made a move to rush out onto the deck, Jet tackled him to the ground.

"Let them have it, Pop. It's not worth dying for."

"Dreams die hard, Jet. Who are these fuckers?"

Jet knew who they were, Sami had shown him photos of Rey Olmos and he was the ringleader on the yacht. "A damn Mexican drug cartel, that's who they are."

"Holy Crap," Nemo whispered, motioning for Sid Franks to come help him.

Beneath the waves, something bumped against Sami's right shoulder and in the next breath a large object passed close by her. She jumped, whirling around. It was a shark. Not a great white, but a shark nonetheless and her heart nearly stopped. Her entire body shook.

"Please, please, Jet," she begged.

As if in answer to her prayer, a moment later she saw a figure coming toward her through the water. Her heart slowed down at the sight of another human being. The figure drew closer. She strained to see and right away she could tell it wasn't Jet and as he grew closer, she realized it wasn't Micah, Tyson or Isaac either.

"No, no, no," Panic began to set back in.

Sami knew she was in trouble. Jet had told her to stay where she was, but a stranger was worse than a shark. Undoubtedly they were there to claim the treasure as their own and kill anyone who got in their way. In desperation, Sami broke from the coral. She didn't know where she was going, but she needed to get away as fast as she could.

Meanwhile, Micah and Isaac had gotten off the yacht with the help of a jet ski and had made their way back to the Seaduction. They had left three men dead and two wounded, but a fresh supply of manpower from the fishing boat made them realize they needed to escape while they could.

Triumphant, Rey Olmos stepped out onto the deck and opened fire on the Cazador. The cigar boat had pulled up beside the yacht and he climbed on, pointing to the fishing boat which now held treasure from the San Miguel. He smiled. The Jaguar would be very pleased. They wouldn't only be bringing fabled gold and jewels, they were bringing an even bigger prize. "Move, you idiots," Olmos barked. "Carlos has the girl, he's bringing her up."

Sami struggled with all of her might, but the man in the water held her tight as she swam to the surface, taking her toward the yacht. When her eyes fell on Olmos, she realized her fate. "Help! Help!" she screamed.

Jet felt like his world was crashing in all around him. He watched helplessly as they loaded Sami onto the yacht, jerking her around and hitting her when she tried to fight back. "Bastards!" Firing toward the boat, he had to be careful to not hit Sami. The rest of them quickly took cover. He could do little from where he was.

Turning, he debated what to do, how to get there. This time it was Nemo's turn to stop him "Wait. It's too dangerous." Gun shots rang out in the air, the fire fight was long from over.

Across the way, Rey Olmos kicked one of his men who was loading treasure onto the cigar boat. "Unload it, you fools. The girl is more important."

The scene looked like a Three Stooges routine, the men who had been scrambling to load the boat for the last few minutes, now worked frantically to unload it. When they were done, the fishing boat began to pull away from the scene, taking much of the treasure from the San Miguel with it.

Olmos instructed his driver to pull up to the yacht that was still fiercely locked in combat with the Cazador. "Put her on!" Olmos commanded.

Sami was pushed onto the bright yellow boat, kicking and screaming all the way.

Her cries of protest tore Jet's heart in half. "Get off me!" He tried to get up, but Victor piled on top of him when it looked as if he was going to shake Nemo off and charge out into certain death. "You can't save her, Jet, let it go," Nemo begged.

"The hell I can't," Jet hissed, his every muscle tense, his chest heaving.

Micah fired on the cigar boat and it began to smoke. Jet watched with rage as it pulled away and went in a different direction than the fishing boat.

"We'll never catch them," Nemo said from on top of him. "Not with this boat or yours. We need to stay here and survive this. Wait until that damn yacht is gone, then we can go after the treasure."

"Get off him." Micah tore Victor off of Nemo and Jet was able to shuck his father with one mighty shrug. "There's a jet ski around the back of the boat," he told Jet once they were behind cover. "Go after the treasure. We'll cover you."

Jet ran to the back. The jet ski had drifted twenty yards from the boat and he could see the shadows of sharks as they circled it. Without missing a stride, he dove off the Cazador and headed for the jet ski, ignoring the danger that lurked right below. Climbing up into the seat, Jet gunned the engine and was off like a shot.

"What's wrong?" Olmos barked at his driver. Crying, Sami attempted to crawl away, and he kicked her hard. "Stay where you are, bitch."

The cigar boat had slowed significantly and Olmos watched as the hard charging jet ski closed in on them. He leveled his gun and fired, but the waters were choppy and his shots missed. Before he knew it, the jet ski had caught up, coming directly to the side. Olmos grabbed the wheel. "Ram him!" He yanked the wheel hard.

Jet veered just in time. Slipping in behind the boat, he ducked when Olmos fired on him, but when they hit a wave, all aboard lost their balance and fell to the deck. Jet seized the moment and climbed on. He moved like a panther as the boat began to slow, still moving swiftly across the water. When Olmos appeared, Jet clutched his shirt and yanked, pulling him off his feet. The driver pulled a gun from a cupboard and aimed it at Jet.

Sami's heart was in her throat. Jet was here! "Watch out, Jet!" Sami warned before throwing herself at the driver.

Her weight took him off his feet and Jet reached for the gun as it slid right over to him. Quickly, he cocked it and fired two shots into the chest of the driver, sending the man reeling and falling over the railing and into the water.

Olmos clutched at Jet's leg, dragging him backward. "Now you die, Foster." He jumped on top of Jet's chest and began choking him, but his hands lost all their power a moment later. "You...bitch," he gurgled and fell to the side.

Olmos clutched at a knife buried deep in his side and Jet saw Sami standing over him. She'd saved him once again. "We've got to stop meeting like this," he quipped. Seeing Sami looked dazed, he decided to get them back to the boat as soon as he could. "Let me take out the trash." Quickly getting to his feet, Jet picked Olmos up by the belt and tossed him overboard before he sped the boat up to get them out of there.

The man would probably be eaten alive by sharks. Jet didn't care. As long as Olmos was off the boat he was no danger to Sami or himself.

Sami was sitting still, staring at the blood on her hands. Jet couldn't take it another moment, he had to get her in his arms. Stopping the boat, he went to her. "Baby, are you okay?"

The world came back into focus and the fog that had invaded Sami's brain began to dissipate. "You came after me," she said in wonder.

Jet pulled her against him. "Well, of course I did."

She didn't understand. "But the treasure. It's on the other boat, Jet."

"No, you're wrong." He kissed her firmly. "The treasure's right here, it has been all along. You are my world, Sami."

Sami threw her arms around his neck. What he was saying was too miraculous to comprehend. "What about the others?"

Jet hesitated. "They'll be okay." There was no way he was taking Sami back to a raging battle, they'd wait it out here and see what happened.

Sami could see the indecision in his eyes and she wouldn't stand for it. "We can't just leave them, Jet."

Jet sat down at the wheel of the boat, turning his back on her. "I can't risk taking you back into danger." It might kill him to sit here and wait it out, but Sami had almost died today and that was totally unacceptable.

Sami looked back toward the battle. She saw Rey Olmos floundering in the water. Just beyond him the jet ski floated away. "The jet ski!" Sami cried as a plan hit her like a tsunami.

Jet glanced at her. "What?"

Sami stepped up to the cigar boat console. "How do you turn this thing back on?" She pushed buttons that might as well have been labeled in Japanese, she had no idea what anything did.

Jet pushed her hands aside. "Stop. I have to keep you safe, I don't know what I'd do if we went back and you were killed."

Sami yanked her hand out of his. "And how do you think I'll be able to live with myself if your father and friends die back there because you stayed with me? I can't live with that knowledge, Jet. It'll kill me. It'll kill us both. The jet ski. Turn the boat around. Drive me over to the jet ski. I'll get on and you can go back to the fight."

Even though his head was spinning, her plan made sense. "You know how to drive one?"

"Sit on it and turn the throttle. If one of those other boats starts to head toward me, I gun it and get out of there."

Jet thought it over for a moment. There was no way the fishing boat would catch her on the jet ski and the yacht was too damaged from the collision to catch her either. "Promise me you'll run, you'll stay out of their way."

"Yes, I will, Jet. Please. Hurry."

He fired the cigar boat. A heavy plume of smoke billowed out from the holes Micah had blasted in the hull but the speedster was up and running and Jet brought it up beside the jet ski, washing Olmos with the wake.

"Go!" Sami ordered when she was safely on the jet ski.

Jet leaned down and kissed her. "I love you. Be safe."

All around her hell was raging, but Sami wasn't aware of a thing but what Jet had just said. "I love you?" She put her fingers to her lips and touched where he'd kissed her.

Jet revved the engine of the cigar boat and headed for the battle with a gun in his hand. As he approached the scene he heard a shot. A few men perched on top of the yacht waved to him as he came closer. They thought he was one of them and Jet planned to use that case of mistaken identity to his advantage. He eased back on the throttle and brought his firearm up, strafing the top of the boat as he passed and hitting two of the enemy targets. He'd announced himself as one of the good guys now, the boat was no longer of use to him. At first he considered the yacht as a target, but the fishing boat was pulling away so he aimed the cigar boat right for it before diving off. If things went bad and they lost the battle, at least both enemy boats would be crippled so Sami could escape to safety.

BAM!

The cigar boat crashed into the hull of the fishing boat. The yellow watercraft disintegrated on contact but the damage had been done and Jet swam to the yacht with his knife in his teeth. Climbing up over the railing, he sliced at the first man he saw. His enemy lashed out with his own knife, but Jet deflected the attack and pushed the man over the railing. He made his way through the boat, disabling enemies as he came upon them.

Shaking, Sami drifted along on the waves. In one direction she could hear the gun battle going on, in the other, she heard Olmos' groans of pain. She did her best not to think about him being torn to pieces by sharks, but she didn't feel bad for him. Olmos and his friends had done far worse things to others and if being eaten by a great white was his punishment, then so be it.

On board the Cazador, Micah, Isaac, and Victor focused their attention on getting to the yacht.

"Let's go," Micah said, leading the charge, piling over the railing and onto the yacht, moving from room to room.

When they found Jet battling two men, they pitched in and together they finished the fight within minutes. But when the smoke cleared, the fishing boat was well on its way, nearing the horizon.

Watching the ship sail away with the gold from the San Miguel was hard for Jet, but he had other things on his mind. Once he was back to their boat, he found Victor tending to Saxon and Nemo's wounds.

"Are they going to be all right?" He wanted to take time to help, but he couldn't.

"We need to get them back to shore as quickly as possible," Victor told Jet.

"Call the coast guard and get some help," Jet instructed Micah. "I'll be back."

Nemo, still in pain, motioned for his son to come closer. "Wait. Did you recover the treasure?"

"Yes, I did," Jet stated evenly. "And she's sitting on a jet ski waiting for me."

Nemo eyed him. "What is that girl to you?"

Jet looked him dead in the eye. "Everything."

CHAPTER FIFTEEN

When Sami saw the Sirena heading her way, she began to cry. Her knight in shining armor was bearing down on her. He wasn't riding a white steed—instead, he stood at the helm of his ship, as grand a figure as any Viking hero who ever sailed. When he came up alongside of her, she held out her arms and he stepped down the ladder to pick her up, abandoning the jet ski. "Are you all right?"

She clung to him and cried, the events finally catching up to her. "They were going to kill me."

"They would've had to kill me first."

The bands of his arms were like steel, it was hard to breathe, but she didn't care. "I was so scared. Thank you for saving me."

Jet rubbed his mouth across her temple. "Did you think for one moment I wouldn't?"

No, she hadn't. Sami realized that now. "I knew you'd come."

"You saved me too, don't forget that." His heart was so full, Jet thought it might burst. Once he had her safe, Jet turned the ship around and motored to where the Seaduction and the Cazador were anchored. Their arrival didn't go unnoticed. Jet pulled up next to the ship where the others were congregated, helping Sami make the leap. Tyson came running up. "Are you all right?" he asked Sami.

"Yea, she's fine." Jet kept one hand on her shoulder, still unwilling to let her go.

Isaac and Micah gathered around. "Damn, pirates. I've got to put this in a book," Micah said, his dry sense of humor lost on no one.

"I think we're pretty lucky to be alive," Isaac said, crossing his arms over his chest. "I've been in some skirmishes in my life, but this is one for the record books."

"What about Nemo and Saxon?" Jet asked, looking around.

Victor came forward from the wheelhouse. "The Coast Guard picked them up and took them into Jacksonville."

"I should go." Jet sighed. "But I can't, I need to…"

"I'll go," Micah said. "Let me take the Seaduction over to Amelia Island and I'll get a car and be with them till they're ready to come back."

"What about the treasure?" Victor asked. "We have to try and get it back."

"You're right," Jet agreed. "Why don't you follow them? The fishing boat's taking on water. Don't confront them, they're armed but at least we'll know what direction to start searching."

"What are you going to do?" Micah asked. "Is Sami feeling okay?"

"I'm fine." Sami insisted.

Knowing Micah knew about the clinic, Jet explained. "We need to make sure. This can't be put off any longer."

Micah nodded, understanding. "Do what you have to do. We'll handle everything else."

Wanting away from prying eyes, Jet took her by the hand and led her below. Polly met them, meowing for a handout. This time Jet ignored her. "We need to talk," he announced as he shut the door behind him.

"You look mad." Sami didn't understand. She felt so bad, nauseated. Not from anything internal, though. "If I hadn't been on board, none of this would've happened."

Jet made a growling noise. "I am angry."

Sami hung her head. "I know. I'm so sorry. If I could do it over again, I would run in the opposite direction. You were right. I was bad luck—the storm, the mutiny and now you've lost your treasure."

"Stop it." Jet sat down and pulled her into his lap. "The treasure isn't what I'm worried about."

He was being so nice, she couldn't help but cuddle up against him. "But you're angry and I don't blame you for it."

Jet huffed. "Honey, I'm not angry at you. I'm angry because I put you into danger. It's my job to take care of you."

Sami closed her eyes. He was saying things that made her hope, made her think dreams could come true. "Don't. This is confusing."

Jet took her by the arms, his lips moving across her face. Chuckling, he confessed, "You think you're confused. Up until a few moments ago, I was in denial about how I felt about you." He leaned his forehead against hers. "Hell, I knew I was in like, I knew I was in lust. I'm attached to you, you're my friend."

Disappointment flooded Sami. "Oh. I like you too," she offered softly as she scrambled from his lap to put some distance between them.

Distance that he couldn't tolerate. "Don't move away from me." He went to her, blocking her path, cornering her between the end of the bed and the door. "You don't understand what I'm saying, Sami." He touched her face reverently. "When I saw those men put their hands on you, taking you away from me—it hit me

392

right then that I don't want to live a day without you. I love you."

Joy. Despair. Hope. Fear. All of these emotions bombarded Sami. "No, no," she protested, pushing against his chest. "Me loving you was a given. Inescapable. You loving me is a completely different thing. I stowed away, I forced myself on you." She threaded her fingers through her hair, which was getting quite long now. "You noticed me because I was here. Literally the only woman on a ship in the middle of nowhere. Any port in a storm."

This upset Jet. "Let's get a few things straight, Samantha. I'm not desperate. If I hadn't wanted you, I could've sent you to your cabin and ignored your sweet ass." As soon as he said it, he smiled. "Your tits on the other hand were hard to ignore." At her pained look, he continued,. "I have lived my life with the policy of not getting involved. I loved the one I was with, a girl in every port."

"Is this supposed to make me feel better?" she asked, a tad sarcastically.

Jet snorted. "Just listen." He knelt at her feet, on one knee, taking her hand. "From the moment you told me about your cancer, I've been dying inside. But I pushed it back because you wanted to prolong the verdict. Knowing that you're sick is eating me alive. Knowing that it's possible I could lose you is almost unbearable."

Tears began to run down Sami's face. She put her fingers over his mouth. "Stop. Don't say anything else."

He jerked her hand down, not roughly but with enough strength to get his way. "I'll say it as much as I damn well please. I love you." He pulled her down to sit on his knee. "And I want to spend the rest of my life with you."

"Don't say that, not until we know what the future holds." Sami wasn't moving an inch on this. "I know my fate isn't set in stone. At this moment, it's deniable. A possibility, not a certainty. But if the treatments didn't work, then I'm getting on a plane to Houston and you're going to forget you know my name."

Tenderness welled up inside of him. "Not a chance, mermaid."

"I never intended…I didn't think there was a chance. I just wanted to be with you."

"Look, Sami. I don't want to be your fling, the one you're with because you're trying to cram a lifetime worth of living into a short space."

"It would be for the best, you don't know what it's like to be around someone who's ill and dying."

Jet's voice grew stern with hurt. "No. You don't get to tell me to walk away. We're in this together. The time I've spent with you on this boat has been some of the happiest days of my life." Seeing her surprised look, he gentled his tone. "I don't want to walk away from you." His voice hitched in his throat. "If you're going to die, I want to take care of you. I'd be honored to take care of you. Whatever days you have left are precious to me. You deserve to be loved and I deserve the chance to love you. If you forget my name, I'll remind you who I am. I'm not walking away!"

Sami surrendered, throwing her arms around his neck. "Well, if you feel that strongly about it." She teased. "Let's go to Mexico and talk to Dr. Rio."

* * *

Being back in Veracruz was nerve-wracking for Sami, but Jet took no chances. She'd known he was intimidating, but when he was protecting what he considered to be his own, the man was downright scary. Being armed in a foreign country was dangerous in itself, but no one challenged him. Arriving in a private plane, they were met by a driver Kyle trusted and escorted to the clinic by two vehicles manned by people the Equalizers counted as friends. To say Sami was impressed was an understatement.

"Are you nervous?" he asked as he sheltered her from the vehicle to the door.

"Yes, terrified," she admitted, trembling from the knowledge that this was it—the verdict—the rest of their lives depended on what the news would be.

"Me too," Jet unashamedly confessed. "Know this, if I could trade places with you, I'd do it in a heartbeat."

Sami closed her eyes. "No matter what the doctor says." She opened them back up and smiled at him. "Don't ever forget that I'm the luckiest woman on the face of the earth to have you in my life—no matter how long that is."

Jet kissed her hand. "Let's have faith. We're going to fight the fight and we're going to win. Come on."

Together they walked into the clinic. Jet had refused to let her call. He didn't want anyone alerted to the fact they were going to be in town. The surprised look on the receptionist's face was obvious. "Señorita Cabot!" she exclaimed, clapping her hands together. "We weren't expecting you!"

Her welcome was in direct contrast to Maria's scowl. If Sami weren't so nervous, she would've wondered more but at the moment the only thing on her mind was her own future...until her eyes fell on a photograph on Maria's desk. Maria was searching for her file when Sami saw it and she forced herself not to react. The answer to who Rafael's sister was sat right in front of her. She'd noticed the photograph before, but not having been at the clinic since the night she'd met Rafael at the Pirate's Lair, she hadn't remembered the face. Sami picked up Jet's hand and squeezed it, moving her eyes toward the framed picture, hoping he'd follow her gaze.

He did. She could feel him stiffen beside her.

Maria turned back around, and Sami tried not to react.

"Dr. Rio will see you now."

She hesitated, not sure if she should go through the door or not.

Was she walking into a trap? Could Dr. Rio know about Maria's connection to the cartel?

Could he have been in on it all along?

The possibilities that her treatments were placebo or fake crashed over Sami.

Jet took her by the arm. "It's okay. Let's go in." He had his phone in his hand and he was texting the men outside.

She didn't know what Jet was thinking, but Sami was completely unnerved.

On the other hand, Dr. Rio seemed genuinely glad to see her, which was a relief. "Come in, come in. I've wondered what happened to you. I had the girls looking for you. We called." He stretched out his hand. "No matter, you're here now. How do you feel?"

Sami tried to smile. "I guess that depends on what you have to say. I feel pretty good. A little nausea, but I've been at sea, could've been seasickness."

"Well, we'll see." Rio gestured toward a chair. "We can run a few more tests…"

"We're heading back to Houston today," Jet interjected.

Sami touched Jet's arm. "Dr. Rio, this is Jet Foster, my—"

"Boyfriend." Jet finished. "I'm her boyfriend." The term seemed a bit tame to Jet, he'd be far happier with the word husband.

"Very good." The doctor stared at Jet as if trying to place him.

Anxious, Sami asked, "What can you tell me? Did the treatments work? Am I going to live…or die?"

Dr. Rio opened the chart, and Jet could've cheerfully strangled him for making them wait.

"I have studied the results and I would like you to undergo a few more tests…" He looked up and met Sami's eyes. "But I think, overall, our sessions have been a success. There was no trace of the tumor in the last round of images."

Jet felt like all the air had drained from his body. He was weak with relief. "Thank God."

Sami stood up, took the papers and turned them around. She'd seen enough lab results and charts to be able to interpret the analysis. The numbers and figures she saw made her smile. "I might not be cured, but I'm sure in remission."

Not caring where they were, Jet pulled Sami close and kissed her soundly. "Let's get out of here."

Dr. Rio wasn't through. "What I'd like to do—"

"I have to go home, Doctor. Perhaps I can get my information transferred to a doctor in Houston, just for follow-ups."

Rio frowned. "Well, I can do that, if you'll keep me in the loop. I want to know immediately if there are any changes. I'm very pleased with your response and I would like to do some further evaluation, not only for your sake but others with the same problem."

Sami could understand that. "I will keep in touch. There's a reason I have to leave now, but it won't be forever." Even as she made that promise, she didn't know if she could keep it. Maria was a danger to her. There were still people here who wanted her dead.

Jet stood and shook the doctor's hand. "We'll be in contact."

Sami went out to complete the final financial transactions with Rosa. She couldn't help but notice that Maria was nowhere in sight.

Jet hurried her out, where they ducked into the car. "Take us back to the airport," he directed.

As soon as they pulled away, Sami was in Jet's arms. "I'm going to be okay."

Jet kissed her face over and over. "I'm so happy. You'll never know how much I love you."

The ride to catch the Chancellor jet was spent in thanksgiving, yet Jet kept his eyes open—something told him they weren't going to get off scot free. He was right. When they arrived at the airport, they'd no more than boarded the plane before two jeeps drove up and the plane was sprayed with a hail of gunfire. "Let's get out of here!" Jet yelled, and Sami held her breath as they taxied down the runway and lifted off.

"Maria," Sami said the one word in explanation. "Rafael told me he had a sister who'd connected me to Marisol. It was Maria."

Jet shook his head. "And to think how many times you've been near her."

"She was even in my apartment a couple of times. Loyola said that it was hard to tell the good guys from the bad guys. He was right. So many of the young people are in gangs and the gangs serve as the footmen for the cartel."

Shivering, Jet realized how much Sami knew about the inner workings of the cartel—too much for his comfort, that was for sure. "I can't wait to get you back to the States. This place is dangerous."

"What's next?" Sami asked. For the first time since she was fifteen, the realization that she had a future washed over her. It was a wonderful feeling.

"We're going home. You can see Marisol and I'll introduce you to the rest of my friends. And we'll live happily ever after." Jet grinned, so relieved he didn't know what to do.

Sami played with the buttons on his shirt. "I sold the house, I don't really have a home or anywhere to go." She wasn't being negative, she was just thinking out loud.

Jet stilled her hands. "You have a place. With me. I live on the Sirena right now, but if you want another house or an apartment or whatever, we'll do it. As long as we're together, it doesn't matter where we are."

"You're right." She leaned into him, giving herself over to the man she'd always dreamed would one day be her rock, her haven, her sanctuary. But he was more than that—Jet Foster was her world. "I just want to be where you are. That will be home."

Chapter Sixteen-
EPILOGUE

The plane winged its way from Veracruz back to Florida where they checked on Nemo and Saxon and made sure they were comfortable and recovering on the Seaduction. Afterward, they boarded the Sirena so Jet could be there when the remainder of the treasure from the San Miguel was being raised. Now most of it was being held by the state until insurance inspectors and lawyers could evaluate it and recompense could be made to the state of Florida and the country of Spain. Jet knew this was a long-drawn-out process, but it was well under way.

As far as the portion of the treasure the cartel had stolen, that wasn't over either. Victor and Tyson had located the ship two miles down the coast, abandoned, with no crew and no treasure on board. Jet and the Equalizers had conferred and decided they were going to begin a campaign to bring the Jaguar down and get the treasure back. It wouldn't be immediate and it wouldn't be easy, but all agreed it was necessary.

Isaac had flown back to Kerrville from Florida, but he'd assured Jet that the McCoys would be ready when push came to shove with the cartel. They hadn't forgotten the help the Equalizers had given when Aron had been rescued—and they never would. He did have a word on Angel Rubio. The PI the McCoys had sent down there confirmed she was alive and well and not at all what she first appeared. He wasn't exactly sure what that meant, but they had decided Noah had a right to know.

After they'd wrapped up the paperwork, Jet and Sami sailed home to Galveston from Florida, a trip neither would forget. This time there was no storm and no trouble. It was a risk, but he didn't register his route with the coast guard, just in case the information was susceptible to the cartel. He did let Kyle and the guys know, and that was just as good. So they used their time to celebrate, make love, and bond.

Once they were back on home ground, Jet took Sami to Marisol and they cried in one another's arms. Marisol was still lying low in Tyson's RV. Jet had laughed at the thought. Tyson was such a grump, he didn't know how the rapscallion was reacting to a roommate. All he'd told Jet today was that she was 'okay,' whatever that meant.

When the tears were over, the questions began and Jet slipped out, using their reunion time to visit with his friend and do a little shopping, a surprise for his soon to be fiancée. Almost unconsciously Jet patted his pocket where a ring box rested.

On their way back to the RV, Tyson had observed, "Marisol is stilling getting information from her contacts, and Saxon is helping her to access other avenues. They'll cage the Jaguar sooner or later."

"I want that, but we have to be alert and keep them safe." Jet was still worrying.

"There's no safer place for them than with us."

"No, I wouldn't have it any other way," Jet admitted, his heart more full of love than he'd ever known it was capable of holding.

The girls were having a blast catching up. "Tell me everything," Marisol encouraged, so Sami did, reciting an account of all that had happened from the time she'd last seen Marisol to the moment they were now enjoying. After she'd finished, Marisol waved her hand. "I don't want to know about the cartel, I want to know how you ended up with Mr. Big."

Sami blushed and giggled. "He is big."

Marisol laughed with her. "You lucky little devil."

Sami sighed. "I'm not really sure how it happened, Mari. Like I told you on the phone, he walked into the bar where I was working and fate just took over. We talked, he stood up for me, I went to watch him fight and that night when he came in the bar there was a scuffle and I brained this guy with a bottle when he was about to hurt Jet."

Marisol was hanging on her every word. "And then what?"

"That was the same night Olmos and Andrade came after me, someone had connected the dots. I later learned it was one of the nurses at the clinic. She'd seen the news report about your demise—which wasn't true, thank God, but she recognized your face as the person who'd come into the clinic to find out if Dr. Rio would see me. Since I had a connection to you, the Lioness, they figured out I was your replacement. To get away from them, I hid on Jet's boat—and the rest like they say, is history."

"I can't believe it. I can still remember the day when you showed me his picture and told me how much he inspired you…and how much you wanted to jump his bones."

Sami blushed anew. "I can hardly believe it myself."

Marisol already knew about the good news concerning her diagnosis, she was the first person Sami had called when she got back to the States, but there were still things to discuss. "Have you made an appointment for some follow-up tests yet?"

"I will tomorrow. I'm going to phone some of my mother's colleagues." Thinking about her parents was still hard, but now that she had Jet in her life the pain was beginning to lessen.

The two girls talked for hours while Jet was patient, huddled up in the front of the RV with Tyson, debating how to invest their booty from the San Miguel. Finally, they had to break up the happy reunion.

"Baby, we need to go." Jet stood at the door, delighted to see her so happy. "Tyson tells me we're having company tonight. It was supposed to be a surprise party, but he had to let the cat out of the bag so we'd go home and be there when the others arrive."

"Oh, my goodness!" Sami jumped up. "Let's go, I have to get everything ship-shape!"

Jet rolled his eyes at Tyson. "She does this all the time, nauti-talk, nauti-talk." He did his hands in the air like talking clams.

Sami swatted him. "You love my nauti-talk, especially when it's spelled n-a-u-g-h-t-y."

"She's got you there," Tyson agreed as they watched Jet pick her up and carry her out over his shoulder, play spanking her on the bottom.

As they climbed on Jet's motorcycle to leave, Marisol cried as Tyson held her. "I can't believe she's alive and well and has such a wonderful future to look forward to."

Tyson vowed in his heart that Sami wouldn't be the only one. Marisol deserved all of those things too.

Later that evening, the Sirena was ablaze with lights and laughter. "We're glad you're here." Hannah hugged Sami. "I didn't know Jet could be so contented. Welcome to the family."

She was so happy, Sami thought she might cry. "Thank you."

All of the Equalizers had come to welcome them home, even Saxon was back. Nemo had actually found a neighbor to check in on him and Saxon gleefully informed them that the neighbor was female.

This gathering of close friends was an impromptu 'boat warming,' so unlike the christening party only a few weeks before. They ate good food, drank fine wine, and toasted that once more they'd been tested by fire and emerged stronger for it. Everyone had brought gifts, everything from bed linens to a magnificent figurehead for the front of the boat—commissioned by Micah. The bare-breasted beauty had an uncanny resemblance to Sami. She'd loved it.

Kyle and Destry had the party catered, and Saxon served as bartender. They chowed down on shrimp, crab, steaks and every side you could imagine. For dessert they made huge ice cream sundaes and planned a trip together to the country as soon as they could all arrange to get away.

As the evening wore on, one by one their friends went home, bidding them goodnight and good luck until only Micah was left. "Thank you so much, Micah. Thank you for everything," Sami told him.

"Yea, that goes double for me, Wolfe." Jet hugged his friend. "Life sure has a way of taking some unexpected twists and turns."

"Hell, isn't that the truth. Oh, I have one more gift for you."

Jet looked confused. Holding out his hand with a package in it, Micah did his best Jeff Foxworthy imitation, "Here's your sign."

Jet unwrapped the package. "A sign?" He didn't understand.

404

It was hard, felt wooden and was triangular shape. With Sami looking over his shoulder, he turned it over and his face broke into a grin.

"What does it say?" Sami asked. "Is it for the boat?"

He held it up. "Yep, it's a sign of the times." Instead of the infamous, 'Baby on Board,' it announced in big block letters:

WOMAN ON BOARD

"I love it!" Sami exclaimed. "Where can we hang it?"

"Right by the gangplank, I'm thinking," Micah added. "It could sorta be a warning."

"We don't need a warning," Sami interjected with a smile. "It's going to be smooth sailing and calm seas."

"I hope so, beautiful, I hope so." Micah kissed Sami on the cheek. "What I do know is that you have made this old pirate smile, and that's saying a helluva lot."

They hated to see him go, but were also anxious to be alone. Sami and Jet stood on the bow and waved him off.

"Well, are you ready to go below, Miss Cabot?" Jet asked. "I have a proposal for you."

Excitement fired through her veins. "I love the things you propose."

Knowing he would meet her expectations, Jet took her by the hand, not telling his proposal would be just that—a proposal. "Come on, Miss Horny, I have something to show you."

Sami was so happy she had the giggles. "I know what you're going to show me and it's worth looking at again."

When they got below, he didn't turn on a light. They were winding their way in the darkness, bumping into things and laughing when a plaintive pathetic meow caught their attention.

"Wait." Sami stopped in her tracks.

Jet had to throw his weight off balance to keep from barreling into her. "What is it?"

"I hear Polly and she's crying. She's in trouble."

Jet flipped on some lights, listening to see if he could hear what Sami was hearing. "Polly!"

"Meow-meow!"

"Where is she?" she asked, moving into the galley.

Jet moved methodically around the room until he came to the locked cabin where he kept his treasure hunting maps and other important papers. "How in the world?" He took the key from his pocket, unlocked it and the cat came bounding out.

"Did you…how…when was the last time you were in that cabinet?"

Jet laughed, locking the door once more. "I haven't opened that door since we left Florida and Polly doesn't have a key as far as I know."

"So how?"

Shaking his head, Jet mused. "I don't know, strange things happen at sea. It was probably Claude."

Sami held up her hands. "Okay, I've been intending to ask you this, but you always have me distracted by your hunky body. Who is Claude?"

Jet faced her, struck a bodybuilding pose and grinned. "What did you say?"

She covered her eyes and asked. "Claude who?"

Relaxing, Jet hooked an arm around her neck. He still couldn't go but a few minutes without touching her. It was like he had to keep reassuring himself she was near and all right. "Claude lives on the boat."

"Where?" Sami looked around. "No, I would have noticed someone else." She looked stricken. "Jet, I run around naked on this boat."

Laughing, Jet kissed her, capturing her mouth mid-word. "Claude is our resident kobold or klabautermann."

"You ka-what?" Sami asked.

Indulgently, Jet explained, "Claude is our ship spirit or gnome. You never see him, but he moves stuff or fixes things or shuts prowling pussies in places where they shouldn't be prowling."

Sami laughed. "Do you think Claude will be after me next?"

"I don't know. Anytime something happens we can't explain, we blame Claude."

"Okay, I understand." She looked around nervously. "As long as Claude doesn't jump out at me, I'll be okay."

Jet's heart softened. "He'll protect you, just like he does this ship."

"I can live with that. Now, come on, I have business with the Captain."

She led him down the hall, his eyes glued to her cute ass as she sashayed in front of him wearing a short jacket and a shorter skirt. He'd picked it out, a sailor outfit that fulfilled several of his own fantasies. When she opened the door to his stateroom and went to his bed, he could tell she expected him to follow.

But he didn't.

"I thought you were about to show me something." Her eyes looked at him questioning. "What's wrong?"

"Nothing's wrong, everything is very, very right." He pushed her up against the wall, holding her hands behind her back, immobilizing her. Jet nuzzled her neck, letting the stubble of his beard rasp against her tender skin.

"You're the best lover in the whole world." She arched her back, tilting her head, giving him all the access he wanted. "I never knew it could be like this."

"You've been a very enthusiastic student," Jet muttered as he began to unbutton her top.

As he pushed the metal buttons through their holes, Sami stopped his hands, a wicked little scenario coming to mind. "Let me. I think it's time I demonstrated my seaworthiness, Captain."

"I damn sure love to look at you, doesn't that make you see-worthy?" He groaned as her questing fingers began divesting him of his clothes.

She took her time, petting and teasing him with slow, warm kisses. "I'd rather make love with you than eat." Boldly, she licked his chest. "I'd rather make love with you than breathe."

Her whispers about how much she adored being with him aroused Jet more than any erotic act with any other woman. Once she had him naked, she walked around him slowly, trailed fingers from his back, around his side and down to stroke his cock. "God, what are you up to, Sami?"

Standing in front of him, she seductively wiggled out of the skirt and tugged off the jacket, leaving herself clad only in a see-through pair of navy blue lace panties and a matching bra. The sight of her voluptuous body had his cock at half-staff and rising.

"I want to show you how well I've learned the ropes." Opening a drawer by her side of the bed, she took out the lengths of rope she'd used to learn to tie knots.

Jet's pulse started to pound. "Now, why in the world would I let you tie me up?"

She stopped with the strands of rope in her hand, her lips pooching ever so slightly. "Cause you'll thank me afterward?" When he smiled, she took that as acquiescence. "Lie down in the middle of the bed."

This he didn't argue with, especially when she crawled up on the bed to join him, her breasts hanging down like the lushest fruit. "Come up here, siren." He crooked his finger at her.

Sami loved it when he talked sailor to her. "I'm coming in a second, I have knots to tie down here first."

Jet chuckled. "You're not coming yet, but you will be." Before he knew it, she had a rope wrapped around one ankle and was in the process of affixing it to the bedpost.

"Hey!" He leaned up on his elbows to watch. "You're so damn sexy."

"You taught me well, see." She glided a hand down his leg to his foot, moistening her upper lip with her tongue. "Make a circle using the inner end and tuck it back under itself and above the long piece." She continued to repeat the words back to him that he'd asked her to memorize. "Finally, tighten the ends. This is called the *soft shackle*."

The way Sami said the last two words made him tremble. "You realize I'm hard as a rock."

"I can see that…" She leaned up and pressed a kiss on the end of his cock. "Patience, Champ." She repeated the process on the other leg, then turned her attention to the rest of his aching body. "Now, how am I going to get past this?" Sami gestured at his cock sticking up like a planted flag pole.

"I don't know." Jet shrugged his massive shoulders, every word a hiss under his breath. "Maybe you should put it away, slip it out of sight, tuck it in some small…wet…"

He grunted when she mashed him down against his stomach and moved over the top of him. "There."

"That wasn't exactly what I had in mind."

Sami was undeterred. "Lift your hands over your head."

He obeyed only because he was hypnotized by her bounteous breasts dangling right in his face and by the time he came around, she was tying him up. No woman had ever even come close to getting Jet Foster in a position like this before—and he didn't mind it one bit.

"Now, this is the handcuff knot. You use the rope to form two identical loops. Then, you overlap them like you're tying a clove hitch."

Unable to stop himself, Jet flicked his tongue out and twirled it around a nipple. To his amusement, Sami never stopped talking, she simply paused and pushed down, giving him more to suck. "Then, thread each loop through the other and tighten. Insert the—uh—victim's limbs into loops, tighten and apply traction."

Once she finished, she lowered her head and nipped his ear lobe. Jet, his mouth full of tit, yelped. "Now that you've got me all hitched, what are you going to do with me?" He didn't wait for an answer, Sami almost came unglued as he nuzzled the top of her cleavage, his darting tongue moving from one solid nipple to the other.

"Love on you," she whispered, giving herself a few moments to enjoy the attention before she began her own quest, licking and kissing her way down his magnificent chest, nipping and nibbling at his firm pecs and tracing the ridges of his chiseled abs.

"Sami, honey, I'm about to blow."

Jet spoke in a low, husky tone that made her quiver from head to toe. "You'd better not, not till I get there."

Raising her head to wink at him, Sami gave him a look of love so intense he shook. "I'd swim the ocean just to see you smile, Samantha Cabot."

"Smiling is easy, you make me happy, Jet." Planting more kisses in a straight line down his happy trail, she stopped when the tip of his cock nudged her chin. "Very happy." To show her gratitude, she drew the wide flared head between her lips, all the while stroking the shaft with a gentle hand.

Jet shut his eyes in bliss, the warm wet velvet of her mouth surrounding him—and when she began to suck, his back arched and his thighs tightened. "Damn…feels so good." His bound hands came down from above his head to stroke her hair. He often wondered how she'd look when it grew long enough to touch her shoulders. She'd look amazing, he would bet his life on it. With every bob of her head, her tits moved, swaying and jiggling, the hard nipples grazing his thighs. Watching her go down on him, those sweet lips wrapped around his cock as she worked him was hotter than fuck.

For long delicious minutes, Sami kept him on the ragged edge. Taking him deeper, she cupped his balls, rolling them between her fingers. Hollowing her cheeks, she sucked and licked, pleasuring him until he erupted in an orgasm so intense it felt like an earthquake. Even then, she didn't stop or pull away, but swallowed every drop.

Jet was panting, blown away by what she made him feel. But what she did next took the cake. "I need you inside me, Jet."

To Jet's amazement, he was still fairly hard. She slid up his body, seeking his mouth and kissing him with such sweetness and passion he felt the familiar hunger rise again. "Put me in."

Rising up, she took him in hand, guiding his aching cock into her body, coating him with her cream. Immediately, he was fully erect and nearly blacking out from pure ecstasy as she rode him until they both came. She shuddered and cried out. "Jet!"

The way she said his name caused a wave of déjà vu to wash over him. "I heard you, you know. Even before we met, I heard your voice crying out to me as I swam—the siren's call." Holding her as she calmed, Jet pulled her down on top of him. "You're my siren. Lie here and let me hold you."

"We were connected, I guess. Meant to be. I used to escape into dreams with you when my life was too scary or painful to endure." She kissed his chest, relaxing on top of him. "Now, I don't have to pretend anymore, my dreams have come true."

"Mine too," Jet admitted. "Even though I didn't know what my dreams really were—until you came along."

"I enjoyed that." She loosened the rope she had bound his hands with. "Thanks for letting me practice tying my knots." She sighed and rubbed his chest slowly.

"Oh, dang! Tying the knot!" Jet reached over the side of the bed for his pants, easing her off of him. Laughing, he pulled his shirt over his head and redressed. "You're so sexy, you almost made me forget something important."

She sat up on the bed. "What are you talking about and why are you putting your clothes on? Should I?" She reached for the sheet, unsure, pulling it up over her.

"No, baby, you're fine. This is going to be a moment I'll want to tell our children about. I don't want to go down on one knee naked." It had dawned on him that she could be pregnant, they'd done nothing to prevent it. But that wasn't why he was proposing. He wanted her with him, it was as simple as that.

By the time she realized what he was saying, he was kneeling next to the bed. Sami's heart began pounding like the incoming tide. "Jet, what are you doing?" Even though he'd said not to, she pulled her jacket on.

"You're beautiful in whatever you have on, even if it's just your beautiful skin." Almost nervously, he cleared his throat and began. "Samantha, you've changed me. You're the only woman I want. I'm a better man because of you."

"Not possible," she interrupted.

He put his finger over his lips to indicate she should shush. "Let me make my speech—I practiced." With a smile, he continued, "You've changed my world. When you look at me with those big beautiful eyes, I can't breathe. I have no defense against you." She reached out to touch his face and he turned to kiss her palm. "Sami, you are the most precious thing in my world. I'm in so deep with you, I have no hope of finding my way out and no desire to do it if I could."

"Jet..." Her heart was melting. "I adore you. I love you so much."

"I want to spend the rest of my life with you." He lifted up a ring, a beautiful diamond with two pearls, one on each side. "Give me your hand, Sami. Will you marry me?"

There was no lapse of time, no hesitation, yet in that moment her past flowed by her like an ocean current—every hope, every wish, every dream she'd cherished close to her heart was coming true. Kneeling before her, looking like the perfect hero, a man so majestically proud that he should never be on his knees to anyone—was her Jet. "Yes, please, I'll marry you."

She held out her hand, and he slipped the ring on her finger. "Now, it's official. You are my treasure. One man's treasure, now and forever."

Jet and Sami's story has just begun. Join the Equalizers with Micah's story.

Enjoy a glimpse into some other Sable Hunter romance!

You Are Always on My Mind

She said nothing, just opened the door, slammed it and fled into the night. Revel didn't even hesitate, he was out of the truck and after her in a flash. Only she didn't run into the swamp like he feared, she ran up to the door, unlocked it with the key he'd given to her and went inside. He was about a dozen strides behind her and when he stepped into the house, he didn't know what he'd find. But what he saw shocked him. There was a trail of very feminine women's clothing scattered on the stairs. A dress. A wrap. A bra…and very small, lacy pair of panties. "Harper?" He couldn't believe his eyes. But oh, how he wanted to. When he came to the bedroom she was occupying, the door stood wide open. "Harper?"

"Come in, Revel. I'm waiting for you."

Her voice was low, sultry—sexy. Revel was breathing so hard, it sounded as if he'd run a marathon. And when he stepped around the corner into the doorway, he almost swallowed his tongue. She was lying on the bed, naked. On her back, legs spread with her hand between her thighs. She was massaging her slit, her fingers dipping and delving, spearing up inside of her, then up to caress her clit. "Holy Fuck," he whispered. "Harper, what are you doing?"

"Seducing you. Is it working?" Harper could see a war being waged in his eyes. Was this a mistake? Mercy, if she had the sense God gave a flea, she'd back off. They had so many issues to work through, and here she was confusing the issue with sex. But wasn't this what it was all about? She'd made him feel inadequate, not enough and it was her mission to show him he was all the man she needed. The insufficiency, the deficit—it was all hers. This could be the biggest mistake of her life, but she had to take the risk. She needed this, she needed him. She needed to be normal. The emptiness inside of her was a constant, pulsing ache which grew stronger with every passing moment.

Revel didn't have to know she was damaged goods.

Harper's hand stilled between her thighs. She stared at him. He was frozen. He wasn't moving. What did that mean? Instead of giving up as she should have, Harper rose and moved toward him, moving right into his space, fitting her hungry body to his. Would he reject her? Despite his words of love, when she was stripped and vulnerable before him, would he want her or would the things she'd done at the clubs repulse him?

Touching him, she rubbed her breasts across his chest, her hands going to his crotch. "I only want to make you happy. Let me love you." She teased the seam of his lips with her tongue, her heart leaping when he trembled against her. The power in his big body wasn't subtle, so it amazed her that she could affect him so. He was an addictive drug.

Revel wasn't fighting the attraction, he was paralyzed with it. Just being this close to her made his brain go haywire. He'd wanted her so badly and for so long, every nerve ending in his body was vibrating and buzzing. With a growl, he surrendered to the incredible pull. Fisting his hand in her long dark hair, he pulled her to him, covered her lips and sank his teeth into her lower lip. Nip! "How's that, baby? Do you like that?"

The small amount of erotic pain thrilled her. He wasn't being facetious, this was him trying to do what she'd asked him to do. "I love it," she admitted. "You turn me on so much." She reached between his legs and folded her hand around his big cock, giving it a squeeze.

Revel growled. Harper could almost hear the threads of his control snap in two. He took hold of her shoulders and hauled her flush to him. With a whimper, she started pulling at his shirt, uncaring that buttons were popping off and bouncing across the floor. The next thing she knew, Harper had gone from pressed to his body to sitting on the dresser with Revel standing close between her thighs. Revel was staring down at her as if he couldn't believe she was real. His fiery black eyes were glittering with hunger and bold flags of color stained his high chiseled cheekbones. With a primal snarl, his mouth crushed hers. Harper didn't have to process, all of his pent-up desire, hunger—it was directed right to her.

"Yes, yes," she murmured. But for all the ravishing hunger, his hands were gentle as he caressed her body.

"It's been so long," he whispered. "I've ached for you. I've touched no one. Only you, you're all I want. So soft. So fragile." He bent his head to place a tender kiss to her neck.

"Revel, I'm not fragile." She wove her fingers in his hair, so much longer now than the last time they'd done this. "I want you to take me, touch me. Dominate me. You have no idea how much I've dreamed of this. How I missed you."

Dipping his head, he buried his face in the valley between her breasts, kissing both sides of her cleavage. When he framed one swollen globe, closing his lips over the distended nipple, Harper moaned. She arched her back, holding his head to her breast. "Bite me," she pleaded.

416

Revel stiffened, so Harper stiffened, pulling back. But she wasn't successful, Revel stopped her—with his teeth. He grazed her nipple, scraping the tender flesh. Harper gasped, cradling his head. "Ah, yes!"

"Like that?" he muttered. When she keened, he plumped her breast, and she was mesmerized, loving the way his big broad hand looked against her white skin. Reaching down, she began working on his belt, releasing the button on his jeans, slowly lowering the zipper.

"Yes, I love it." Slipping her hand inside, Harper closed her fingers around his manhood and stroked. "We're making progress, guess next time we'll just drag out the whips and chain." She teased.

With a harsh groan, he jerked her forward, taking her lips in a complete and thorough kiss. Those wicked little fingers could steal his reason if he wasn't careful, or maybe it was too late, for he confessed way before he was ready. "We don't have to wait till next time, the whips and chains are ready and waiting for you. Ever since you left, I've been training."

With a gasp, Harper clung to his neck as he pulled her close, picking her up and taking her to the stairs that led to the area below, under the front gallery. "Where are we going?"

"To my dungeon, little submissive. Are you ready to play?"

myBook.to/AlwaysOnMyMind

About the Author:

Sable Hunter is a New York Times, USA Today bestselling author of nearly 50 books in 7 series. She writes sexy contemporary stories full of emotion and suspense. Her focus is mainly cowboy and novels set in Louisiana with a hint of the supernatural. Sable writes what she likes to read and enjoys putting her fantasies on paper. Her books are emotional tales where the heroine is faced with challenges. Her aim is to write a story that will make you laugh, cry and swoon. If she can wring those emotions from a reader, she has done her job. Sable resides in Austin, Texas with her two dogs. Passionate about all animals, she has been known to charm creatures from a one ton bull to a family of raccoons. For fun, Sable haunts cemeteries and battlefields armed with night-vision cameras and digital recorders hunting proof that love survives beyond the grave. Welcome to her world of magic, alpha heroes, sexy cowboys and hot, steamy to-die-for sex. Step into the shoes of her heroines and escape to places where right prevails, love conquers all and holding out for a hero is not an impossible dream.

Visit Sable:

Website:

http://www.sablehunter.com

Facebook

https://www.facebook.com/authorsablehunter

Amazon:

http://www.amazon.com/author/sablehunter

Pinterest

https://www.pinterest.com/AuthorSableH/

Twitter

https://twitter.com/huntersable

Sign up for Sable Hunter's newsletter

http://eepurl.com/qRvyn

SABLE'S BOOKS
Get hot and bothered!!!

Hell Yeah!

Cowboy Heat

Hot on Her Trail

Her Magic Touch

Brown Eyed Handsome Man

Badass

Burning Love

Forget Me Never
With Ryan O'Leary & Jess Hunter

I'll See You In My Dreams
With Ryan O'Leary

Finding Dandi

Skye Blue

I'll Remember You

True Love's Fire

Thunderbird
With Ryan O'Leary

Welcome To My World

How to Rope a McCoy

One Man's Treasure
With Ryan O'Leary

You Are Always on My Mind

If I Can Dream

Head over Spurs

The Key to Micah's Heart
With Ryan O'Leary

Love Me, I Dare you!

Hell Yeah! Sweeter Versions

Cowboy Heat

Hot on Her Trail

Her Magic Touch

Brown Eyed Handsome Man

Badass

Burning Love

Finding Dandi

Forget Me Never

I'll See You In My Dreams

Moon Magic Series
A Wishing Moon

Sweet Evangeline

Hill Country Heart Series
Unchained Melody

Scarlet Fever

Bobby Does Dallas

Dixie Dreaming
Come With Me

Pretty Face: A Red Hot Cajun Nights Story

Texas Heat Series
T-R-O-U-B-L-E

My Aliyah

El Camino Real Series
A Breath of Heaven

Loving Justice

Texas Heroes Series
Texas Wildfire

Texas CHAOS

Texas Lonestar

Other Titles from Sable Hunter:

For A Hero
Green With Envy (It's Just Sex Book 1)with Ryan O'Leary
Hell Yeah! Box Set With Bonus Cookbook
Love's Magic Spell: A Red Hot Treats Story
Wolf Call
Cowboy 12 Pack: Twelve-Novel Boxed Set
Rogue (The Sons of Dusty Walker)
Be My Love Song

Audio
Cowboy Heat - Sweeter Version: Hell Yeah! Sweeter Version

Hot on Her Trail - Sweeter Version: Hell Yeah! Sweeter Version, Book 2

<u>Spanish Edition</u>
Vaquero Ardiente *(*Cowboy Heat)

Su Rastro Caliente (Hot On Her Trail)

Printed in Great Britain
by Amazon